MONSTER SQUAD

BOOK 7

OBSESSIONS

HEATH STALLCUP

Obsessions

A Monster Squad Novel

Heath Stallcup

Edited by TW Brown
Cover Art by Jeffrey Kosh

Obsessions; A Monster Squad Novel

Printed in the U.S.A.

ISBN-13: 978-1506017563
ISBN-10: 1506017568

DEDICATION

For my children. Aim for the moon and you may hit the barn. Aim for the stars and you may hit the moon. Aim for forever and reach the stars.

ACKNOWLEDGMENTS

Yes, I always thank my beautiful wife, Jessie. She's the one who has given up so much so that I can live the dream.

I always have to give a shout out to the Tufos. Sometimes those who offer so much ask the least.

Linda Coffman who proofread and polished these before Todd can work his magic.

Todd Brown who has taught me so much over the past few years and who polishes these stones into gems.

Jeffrey Kosh for covering these stories in his fantastic artwork.
Last, but certainly not least, my kids. You still believe.

Thank you.

-Heath

Obsessions

A Monster Squad Novel

by

Heath Stallcup

1

Spalding and Apollo strode out into the aftermath and reviewed the carnage. “Damn, I’m glad I’m not part of the clean-up crew.” Apollo kicked a body over, watching as it slowly transformed back to something like a human-wolf hybrid. “Ugly sons of bitches, ain’t they?”

“They aren’t so pretty in either form. They’re even less pretty in between.” Spalding keyed OPCOM and requested the clean-up crews converge on his location. He looked up at his haggard squad. “Donnie, you and Sullivan double-check the containers. Make sure everything inside is no longer breathing. Jacobs, Lamb, take the main gate and escort the clean-up crews in.”

Spalding made a wide circular motion with his hand to attract the attention of Second Squad. Keying his throat mic, he announced, "We're mopping up down here. Keep your eyes and ears open and do not secure your stations until the clean-up crews are finished."

"Roger that." Bravo Four was the first to respond. The other two chimed in as well.

Spalding turned and began walking toward the main warehouse. "Brother, how about you point me to Sheridan's personal stuff and then you need to disappear before folks start to arrive."

Apollo stood tall and nodded. He inhaled deeply, the scent of spent gunpowder still lingering in the air. He glanced about the site then back to Spalding. "I'm really going to miss it, ya know."

"I know. Once an operator, always an operator." Spalding turned and walked slowly with him toward the main building. "But they meant it, buddy. No popping up on radar. No mercenary stuff. Just…disappear."

"I ain't the merc type, man. You know that." Apollo paused and stared off into the darkness. "The hardest part is not saying goodbye."

"It's probably for the best, brother. There's a lot of people at the base that won't be happy with our decision…we haven't told them yet."

"I understand. I don't like it, but I understand. I just wish there was some way to turn back the clock, ya know?"

"I know. Believe me, buddy. I know." The two stood in silence for a moment longer. Apollo turned and motioned toward the main doors of the hangar. "Come on, Sheridan's crap is in the office in here. Probably got contact info for that Simmons cat."

"That's what I wanted to hear." Spalding fell into step with him and the two began working their way across the expanse.

A muffled shot echoed in the darkness, the flash hidden by the suppressor attached to the barrel. Apollo jerked suddenly and froze in mid-step, his eyes dropping to his chest.

Spalding stopped and turned to him. “What’s wrong, buddy?” He didn’t notice the fresh blood splatter on Apollo’s tactical vest. He was already covered in blood, flesh, and spittle from the earlier wolf attack.

Apollo turned and stared at him blankly, his mouth opening to say something, but the words never came. A second shot hit him in the temple, dropping him where he stood.

Spalding leapt to his side, catching the big man before he hit the pavement. “Medic!” His scream was instinctive from years in the field, as no medic had ever gone out with the squads in missions past.

Spalding cradled Apollo as he quivered and shook, his nerves firing, causing his body to jerk. Keying his throat mic, Spalding screamed into the coms, “Stand down! Stand down! Hold fire!” He lay Apollo down gently on the ground, “Stay with me, buddy! Stay with me!” He glanced around with desperate eyes, “I need a medic over here! Man down!”

Jacobs and Lamb rushed to his side, pulling their emergency packs as they slid in beside Spalding. “What happened?”

“Gunshot!” Spalding stepped back as Lamb and Jacobs did their best to stench the flow of blood.

Lamb gently turned Apollo’s head only to realize that the other side of his skull was missing. He turned shocked eyes to Spalding and shook his head. “There’s no way, Spank.”

Jacobs pressed his fingers to the big man’s neck and felt for a pulse. “I got nothing.”

Spalding slowly came to his feet and stared off toward the points where his Bravo members supposedly sat overwatch. Hatred flashed in his eyes, and he ground his teeth as he tried to calculate which man had murdered his friend.

*****

The sniper rifle slipped away from his eye, and he let it drop to the ground below. The patch of grass below him muffled the impact as he turned and slid from the rafters of the dilapidated maintenance building.

Bigby's feet touched the ground, and he slipped into the shadows of the building, doing his best to stay out of the line of sight of the three lookouts planted along the perimeter. He spotted them on their approach and watched as they set up their overwatch stations before their brethren began murdering the wolves in the cargo containers. It had taken him this long to sneak past them and establish his own position out of their view.

He hadn't allowed himself the luxury of mourning Sheridan. His shock that Apollo and the other operator got the drop on him was bad enough, but Sheridan being absentminded enough to let himself be killed by the likes of those two? The old boy had slipped a lot further than Bigby would have thought.

He left the sniper rifle on the ground for the squad to find later. He wanted them to locate it and discover the weapon. He wanted them think that it was one of Simmons' men that dropped the great Apollo Creed Williams. When the time was right, he'd let them know it was him. As he was crushing them under his heel, he'd gladly tell them himself.

Bigby watched from his position until he felt he was clear then broke away. He knew where Sheridan had hidden a good portion of the munitions that Simmons' had bought. He knew the weapons would come in handy when the rest of Simmons' men arrived later.

He had considered simply using his knowledge to take the war to the squads himself but that would be suicide. If he truly wanted revenge, it was better to stand back and direct others to run into the rain of bullets. With Sheridan gone, Bigby would be the contact man for Simmons. He'd be the one to give the orders now. He'd be the one to pick up the reins and take over for his best friend, mentor and commanding officer.

Glancing back over his shoulder when he knew he was well beyond hearing range, Bigby paused and watched as the trucks rolled into the abandoned industrial zone. True to their standard operating procedures, they had called in the chaps to clean up after them. Men in rubber suits and fancy space-age equipment would go over every inch of the facility. They would pick it clean like white suited vultures, leaving nothing behind that could possibly indicate what had happened.

Bigby spotted the black trucks parked outside the gate of the facility; nearly identical trucks to the one that decimated their team at the hangar. He growled low in his throat and wished he had a couple of RPGs to spare. Bigby forced himself to breathe and calm down. His time for revenge would come. He turned back to the crowd of people collecting in the middle of the facility below.

"I'll be back, old boy. And when I come, I'm bringing the Devil himself with me."

*****

Mark slipped his headphones off and laid them down quietly on the console at his station. His eyes stared at the screen and the body of Apollo splayed on the ground. He opened his mouth to speak but no words came. He could hear the buzz of activity in the OPCOM but nothing registered with him. He stood slowly and approached the command chair.

Jericho was still barking commands as Mark gently squeezed the man's shoulder. "How did that happen?"

Jericho shook his head, his eyes still scanning the heat signatures displayed on the smaller screen. "All of First Squad was accounted for. None of Bravo Team fired that shot." He pointed to the video replaying for the fourth…or was it the fifth time? "All of them are static when that shot was fired. No increase in heat on any of their weapons."

"Hold on." Mark went back to his station and pulled up a three dimensional representation of the facility. Placing Apollo where he was standing when he was shot, the way he was facing and the entry of the bullet into the side of his head, he was able to extrapolate, within a seven degree arc, the approximate location of the shooter. He sent the data to the big screen. "Cap, our shooter was somewhere along this vector."

Jericho studied the 3-D layout a moment then typed in the commands to send the information to Spalding. "Team Leader, OPCOM, your shooter is somewhere along this vector."

"Copy, OPCOM." Spalding's mic went dead and the men in the command center watched as three heat signatures took off at full speed.

Jericho pulled the drone out of high orbit and put into a low arc, searching for the shooter as well. "If he's anywhere nearby, we'll find him."

Mark stared at the drone's video feed and prayed something tangible could be found. "Let's hope for the shooter's sake that we find him before Spalding does."

*****

"Monsieur Thorn, you have a call." The enforcer held the phone to his chest waiting to see if Rufus would accept the call. Rufus slipped from his bed and nodded, waving the man closer and reaching for the phone.

"Viktor, I appreciate you calling so soon."

"You said it was important." The fatigue in his voice was unmistakable.

"*Oui, mon ami.* I must ask a very large favor. One that I fear you will not like."

"I am listening." Rufus could hear rustling in the background as if Viktor were dressing while speaking to him.

"I need to speak to your aunt. The witch."

"I do not personally know the gypsy." Viktor spoke slowly, choosing his words carefully, "However, I could speak with my mother. It may be possible to get you an audience with her. If she still lives."

"That is all I could ask, *mon ami*. I cannot express how much I appreciate—"

"I must ask," Viktor interrupted, "if what Nadia tells me is true?"

Rufus inhaled deeply and sighed. "If she has told you that I acted behind Jack's back and broke his trust, then *oui*, it is true."

"And you created a weapon that could destroy all non-human beings?"

Rufus couldn't be sure from the deadpan tone of Viktor's voice what the wolf was thinking, but he knew better than to lie to him. "That is not a simple answer. The weapon had the potential to kill any non-human it was used on, but it was made to combat only one."

"And yet you used it."

"In an emergency situation, *oui*." Thorn feared where this was about to go.

"Against attacking wolves."

Rufus sighed again and hung his head low, his free hand rubbing the back of his neck. "*Oui*. Against an attacking force of wolves."

Silence echoed across the phone line for an extended period of time. Rufus could barely hear Viktor breathing on the other end. When he finally spoke, Rufus was surprised he did not yell. "Did the weapon work?"

"*Non*. It was destroyed." He lifted his eyes and stared at the ceiling of the hotel room. "It nearly killed me in the process."

Viktor exhaled hard into the phone, and Rufus feared what he may say next. "I suppose we should all be thankful that it did not."

"*Oui*, I am very thankful. Monsieur Thompson, on the other hand, I do not think shares such sentiment."

"Then he is a fool." Viktor's sharp tone surprised Rufus. "I will contact you once I have arranged the meeting with the witch."

"Thank you, *mon ami*."

*****

Laura stared at the clock, the second hand seemingly slowing as the clock continued to tick away. She knew that once Matt was out of his cell, she would have little time to press her position or he'd find another reason for her to stick around. She walked through her office for the third time, ensuring that everything she needed was packed. She lifted the single duffle bag and carried it to the door. She turned back and stared at the room that had essentially been 'home' for the past six years and slowly pulled the door shut.

"Need a hand with that?"

Laura spun and saw Dominic approaching. She relaxed her grip on the bag as he reached for it. "I think I can handle it."

"Aw, come on, Ms. Youngblood. If you're really going to leave, let me at least be a gentleman and carry the lady's bag once." He pulled it from her grip and hefted it as though it were weightless.

She nodded and waved him on in front of her. "To the parking lot, my knight."

"I like the sound of that." Dom turned and headed for the elevators. After she stepped in, he punched the button for topside. "So this is really it, huh?"

"Once Matt is back up and in charge, yeah. Major Tufo is out of harm's way. The colonel's girlfriend has been delivered. There's no reason for me to stay."

"No reason?" Dom gave her a sideways glance. "What about Doc? I bet he's gonna miss you something bad."

She stifled her smile and avoided his watchful gaze. "I'll come back and visit from time to time."

"And Doc's okay with that?" Dom shook his head. "Sorry, ma'am, but if I was Doc, I'd have dragged you off to some dark, secluded spot, tied you up, and not let you leave." She gave him a cautious stare and Dom suddenly stiffened. "Sorry. It didn't sound nearly as creepy in my head."

"Evan and I have an understanding."

"Maybe you do, ma'am, but he's a guy. I can tell you from experience that we're not the best at putting how we feel into words." He held the door for her as it opened. "I'd bet money he's hurting inside a lot more than he'll admit."

She stepped outside of the elevator and opened the door leading to the main hangar. She held it open as Dom stepped out and toward the overhead doors leading to the parking lot. The first rays of dawn were just beginning to break over the eastern horizon, and Laura felt an anxious pang as the two stepped out to the gravel parking area. She unlocked her Jeep, and Dom placed the bag in the back for her then shut the rear door.

He turned to her and lowered his voice. "Ma'am, I'm sorry. I know it's not my place to say anything. I know you got your reasons for leaving." He glanced back toward the hangar and then to her car. "I know you've wanted to leave for a long time. But if you have any kind of second thoughts, now would be the time to let them know."

Laura gave him a sad smile and pulled the large man into a soft hug. "I'm going to miss you, Dom. I really will." She stepped back and smiled at him. "But I need this."

"Well, okay then." He tipped his cap to her. "Be safe out there, Miss Laura. You know as well as anybody what's really out there."

"I will." She turned and marched back inside. She felt it best to wait for Mitchell inside his office.

*****

Matt's first memory after shifting back was of a burning sensation across his shoulders. He looked down at the raw, red marks where the silver bars had scalded his wolf. His arm lay between the bars and rested on Jenny's bare hip. She lay on the floor, as close to the silver bars as possible without touching them, sleeping.

Matt sat up and stretched, the cold concrete floor having stiffened his body; aches and pains the result of a night spent on a surface not designed for sleeping on. He glanced around and saw Jack, still in the form of his Halfling, sitting at the back of his cell, his eyes glued to the clock.

Mitchell cleared his throat and nodded to Jack. "Chief, I think you can shift back now." Jack's Halfling turned and stared at him then back to the clock. In a brief golden glow, Jack shifted to his human form, his bodysuit now hanging loosely from him, but slowly starting to pull back to its original size.

Jack stretched, his body popping as he groaned. "You really should consider putting bunks in here."

"Had some for a short while. My wolf kept destroying them."

Mitchell walked to the door and waited for the time lock to open them. He saw Jenny stir on the floor, her soft moans from laying on the cold surface pulling at him.

Jack waited at the door and pushed it open as soon as the locks clicked. "I have something I need to do. I'll catch up with you."

Mitchell was picking up the clothes outside the cells as he turned to Jack's retreating form. "What's so important, Chief?"

"I think I know where Thorn might be." He took the stairs two and three at a time and disappeared.

Mitchell slipped on his boxers and pants then hung his shirt over his shoulders. He scooped up Jenny's clothes and stepped into her cell. She was just sitting up slowly, the cold concrete having stiffened her body as much as it had his. He handed her the clothes she had tossed out of her cell and turned his back to allow her to dress.

"I, uh…I wonder how our wolves reacted last night?"

She placed a hand on his shoulder and turned him around to face her. "We're wolves, Matt. Nudity means nothing to us, remember?"

He tried to avert his eyes as she turned him to face her. "It's not…I mean, I…" He exhaled hard and turned his gaze back to her, their eyes meeting. "It's more out of respect, Jenny."

She reached up and caressed his cheek. "That's very sweet. But after last night, I don't think you need to be so bashful." Her smile made him tingly inside, and he felt like a teenager again. Someone had released butterflies in his stomach and words couldn't form in his mind, much less in his mouth.

"After…last night?"

"Our wolves accepted each other." She smiled sweetly at him and then began dressing. Matt didn't want to look at her, but his eyes soaked in every inch of her body as she slipped back into her clothing.

"Uh, what…how do you mean, 'accepted'?" He rubbed a hand through his hair and stared at her. "Did we…I mean, are we…"

"Are we mated?" She laughed gently and shook her head. "No, we're not. But it isn't from a lack of trying. I think those silver bars worked a little too well." She pointed to the burns along his shoulders and the backs of her thighs. "I remember just enough to know that our wolves tried though."

"I am so sorry."

"Don't be." She worked her bra back on, and Matt had to turn away, the butterflies fluttering in overtime. "It's natural."

"It may be natural, but…I mean. I thought that 'we' had to accept each other. I mean…" He trailed off, unable to find the right words.

"Our wolves are part of us, Matt. They know what we truly want, even if we aren't sure." She pulled her shirt on and slipped in next to him. "All I know is that I remember the dreams after I slept. Our wolves were together and they were happy."

"Does that mean we'd be happy together?" He truly didn't understand, but he wanted to so desperately.

"As long as we don't mess it up, I think so." She turned and headed for the cell door. "Are you ready?"

Matt squared his shoulders and nodded to her. "As ready as I'll ever be."

*****

Donovan held the rifle in his hands and inspected it. "Sniper rifle. What do you want to bet that once we trace it, the rifle will have come from South America?" He handed the rifle to Spalding who gripped the weapon so tightly in frustration that he feared the stock might break.

Lamb appeared from the small building. "Looks like our shooter was in the rafters and fired from under the roof overhang. This part of the wall is missing. We'd never have seen him."

"Not with a suppressor on it." Donnie pointed to the end of the barrel. "Bravo units couldn't have spotted him."

"Neither could the drone." Jacobs studied the ground where a set of boot prints went off toward the chain link fence. "Looks like he exited this way."

"Donnie, you and John track him. See if he's still on foot or if he scavenged a vehicle. Radio back if you find anything." Spalding turned to Jacobs and Lamb. "You two, back on security detail for the clean-up crew."

Spalding watched as the two sets of operators broke apart and went in separate directions. He waited a moment then stepped inside the building. He stared up into the rafters where the shooter had laid in wait. Jumping up into the overhead, Spalding suspended himself across the rafters and peered out through the missing gable. He had a clear view of the entire yard. The shooter could have taken out any of them at any time…yet, he'd chosen to only shoot Apollo.

Spalding watched as his men provided security to the clean-up crews and considered the situation. Either the shooter had a personal axe to grind against Apollo or was under orders from somebody who did. Could Sheridan have given an order prior to shifting? Wouldn't that mean that at least some of the men under Sheridan's command were human and not wolf?

Spalding slipped down from the rafters and walked out of the small building. "Too many questions, not enough answers." He turned and headed out to the main yard. He paused as he noticed the clean-up crews placing Apollo into a body bag. He watched as the men zipped the bag shut then lifted the body and placed it into the back of a truck.

Spalding vowed to find out who was responsible, even if it took destroying every last wolf at Simmons' disposal.

*****

Kalen lay in the dark and stared at the ceiling, sleep refusing to return to him. He placed his hand back against the cinder block wall and tried to feel the leather clad woman on the other side. All he could feel was the cold cement under his fingertips.

He rolled to his side and tried to force the thought of her from his mind. Why had these thoughts invaded his mind like this? He had never been so attracted to a female before that it left him distracted. Was it her skill? Was it her flippant attitude? Was it her defiance?

He sighed and rolled to the other side, unable to get comfortable. He ground his teeth together and fought to force the female vampire from his mind. He tried to think of anything else. His brother Horith. His homeland. The many battles he had fought. Nothing could completely remove her. When he thought of his home, she would be lurking behind a tree, waiting for him to spot her. When he thought of the battles he had fought, she was there as well, fighting alongside him. When he thought of Horith, she always invaded his mind, sitting atop him, unzipping her top, and biting with such speed that it shocked him.

It frightened him.

It shook him.

It excited him.

Kalen sat up and went to the sink once more. He ran the cold water and splashed it across his face. He snapped on the light and stared at the reflection in the mirror, water dripping from his sharp features. Turning his head, he looked to the area on his neck where she had bitten him in his dream. He wasn't surprised that nothing was there. No matter how real the dream felt, it was still just a dream.

Kalen turned and opened the door of his room. He turned down the hallway toward the bathroom and ran into Brooke, heading the opposite direction. She wore the same shocked expression he did at that moment. "Apologies. I was just…" Kalen pointed behind her. "The lavatory is there."

She blushed and averted her eyes. "Yes. The ladies room is…" She pointed behind him.

Kalen nodded slightly and stepped out of her way, allowing her to pass. She stepped past him and disappeared through a doorway. Kalen watched her and felt a pang in his chest as she strode purposefully through the hallway. He turned slowly and made his way to the restroom. Once inside, he pulled a towel from the rack and stripped off his robe.

Stepping into the shower, he turned the water on hot and let the steaming water beat his skin until it shone bright pink. He couldn't help but wonder why she acted the way she did in the hallway. It seemed so out of character for her. She actually blushed when she saw him. He chuckled to himself as the water beat his skin.

Kalen slowly lifted his eyes and stared at the tiled wall. *She blushed?* Why would she blush? What could possibly make her react in such a manner unless…

He turned quickly and shut off the water, toweling off absentmindedly. He dropped the towel in the basket and slipped his robe back on. He slowly approached her door and held his hand up, ready to knock. *What am I doing?* He stepped back and stared at the door. Slowly, he retreated the short distance back to his own room and opened the door. He stepped inside and sat on the edge of his bed. How could he ask her what he wanted to ask? *Did you have the same dream I had?* He snorted a short laugh to himself as he realized how ludicrous it would sound.

Kalen turned off the light and lay back on his narrow bed, staring at the ceiling in the darkness. "Surely she didn't share the same dream as I did…did she?"

He rolled over and stared at the block wall he shared with Brooke. He raised his hand and placed it gently against the cold cement. "Did you?"

On the other side of the wall, Raven lay in her narrow bed facing the block wall she shared with Kalen, her hand pressed to the concrete block. "Did you?" she whispered in the darkness.

*****

Lilith stood and paced slowly, inspecting those who had already arrived. She cocked her head to the side and whispered to Samael, "Why would some of them take the bodies of women?"

"Women have power and position in this day. Those who can serve a purpose have been taken."

Lilith nodded and continued walking between the rows of her legion. Satisfied, she turned to Samael, "How many more are coming?"

"About half." He lowered his voice and pulled her aside. "They've taken bodies of people in key positions in order to expedite your rise to power."

Lilith purred as she rubbed against him. "I like the way you think." She turned and glanced back over the crowd. "I suppose there are presidents and politicians out there?"

Samael shook his head. "This is an army, my love. We have soldiers, police, those who can operate military machinery and those who can get us access to weapons. We don't need politicians."

She pouted and leaned against him. "Politicians can simply hand us over their lands. Armies have to fight to dominate."

"And they are an army. Fighting is what they know." Samael squeezed her bottom. "They would be outed quickly if they tried to emulate a politician, but a soldier?" He shook his head.

"Very well." She turned and he watched as she made her way back to the warehouse office. "Have somebody notify me when the rest of my army arrives."

Samael nodded to Gaius. "You heard your queen."

Gaius dropped to one knee and bowed. "As she wills, so shall it be done."

Samael turned and followed Lilith into the office. He stuck his head back out and looked to Gaius. "Bring us water and wine. We'll be thirsty soon." He gave the man a wicked smile before shutting the door.

2

Mark stepped out of the OPCOM and leaned against the wall, his thoughts turning to the past when he and Apollo had interacted not only as coworkers, but as friends. He tried to shake off the anger he felt as the images replayed in his mind. He knew that Apollo had turned against them. Hell, he was the reason he had been attacked and infected. But still…it just didn't seem *right* that somebody should shoot the man like that.

Had it been in the heat of battle and he had been injured, that's one thing. If he had been tagged for a body bag and taken out by one of the squad members, that was another. But to be sniped once the dust had settled? That was chicken shit. If you're going to drop a guy, do it face to face.

Mark pushed off the wall and felt the pangs of hunger tearing through his midsection. He made his way down to the chow hall and absentmindedly filled a platter, his mind still replaying the events of the night. As he sat alone in the furthest corner, he continued to replay the events. His body went through the motions of stemming his appetite without ever truly tasting the food or remembering what he had eaten.

He pushed the platter away and stared at the stack of bones, a momentary lapse in memory causing him to question where they originated. He sighed heavily and leaned back in his seat, his mind playing back to the battlefield. If all of Simmons' men had shifted, then who fired the shot? Surely this Simmons character wouldn't trust humans to work alongside his wolves? Mark scratched at his chin as his mind raced. If not another human, then who else could have…he shot from his chair and practically ran from the chow hall.

"What's your hurry, Major?" Hammer asked as he darted past him.

"I need to make a call." Mark skidded to a stop and turned on the man. "Any idea what time it is in England right about now?"

*****

Rufus hung up the phone gently and turned to Foster. "We have our audience. The gypsy witch will see us."

"Hooray for us." Paul stretched on the bed and flicked at his nails. "And you truly think this witch will tell you the truth? What is to prevent her from lying to you for shits and giggles?"

Thorn called his valet and ordered his bags readied. Preparing a cognac, he spoke to Foster absently. "She will speak truly. It is her way."

"How can you be assured?"

"She is sworn to her sister. That sister is Viktor's mother, and if Viktor has arranged the meeting, then she has sworn an oath to him to serve my purpose honestly. Viktor will have seen to it." Rufus sat down gently and sipped at the cognac.

"You put an awful lot of trust on an awful lot of maybes." Foster slid his legs off the edge of the bed and shook his head. "I fear I will never be as trusting as you are, brother."

"I must be." Rufus stared deeply at the snifter of cognac, his mind playing out possibilities. "My fears are not with whether Angelica may lie to us. My fears are with if she tells us the truth." He turned and faced Foster. "Then we will have to face Damien and possibly the demon whore Lilith."

Foster snorted with derision. "He shall answer the call of his maker or be undone." He stood and marched to the door separating the rooms. "And as for Lilith, if she has truly been reanimated, then we shall do the world a favor and shred her heart once more."

Thorn watched as his brother marched purposefully back to his room and prepared to leave. His own valets entered and began packing his belongings while he contemplated the future. If Lilith was once more walking the earth, surely they'd know. Wouldn't they? She would have made her presence known the moment she became whole.

He swirled the cognac in the snifter and sipped at it, his mind considering the numerous possibilities. If Lilith was once more amongst the living, their safest course of action would be to allow the Monster Squads to deal with her. If he could only *know* for sure one way or the other.

"Monsieur Thorn, your belongings are ready."

Rufus looked up and nodded to the valets. "Very well. See them to the car." He drained his snifter and placed it back on the tray. "Notify my brother that I'll be waiting downstairs."

*****

Jack sighed heavily into the phone. "No, I don't know where he might be staying. I only know that the Council demanded that they meet on the full moon and that—" He pulled the phone back and rubbed at the bridge of his nose. "Yes, I understand that was two nights ago for you, but he may still be in town."

Lieutenant Gregory reached for the phone. "Chief? Can I give it a try?"

Jack shrugged and handed the phone to the junior officer. "Give it a whirl."

"This is Lieutenant Gregory with Team Four. With whom am I speaking?" Jack watched as the man jotted down the name. "Captain, we've been asked to coordinate with Team Two in trying to apprehend a wanted fugitive who has stolen classified data and attempted to build what we believe is a Doomsday weapon. This person of interest had an appointment in Geneva yesterday evening and we have reason to believe he may still be in the area. All we are asking is for you to send some of your people to check it out. If he's vacated the area, we'd appreciate the feedback. But if he's still in the area and you can apprehend him for us, we'd be very much in your debt."

"It ain't gonna work." Jack leaned back in his chair and crossed his arms behind his head. He stared at the ceiling and shook his head with frustration.

"Thank you, Captain. You can call me back at this number, day or night. I truly appreciate your cooperation in this matter." Gregory shot Jack a smirk as he hung up the phone. "He's got spotters in the area, and they're going to hack the local hotel registries to see if Thorn signed in under his own name. If anybody from the States checked in with an entourage, they'll check it out and get back to us."

Jack leaned forward and stifled a smile. "How in the hell did you…"

"You catch a lot more flies with honey than you do with vinegar." Gregory shrugged.

"I was using honey!" Jack stood as Gregory stood and left the room. "I was! I know how to use…" He stammered after the man's back. Jack fell back into his chair and chuckled. "I don't care if you used black strap molasses, as long as they'll cooperate."

*****

Matt opened the door to his office and stopped dead in his tracks. Laura stood so quickly that he nearly jumped. "Ms. Youngblood." He nodded to her then slipped behind his desk and poured a cup of coffee. "I suppose I have you to thank for brewing this?"

"Yes, sir. I assumed you'd want some as soon as you got out." She sat as he took his chair.

"Thanks." He sipped the dark bitter nectar and sighed. "Ahh, now that hits the spot." He smiled at her then noted the look on her face. His smile slowly faded, and he placed his coffee mug on his desk. "I'm not going to like this, am I?"

"I'm ready, Colonel."

Mitchell gave her a confused look at first then realization struck him. "Oh." He glanced around his office, hoping to find something else that needed doing before she could officially 'leave' their service. "I, uh…"

"I brought her in just like you wanted. You don't need to travel any longer and leave the squads behind." Laura cleared her throat and rubbed her palms across her pants leg, attempting to dry them. "Mark is all but healed completely. He's more than capable of taking over all of my duties."

"And, uh…Evan? He's okay with…"

"We've talked. He knows that I need to go and he understands that I'll be back." She stood and nodded. "Colonel. I *need* to go."

Mitchell stood slowly and shook his head. "I guess you do." He stepped out from behind his desk and shook his head. "I just don't understand why you have to go so quickly."

"If I don't get out of here, I'll never go. This place has a way of sucking me back in. It seems like every time I turn around there's something else that is threatening the world, and if I could just stick around a little bit longer…" She gave him a tight lipped smile. "I will be back. Eventually. But right now? I have to get out of here or I'll go insane and take everybody else with me."

Mitchell nodded as he held out a hand to her. "Understood."

Laura reached for his hand then paused. She stepped forward and wrapped her arms around the man that had become a surrogate father to her. "I'll come back. I promise." Her voice sounded tiny and small, buried in his chest.

"I'll hold you to it." Mitchell stroked her hair gently and allowed her to let go and wipe at her face. "If you don't, you know a certain vampire that will definitely come looking for you."

She sniffed back a tear and nodded. "Yes, sir." She stood at attention and snapped a perfect salute. Mitchell sobered then returned it. He felt his chest tighten as she spun and marched out of his office. As he watched her walk away, he felt like his family was being torn from him once again.

He stood alone in his office for a moment, unsure what to do next. He turned slowly back to his desk and sat down, suddenly weary. He reached for his coffee cup as his door opened again. Captain Jones stepped just inside. "Have a moment, sir?"

Mitchell glanced up and waved him in. "How did the op go

last night, Jericho?"

Jones approached his desk and laid a report down gently. "It could have gone better."

Mitchell snapped to attention. "Casualties?"

Jericho nodded. "One, sir." He tapped the report. "Apollo."

Mitchell released the breath he had been holding and nodded slowly. "So that's what the men decided."

"Negative, sir." Jones seemed to be in a state of shock, or disbelief. "The men took a vote and decided to banish Apollo. He could no longer be a part of the squads, never pop up on our radar or face their wrath. They were going to tell him to just fade away. Maybe find a pack and lay low."

"What happened, Captain?"

Jericho slowly shook his head. "Sniper, sir. And he got away. He's still out there somewhere."

"It wasn't any of our perimeter watches?" Mitchell picked up the report and thumbed through it.

"Negative, sir." Jericho nodded toward the report. "It's all covered in there."

Mitchell closed the report and looked up at Jones. "Are you okay, Captain?"

Jericho inhaled deeply and let it out slowly while he chose his words. "We lost an operator tonight, sir. Whether he was actually still with us or not, that doesn't matter. He was one of us." He turned toward the door then spun back toward Mitchell. "I know this makes no sense, but it would have been different if the squad had decided to…" He trailed off.

Mitchell stood and approached the man. He placed a comforting hand on his shoulder and nodded. "I understand what you're saying, son. Somebody took it upon themselves to lay down judgment on one of our own."

"Exactly, Colonel. They don't have the right." Jericho turned reddened eyes to him and shook with rage. "If we had decided that, it's one thing, but we didn't."

"This isn't over, Captain. If there's still one of theirs out there, we'll keep hunting until we find him." Mitchell squeezed his shoulder gently.

Jericho inhaled deeply and nodded. "Apologies, Colonel."

"No need, son. Apollo was with us for a very long time. He may have strayed and done things that we have trouble understanding, but I understand exactly where you're coming from."

Jericho nodded his thanks and turned for the door. "Oh, by the way, sir, Major Tufo is on the horn with Team One in England. I think he may be following up on a hunch."

*****

Bigby maneuvered his stolen car through the industrial park and toward the interstate. Once he was back onto the freeway, he quickly blended with the early morning traffic of those who diligently trekked to and from work like drones. He drove aimlessly until he found himself north of the city and passing well to do homes. He saw a billboard for model homes and without thinking took the exit.

His body was exhausted and his mind raced at what to do next. He knew he needed to let Mr. Simmons know what had happened. He debated on whether to paint Sheridan as an idiot for having trusted the Yank or not. He finally decided against that move. If he made Sheridan out to be inadequate, there was a good chance that Simmons would consider him to be as well.

Big pulled the stolen car into the housing complex and noted the finished homes near the front of the entrance and the new construction in different stages of completion the further you drove. He drove the car through the area and once he was satisfied that the crews had yet to arrive, he turned back and pulled to one of the last homes that appeared finished. He pulled the car up to the garage door and stepped from the running vehicle. The garage door was locked as was the front door. The back door was locked as well, but a quick elbow to the glass gained him entry.

He walked through the semi-furnished home and through the garage, opening the garage door for the car. He pulled the car in and killed the engine. Shutting the garage door, he noted that the first of a line of work trucks had just begun to enter the subdivision. He walked back to the living room and pulled slightly at the blinds. He smiled to himself as the trucks all pulled to the other side of the small subdivision and crews began their daily trudge.

Big fell into an overstuffed chair in the living room and slipped his cell phone from his cargo pocket. He scrolled through the numbers until he found the one he wanted. Punching in the code, he waited for a tone.

When the voice on the end answered, he patiently stated, "Walter Simmons, please." Big closed his eyes and waited.

"Mr. Simmons, my name is Archibald Bigby. I worked with Major Sheridan." Bigby waited for the man to say his piece then interrupted, "Sir, we've run into a spot of trouble. Major Sheridan is no longer with us. Neither are your wolves. It would seem that Mitchell's boys stumbled upon us during the full moon, and they assassinated the lot of them while they were confined."

Bigby waited while his comment soaked in and then listened while the man went off on his tirade. "Sir, if I might..." He tried to interrupt. Bigby held the phone away from his ear while the man yelled. When the volume reduced enough, he brought the phone back to his face. "Sir. I may have a solution. Not all of the weapons were lost, and if you still have wolves incoming, then I believe I can pull off a counter attack that will level them. They believe that they've destroyed your forces entirely. They aren't aware that there is a second wave incoming as support."

"You want me to sacrifice the rest of my manpower?" Walter Simmons screamed into the phone. "Are you daft?"

Bigby inhaled deeply and closed his eyes again. "Negative, sir. I'm simply saying that if you still want your revenge, I can assure it. They won't be expecting a secondary force to muster so quickly and strike. We have the weapons and you have the wolves incoming, do you not?"

Walter Simmons paced the floor of his grand office, his eyes darting from corner to corner. "There is a possibility that my daughter is on her way there. Can you guarantee her safety if she arrives before my wolves do?"

"If you can get me her picture, I can guarantee that we will do everything in our power to secure her prior to the attack. Perhaps we can even intercept her."

Walter slammed his fist into the wall and clenched his teeth. "How did this happen? How could they have known that my men were staging there?"

Bigby sighed and shook his head. *Better to be truthful, old boy.* "In all honesty, sir, Major Sheridan recruited an inside man. It is my belief that he may have tipped our hand. Perhaps inadvertently, but regardless of whether it was him or not, he's no longer part of the equation. I removed him myself."

"You…how?"

"A silver bullet to the head. I refuse to suffer a traitor to live. Even a suspected traitor." Bigby listened to the older man breathe heavily into the phone.

"You *suspected* that he was a traitor so you killed him?"

"Correct."

The old man laughed; Bigby wasn't sure if that was a good sign or not. "You are a hard son of a bitch, aren't you?"

"Operationally tactical, sir," Bigby corrected.

"Either way, I think you might be one I can work with. Just between us, I wasn't sure if I could trust Sheridan." Bigby heard rustling over the phone as if the old man were settling it in the crook of his shoulder. "My men are still on their way. And if you need support equipment, it's yours."

"Very well, sir. I'll check back in with you this evening after I've secured another location to base operations from." Bigby clicked the end call button and glanced out the window once more. Satisfied that the construction workers would be staying on the other side of the subdivision, he leaned back in the chair and closed his eyes. After the night he had, he needed to rest his exhausted body.

*****

First and Second Squads pulled into the gravel parking lot behind the large, green two-ton trucks that the clean-up crews used to transport the bodies of the wolves. Spalding stepped from the truck and felt both physically and emotionally spent. "Ing, do you mind escorting the clean-up crews?"

Jacobs shook his head. "Whatever you need, boss." He elbowed Lamb. "Wanna tag along?"

"And miss them incinerating these guys? I'd rather have my eyes gouged with hot pokers." He tossed his pack to Little John. "Want to hang that up for me, brother?"

Little John caught the bag and gave him a mock salute. "Gotcha covered. You two have fun." He turned and jogged to catch up with Spalding. "They just incinerate the dead?"

Spalding gave him a weary nod. "Reduces the chance of spreading the virus." Spalding held the door for him then hit the button for the roll away door. "Used to be, they would do autopsies and whatnot, but…we already know what killed them. There really isn't a need. They bag up the bodies, spray that bio-foam crap anywhere there's biological contamination then bring 'em back here and torch 'em."

Little John paused at the staging table and hung up Lamb's pack then his own. "What about…" He trailed off then met Spanky's eyes. "When it's one of our own?"

Spanky nodded. "Same thing, brother. No fancy funerals for us. No coffins to be buried in Arlington National. No twenty-one gun salute." Spanky leaned against the table and sighed heavily. "That short memorial we had for Carbone? That's actually pretty rare. Part of the requirement for being a member of the squad is no ties. That way, nobody will miss you when you're dead. No screaming families demanding a body to bury. No wife or kids demanding…" He trailed off and ran a hand over his face. "Sorry, buddy."

"No, I'm…I shouldn't have asked. I know you and Apollo were really tight. I barely knew him. He seemed like a good guy, what little I did know."

Spalding nodded. "He was." He turned and stared at the hook holding Apollo's gear. "I still can't figure out what made him snap like that."

"I thought it had something to do with that gal that didn't make it out of Nevada."

Spalding nodded solemnly. "Yeah, but, there *had* to be more to it than that." Spalding turned to face him and fought back his emotions. "I just can't accept that everything that went south was because someone like Sheridan was able to get under Apollo's skin."

John shrugged. "Maybe Apollo saw an opportunity to infiltrate the bad guys and took it?"

Spalding shook his head. "Nah. He turned to the dark side. Even if he lived to regret it, he still did it."

Little John watched his team leader as he played out events in his mind, trying like hell to make sense of it. When he couldn't, he watched as Spalding tightened up, ready to put his fist through an inanimate object. He took the opportunity to lay a gentle hand on his shoulder and remind him that striking out did little more than hurt yourself. "If you want to work off some of that anger, let's go grab some chow and then hit the heavy bag in the gym. I'll spot you if you'll spot me."

Spalding turned to him and gave him a questioning stare. "What do you need pounding therapy about?"

"I'll give you a hint." Little John turned and started walking for the stairwell. "She's about 5'8", shares the same parents I do and drinks blood."

*****

Evan watched the monitors as Laura carried out the last of her belongings and climb into her Jeep. He could feel his heart threaten to start beating again just so it could break on him. His gut tightened and he fought the urge to dart upstairs and out into the sunlight to scoop her into his arms. If he didn't think that he'd burst into flames for trying, he would have pulled her back down to his lab and shackled her ankle to the corner of his desk.

He felt his lower lip tremble as she loaded the last of her bags into the back then walked to the door of the Wrangler and opened it. She paused and took a lasting look at the rusty old hangar then slipped in behind the wheel and started the engine. He watched the monitor as she backed away and drove off.

Evan slumped in his chair and fought the urge to cry. He knew that she'd be back, but in his mind and in his heart, he felt that she was leaving him. She was rejecting him. The logic portion of his brain screamed at him that it just wasn't so. Of all of the humans he knew, she would never abandon him. She loved him. She stood up for him when nobody else would.

He backed up the digital recording and watched her again, his vision blurry from unshed tears. He watched as she tossed her gym bag into the back then rearrange things. She picked up her other duffel and shoved it on top of a box then reached for the back door and slammed it shut, her head turning on a swivel before walking to the door of the Jeep.

Something piqued Evan's interest, and he backed the image up again. He watched her actions. Something didn't *feel* right. She wasn't acting appropriately. Why would she check her surroundings before getting into the car?

He watched as she loaded her bags again then shut the door, her head turning both directions, looking for…what?

Evan rewound the recording and watched again. He backed it up further and watched as she carried out other items. A box, another bag. There was already a large box in the back of her Jeep that she scooted to the side to make room for…he zoomed in on the box she carried.

He could barely catch it, but it was there. An aluminum case. He didn't remember her having an aluminum case in her office. Where could this one have come from? Evan rubbed at his chin as he studied what he could see of the case.

He adjusted the image again and tried to focus on the contents. For the briefest of moments he became distracted by her cleavage as she bent over to move things around in the back, but there it was. He sat back and stared at the image that he paused on his monitor.

A confused smile crossed his pale features as he reached for his telephone. Punching the numbers he waited for her to answer. "Miss me already? I'm barely out the gate."

"Why, yes, Pumpkin, I did miss you. Actually, I missed the case that you took when you left." He waited and listened to her on the other end. He could hear the Jeep slowly roll to a stop and her voice dropped to a whisper.

"I can explain."

"You had better."

*****

Lilith awoke and stretched, her body aching in all the right places. She allowed her eyes to adjust to the gloom, and her hand reached out beside her expecting to feel the warmth of Samael next to her. Her hand brushed the soft crumpled sheet, still warm from his body. He was not where she expected.

Rising from her bed, Lilith strode to the door and reached for the light. "Leave it off."

She snapped around, her attention drawn to the depths of the shadows. "You surprised me. I thought maybe you had stepped out."

"I was watching you sleep."

She squinted in the darkness but couldn't make out his form in the shadows. "Why do you stay in the shadows, my love? Step out so that I may hold you." She stepped toward him, putting the full sway of her hips to good use.

"Stay there. I like seeing you in silhouette. The light from the windows…it allows me to see you just the way you should be seen."

She paused and stared into the shadows. "And how is that?"

"As a beautiful creature of the dark."

She heard him rise, and the chair he had been sitting in creaked under the strain of his weight. A rustling sound caught her ears and she smiled. "Your wings?"

"Yes." He stepped forward and she caught the first glimpse of his completed self. She looked up at his chiseled jaw, the bright blue of his eyes, the blonde locks curling just above his brow. "Although not as I expected."

She stepped forward and ran her hand across his massive chest. Her fingers brushed his strong shoulders and she squeezed when she felt the meatiness of his massive arms. "What do you mean, my love?" Her voice was breathy as she drank him in with her eyes. "You look perfect to me."

"My wings. They're not like they were." He pulled them in and they settled over his shoulders like a great leather cape. "They're no longer feathered."

Her eyes widened as she ran her fingertips along the black leathery cape. She could feel the veins and connective tissue under the thin black skin. "What happened, my love?"

"I do not know. I can only surmise it is because I took this dead flesh as a palette."

"And it is reflected in your wings?"

He shrugged his massive shoulders and she noted the bat like wings rising with the action. "I can only assume so." He turned and stepped away from her. "It's not like I can go to my brethren and ask them, now can I?"

"What does it matter, my love? Wings are wings. You never needed them before. You can travel at the speed of thought." She ran her hands across the back of his shoulders and felt where the wings connected to his massive back.

"An angel is an angel, my dear. But it is all about perception." He spun on her and extended his wings, letting the blackness blot out what little light shone into the room. "They will see me as a demon on this plane."

Lilith sighed and wrapped her arms around his waist. She laid her head against his chest and felt him relax, his wings lowering and wrapping around her. "Once we have dominated them all, who cares what they think. All will bow before us."

Samael closed his eyes and squeezed her gently. "It matters, my love. For the subterfuge to work, they need to believe us holy at first."

She smiled wickedly and pulled away from him. "So we skip the holy part and go straight to domination."

"It will be much more difficult." He stroked at her hair with his massive hand.

"Perhaps. But we have a demon army that cannot be destroyed." She chuckled as she pulled back and stared up at him. "One thousand may as well be ten million when their numbers cannot be depleted."

3

Mark hung up the phone and went over the names on his list. He shook his head at the potential shit storm he had written down on paper and got up from his chair. Mitchell knocked just as Mark stepped out from behind his desk. He glanced up at the face poking through the door. "I heard you were running up the phone bill."

Mark waved him in and took his seat again. "I was running a hunch." He tossed the tablet across the desk. "Those are people who used to be with Team One."

Mitchell picked up the notebook and scanned the list of names. "What do you mean, 'used to be'? I thought Sheridan was the only one removed from—"

"The rest are either MIA or confirmed dead." Mark chewed absently at the end of the pencil in his hand. "I have a sick feeling in my gut, and it isn't from eating in the chow hall."

"So let me get this straight. Roughly a third of Team One has been killed or is MIA and nobody thought to say anything?" Mitchell slapped the notebook down on the desk and glared at Mark.

"Apparently it was one here, another there…it all took place over the last five or six months." He shrugged. "They didn't have reason to believe it was anything other than normal casualties during high risk missions."

"Normal casualties?" Mitchell sat down hard and stared at Mark disbelievingly. "How often do they lose people, I wonder?"

"They would find just enough evidence for them to convincingly place the person in the 'deceased' pile. Whether it was a bloody uniform or…hell, what does it matter? They're pissed that we didn't inform them that Sheridan slipped WitSec."

"Like we'd have any idea that weasel had. There's a reason it's called witness protection. They don't even tell us where the son of a…" Mitchell forced himself to stop and take a deep breath. "So the weasel not only slipped from WitSec, he recruited from his old team."

Mark nodded and tapped the list. "The ones who wouldn't join, he removed from service. Permanently. I guess he couldn't risk them telling anybody that he was back and about to stir up trouble."

Mitchell reached for the phone. "Get me the clean-up crews." He turned to Mark. "We need them to wait on incinerating the bodies. I want every one of them bounced off this list until we can tell if any of the MIA are with the dead."

*****

Rufus loaded the plane just as his phone rang. He took his seat and answered it. Foster fell into the chair across from him and watched his brother's eyes widen slightly. He spoke quietly into the phone then thanked the caller and ended the call. "Who was that?"

Rufus tucked the phone back into his coat pocket and buckled his seat belt. "That was one of our hired security. It would appear that representatives from an unknown military group came to the hotel looking for a party meeting our description."

Foster sat up, his curiosity piqued. "What did he say?"

"Only that they inquired as to whether or not we might have stayed at the hotel." Thorn sat back and closed his eyes, his face unreadable.

"And?"

"And the hotel staff is worth every Euro." He opened his eyes and a slight smile crossed his features. "They said that they've had no large parties check into the hotel in months. The human hunters left, accepting their answer."

"Something must have led them to that particular hotel."

"*Non*, security followed them to the next hotel where they asked the same questions. We are safe. For now."

Thorn closed his eyes again as the plane's engines began spinning up. Foster chewed nervously at his lower lip. "Was Thompson with them?"

"*Non*, Jack would be in the States still. Remember, he had to shift with the moon. I doubt that he would be in any condition to travel."

Foster leaned back in his seat and stared out the window. "Still, we had better keep on our toes. If Viktor had not secured the meeting with the Gypsy…"

"*Oui*, we would have been caught. Rather, we *could* have been caught. It truly would depend on the diligence of the hunters."

"Tell me where we are going next. I need to set up security

ahead of our arrival." Foster pulled his PDA from his coat pocket and began tapping into it.

"*Non*. We will not need additional security. We are invited by the wolves, we will be under their protection. We have the pack master's word."

Foster glared at his brother. "You, of all people, should know better than to trust your life…no, *all* of our lives, on somebody's word. We need extra security before we get close to—"

"*Non*!" Rufus sat up and shot Foster a stern stare. "When it comes to wolves, who knows better how to deal with them? Only I. If I say that Viktor's word is good enough, you shall accept it."

Foster prostrated himself in his seat and bowed his head. "Forgive me, m'lord. I meant only to keep you safe."

"The best way to keep me safe when dealing with wolves is to keep your mouth shut, your opinions to yourself and be grateful that they are willing to be of service. Regardless of your personal feelings toward wolves, they are a proud people with a strong sense of honor. You would do well to respect them and the power they wield."

"Of course. I meant no harm." Foster cast his eyes to the carpeted floor and only chanced a glance upward when the plane pulled forward and began taxiing toward the runway.

"Rest now, brother. We have a long flight."

*****

"What's in the case, Laura?" Evan continued to stare at the image of the aluminum case stuffed into the rear of her Jeep and listened to the phone while she shifted it, the sounds of traffic driving by highlighted by her breathing.

"I don't want to say." Her voice trembled as she spoke. "If I don't tell you, then you won't have to lie for me."

"Nobody but the two of us even knows about it. I won't have to lie, because nobody is going to know to ask me, will they? Please don't make me do a complete inventory. It will take far too long and you know how I am. I *will* do one if I think you are less than truthful."

Laura sighed into the phone and Evan knew the truth was about to pour from her along with some kind of explanation. "My father isn't well, Evan."

"And?"

"And, he's too young to suffer like this." She shifted the phone again and he could hear her putting the Jeep back into gear. She began driving again, and he wasn't sure if she was returning or driving away. "I had to do something."

"What did you take, Laura?"

"I took the protocol for the squad members." Her voice had changed to defensive, and Evan was too floored to understand why.

"You took the...*why*?! You know what that will do to him!"

"Yes, I do. It will save his life!" He could hear the engine accelerate as she spoke, her emotions taking over, causing her to 'run away' as she admitted to him her wrong doings. She knew it was wrong, but she did it anyway.

"Laura, you don't want to do this. Take it from me. I know. If I could refuse or remove what I am and be human again, even if it meant death."

"But that's because you're a vampire, Evan. This is the wolf. He can live a perfectly normal life as long as he takes the bane. He may get a little antsy around the full moon, but..." Her voice trailed off.

Evan felt his guts twist as she spoke. As if being infected with one virus wasn't 'as bad' as the other. Apparently all of their talks about being human and what that truly meant had fallen on deaf ears. He tried not to take it personally. This wasn't about him, this was about her. And her father. He inhaled deeply and blew it out slowly.

"Laura, you still aren't thinking this through."

"Yes, Evan, I am. When I left Nevada, I came back to Tinker to grab a few things from my office and grab this. He was sick then, but he's getting so much worse. I was getting desperate. It was now or never. So I grabbed it. Not a lot, just a couple of doses. I needed to be sure it took."

"How many did you take?"

"Two vials. That's all I planned to take. I know that one will do it, but with two…it *is* a gene therapy 'thing', right? I mean, he'll only need the one real dose."

"What color are the caps?" Evan rubbed the back of his neck as he saw the different dosages in his mind.

"One is blue. The other is a burnt orange. Almost red."

"Give the red first. Three days later, shoot him with the blue. The day after that, shoot him again with the blue. Just make sure you destroy what you don't use. Don't give more than 15ccs per dose. You got that?"

She sniffled into the phone. "Thank you. I mean it, Evan. Thank you. I don't know what I'd do without you."

"You'll get us both arrested if you get caught. Maybe even get your dad…never mind. Just make sure he understands what you're doing to him. Don't tell him it's some miracle cure. Make sure you tell him. I mean it, Laura. Give him the choice. Don't you dare decide for him. No matter how much you love him and want to save him. Promise me that."

"I love you."

Evan chewed at the inside of his cheek as he waited for her to promise. “I love you, too. But I mean it. Promise me you’ll tell him.”

“I’ll tell him.” There was something about her voice that he didn’t quite believe.

“Before you give him the shot. Promise me, Laura. Let *him* choose.”

She paused a little longer than he would have liked, but she finally capitulated. “I promise. I’ll let him choose.”

“Call me once you’re done. Just so I know there aren’t any complications.”

“I will.”

Evan heard the phone click and he leaned back in his chair. He reached for the mouse and deleted the images of her and the aluminum case from the computer systems. “What the hell have I just done?”

*****

Mitchell walked back to his office, the list of Team One soldiers still on his mind when a familiar voice called out. “What’s a girl got to do to get a meal around here?”

He turned and knew he had a goofy smile before he ever laid eyes on her. “Please excuse my lack of manners.” He held an arm out to her and she wrapped her arm around his. “Allow me to escort you to our fine dining facilities.”

“Fine dining? I’m impressed.” She fell into step alongside him and was just realizing how large and imposing he might be to someone he wanted to intimidate.

“I may have stretched the truth a little. *Fine* might not be the best descriptor. But it *is* a dining facility.” He punched the button for the elevator and held the door open while she stepped inside. He studied her and his brows knitted in confusion. "Say, weren't you a brunette when you arrived here? When did you change your hair to blonde again?"

She patted his arm. "That's a byproduct of the shift. If a gal wants to keep her hair dyed, she better buy stock in Miss Clairol. Every time you shift, your hair returns to its natural color."

"Must be really rough once someone goes gray." He absently ran a hand alongside his own hair.

"We age so slowly that very few wolves actually go gray. Those who do are usually quite proud of it." She gave him a knowing look. "Besides, it makes you look distinguished."

"I was thinking old, but I'll take what I can get." The doors opened and the smells of food wafted into the elevator. "As you can tell, the chow hall is right down here." He motioned down the hallway and escorted her inside.

"It's bigger than I would have thought." Jenny stepped in and found a few people milling about, some eating, others simply sitting and drinking coffee, reading while waiting to start their shift, or relaxing after coming off of one.

"We have a couple hundred people that we service. Naturally, the operators have pretty healthy appetites, so it's like having to feed three hundred. We go through quite a bit of meat."

"That goes without saying." She nodded to the stacks of bacon, the hams, and large chunks of roast behind the sneeze guards.

"We serve just about anything you could want at all hours. If you want breakfast at three in the afternoon, just come down here and tell the cooks what you want. They'll whip it up in no time."

"Oh, I'm liking this. This is better than room service." She elbowed him in the ribs. "A girl could definitely lose her figure with a place like this."

"Believe it or not, you get tired of the same foods. They have pizza night, steak night, Chinese food…it just depends on the day of the week. They try to switch things up pretty regularly. Still, the wolves usually stick with red meats."

"Have you already eaten?" She nodded to his empty hands and he shrugged.

"I was actually pretty hungry until I saw you. Then…"

"You're saying I killed your appetite? I'm not sure how to take that." She raised a brow at him.

"No, I just meant that, I dunno, it's like you calm my wolf. And when he's calm, I'm just not…I mean. I just don't…" He sighed heavily and leaned against the counter. "I just don't want anything else."

She gave him a wicked smile then handed him a tray. "Eat up, big boy. You keep talking like that and you just might need your strength built up."

*****

Mick sat alone in the tiny chapel that served the squads. A fine layer of dust covered the few pews inside, and the altar had assorted bric-a-brac stacked on it. The candles had all been burned to nubs and the place had obviously been forgotten.

He sat quietly and stared at the crucifix hanging on the wall behind the altar and noted how it had been knocked crooked. His first impression was that somebody had purposely thrown something in the tiny chapel, knocking the crucifix to the side, but not off the wall.

He continued to stare at the image of the son of God hanging broken on the cross and he dropped to his knees. He wasn't sure if he was simply begging to the universe or if he were praying to God. He had never really prayed before, even though he believed that there was a god. He wasn't sure which god might be the real god, but he knew that something had to have created everything. The very idea that the universe and all life was all some cosmic accident was just too big a leap of faith for him. It was much easier to believe that a much higher power, an all knowing being created everything.

Mick felt his heart break and he cried out softly. "Please, don't let her stay here with this buffoon. She deserves so much more. She deserves someone who knows her. She deserves someone who can truly love her for who she is. Not someone who is *told* they have to love her because some unseen force says so..." Mick suddenly realized what he was saying.

Here he was praying to an unseen force and begging for the girl he loved, all the while claiming that her being with her Fated Mate shouldn't happen because it was dictated by an unseen force. Could the two be the same? He collapsed in the floor and sobbed. Were the cards stacked so firmly against him? Would she ever forgive him?

Mick slowly pulled himself to his knees and stared at the crucifix again. "Can't you do something?"

The crucifix didn't answer no matter how much he willed it to do so. Mick hung his head and felt the sting of hot tears run down his cheeks.

*****

Bigby woke with a start. The banging had increased in volume, and he rolled from the chair he had been sleeping in. He slipped to the window and spread the blinds ever so carefully.

Outside, workers were constructing a fence around the front of the property he was currently in. He watched carefully and was about to slip back to another part of the house when a black SUV pulled to the front of the house and into the driveway. The vehicle stopped, and a man in a business suit stepped out, followed by a young couple.

Bigby cursed to himself as the trio walked to the front of the house and he heard the jingling of keys. "They'll have the fence done shortly, but this is just a model home. You'll be able to see the layout and pick and choose exactly how you want your own unit finished out."

Bigby slipped down the hallway and into a bedroom. He contemplated his options. He could exit from a bedroom window and work his way around the rear of the green field to another area where he might be able to steal another vehicle. He could kill the trio, take the SUV and pray that none of the work crew outside noticed. He closed his eyes and tried to imagine the outcome of each option. He knew that even if he evaded the invaders, it was only a matter of time before they looked in the garage and saw his stolen car.

Bigby heard the trio walk through the living area and into the kitchen. If he were going to make a break for it, he'd have to cross to the other side of the house now, while they were preoccupied.

Big glanced out the bedroom door then slipped silently to the bedroom across from where he was. He shut the door behind himself and went to the window. Lifting the glass, he pushed the screen out and slipped out to the back yard. He pulled the window shut then replaced the screen. Keeping low, he made his way to the corner of the house.

Bigby stepped out from behind the house and walked purposefully toward the road. He glanced back once and noted that nobody came running from the property, no shouts of alarm. He paused by one of the trucks parked by the front of the property and waited. After about five minutes, the trio walked out, and the three talked, the salesman pointing out different aspects of the property. Big watched from his vantage and wondered if they had ever entered the garage. Had they not seen his stolen car?

He shook his head at the unwitting trio as they stepped back into the SUV and backed out of the driveway. He stood near the back of the truck and watched as the black vehicle drove away. Did he dare risk going back for the car? What if they got the plate and reported it? What if they returned with the authorities? If he'd had his weapons, he wouldn't care.

Bigby sighed heavily and leaned against the truck. He considered possibly stealing one of the numerous work trucks parked around the site, but construction workers tended to keep a close eye on their tools and those tools were stored in their trucks.

"Looks like I'm walking."

He turned and worked his way back toward the main road. He'd find a stop and go gas station or fast food place to pick up his next ride. He glanced at his watch and realized, he'd better do it quickly. He still had to scout out a new base of operation.

*****

Kalen pressed his ear to the door and listened intently. Once he was assured that there was no movement in the hall and that Brooke was still asleep, he pulled the door open and stepped out. He was nearly knocked over by her returning from the ladies showers, her dark hair still dripping and her robe pulled tight around her pale body.

"I'm sorry. I didn't…" Kalen stammered as he tried to step to the side.

Brooke paused and lowered her eyes to the floor, her hand clutching the ends of her robe and pulling it tighter to herself. "Excuse me." Her voice was like a whisper, but seemed to echo in the empty corridor.

Kalen stepped aside and allowed her to pass. He tried not to watch her as she walked quickly to her room and slipped inside. He released the breath he had been holding and felt faint. He leaned against the wall and stared after her.

"Are you okay? You look pale."

Kalen spun to see Azrael and Gnat staring at him, concern etched across their features. He nodded absently. "Yes, I am fine. I just…" He turned and stared down the hallway again. "I was just wondering if we should bother to get Raven for morning meal."

Azrael shrugged. "She is vampire. I doubt they serve fresh blood at the banquet hall."

Kalen nodded absently, his eyes still glued to her door. "Perhaps you are right." He felt Azrael lay a hand on his shoulder and pull him gently toward the stairs.

"Come, dine with us and regale us with tales of your conquests on the battlefield."

Kalen turned to him and gave him a confused look. "Yes, and you as well."

Gnat grunted as the two took the lead. "Nobody cares about my conquests. I may as well stay under the table and eat the crumbs you two drop."

Azrael nodded. "As you wish, Gnome." He pushed open the doors to the stairwell and held it for the two others. "It might be best if you did. I doubt they have chairs tall enough for you to reach the table."

Gnat drew a dagger as the two larger warriors disappeared into the darkness of the stairs. “Perhaps I’ll start with a slab of Gargoyle.”

*****

Lilith slid her robes over her shoulders and stepped out to the warehouse. She felt Samael’s presence more than saw him. His shadow covered her from behind and she felt comforted by his closeness.

The pair watched as scores of demons entered the large overhead doors and milled about, preparing to be addressed by their queen. Many had begun to form up in ranks, lining up in columns and rows while others stayed in small groups, making small talk.

Lilith began to step forward when she noticed that the demons seemed to be frozen in place, none speaking. None were moving. None so much as blinked their eyes as they stood at attention. She turned back to Samael who was staring upward.

“What’s happening?” A cold chill settled upon her as an unearthly green glow began shining throughout the warehouse. “What’s going on, Samael?”

“My brother.” His face curled into a grimace as his hands clenched into fists and he set his feet. She noted that his great muscles were taunt as if ready to strike and she felt that familiar tugging in her loins. His arm shot forward and pulled her back behind him. “Do not look directly at him until he has made himself known.”

“Why would—” A brilliant flash of green light reflected off of all of the metallic surfaces, intensifying the magnificence of it. She slid behind Samael’s wing and hid her face in his back. “Tell me when it’s over.”

A strange voice boomed throughout the warehouse. “It is over. You may come out now, little mouse.”

“State your purpose, brother.” Samael stiffened even more as he held Lilith behind him.

She cast a furtive glance from around Samael’s arm and her eyes went wide with wonder. She spied the most brilliant of creatures…one that rivaled Samael in beauty and size, his armor glimmering as if aglow in the dim interior of the warehouse. The large, white feathered wings stretched out and flexed silently as the creature stepped toward her lover.

“I have come to warn you, brother. Nothing more.”

“Then state your warning and be gone.” Samael puffed out his chest and flexed his own wings, spreading them out behind him like a large black dragon.

“Oh, brother. What has become of you?” The angel tsk’d as he stepped closer. He paused and cast a disapproving eye at the Samael.

“Nothing for you to concern yourself with, I assure you.” Samael pushed Lilith further behind him, blocking her view. “Say what you intend to say, Azazel.”

The large angel sighed and Lilith could smell the most heavenly of scents, as if fresh breads were baking, smothered in honey and cinnamon. She closed her eyes and inhaled deeply, letting her ears cherish the sound of his voice as he spoke.

“Samael, you and your little war party are in danger.”

“I highly doubt that, *brother*.”

Azazel sighed and stepped closer. “While you may have chosen to stand against the Father, you were, and are still, my brother, Samael. He may have disowned you, but that doesn’t change who we are.”

“It changes what we stand for.”

Azazel shook his head and leaned against a large concrete pillar supporting the roof. "Samael, whether you believe me or not, it is so. Abaddon has seen it."

Samael snapped to attention, his brows knitted in worry as he studied Azazel. "Swear it."

"Do I have to, brother? I came all this way to carry his word to you."

"Swear it or it isn't so!" Samael growled, his fists clenched so tight that Lilith started with fright.

"I swear it. By the Father, by Abaddon's word, by my love for you, I swear it to be so." The look of pain and dejection on Azazel's face told Samael more than his words ever did.

"Then tell me Abaddon's vision." His body relaxed and he stepped away from Lilith, his wings draping off of her as he moved forward.

The two stepped to the far end of the warehouse, and Lilith slowly moved closer, tilting her head to listen to the conversation. "Abaddon has seen the upcoming battle and your attempt at placing your whore at the throne of Earth. It will fail."

"It cannot fail. I have given her a legion of demons." Samael stood tall, his shoulders squared.

"Aye brother, you have. But your efforts will fail. You will achieve only in being banished from this realm once more and having your lovely demoness torn to shreds once again. Your legion will be killed and…"

"Impossible! They are demons. They cannot be killed!" Samael crossed his arms in defiance and glared at Azazel.

Azazel sighed heavily and placed a heavy hand on his shoulder. "Aye, brother, they *can* be killed. And they will be."

"How? I tell you, it is impossible."

"Angelic weapons. From the Battle of the Fall. They are

stored here on Earth. And Gabriel has told a non-human where they are stored. She has put in place a team of warriors, young at heart…"

"No…" Samael's eyes widened. "The prophecy."

"Yes, my brother. The prophecy. Warriors five, young at heart, with angel swords and armor marked…"

Samael swallowed hard and nodded. "They'll hunt by night with all their might, 'til the lands be cleansed of the Darkness' plight." He turned and faced Azazel once more. "Have these warriors laid claim to the angelic weapons yet?"

"I honestly do not know, but Abaddon has seen that their location will be revealed to their benefactor." Azazel crossed his arms and studied Samael. "And since none but Gabriel and Rafael know where the weapons cache are…"

"And neither are likely to tell either of us," Samael growled in frustration.

"They definitely won't tell you, Samael. You're a Fallen brother."

Samael turned slowly to him. "But you're not."

"I wouldn't even try. They're both Archangels."

"So?"

"So there's no deceiving an Archangel. They can see right through the attempts." Azazel shook his head. "I'm sorry, brother, but you're on your own with that endeavor."

He turned to leave and Samael grabbed his wrist. "You're in this with me, brother. You brought word of Abaddon's visions. If the Archangels discover your treachery, your life isn't worth a bucket of warm piss."

Azazel smiled as he pulled his arm free. "It was Michael that sent me."

Samael's eyes widened at the name. "Why would Michael, of

all angels, send you to warn me?"

"In an effort to prevent innocent blood from being shed. Nothing else."

Samael opened his mouth to continue the argument when Azazel vanished in a flash of green light. He stared at the spot where his brother once stood and trembled. "If the angels on high want me to stop, then perhaps we're on to something greater than we imagined."

4

Mark paced outside the small outbuilding where the clean-up crews incinerated the biological waste. He checked his watch for the twelfth or thirteenth time when the outer door opened and a technician in a white biohazard suit stepped out. He removed his oversized helmet and tucked it under his arm. "We checked every body in there against the stack of pictures you gave us, Major. The only match was ex-Major Sheridan." The man handed a clipboard to Mark who stared at it as though it were infected.

"You can burn that, too." Mark took a half step back and eyed the man warily. "You're absolutely certain?"

"We double checked, sir. The only one was Sheridan, and all of the bodies have finished shifting back to their human forms. There was no mistaking the idents."

Mark hung his head as he turned. "Great. There's no telling how many may still be out there."

“Sir?” The tech stepped toward him, concern across his features.

“Nothing, sergeant. I was just hoping that those men were with the bodies, that’s all.”

“I can’t make that happen, Major, but I bet we both know the guys who can.” The tech gave him a knowing grin.

“We have to track them down first.” Mark spun and headed back to the hangar, his mind racing. “Where the hell are your other players, Sheridan?”

“What other players?” Jack asked as he approached Tufo.

“Jack. I’m sorry, I was just talking to myself.”

“Well, when you need expert opinions, who better to turn, to, right Major?” Jack turned and walked alongside him. “I was looking for you to ask a favor, but if you’re having issues with Sheridan.”

“Sheridan is dead. They’re disposing of his remains now.” Mark hooked a thumb over his shoulder.

“Couldn’t have happened to a nicer guy. But I heard you mention his name and something about other players?”

Mark stopped and considered having to rehash the entire situation again. He knew that Jack and Sheridan were friends at one time. Perhaps he had the insight to assist? “Feel like listening to a hell of a theory?”

“I’m all ears.” Jack fell into step as Mark headed for his office. “But I do have a favor to ask.”

“Spill it.”

“Since you’re still technically in charge of training, I was going to ask if I could borrow Jacobs and Lamb to help train my pups.”

Mark nodded. “Have them home before midnight or they turn into pumpkins.” He held the door as Jack went through. The two worked their way through the workstations and to the elevators. "What's the word on these 'other' operators of yours?"

Jack shrugged. "Beats me, Major. Word came down from the Wyldwood, and since we're sort of beholding to her, I'm stuck on babysitting duty."

The door to the elevator opened on the admin level and Mark held it for him. "I didn't realize they were all so young. I guess it's sort of hard to tell."

"Tell me about it. Who would have thought that a teenage gnome would have a beard hanging to his waist?" Jack cracked a grin as he opened the door to Mark's office. "So, tell me this theory of yours."

Mark explained the discovery of Sheridan and his missing mates from Team One while Jack listened intently. Once the pieces were laid out and put together, the two had an even clearer understanding. "It sounds like Sheridan was a busy guy while he was supposed to be in WitSec."

"And we have at least two missing team members. Possibly a third, but they did find…well, something that could have been remains." Mark leaned back in his chair and studied Jack. "What's your gut tell you, Chief?"

Jack closed his eyes and tried to put himself in Sheridan's shoes. "Honestly, I think you're right that any that wouldn't join his little merry band of misfits were probably erased. Now, whether he would leave a body to be found…I highly doubt that."

Mark sat up and leaned across his desk. "Why? I mean, if he's going to kill them, why not leave the body? That way there'd be no doubting that they were dead."

"True, but if the body wasn't 'killed' in action as originally thought, then Team One would know that somebody was targeting their men. Specifically, the men that Sheridan worked with and supposedly trusted."

"I have to give you that one. I guess I'm not used to thinking like a bad guy."

"I'm not either, but try to imagine you're a double agent or that you've infiltrated the bad guys. You have to assume the same line of thinking or you're dead. Sheridan had to live like that for…what? Six months or more?"

"True." Mark sat back again and tried to wrap his mind around Sheridan and his actions. "So what is his end game?"

"Truthfully? Knowing Sheridan, it's all about the money. My opinion is he was a hired gun."

"We sort of knew that. This Simmons guy hired him to attack both us and you." Mark shook his head. "I'm still not sure why they'd attack you though."

Jack sighed heavily. "That would be because of Apollo if I had to guess. He would want anybody that his twisted mind blamed for Maria…for not telling him about Maria and the Padre." Jack shook his head. "I still can't wrap my mind around that one, Major."

"I don't think anybody really saw that one coming." He poured a cup of coffee and offered Jack one. "But regardless, Sheridan pulls Apollo into the fold so now he has to fight Apollo's battles in order to gain his trust. And all of this is so he can get a payday?"

Jack nodded. "Sounds about right to me."

"Okay. Then what about his operators that he recruited from Team One? Are they in it for the money as well?"

"That and some misguided sense of responsibility to the officer that led them through the fires of hell." Jack sipped the coffee and reclined on the couch. "Look, I can't begin to try and figure out how these guys are all thinking, but I'm betting that

Sheridan probably sold them all a bill of goods. Probably told them about the augmentation and how they were sold down the river by queen and country. Whatever. The end result is the same. Those who would follow him, did. Those who wouldn't, died."

"Were murdered," Mark corrected.

"Their ticket got punched." Jack set the coffee cup down and eyed the man cautiously. "Same result. They're out of the game."

"So, can you think of a way that we can figure out which operators might still be working with him?"

Jack rubbed at his jaw and thought hard. "Where's your list of missing members?"

Mark pulled another copy from a file folder and handed it to him. Jack ran a finger down the list and tapped it twice. "I can guarantee that this little cockbite is with him." He looked up and smiled. "Well, *was*. If Sheridan is out of the game, Bigby here might still be playing, or he may have pulled up stakes and hauled ass for safer ground."

Mark looked at the list and circled the name. "Any others?"

"Silverman and Winchester are both true blue Brits. They wouldn't sell out for any price."

"They're both dead. Confirmed dead. Their bodies were found." Mark hovered over the list as Jack went down it again.

"Sammons and Cowley I didn't know that well." He rubbed at the back of his neck. He slowly shook his head. "It's truly anybody's guess on those two."

"Cowley is confirmed KIA. Sammons…hold on." Mark turned back to a report and fished it out. "Ah. That's the pile of biological goo that *could* have been a human body, but…" He trailed off.

"So they didn't test it?"

"Negative. They found shreds of his uniform mixed in with

the Jell-O and just assumed it was him."

Jack stared at the list again and shook his head. "Bigby is affirmative. Sammons is a possible."

"So there may be two more out there."

"It would appear so, Major." Jack handed the list back to him and stood. "I wouldn't want to have to try to track them down. They're both ex-SAS."

*****

Laura played out different scenarios in her head. Rushing home with a 'miracle cure'…oh, but there is this tiny little side effect. If you don't take this other pill every day for the rest of your life, you'll grow hair in funny places and start barking at the moon. She shook her head and sighed heavily.

How do you explain to your no-nonsense father that monsters are real? How do you convince him to become one in order to save his life? True, it would add many, many…*many* years to his life. Healthy, strong, vibrant years. But how do you explain to a man who had already suffered the loss of his wife that he could live healthier and happier than ever if he accepted this? How do you explain to him that if you'd known in time, you might have been able to save your mother?

She felt the hot sting of a tear running down her cheek and she swiped it away. She wouldn't allow herself to do this. She had served well for far too long, asking little to nothing in return for all these years of service. This one thing was not asking too much.

She looked at her reflection in the mirror and saw the accusatory stare that her image shot back. "What?" she shouted. "It's not like you wouldn't do it, too."

She turned her attention back to the road then realized she had just yelled at herself. *Good lord, I'm losing it.* If only Evan hadn't made her promise to tell him first. She could have stepped in, saved his life, and then explained how. Far better to ask forgiveness than permission.

She increased her grip on the steering wheel, her determination firmed as she increased the speed of her Jeep. She *would* save her father, whether he wanted her to or not. If he said no to the protocol, she would simply dose him in his sleep.

She clenched her jaw, her will resolute as she drove. Slowly she loosened her grip, her determination waning as the many different reactions her father could have struck home.

She glanced upward and muttered a silent prayer that whatever power above would give her the strength to see this through.

*****

Bigby pulled the Super Duty pickup up to the chain link gate of a rundown building that looked suspiciously like a school. He turned off the ignition and stepped out of the large truck. As he approached the chain link fence, he noted the various signs posted warning people to keep out, but it was obvious that that warning had gone unheeded.

He glanced at the main building and nodded. "This will do in a pinch." He pulled up his PDA and punched up the GPS location and stored it to memory as a possibility.

He walked across the grounds and found the old gymnasium set apart from the rest of the school. It appeared as though it had been saved from the vast majority of vandalism. He wasn't sure if it was because the doors had been chained or because the windows were mounted too high for trespassers to enter easily, but either way, the building was in far better condition.

"I think we can stage here."

Stepping out of the back of the gym, he marched to the rear of the grounds and eyed an area where they could stage vehicles. "A dozen transports parked here would never be seen from the roads." He tapped at his chin as he continued walking the grounds. "But how to get them here without being seen?" There were too many residences in the area and prying eyes and nosy neighbors could go a long way toward detection. *How difficult would it be to remove a dozen or so neighbors?*

Bigby shook his head as he considered the ramifications. He glanced at his watch and decided it was time to gather the weapons. Perhaps he could find a suitable staging location in transit. He walked back to the truck and climbed into the cab. As the big engine roared to life, he backed out and began working his way across town to the storage unit that Sheridan had rented.

The wheels in Big's mind started spinning as he thought about the storage rental place. Remote location, little to no traffic. Plenty of storage bins. Security was practically nonexistent. He smiled to himself as he drove. Maybe he had the proper place the entire time without knowing it. He simply couldn't see the forest for the trees.

*****

"And you didn't have any trouble sleeping?" Kalen looked to the two sitting across from him.

Azrael shook his mighty head. "None. I didn't even achieve stone sleep and still I slept without issue."

Gnat lifted a bowl of oatmeal to his mouth and slurped loudly. "I never have issues sleeping." He belched loudly and set the bowl down on the table, reaching for a handful of sausage links. "I could sleep through battlements if need be."

Kalen nodded, his brow furrowed. “I suppose it is just being in a new place.”

“What troubles you, elf?” Azrael scooped a large slab of ham from his tray and bit off a chunk.

Kalen shook his head. “Just dreams. Perhaps it is all of the unknowns we face. Perhaps if we knew what our quest was, who our enemies are…”

“That has never prevented me from sleeping.” Azrael bit through the large ham bone and crunched it as he chewed. “Usually the stone sleep takes me too soon and I still crave battle, but being here, underground? It was of no issue.”

Kalen waved off their comments. “It is of no concern. I was only curious.” He picked through the fruits and vegetables on his plate. Their lack of venison or fish had caught him off guard. The beef and pork they served had little flavor.

Gnat shoved a handful of bacon into his mouth. “I tell you, the humans have discovered the greatest way to cure pork. This bake-in is one of the best foods I’ve ever eaten.” He grabbed a large handful and tossed it onto Kalen’s plate. “You must try it.”

Kalen watched as the gnome licked the grease from his fingers then blanched. He flicked the pieces of meat from his plate and onto his platter. “Perhaps another time.”

“There you are.” Lamb sat down at the table and smiled at the crew. “Looks like I get to be your weapons instructor.”

“We know how to use our weapons, thank you.” Azrael turned from him and back to his two friends.

“True enough, my large, winged friend.” Jacobs patted the gargoyle on the shoulder and settled in on the other side of him. “But we’re going to teach you fellas how to use human weapons.”

Gnat’s face fell. “If I wanted to learn human weapons, I would have been born one.”

"I thought Chief Jack would be teaching us these things." Kalen leaned away from the pair and studied them carefully.

"Normally, he might," Lamb answered. "But he wanted you boys to learn from the best."

"So he sent us." Jacobs smiled at the trio. "As soon as you're through eating, how about you muster at the training center."

Kalen gave them a curious stare and opened his mouth to question when Lamb stood up and hooked a thumb over his shoulder, "Big double doors one floor up and down the hall. Opens to a large two story room with mock buildings inside."

Kalen nodded. "I am familiar with it."

"Excellent." Lamb turned to leave. "Don't forget to grab your girlfriend before you show up."

"She's not my girlfriend!" Kalen replied a little too enthusiastically.

Lamb and Jacobs both paused and turned on him simultaneously. "It was just a figure of speech, pal."

Jacobs nodded. "No need to get worked up."

Kalen sat back and nodded. "Very well. We will be there shortly." He watched the two humans leave then he turned back to his friends. Azrael stared at him and Gnat forgot to close his mouth.

Azrael nodded knowingly. "I think I know what your 'dreams' were of now."

*****

Little John fought the urge to put his fist through a wall. He turned to Spalding and pleaded with his eyes. Spalding threw his hands up. "It's not up to me, John."

"Surely he must know that I need to talk with her." John paced back and forth through the lounge, his jaw ticking as he walked. "Why would he ask those two frogmen to help train them? That makes no sense."

"Jack was a SEAL, both Jacobs and Lamb were SEALs. It makes perfect sense. He trusts them because he understands what they've been through."

"But she's *my* sister!"

"I understand that, but John, she's his operator now."

"Yeah, how the hell does that even happen?" Little John stopped pacing long enough to stifle a scream. "We finally get her back and not only do I not get a chance to talk to her, this guy just waltzes in and says, 'I need her, she's mine' and everybody's okay with that? Really?"

"Look, John, you don't really know this guy, but I do. He was with the squads for a long, long time."

"Yeah, I know. You told me. He went native, got married, blah, blah, blah. But where does that give him the right to just step back into the scene and then pick my sister to be his new attack dog?"

Spalding hung his head and exhaled hard. "Have a seat, John."

"No, I've taken a knee enough in this. All I want is a chance to talk with her. Find out what happened. Try to…I dunno, connect with her somehow."

Spalding nodded, his desire to be sympathetic diminished by the loss of Apollo. "I wish I knew what to tell you. Really, I do. All I can say is for you to be patient. She'll come to you when she's ready."

"That's horse shit and you know it." He began pacing again. "She's wrapped up in this Jack guy now, and he's got every moment of her time claimed."

"She hasn't been here long enough for you to say that."

"Long enough." John stopped and clenched his teeth. "All I'm saying is that it isn't right that he monopolizes her time like this."

"And I'm trying to tell you that he isn't. He just has a lot of work to do and little time to get it done." Spalding stood and stepped in front of John's pacing. "Are you listening?"

"Of course I am. I just don't accept it."

"Well you better." Spalding pointed toward the door. "Because if you push too hard on this, you're likely to push her away and never get her back."

John stared at Spalding, his mind racing, but the words sinking in. He fell onto the couch and held his head in his hands. "I feel responsible."

"Don't." Spalding clapped him on the back. "Dude, you were what, ten years old when she disappeared? Try to accept the fact that she's back and she's alive and well and you *will* get the chance to catch up, but not until she's ready."

John looked up at him and smirked. "Alive and well? Bad choice of words there, boss man."

Spalding smirked. "You know what I mean. At least she's back, bud. That's a whole lot more than most of us get."

John had to agree. "So…patience?"

"Patience."

"Can I get a double order of it? Yesterday?"

Spalding shook his head. "Doesn't work that way, buddy."

*****

"So this is my room? Hmm." Jenny looked around the small quarters and wrinkled her nose.

"I'm sorry. It's the best we can do on short notice. And trust me, it's a lot nicer than most of the other quarters. This is officer quarters. You should see what the enlisted men get." He offered a wan smile and shrugged.

Jenny turned and gave him her best sultry smile. "And where is *yours*?"

"Mine? Oh, you mean…uh, my quarters?" Mitchell suddenly felt as though the ventilation system had failed and the hallway had gotten hotter. "I, uh…I mostly stay in my office, but I do have a room similar to this. It's just a bed and wardrobe where I keep spare uniforms."

Jenny withdrew and gave him a curious look. "Really? You're like…the boss here…and you don't live in the lap of luxury?"

Mitchell snorted a laugh and shook his head. "No, no luxury." He ushered her inside and pushed the door shut behind him. She sat on the bed and he pulled up a chair. "We live pretty basic here. Our quarters are really just places to sleep and keep clothes. We're usually too busy to…well…I mean, there is married housing on the base, but…"

He stumbled as he tried to find some redeeming quality to the life he led. He sighed heavily and leaned back in the chair. "Up until you, I never had a need for any of that. My job was my life and as long as I had a roof over my head, food on the table, and a clean uniform to put on, I had my needs met."

"That sounds like a bleak existence." She reached a tentative hand out and rubbed at his arm. "It sounds lonely."

Mitchell shook his head. "No, not really. My men were my family. All of my people are. We're a small enough outfit here that I know them all by name. All the way down to the cooks in the kitchen."

Jenny smiled. "You should definitely make a point of getting to know them." She winked at him.

"Yeah, well, to somebody on the outside looking in, it might seem lonely, but we stay pretty busy. And when I'm worried about my guys out in the field, it just didn't leave time for…well…you know."

"Dating?"

"Yeah. I mean, I guess I could have, but how do you tell a prospective date that once a month you turn into a wolf and bark at the moon?"

"True." She patted his arm. "But the thing is, you don't have to do this alone anymore. Not if you don't want to."

"What are you saying, Jenny?" Mitchell eyed her cautiously.

"I'm saying, my wolf accepted you. The more time I spend with you, the less apprehension I feel…"

"And that means…what?"

"That means I don't need to be on the outside looking in." She met his eyes and he felt that familiar flutter in his guts again. "If you'd let me, I could be on the inside. With you. Making things less lonely."

Matt felt the smile tugging at the corners of his mouth. "I think I'd like that very much."

Jenny leaned in and kissed him. Softly at first, then more deeply as she allowed herself to drop her guard. In the echoes of his mind, Matt could hear a wolf howling…he just didn't know if it was his or hers.

*****

"What do we do?" Lilith paced as Samael considered their options. "You heard Azazel's warning. If we continue on this path, we're both doomed."

"Bah! Foolishness." Samael crossed his arms and tapped at his chin as he continued to think. "Michael sent him here to throw us off. There is no way we could lose and they know it. They just want to try to save 'innocent' blood. I have no care for innocent blood."

"Nor do I, my love, but I do care about saving my own skin. I just got it back and I'd really like to keep it a little longer." She continued to pace, pausing only a moment to notice her demons had finally gathered into ranks and waited for her command. "And what do we do about them?"

"Huh?" Samael turned and noted the demon legion standing at attention, their commanders standing at the front of each troop. "I am thinking. Give me a moment."

"But what do we do about them?"

"They've waited this long, let them continue to wait." Samael's brow knitted as he continued to consider the possibilities. "If we had an inkling where Gabriel hid the weapons, we could send them after the cache. If we could gain control of the angelic weapons before the humans do…" His voice trailed. He turned to Lilith, "Tell me you know who this 'non-human' is that Azazel spoke of."

Lilith shook her head. "What makes you think I would know that?"

"You cavorted with vampires. They're non-human," Samael snorted in derision. "It's not too far of a stretch."

"If I didn't love you dearly, I would tell you to kiss my ass."

"I already have. Numerous times. It was fun, but this is not the time for sex." Samael continued to ponder the possibilities. "If not vampire, then who?"

"Oh, it could still be a vampire. It's not like I know them all personally. I just used them to my advantage." She gave him a knowing smirk then went back to her pacing.

"Who would the on high trust with angelic weapons?" He tapped a tooth nervously with an extended claw. "It would have to be one of pure heart. The temptation that the cache would bring would simply be too much for any less."

"What are you saying?" Lilith paused her pacing and studied him.

"I am saying that a collection of angelic weapons would tempt even the purest of human hearts."

"So that's why they revealed it to a non-human." She pointed to him as though an idea had come to her. "And vampires were once human. Whatever traits they had in life, they're amplified in death. If they are greedy in life, they are overwhelmed with greed as a vampire. If a glutton, then a glutton too shall they be. If a liar—"

"Your point is made," he interrupted. "Which explains your appetites."

"I wasn't a vampire, I was…" She turned and glared at him. "You helped create me."

Samael gave her a sideways glance. "A decision I have never regretted."

Lilith narrowed her eyes at him and raised a brow. "Your voice says one thing but your tongue another. I think—"

"And therein lies your problem," he interrupted again. "Allow me to figure out angelic issues."

"Why you self-righteous—"

"Which led to my fall. We already know this, my love. Now stop so that I may think." Samael paced slowly, his wings opening and closing as he marched. "Who would the angels have entrusted a secret like this to?"

Lilith stood and watched him, deciding to keep her opinions to herself for the moment. She watched as his mind raced. She swore she could almost see the gears turning within his skull. When he stopped he turned to her. “Somebody *pure* of heart. Who on this planet is still pure of heart?”

“Certainly not a human.” She stared at her nails as though there was suddenly something quite interesting to be found there. “In fact, I would have to say, *none*.”

“Normally, I would as well.” Samael gave her a wicked smile. “Are there still elves or fairy folk?”

Her eyes widened and she turned to him. “There most certainly are. But…I don’t think they live *here* any longer.”

“Do not speak in riddles, woman. Spill it.”

She gave him a wicked smile. “They live in a different place. A place that neither we, nor humans can reach unless they want you to be there.”

Samael’s face fell. “Then how do we discover which one might have been given this insight?” He punched at the concrete column and ignored the huge chunk of manmade rock that shot from the support.

“One has to be invited to enter the land of the elves or the fairy.” She sidled up next to him and ran a hand across his massive chest. “But that doesn’t stop them from coming out here to our world.”

He turned to her and studied her face. “You speak truly?”

“Of course I do. The wee sprites and those white haired do-gooders are coming across to our realm all the time. Every once in a while a vampire gets lucky and catches one. Rare, but it still happens from time to time.”

“Then it sounds like we need to set a trap.”

5

Mitchell had to pull himself away from Jenny before things got too heated. His head spun while his wolf tore at him, urging him to go back and claim her, make her theirs for all time. He paused more than once and forced his breathing to slow, trying in vain to push the image of the young, blonde haired woman from his mind. Her face haunted his dreams to the point that he wanted nothing more than to be by her side and it caused his body to ache. It caused his heart to ache. It caused his wolf no end of pain.

He felt as though his legs were dragging iron chains as he carried himself back up the stairs and to his office. The air inside felt stale and stuffy as he entered his workspace and took his place behind his desk. His mind seemed muddled and dragging as he tried to do his work. He just couldn't focus. She was always there. Popping up in his thoughts when he didn't need her there.

He read through the daily reports and had to reread them a second and third time before finally surrendering and tossing them aside. Another cup of coffee did nothing to help clear his mind and the image of her rising on her tip-toes to kiss him kept returning. He could still taste her on his lips, smell her on his skin.

Mitchell leaned back in his chair and tried to will her from his mind as the knock on his door shattered his concentration. "Come."

Mark stepped in and plopped onto the couch across from his desk. "Bad news, and more bad news."

"Okay then, hit me with the bad news first." Mitchell pulled his coffee mug to him and sipped while he tried in earnest to pay attention to his XO.

"I spoke with Jack. I figured since he and Sheridan were so close, he might be able to shine a little light on this subject."

"And?"

"And there's a distinct possibility that at least two more of his men are still alive and kicking."

Mitchell nodded, his distracted mind not quite making the connections. "Okay. So we need to keep an eye out for these guys."

Mark tilted his head at him and gave him a quizzical look. "You mean we need to figure out their next move and get a step ahead of them."

Mitchell stared at him a moment before nodding. "Okay. That sounds good. Make it happen." He turned back to the stack of papers on his desk shuffled through them.

"You seem distracted." Mark sat on the edge of the couch and studied the man. "What's up?"

Matt groaned and gave up his charade. "I'm sorry, Mark. I'm just…I can't think. I can't concentrate on anything. She's got me so worked up that…"

"She? Who…that Simmons girl?"

"Yeah. My Fated Mate." Matt shook his head and threw his hands in the air. "I can't stop thinking about her."

Mark sighed and leaned back again. "You need to get your head in the game again, boss. This isn't good. With Laura gone and me having to check in with Doc every day, he could pull me at a moment's notice. We need you four-oh, squared away."

"Laura's gone?" Matt gave him a confused stare then realization struck. "I had forgotten that…" He stood suddenly and began pacing. "You're right. I need to figure out something. I don't know why that struck me as news."

"You need to figure out what's causing this and fix it. Even if it means sending her away."

Matt turned on him suddenly, his head shaking. "I can't…I don't think I can do that."

Mark shrugged. "Then you need to figure out how to work around this." He stood slowly and placed a reassuring hand on his shoulder. "It ain't good to have a werewolf with Alzheimer's running around here. You'll be chasing your tail and hiking on electrical outlets."

"Ha-ha-ha."

Mark shrugged. "If you don't want to electrocute your junk, you better get a grip on…well, your mind." He turned for the door. "'Cuz, I'll be damned if I'm gonna be the one to paper train you."

*****

"I am very uncomfortable with this." Angelica turned to her sister and shook her head. "I've never tried to 'read' a vampire before. I don't even know if I can."

Victoria patted her sister's hand. "All Viktor asks is for you to try." She pulled her sister gently toward the table and pulled her chair out. "They will be here shortly, and we've traveled all this way to meet them."

"If he were not my nephew, I would tell him no. I have no obligation to the pack." Angelica stared over Victoria's shoulder anxiously.

"I know, my dear, and I love you all the more for this." She gently pushed her sister into her chair. "Trust me when I tell you that Viktor would not allow any harm to come to you. When he says that this vampire can be trusted, then he can be trusted."

Angelica trembled and tried to shake off her trepidation. "I would be lying if I said I am not without fear."

"I know, darling, but we will all be close. I promise."

A young man stepped closer and pulled back the heavy covering to the makeshift tent. "They have arrived."

"I cannot do this." Angelica stood and turned for the rear of the tent.

"Sister, please, I assure you, no harm shall come to you or your party. Simply try to read him. That is all we ask." Victoria pulled her gently back to her seat.

The young man stepped within the tent again and announced, "Monsieur Thorn." He held the tent flap open and Angelica stiffened. She relaxed somewhat when a young man dressed in a white suit bent low and stepped within. Other than pale skin, he appeared perfectly normal. Nothing at all that she had expected.

"Please forgive this rather rushed meeting, and accept my sincerest gratitude for agreeing to do this for me and my people. You may very well save us extremely valuable time in preserving the human race." Rufus bowed deeply to the Romanian woman seated behind the table. "I am Rufus Thorn, at your humble service."

Angelica turned wide eyes to Victoria and whispered, "He's not at all what I expected."

"And that, too, is my fault, *mademoiselle*. We had no time to prepare once the plane landed. I fear my appearance is most dreary."

"On the contrary, sir. You look…impeccable." Angelica stood slowly and extended her hand. "I am Angelica Veres. I shall be performing your reading this evening."

Rufus accepted her hand and placed a chaste kiss upon her knuckles. Angelica did not miss the coolness of his touch and withdrew her hand slowly, resisting the urge to wipe at it with her warm hand. "Please, take a seat, *monsieur*."

Rufus sat quickly and placed his hands carefully in his lap. "I am not sure how this is performed."

"There are many different ways to see the future." Angelica cleared her throat. "But, to be completely honest, I'm not entirely sure if it will work with somebody in your…"

"Condition?" Rufus gave her a winning smile.

"Yes. Exactly." Angelica pulled a stack of tarot cards and placed them on the table next to her 'crystal' ball. "Exactly what are you hoping to discover, sir?"

"Please, call me Rufus. And I am seeking information about a young vampire that my brother created. His name is Damien Franklin, and I fear he may be involved in some very dangerous extracurricular activities."

"I see." She reached down by her feet and retrieved a bowl. "And do you have anything that may have belonged to the young man?"

Rufus thought for a moment and shook his head. "*Non*, the only thing that I am aware of is that he shares the blood of my brother."

"And did you happen to bring any with you?" She reached inside her robes and pulled out a small leather bag.

Rufus turned and closed his eyes, his arm extended toward the opening of the tent. A moment later, Paul appeared at the tent opening. "You called?"

"We need your blood."

"All of it?"

"*Non.*" He turned and gave Angelica a quizzical look. "You do not need all of it, do you?"

"No, just a small sample will work." She handed him the bowl and Rufus handed it to Paul. Paul extended his fangs and bit into his wrist, allowing the blood to pour into the bowl quickly before his wound healed. "That should be plenty."

They placed the bowl back on the table and Angelica began reciting an incantation. She shook the leather bag and dumped the ancient small bones into the bowl then opened her eyes and stared deeply. She turned the bowl first one way, then the other. With a long finger she mixed the bones and blood then stared again.

"What do you see?" Rufus asked.

She shook her head slightly. "I see…nothing." She gave him a less than hopeful glance. "I don't know if it's because the blood is dead or he is."

Rufus sighed heavily and looked to Paul who simply shrugged. "I can't feel if he's departed."

Rufus turned back to Angelica. "Is there anything else you can try?"

She pulled the tarot cards and had both men shuffle then cut the deck. She began dealing the cards out and attempted to read them. "The Magician. This means that one of you is a channel for great power. Whether that power is for good or evil, I cannot tell."

She turned over another card. "The High Priestess. Somewhere along this journey, a woman of great power will come into play and once she meets with the Magician, she can take all of his power as well." She flipped another card. "The Lovers. This can have numerous meanings. Let's see what else the deck shows." She flipped another. "Death." Angelica noticed the look that both vampires gave her and she held her hands up to calm them. "The Death card doesn't mean 'death' in its purest sense. It can mean change or transformation."

"But it can also mean death, right?" Paul's voice cracked when he spoke, and he noticed his mouth was dry.

"It can, but rarely." Angelica flipped another card and placed it on the table. "Strength. This means just that. An inner strength or a newfound strength. Perhaps to complete a journey?" She gave both men a smile as she flipped the next card. "The moon." She tapped at her chin as she studied this card. "The moon is an odd card. It has no light of its own. It reflects sunlight. It often means the negative of something. Like nightmares are to a happy dream."

"Could it also mean that since we are vampires, we can only come out at night?" Foster asked hopefully.

Angelica shook her head. "No, not this time, I'm sorry." She flipped another card and her brows knitted together. "The Emperor. Usually, this is a strong masculine head. A leader. Someone who gives advice or…rules from the sidelines." She scratched at her head as she looked at the cards. "I'm curious…" She flipped another card and sat back, her eyes wide. "Wheel of Fortune. If this is a negative reading, then…it's Fated. Whatever you're supposed to do, it won't be easy, but this action is destined to occur."

"So we cannot change it?" Rufus asked.

"Oh, you can always change something. It just may seem

monumental to do so."

Foster waved his hand over all of the cards, "So what is this saying?"

She cleared her throat and gave the two a wary eye. "Whatever your friend is up to, he's neck deep in it. He's started the wheels of fate spinning and it won't be easy to stop him."

Rufus turned to Foster. "Lilith has been made whole."

*****

Bigby opened the roll away door and stared at the weapons and equipment that Sheridan had stolen and squirreled away. He let a low whistle escape his lips then stepped inside. It would take a while to unload all of this. He hadn't realized just how much had been secreted away until it was left to him to utilize it.

With the truck backed to the door, he began lifting the heavy crates and pushing them into the bed. He filled the bed of the truck then began stacking the wooden crates atop the others. He made certain to turn the crates so that their printed contents were turned to the inside of the stack and unreadable to prying eyes. Once he had the truck loaded he pulled out slowly and parked it.

He walked slowly through the rental units looking for open units. If he could find three or four that were unlocked that they could borrow for a short time…but there was only one other unit. Bigby cursed to himself and reluctantly picked up his cell phone. He checked his messages and found the text from Simmons' men. They were at the airport and about to secure transportation.

Bigby called the number and was grateful the man spoke English. He explained the situation and the lack of suitable abandoned properties.

"What about the warehouse you were using? Did they set up

surveillance?"

Bigby paused, his mind racing. Would they have? Would they have a reason to? Would they even suspect that anybody would go back once it had been raided? He wouldn't expect an enemy to return to a raided stronghold...why should they? "I can find out. I'm not that far from there. Give me thirty minutes to scout the place." He clicked his phone shut and jogged to the truck.

As he slipped behind the wheel and started the big engine, he felt a smile curving the corners of his mouth. Wouldn't they be shocked to know that they had set up again in the exact same spot? He chuckled to himself as he pulled away from the storage rental units.

Big drove to the location and parked far enough away that surveillance cameras wouldn't detect the motion, then he entered from the wooded side. He slipped under the chain link and darted from building to building, his eyes constantly scanning for cameras, motion sensors or any other foreign devices.

As he crossed the short area between the outbuildings and the main warehouse, he paused. He noted the brown stain in the gravel; the stain that was once his commanding officer. Bigby stood in the open and shook with rage as he remembered watching Sheridan's Halfling form fall, the Monster Squad operator and their traitorous ally working together to remove him from the equation. His jaw ticked as the images flashed through his mind's eye.

"I shall avenge you, Sherry. You have my word."

He quickly turned and finished his assessment of the grounds. Satisfied that it was clear, he texted the location to the incoming wolves. Bigby walked out through the open gates and pulled the truck through and into the warehouse that was home just days before.

He began unloading the crated gear, all the while his mind raced. Different scenarios on how he would decimate the Monster Squad for what they had done flashed before his eyes. When he finished, he hadn't remembered half of the job, his anger having taken his mind to a darker place. A place where revenge was sweet and served cold.

*****

Kalen had purposely separated himself from Brooke when they arrived at the training area. The group broke into two sets of two, each set of warriors working with a different squad member. He had assigned Azrael and Brooke to work with Lamb while he and Gnat worked with Jacobs. He found the exotic looking man's voice to be calming.

"None of your human weapons fit my hands." Azrael sounded frustrated as he tossed the SCAR to the side. "They are too small for my frame, as well."

Lamb rubbed at the back of his neck. "Yeah, I noticed that as well." He picked up the SCAR and extended the stock all the way to the rear. "How much more before this feels comfortable?"

"Can you attach another one to the rear of this one?" Azrael wasn't joking.

"Uh…no." Lamb pulled the weapon from him and examined it again. "Maybe a .50 cal?"

"Maybe if he didn't have gorilla arms." Brooke punched the gargoyle lightly in the arm.

"I do not. I have gargoyle arms." Azrael flexed his mighty muscles and even Lamb was impressed.

"Okay, Schwarzenegger. Quit showing off for the ladies." Lamb pulled a Barrett .50 caliber rifle from the weapons locker and handed it to him. "Try this on for size."

Azrael hefted the weapon and nodded. "This feels more appropriate. But this part is still too short." He pointed to the stock.

Lamb shrugged. "Try to make do until we can get you a custom stock made. Can you fit your finger in the guard here?"

Azrael wiggled his trigger finger into the guard, but it was too tight. "No." He handed the weapon back.

Lamb laid the weapon down and scratched at his head. "Maybe we'll just have to have one custom made for you."

"Try the M2." Major Tufo stepped closer to the railing and nodded over their heads. "You'll have to pull one from the stocks. He can hook an ammo can to his belt or wrap a few bandoliers across his chest." Mark shot a cheesy grin to the crew. "Those ginormous meat hooks of his should be able to hold and operate one of those."

Lamb snapped his fingers and smiled. "And as big as you are, the recoil shouldn't be a problem."

"What is recoil?" Azrael gave him a quizzical look.

"It's when the gun kicks you." Lamb turned and trotted off for the weapons supply.

Azrael turned to Brooke. "Then I shall kick it back."

Brooke patted his large shoulder. "You do that, big guy. You just do that."

Jacobs sat on the ground and tried to figure out how to make any of their weapons work with Gnat's stubby little hands. He threw his hands in the air and shook his head. "Major, none of our weapons will fit him. I'm sure he's stout enough to handle the FiveseveN, but the grip is too wide. He can't wrap his hand around it."

"Did you try the MP7?" Mark asked from the balcony overlooking the training arca.

“Affirmative, sir. The grip is too wide. He can’t get his thumb and trigger finger to wrap around…” Jacobs paused and stared at the little Gnome. “What about a .22, sir?”

“We have no silver ammunition that will work for a caliber that small.”

“Never mind, Ing.” Jack stepped into the training area and crossed his arms, his eyes scanning his ‘team’. He turned to Kalen, “You’ll never guess who just contacted me.”

Kalen shrugged. “I have no idea, Chief Jack.” He swallowed hard, hoping that Azrael said nothing to him about Brooke.

“Loren.” Jack shook his head. “Apparently *our* weapons are not the order of the day. She’s been in contact with…I dunno, somebody. There are supposedly *special* weapons that we need to pick up.”

Lamb stepped back in lugging the M2. “What do you mean, special, Chief?”

“I mean, not human. She didn’t go into detail. All I know is that we’re wasting our time here.” He cast a disapproving look to Kalen. “How I’m supposed to train you guys without having all the facts is beyond me.”

“I’m sorry, Chief Jack, I did not—”

“Save it.” Jack turned for the door. “For now, run them through the drills using their own weaponry. I have no clue what the special stuff is supposed to be, there’s no sense in risking their lives with stuff they don’t know. Just get them working together tight. As a team.”

“Got it, Chief.” Lamb dropped the M2 and stepped toward the door of the trainer. “Grab your gear and get ready to run the gauntlet.”

Azrael perked up. “The gauntlet? I enjoy gauntlets.”

“Sorry to disappoint, big guy. It’s just an expression.” Brooke patted his shoulder again as she walked by.

Azrael's shoulders slumped and his face fell before he turned to retrieve his own weapons.

*****

Matt wasn't sure how he ended up back at Jenny's quarters but he was just about to turn and try to walk away when she opened the door and leaned against the doorjamb. "Are you going to keep pacing out there all evening or are you going to knock?"

"I was…I mean, I…" He glanced first one way, then the other. "I have no idea how I even got here."

"Join the club." She stepped away from the doorjamb, inviting him inside when he noticed that she wore only boxer briefs and a thin t-shirt. He swallowed hard and found that his feet were moving him inside on auto-pilot.

She shut the door behind him and turned to find him looming over her. "I can't stop thinking of you." His voice was low and breathy, and she felt chill bumps break out over her skin. A shiver ran up her spin as his hands reached out and grasped her gently by the elbows. "Why can't I get you out of my mind?"

She leaned into him and inhaled deeply, doing her best to imprint his scent in her mind. She slowly opened her eyes and stared at him. "I don't know. I've had the same problem since I…since we…I mean, since our wolves…"

He leaned down and kissed her, pulling her up and closer to him. She stood on the tips of her toes, placing her hands against his wide chest and pulling herself higher to better reach him. She barely realized that his hands had slid down and cupped her bottom until he lifted her effortlessly and held her against him. She groaned in his mouth and wrapped her arms around his neck, pulling him to her.

He turned slowly and placed her gently on the narrow bed. She wrapped her legs around him more tightly and squeezed, holding him close to her. Matt pulled his mouth from hers only long enough to draw in a gasp of breath before she pulled his mouth back to her own.

He turned them both and sat on her bed, the springs creaking under his weight. She slid further up in his lap and wrapped her legs tighter around him, struggling to keep her grip on him. He ran his hands up her back and soon found them sliding under the thin material of her t-shirt. Without trying, he had the shirt pulled to her neck and slid his mouth from hers long enough to pull the shirt off and toss it to the corner of the room. She was back on him before he could speak and his hands slid slowly across the silky smoothness of her bare skin.

She moaned as he pulled his calloused hands to her front and cupped her bare breasts, his fingers brushing her sensitive spots. He slowly kissed his way to her neck, pausing only a moment to tug and nip at her earlobe before kissing his way to her chest. She threw her head back and bit back a scream as he deftly took each bud in his mouth and sucked at her, nipping her gently with his teeth, his whiskers rasping her tender flesh with each brush.

She threw herself forward, her arms wrapped around his neck once more, pulling herself up and tighter to him. "If you don't fix this soon, I'm going to go crazy."

He gave her a confused and half-dazed stare. "Fix what?"

"This." She leaned back and thrust her breasts into his face. "Get your clothes off now before I rip them off!" she growled from low in her throat.

He felt a chill run up his back and settle in the base of his neck. He knew that her voice had stirred his wolf, and he was quickly pulling at his uniform, tossing pieces aside as quickly as he could remove them.

His hands slid into the waistband of her boxer briefs and slide them off her hips, his roughened hands scratching at her legs as he tugged them off. He paused only a moment as he stared at her beauty then lifted her gently in the air and settled her on him. Her eyes went wide just before he entered her, and she placed both hands on his shoulders. "This is forever you know."

His eyes darkened and he smiled at her knowingly. "I know." He pulled her close and sucked her tongue into his mouth just as she relaxed her thighs and allowed herself to lower onto him.

*****

"What kind of trap can we set that will draw them out?" Lilith paced in the confined area of her office/bedroom.

Samael hunkered in a dark corner, his mind wondering about that very same problem. "Perhaps we need to draw them out by sticking to the plan? Use our demons to stir up the humans and when they come out and offer the cache to help, we strike."

"Who would they offer them to…" She snapped her fingers. "The hunters."

"The hunters." Samael stood and leaned against the support column. "We will need eyes on the hunters."

"Easy enough. There are humans all around them according to Damien."

Samael shuddered. "Do not speak that name any longer."

"Why, lover? Surely that flesh no longer remembers being him. It surely looks nothing like him any longer." She ran a long and pointed finger across his chest.

"The fact that you allowed that dead flesh to touch you…" he trailed off.

"No, lover. I allowed it to touch a borrowed body." She shuddered as she remembered the buxom redhead. "One that almost corrupted my mind."

"Regardless, that name is dead to us." Samael snapped as he pushed away from the column. "Now, let us check with our legion and see if the preparations have been made."

Lilith held the door for him as he ducked and walked outside. As soon as his presence was noted, the demons rushed to form up once more. "Commanders!" he barked. "Do you have your supplies?"

"Yes, m'lord." The company commanders stepped forward and marched toward him.

The lead commander spoke first. "We have those with the technical knowledge creating the devices now."

"Very well. How much more time is needed?"

The commander turned and looked to the others who gave a slight shrug. "A day, two at the most."

Lilith held up a white ball. "And these will do the trick?"

"According to the host, yes, my queen. Those are ceramic and will not be detected by metal detectors."

"Damn the technology," Samael growled as he snatched the white sphere from her hand. "And what of the rest of it?"

"Fiber optics instead of wires. Two part explosives, virtually undetectable by most of their scanning machines. Even the canines they use are not trained for this."

Samael nodded as he tried to crush the white sphere. It seemed as solid as the steel he wanted to use. "And the triggering devices?"

The commander held up a cell phone. "Everybody has one these days." He turned to another of the lesser unit commanders.

"Retrieve one of the devices." They watched as he ran to the far side of the warehouse then jogged back carrying the vest. "They are lightweight, easily concealable, the explosives are layered in as a paste and it takes very little. The ceramic spheres will act as mortars once the device goes off. Everything within two hundred yards will be decimated." He smiled as he held the device up.

"And how many are there now?" Lilith asked as she handed the ceramic sphere back.

"Somewhere between five and six thousand. Each of us should be able to suicide our host, return with a new one and be back out in a matter of days."

Samael nodded. "How many total will there be once all of the materials are used?"

The commander did some quick calculating in his head. "I'd estimate perhaps seventy-five hundred. Perhaps even eight thousand. It just depends on how frugal we are with the spheres."

Samael turned to Lilith and smiled. "Commander, I do not care about being frugal. We want maximum carnage."

"Understood, sir." The commander retrieved the vest from him and handed it back to the sub-commander. "And once we have brought them to their knees?"

Samael sighed heavily. He extended his wings. "Our intent was to have me pose as a Heavenly being and assign our queen as guardian. Obviously that isn't possible now."

"Perhaps you can still be of service, sir." The commander raised a brow, his eyes twinkling with mischief.

"What are your thoughts, Commander?" Lilith asked, stepping between the fallen angel and the Roman.

"Who says the angel that appears has to be 'heavenly'? What if an angel from the Fallen appeared…and took credit? Then our queen steps in and saves the day?"

Samael gave Lilith a sidelong glance and smiled knowingly. “You’ll need to watch this Roman, my love. I am beginning to think he is far too smart for his own good.”

6

Matt lay on the floor of the cramped room with Jenny curled beside him. The room was a shambles, the desk and chair knocked over, the mattress from the small bed now acting as a pillow against the wall, and sheets and blankets scattered everywhere. His chest rose and fell quickly as he tried to slow his breathing, sweat running down his sides and soaking the blanket underneath them.

"That was…" He trailed off, unable to find the words.

"Incredible." Jenny nuzzled him and draped a leg over him. "When I think of the time I spent running when we could have been doing this?" She giggled at herself, drunk on the emotional high she was feeling.

Mitchell wrapped a protective arm around her and pulled her closer to him. "I never knew it could be like that." Her hair tickled his chin and nose as he whispered to her.

She smiled and bit at her lower lip. "Me either. I guess those

Fates get some things right."

Mitchell stared at her leg draped over him and his face became solemn. "I guess it's done now…isn't it? I mean, we're sealed now, right? Connected?"

She nodded almost imperceptibly. "Yes." She turned her face to his and studied him. The way his eyes took in every little detail, the dimple in his chin, the ridge of his nose, somehow he just oozed masculinity. "Are you okay with it?"

He gave her a slight smile and pulled her tighter to him. "Yeah, I am. I didn't know if I would be, but I am. Somehow this just feels right."

She relaxed and exhaled deeply. Her body seemed to melt against his and she laid her head against his chest. "Good, because there's no going back now."

"For better or worse. Right?"

"Something like that. Definitely 'til death do us part."

Matt stared off into the shadows of her room, his eyes focusing on the future. He nodded more to himself than to her. "I can live with that."

*****

"Major!" Jack trotted to his side, waving for the man to slow down. "Spare a minute?"

"Make it quick." Major Tufo spun and headed back to his office with a stack of papers under his arm.

"I need another favor."

"Why am I not surprised."

"I got word from the Wyldwood and we have traveling to do. I could use some transportation." Jack kept his voice low while they walked.

"Can't your elf open doorways to just about anywhere?" Mark gave him a sideways look.

"Yes, sir, but…" Jack trailed off then pulled him to a stop. "We're supposed to retrieve a weapons cache. Possibly more than we can carry."

Mark shrugged. "So make two trips, Chief. I really don't have transportation that I can legally lend to you. Technically, you're a civilian."

Jack gave him a cockeyed stare. "Really, Major? Don't go down that alley."

Mark raised a brow. "That a threat, Chief?"

Jack grunted a laugh. "Hardly." He pointed to the wall behind him. "Mitchell has his new girlfriend here, we have a vampire on staff that's supposed to be dead, our own men were infected with…"

"Point taken, Chief." Mark huffed and glanced around. "What kind of transport are we talking here? Humvee, truck, plane, chopper? What?"

Jack shrugged. "I'm not sure yet. I want to take my guys there and check it out, then we'll radio for support. But only if it's needed."

"What kind of weapons are we talking here, Chief?" Mark turned and headed to his office again.

"To be honest, I'm not sure. The Wyldwood hasn't been very forthcoming with her information. She knows that there is another big threat coming, but she can't pinpoint exactly what. She knows that we'll need these weapons and these particular fighters will be key…somehow. But she doesn't say exactly how."

Mark turned a curious eye to him as he opened the door to his office. "She doesn't say a lot of stuff, does she?"

"Tell me about it. It's really starting to get under my skin."

Jack entered and fell into a chair

"Yeah, just make yourself comfortable." Mark smirked as he dropped the pile of papers on his desk. "So, it's some kind of special weaponry that will be key to taking out a big unknown threat." Mark scratched at his chin and reclined in his chair. "Funny thing is, we haven't got anything on the leaderboards. No hits, no tags, not a whisper of anything brewing out there."

"Believe me, there's times I want to tell her to deal with it herself, but I owe her. We all do. And she hasn't been wrong before, so…"

"So…better safe than sorry." Mark sighed and rubbed at his eyes. "Okay, fine. You check out her story on the weapons depot. If it pans out and you need help, radio and we'll send support."

"Thank you, Major."

"Don't thank me yet. There's still a chance you'll get to wherever she sends you and there's nothing there." He shot Jack a cautious glance. "If that happens, I'll try not to say 'I toldja so'."

"Copy that, sir."

*****

Laura pulled her Jeep into the driveway of her father's house. She sat in the vehicle and stared at the house that she and her brothers had called home; the place that they had grown up and shared so many memories. She remembered the last time she was here, her father was so proud of her. The work that she had been doing, that she had been involved in, it was so important in his mind. He couldn't understand how she could leave the Company to become a contractor for the military.

She opened the door and stepped from the car, her feet crunching the gravel under her boots. She inhaled deeply and smiled as the pine scented air filled her lungs. She had always loved the mountains and her father's house sat at the foothills of the Zuni Mountain range near Gallup.

She walked slowly toward the front door and pushed it open, reminding herself that she was 'home'. The fears and trepidation she felt at entering her childhood home left the moment she stepped inside and saw things exactly the way she remembered them. She smiled inwardly as she walked past the trophy case that contained the majority of her family's athletic trophies. She ran a hand slowly across the glass and remembered how proudly her father would include each new addition. "I'm going to have to build a bigger case if you don't slow down, Peanut."

She remembered the pride she felt each and every time he'd brag on his children's accomplishments. Their grades, their being accepted to this school or that. Their winning another swim meet or track meet or…

"Laura?"

She turned and felt relief to find her older brother standing in the hallway. "Derek, I didn't know you were home."

"I was just grabbing a change of clothes for dad." He stepped closer and pulled her into an embrace. "It's good to see you again."

"You too, D." She stepped back and stared at her older brother, the spitting image of her father in his younger years. "But what did you mean that you were getting some of his clothes? Isn't he home?"

Derek dropped his eyes and shook his head. "I'm sorry sis. He's taken a turn for the worse."

"Where is he?"

"He's in ICU. They only let a couple of us in at a time. And *she* stays in there with him all the time."

Laura's heart dropped. The reason she left things unfinished with her father for so long…and she was still here. "I had hoped she had moved on to greener pastures."

Derek shook his head. "I dunno, Laura. I always thought she was a gold digger, but Crystal has stuck with him through all of this."

Laura shuddered at the sound of the woman's name. She turned away from her brother and tried to hide her emotions. She could still see the blonde headed hussy's features when she closed her eyes. Barely a year older than she was, Laura believed that her father would snap out of whatever spell she had cast and come to his senses.

Derek laid a hand on his sister's shoulder. "He waited nearly twelve years after mom passed. We couldn't expect him to be alone forever, could we?"

"But why her?" Laura didn't mean for her voice to crack when she spoke. "Why couldn't he see her for what she was?"

Derek sighed heavily and wrapped an arm around her. "I don't know. I honestly don't. But she made him happy. We should try to take comfort in that."

Laura glanced around at the house and shook her head. "And she'll inherit all of this and the kids will be cut out completely."

Derek shook his head. "No. They never married." He pulled her around to face him. To his credit, he said nothing of the tears running down her cheeks. "She even offered to sign a pre-nup, but Dad wouldn't have it."

Laura gave him a wide eyed stare. "He didn't marry her?"

Derek shook his head and gave her a tight lipped smile. "Nope. He said that if he couldn't get his kids' blessings, then it wouldn't happen." Laura didn't realize her mouth had fallen open. "And he meant *all* of his kids."

*****

“Twenty-seven? I have twenty-seven of you to work with?” Bigby shook his head as he marched between the newly arrived wolves. “That’s a far cry from an army.”

“Unlike the others you worked with, we all have military training.”

Bigby turned and gave a raised brow to the wolf trailing him. “Any of them special-ops?”

“Most of them, in fact.” The leader of the wolves paused and crossed his arms. “Trained by a legionnaire.”

Bigby shook his head. “Bloody French.” He shrugged. “Better than nothing I suppose.”

“I suppose you’ve done better?”

Bigby bit back a smile but turned and gave the man a curt nod. “SAS as a matter of fact.”

“Bloody English.” The warrant officer smirked. “Better than nothing I suppose.”

Bigby refused to rise to the bait. Instead he simply nodded. “You have enough spunk, I might can deal with you.” He turned toward the office that he and Sheridan once shared, “Muster your men and get me a list of names. Have them go through the crates of weaponry at the end of the warehouse and divvy up the equipment. Make me a list of anything you feel we may need.”

The warrant officer saluted, “Aye, Major.”

Bigby slipped into the office and pulled Sheridan’s officer’s beret from his head and tossed it aside. He knew that he was no longer in the military and couldn’t be held accountable for impersonating an officer, but he also knew that if the men in the warehouse found out that he was a Staff Sergeant impersonating an officer? He would be torn to pieces. He already felt like he was no longer worthy of the Special Air Service. He took his seat and pulled out Sheridan's hidden bottle of brandy. Taken a long pull to try to calm his nerves he closed his eyes and let the thick liquid burn his stomach.

He opened his eyes and stared out the window of the office as the men outside dug through the weapons that Sheridan had stolen. He knew that in order for him to 'lead' these men, they needed to believe that he was more than what he truly was. He had stolen Sheridan's beret and insignia, affectively giving himself a field promotion to major.

Bigby pulled the plastic baggie from his coat pocket and withdrew another black pill and slipped it into his mouth. He took another long pull from the brandy bottle then slipped it back into the desk drawer. He shuddered as the bane mixed with the alcohol and entered his system. It seemed the only way alcohol could affect him was if he took the bitter pills with a snort, but even then the buzz was short.

He turned and stared at the hand drawn plans that Apollo had made for them. "If we want to cause real damage, we need to strike quickly and quietly." He scratched at his jaw as he studied the plans. "I think maybe chlorine gas through the ventilation system. Come in afterward and put a silver bullet through the brain pan of anything still moving." He nodded to himself when a knock at the door caught his attention.

"You wanted a list of desired equipment." The warrant officer handed over a short list and Bigby scanned it.

"I think this is doable. I'll just have to make a few calls."

"Very well, sir. Meanwhile, I'll get the men settled in and we can begin drills in the morning."

"Mister Martinez? Do you have any idea where we may be able to obtain chlorine gas?" Bigby knew that man was unfamiliar with the area and those who supplied the black markets locally, but he wanted to test him.

"Negative, sir. But it could be manufactured easily enough."

Bigby nodded. "We may have to." He waved the man off. "Get some rest, Mr. Martinez. We'll have a busy day tomorrow."

"Good evening, sir."

Bigby watched him march away and studied the man. "French Foreign Legion, eh?" He shook his head as he picked up his phone. "Time to see how well connected your boss is, Mr. Martinez."

*****

"I am not familiar with this area, Chief Jack. I do not know how close I can get us." Kalen studied the map with Jack, but his voice betrayed his lack of confidence.

"Just do your best. Loren said the weapons were buried inside the mountain near here." Jack turned to Azrael. "I need you on your toes out there."

"Always."

Jack stood and squared his shoulders. "Listen up, all of you. We don't have a whole lot of time to dick around out there. From what I can tell, it will be sunrise in this area in about five hours. That means we need to locate the weapons and then get it all back here before sunrise in *both* locations. Major Tufo said that he can send transportation if there are more weapons than we can carry, so we have that to fall back on."

"Transportation doesn't necessarily mean sunlight-tight though, does it?" Brooke didn't sound nervous but her eyes shot to Azrael.

"No, it doesn't." Jack shook his head. "I know we have both of you to worry about when it comes to—"

“Only him,” Brooke interrupted. “I have found ways around the sun.”

Jack gave her a quizzical stare. “Oh really? And just how do you do that?”

Brooke shook her head as she pulled her hood up and over her face. “It covers everything. I can see the ground, I just can’t see very far in front of me.”

Jack studied her outfit and noticed that her pants tucked into her boots, her gloves came halfway up her forearms…no skin was exposed. “We still don’t want to be caught out in the sun if we can avoid it.” He pushed the smaller door open and ushered the group outside. “Let’s move, people.”

Kalen took the lead and trotted to the large boulder behind the hangar. Jack and Azrael took up security positions on the boulder’s sides, and Brooke covered their rear while Gnat climbed the boulder and covered the forward area. All could see a golden glow emit from the rock before the door slid to the side, and Kalen stepped out of the way. “It’s open.”

“Go, go, go.” Jack tapped each on the shoulder and watched them rush into the boulder. He covered over Kalen’s shoulder as he sealed the rock behind them.

“Is this really necessary in your own backyard, Chief?”

“Brooke, we got attacked here not long ago. There’s no telling who might still be watching.” He motioned for Kalen to take the lead. “See if you can sniff out this weapons depot.”

Kalen drew his bow and took off at a trot across the foothills of the mountain. “Without a bearing, it’s difficult to know where we are.”

Jack pulled a GPS unit from his tactical vest and took a reading. He pulled the map and marked it. “We’re here.”

Kalen studied the location then glanced at the stars. “The stars are wrong." He looked at the map again and then stared at the stars.

"What's wrong, kid? I told you where we were." Jack seemed more than a bit rushed.

"I think we are elsewhere," Kalen answered softly.

"I can take to the air and get a better view." Azrael kept his voice low, but was unsure why they were all whispering. He wasn't sure where they were, but it appeared to be in the middle of nowhere.

"Be careful." Jack stepped aside to allow the gargoyle room for liftoff. Azrael opened his wings and allowed the breeze to billow them. He bent low and leapt into the air, pushing with his mighty wings to gain altitude. Jack watched as he pushed further and further into the darkened sky, a sly smile forming as he disappeared. "Damn, I wish I could do that."

Kalen folded the map and held it loosely while they waited for Azrael to return. "I could be wrong about the stars."

Jack shrugged. "Electronic gizmos shit the bed all the time. If your gut tells you that it's off, then it's probably off."

A few moments later the group heard the beating of Azrael's wings as he came in and settled next to them. He folded his wings behind him as he strode toward Kalen. He reached for the map and spread it out on a flat rock.

"This spring? If we are here, then the spring is not. It feeds this small creek." Azrael pointed to the map and Jack lit it up with his red lensed flashlight. Azrael turned the map and then glanced over his shoulder. "The creek and spring are here, which means we are here." He pointed to the map and extended his claw like nail to scratch an X on it.

Kalen lifted the map and turned it, holding his finger where Azrael had marked it. "I believe he is correct."

"Great," Jack sighed. "That means we need to get on the other side of this thing, find the depot and then make it back before sunrise." He pulled the sleeve of his BDU up and glanced at his watch. "We can't make that. Let's wrap it up and head back to the hangar. We can try this another time."

"We can do this, Chief Jack." Kalen stood in front of him to stop him. "Let me try to open a portal to the other side of the mountain."

Jack glanced at his watch again. "You'd better move quickly."

*****

"If we can't track Damien down, how the hell are we supposed to stop him?" Foster paced inside the small tent, his hands wringing.

"We are not done yet, brother." Thorn turned back to the Angelica. "Please, can you assist in any way?"

She picked up the tarot cards and slipped them away. "I don't know what it might be. You have nothing of his. You're not living flesh. I can't pull from your energy…you have none."

Thorn smiled softly and patted the woman's hand. "That is where you are mistaken, my dear, dear lady."

"You have something of his then?"

"About the power." Rufus let loose a wave of his power and she felt it. She wasn't the undead and should not have been influenced by his ability, but she was a familiar…the wave nearly knocked her over. She fought to catch her breath and leaned heavily against the small table within the tent. "Forgive me!" Rufus stood quickly and steadied her. "I didn't realize you would be affected so strongly."

She nodded to him and gently waved him back. "You're right.

I was wrong." She sat upright and steadied herself, her breath still fighting to escape her. "Give me a moment, please."

Victoria stood behind her, unsure what had just taken place. "Are you okay, Angelica?"

"I will be fine." She patted her hand as she settled into her chair. "Fetch me my crystal ball, please."

Victoria pointed to the table. "It sits here."

"No, darling. My *real* one." She gave Rufus a wan smile. "This one is for decoration." She lowered her voice as Victoria exited the tent. "They're so expensive. I hate to risk the real one getting damaged."

"I understand completely." Thorn gave her a curt nod.

Victoria entered once more carrying Angelica's case. "Please tell me it is in here."

She stood quickly and unlocked the case. "I keep it locked up for good measure." She lifted it gingerly and placed it on the stand on the table. Rufus stared at the crystal ball, his brows knit together. The ball appeared cloudy and misty to him. Not at all clear as he would have expected.

Angelica rubbed an oil on her hands and began massaging the ball, reciting an incantation she had learned hundreds of years prior. As Rufus watched, the ball seemed to almost glow. The imperfections within the crystal seemed to move, like mist on the water or smoke in a room. She continued to chant, her eyes closed, head tilted back.

Thorn watched the ball carefully as shadows danced along the table top, images appearing within the ball itself. "I think it's working."

Foster moved in closer and stared, his eyes glued to the shadowy images inside the ball. Angelica slowly lowered her voice and tilted her head forward, her eyes opening, and her gaze locked on the ball. She stared into the crystal, her lips still murmuring the incantation.

"What do you see?"

"I see the young man you seek. He is with a woman…a woman he cares for very much." She narrowed her gaze and inhaled deeply. "Oh my…she has betrayed him for her first love."

"Where are they?" Thorn's voice took on an edge that surprised Foster. He turned and stared at his brother while the witch continued to commune with the dead.

"They are…in a warehouse…a dead place. In a dead city."

Rufus turned a confused stare to Paul who simply shrugged.

"A name. I need a name."

"Samael…" she whispered. "Samael…"

"Perhaps in Canada?" Foster offered.

"No, that is the name of Lilith's first lover. A fallen angel." Thorn turned a stoic look to Foster. "I fear that Damien is no more."

"There goes our shot at surviving the Council." Foster turned and headed for the exit of the tent.

"Where are they, witch? I need the name of the city."

"Detroit." Her voice sounded dry and raspy as she continued to stare into the ball. "Beware the legion. Beware the legion! They come to destroy! They will bring the world to its knees!" She screamed and collapsed on the table, the light of the crystal ebbing then dying out completely. Victoria rushed to Angelica's side and held her up in the chair as she collapsed in place.

Rufus stood and turned to Foster. "Prepare the plane. We go to Detroit."

*****

Lilith studied the map stretched out on the wall of her lair. She tapped her foot as her eyes studied the different red circles scattered across the world. "I worry about those traveling."

"Don't. If they are detained for whatever reason, they are instructed to detonate there and then return here." Samael flexed his muscles in the full-length mirror then snapped his wings out for dramatic effect.

"Stop admiring yourself, my love. We have work still to do." She tapped the map and turned to him. "What of the centurions working the eastern seaboard?"

"What of them?" Samael folded his wings and stepped closer to her, wrapping his great arms around her middle. "They will begin on the east coast and work their way across the nation."

Lilith shook her head as he nibbled at her neck. "Won't they increase security? Especially at the capitol?"

"So what if they do?" Samael nipped at her ear. "Imagine, if you can," he spread his hand before her, his mind painting an image before her, "a hundred Centurions racing toward the White House, bullets not affecting them as they rip into their human hosts. The first wave hitting the fences and blowing them apart, their shrapnel levelling anybody who is within shouting distance. The next wave rushing in, hot on their heels, getting closer and detonating nearer to the capitol, removing even more of their security. Wave after wave of suicide bombers, impervious to their weapons, wrapped in explosives with ceramic bearings capable of doing more damage than any other projectile." He smiled as he nipped at her chin. "It will be glorious as they remove those in power in a matter of moments."

"What's to keep the president from escaping in his helicopter? Or locking himself in a bunker?"

"And if he did? We'd simply rush the machine and detonate

another human body. The shrapnel would remove the flying machine from the sky." Samael laughed as he spun her around. "You think too linearly. We will send our bombers from all directions. We won't just be attacking from the front."

"If we played our cards right, we might be able to get one or two inside before the others attacked." She hiked a brow at him hopefully.

"Possibly, but I wouldn't hold my breath. These days, unless you have business there, they don't let you close. We'd have better luck getting people inside the offices of Congress."

"Attack both branches at the same time?" She closed her eyes and swayed in his arms while he nibbled and bit at her neck and ear.

"Of course, my love. The judicial branch isn't important to our cause, but the legislative and administrative branches are key." He pulled back and studied her map. "If we could coordinate the attacks so that the capitol area was first…we would definitely catch them by surprise."

"Cripple them before they can react to the news. I like that idea." She pulled form him and stood before the map again. "Make it so. I want Washington D.C. targeted first. All other targets become secondary."

Samael gave her a mock bow. "As you will, my queen." He walked to the door and bellowed for the watch commander. When the man came huffing to the door, Samael relayed the message. "Nobody else makes a move until D.C. has been leveled. Understood?"

"Understood, my liege." The commander bowed deeply then spun and trotted off to spread the word.

Samael walked back inside and fell to the bed. "I think we send Gaius to D.C." He stared at the ceiling blankly as he spoke.

Lilith turned and gave him a questioning look. “To ensure that our orders are properly enacted?”

Samael snorted. “To ensure that he blows himself up as many times as possible. If he’s in the first wave, then he’ll be amongst the first to return with a new body and get back into the field.” He turned and glared at her. “He needs to feel as much pain as possible for his insolence.”

Lilith smirked and stepped toward him, putting as much sway into her hips as she possibly could. “You truly hate the man, don’t you?”

“He dared to touch you.”

“Because his queen ordered him to please her.” She slid across the bed and ran her hands across Samael’s broad chest. “I *made* him take me. I made him please me.” She grabbed Samael’s chiseled jaw and pulled his face toward hers. “Does that displease you?”

“You know that it does.”

She smiled and crawled on top of him, straddling him. “I enjoyed it, you know.” She thrust her jaw out at him. “I *enjoyed* his taking me. I screamed out when he thrust his manhood into me.” Her eyes glinted with mischief. “I bit his flesh when he slapped my buttocks.”

Samael snarled and narrowed his gaze. “Why do you dare speak such things?”

“Does it anger you, my love?”

“You know that it does.” She could feel him trembling under him.

She leaned down and whispered into his ear, “I could *feel* him spilling his seed into me—”

Samael struck with such speed and ferocity that it took her breath away. His hands reached for her, pulling her off of him and pinning her face first onto the mattress. She felt him lift her hips into the air and her shocked expression quickly changed to a smile as she felt him rip her robes from her lower body.

"What do you think you're doing?" she asked in mock protest, wiggling her bottom against him. "Stop, you can't do this." She buried her face in the sheets lest her smile give away her joy.

Samael quickly took her, forcefully and viciously, his intent to pound any memories of another from her mind and body. She responded in kind, thrusting back to meet him, stroke for stroke as her voice screamed, "Yes! Yes! Yes!"

She felt his large, strong hands grab her hips and pull her to him with each thrust. She could feel his grip tightening and feared she would be bruised, but didn't care. She curled her fists into the sheets and shoved a handful of the cotton into her mouth to stifle the scream building in the back of her throat.

When he withdrew and spun her around, her eyes shot wide, not expecting to see the feral look in his eyes. He plunged back to the task and pounded her for all that his angelic body was worth. She wrapped her legs around him and grabbed a double handful of his leathery wings in an attempt to hang on.

Once Samael was finished, he lifted himself from her spent body and wiped himself off on her inner thigh. "Do not…mention…his name…again." His voice came in ragged gasps as he stumbled back and leaned against the column.

Lilith lay on the bed, her mind still reeling and her body completely spent. She felt as though someone had replaced her bones with gelatin and wrapped them with rubber, calling it muscle. Her eyes rolled back in her head and she gasped for breath. "If you…say so…my love." She tried to move and found that she simply had no strength. She knew the only thing that allowed her to survive the encounter was the fact that she was the queen of the dead.

"I know what you did just now." Samael stepped to the corner of the room and lifted the large cask of wine. He pulled the cork and drank from it greedily. "Do not tempt me again."

Lilith sucked in a large amount of air and shook her head. "Wouldn't dream of it, my love." She mustered her strength and rolled to her side. She felt as though she were bruised from the neck down. She cast a glance to his oversized form in the corner, still holding the wine cask. "Not for another few days anyway. Got to give a girl a chance to recover." She tried to smile before she passed out.

7

Matt stepped back into his office and felt like a changed man. His mind was clear and his wolf was at ease for the first time in months. He sat down behind his desk and the mountain of paperwork that had been building up was finished in no time. As he sat back and noted the finished pile, he also noted the cup of coffee he had poured when he first sat down was still half full. He smiled to himself as he made the mental connection between Jenny and his sanity.

Matt stood and stretched, feeling anew. He stared out the window at the different operations going on like any other day, and his mind wandered to Jo Ann and Molly. He felt a minor pang of regret, a sorrow that he hadn't felt in a very long time…almost like he had betrayed their memory.

Mitchell stepped over to the file cabinet and pulled the photo out from behind the files. He stared at their images and ran a finger along the edges of their faces. "It's been so long." The pain he normally felt when staring into their eyes was either diminished or gone. He still loved them both dearly, but another part of him, a bigger part of him, had found Jenny. He had bonded his life to hers. He had become one with her.

He placed the photo back in the cabinet and locked it then leaned on the corner of his desk. His mind raced back to their consummation of the mating and he smiled to himself. "It's real now, Mitch. No going back."

A knock at the door pulled him from his reverie and he stood and answered it. Major Tufo looked up and actually took a half step back. "Damn, you look almost human. What gives?"

"I feel a lot better." Mitchell turned back toward his desk and took a sip of the cold coffee before sitting down.

"You look a lot…" Tufo paused and sniffed the air. "I'll be a son of a bitch."

Mitchell paused and gave him an odd stare. "What?"

"You did it, didn't you?" Mark smirked at him. "I can smell her on you."

Mitchell's eyes widened as he realized what Mark was saying. "You can smell her on me?"

"Don't worry. I doubt anybody else can." He fell into the chair in front of Mitchell's desk. "It's subtle, but it's there."

"Great." Mitchell rolled his eyes. "But yeah."

Mark chuckled lightly and shook his head. "Well good for you. You needed someone in your life, buddy." He kicked his feet up and propped them on the corner of Matt's desk.

Mitchell glared at him until he removed them. "What did you want before you came in here and started sniffing my crotch?"

Mark cleared his throat and dropped a pile of reports on his desk. "Dailies. And I promised Jack backup and transportation if he needs it. He's out on a weapons run."

"Weapons? We have plenty of weapons right here." Mitchell picked up the daily reports and thumbed through them.

"These are some kind of special weapons. Apparently the head Elf lady said that his Kid Squad would need them…I don't understand."

"Kid squad?" Mitchell shrugged. "The operators he's working with are…*kids*?"

"So to speak. I think the youngest is seventeen. Or the equivalent." Mark held his hands up. "I don't know the importance of it, but according to the head Elf lady, it needs to be these kids."

Mitchell leaned back in his chair and rubbed his eyes. "This is nuts, you know that?"

Mark shrugged again. "Look at it this way. That vampire? She's gotta be pushing forty in human years. The gnome? Hell he has a beard that hangs to his—"

"I get what you're saying." Mitchell interrupted. He poured another cup of coffee and cradled it. "I guess if the Wyldwood dubbed these guys the army she wants, who are we to argue?"

"Agreed. The way I see it, we still owe her pretty big."

"What do we know of these weapons?" Mitchell sipped at the bitter brew.

Mark shook his head. "Just that they've been hidden for a long time. But, I'm telling ya now, if they come back with a Viking sword, I'm claiming it."

"Somehow I doubt that it's Viking weapons." Mitchel rubbed at his neck as he thought about it. "I don't guess she gave a better clue what it is they're supposed to be fighting, did she?"

"Negative. As of now, the leaderboards are quiet. The only thing happening is Jack and his team are out scavenging." Mark sighed and stood up slowly. "So, I'm going to the chow hall, swallow a cow and maybe a pig or two, then I thought I might try to catch a few hours of sleep."

"You heading home then?"

Mark shook his head. "My shift starts again in about five hours. Might as well stick around."

"At least call your boss and let her know you're okay." Mitchell narrowed his gaze on his XO. "Consider that an *order*, Major."

Mark sighed. "Sir, yes sir."

*****

Jack stepped out of the glowing rock and took another GPS reading. It gave almost the identical reading as before. He glanced at the map and shook his head. "I think we came back out where we started."

Azrael shook his head. "No, the creek is down there." He pointed with a massive arm to below their position.

"The stars appear correct." Kalen stared upward.

Jack shook his head. "They look identical to me."

"They are different, Chief Jack." Kalen pushed past the group and pulled his own map. "If this is correct, then we need to go up that ridge."

Jack shrugged. "Lead the way."

Kalen glanced to Brooke who stared off in the distance. He quickly shifted his attention back to the task at hand and began trotting up the ridge, the others falling into step behind him. Gnat had to practically run to keep up to prevent Azrael from stepping on him. More than once the large gargoyle offered to carry him but Gnat seemed more aggravated by the offer than thankful.

Kalen crested the highest point of the ridge and paused long enough to refer to his map again. Jack and Azrael closed on either side of him and looked over his shoulder as he pointed down the slope. "Past these trees should be a rock outcrop. The entrance is close to this."

Azrael turned to Jack, "I can glide down and scout the area, with your permission."

"Radio back if anything doesn't feel right." Jack turned to Brooke who was watching the way they had come. "Just below those trees. That's where we need to be."

She nodded absently, her eyes still glued to their rear. "I feel eyes upon us."

Jack stiffened. "Where?" His voice dropped to a whisper and he lowered himself to a crouch.

Brooke shook her head as she slowly backed toward him. "I don't know…but I know how it feels when I'm being watched. It feels that way now."

Jack motioned to Kalen who had slipped into the Anywhere. He was effectively camouflaged and making his way past the pair. Brooke couldn't see him, but she sensed him as he passed by. She sniffed the air and the scent of sugar cookies barely wafted to her nose. "He's good." Her own voice was a barely a whisper as she spoke.

Jack nodded as he crouched behind a large rock. "Yes, he is." He scanned the area behind and below them with nothing catching his eye. "Are you sure there's somebody back there?"

"I can't see them. I can't smell them. I can't hear them. But I can *feel* them. They're there." She lowered herself further until she was barely off the ground.

Gnat popped his head up under her chin, his body slithering past her. "I'm not seeing anything either."

Brooke glanced down and noted that he was nearly between

her breasts and wanted to swat the wee beastie from under her until she caught her breath and realized that he wasn't paying any attention to her dangly bits. She raised herself slightly and watched as the gnome continued to slither past her and behind another rock. He motioned to Jack using hand signals and Jack nodded, giving him the go ahead. Broke wished at that moment that she'd actually taken the time to learn the silent language before now.

She watched as Gnat slipped from rock to rock, working his way back the way they came until he was at the trail head. Their radios all crackled to life. "Chief Jack, this is Azrael. I see nothing of concern here."

"Stand by." Jack glanced toward Gnat and tried to see if he could spot where Kalen may be. "We may have somebody on our tail."

"Do you require air support?" The urgency in Azrael's voice was unmistakable. The giant ached for battle.

"Negative." Jack slid out from behind his protective cover and brought his scope to bear on the trail. He switched on his IR and scanned the area. Other than Gnat, he saw nothing lighting up the night. Shaking his head, he keyed his coms. "Gnat, stand down. I'm not spotting anything on the scope."

"I'm telling you, something is out there."

Jack shrugged at Brooke. "Whatever it is, it isn't acting in a hostile manner. We push on."

Kalen suddenly appeared beside Brooke and his eyes were wide. "Chief Jack, something is out there and it moves quickly. At the base of the ridge, on the other side, near where we exited the gate."

"Did you see what it was?"

He shook his head. "No, it was too quick."

"If these weapons are that important to the Wyldwood, we

need to retrieve them and move out." He motioned to Gnat who was double timing it back toward the group. "Down the slope. Now."

All of them turned and began sliding down the rocky slope, their feet slipping in the loose dirt and rock until they hit the tree line. "Move, move, move!" Jack waved them past him as he covered their rear. "Kalen, find that doorway."

"On it, Chief Jack." He ran past him, the map in hand. "Give me a moment."

Jack scanned the ridge with his scope, his eyes darting from side to side looking for any movement. He thought he saw something once then decided it was a tree branch swaying in the wind. He walked backward, his eyes toward the ridge until he came alongside Brooke. "Any luck?"

"Keebler's working on it."

Jack stole a glance and noted Kalen standing before another large boulder, his arms raised and his bracelet glowing. He was muttering something as the rock attempted to glow. Slowly, light began to escape the seams of a hidden doorway then it suddenly slid open. "It won't stay open for long, Chief Jack. This is not Elven majik."

"Move, people, everybody inside." Jack tapped each one at the shoulder to get them to go inside the large cavern.

He began working his way toward the rock and could almost swear he saw something moving in the shadows of the trees. He couldn't be sure what it was as it moved too quickly and with the bright golden glow behind him killing his night vision, the intruder was quickly lost.

Jack heard the rock start to slide shut and turned and dove inside, the rock door slamming hard behind him. He rolled to his stomach and pulled his flashlight from his belt. Flipping it on, he came to his knees. “Everybody okay?”

“All accounted for, Chief Jack.” Kalen stepped beside him and helped him to his feet.

Jack swung the light in a low arc and examined the inside of the cavern. “Holy…”

Azrael stepped forward, a smile crossing is face. “Finally.”

*****

Laura walked the hallway of the hospital, the smell of antiseptic heavy in the air. She paused at the nurses’ station and noted the thin woman behind the counter speaking in hushed tones on a telephone. She glanced across from the desk where a board with room numbers with last names sat directly in eye sight from the station. She scanned the board until she saw, ‘Youngblood’ and noted the room number. Turning and glancing at the rooms behind her she took off in the direction of her father’s room, the nurse behind the counter still engrossed in her call.

She approached the door cautiously and raised her hand to knock. She paused and realized she wasn’t ten years old anymore and entered her father’s study. She was a grown woman coming to visit her ailing father. She pushed the door open and stepped into the darkened room tentatively. Her eyes adjusted quickly to the gloom and she saw her father lying in the bed, his once strong body now ravaged by time and disease, withered to a mere husk of who he once was.

Laura felt a lump rise in her throat, and the room seemed to tilt slightly as the walls spun. *Breathe!* She fought to stand straight and stepped further into the room. A body sitting in a chair stirred and caught her attention. It was Crystal; and Laura felt a momentary spurt of anger before her senses kicked in she forced the emotion to subside. She paused and stared at the woman who apparently wanted nothing more than to love her father for the years he had remaining. She slept in a chair next to him, her hand wrapped gingerly around his as both slept through the middle of the day.

Laura squared her shoulders and stepped further into the room. She laid a gentle hand on Crystal's shoulder. "How's he doing?" Her whispered voice seemed unusually loud in the quiet room.

Crystal started in her chair and tried to sit up, her body protesting as she moved from what appeared an uncomfortable position. She sat, blinking at Laura, her mind unable to comprehend that Laura had spoken to her without screaming. She cleared her throat and nodded. "He has his good days and his bad days." She stole a glance at his sleeping body. "Today isn't a very good day for him."

Laura squeezed gently at her shoulder and sat beside her. "I can sit with him if you'd like to walk around a bit. Maybe get some air."

Crystal sat forward and stared at Jim sleeping in the bed. Her eyes watered slightly as she stroked his hand. She finally turned to Laura and slowly stood. "Thanks, I'd like that." She turned past Laura and paused, unsure exactly what to say. "He's missed you the most, I think. He'll be very happy to see you when he wakes up."

Laura patted her hand then turned to her father. She slipped into Crystal's chair and took her father's hand in her own. "I'll keep watch while you stretch your legs."

Crystal watched her for just a moment then turned for the door. "I'll bring back some fresh coffee."

Laura gave her a soft smile and nodded then turned her attention back to her father. As soon as she heard the door shut she leaned forward and brushed a stray hair from his face. "Well, don't you just look a mess." She didn't bother to whisper this time.

Jim Youngblood's eyes cracked open and he stared at his youngest child for a moment before recognition struck him. His eyes flew open and his bottom lip quivered as he reached for her. "Punkin." She wrapped her arms around him and dared not squeeze too hard. Her breath caught in her throat as she felt his bones for the first time in her life. The realization that her daddy wasn't superhuman sunk in and she refused to face his mortality.

"I missed you, Daddy."

"I missed you, too." His weak body let her go, and he lay back in his bed, eyes threatening to cry. "You look good, kiddo."

"Yeah, if you count road grit." She sniffed back tears and ran a hand through her hair absently. "I wish you had told me how bad it had gotten."

Jim shook his head. "You had things to do. Important things."

"Yeah, right. Nothing's more important than you, you know that." She sat back in the chair and studied his face. When had he gone so grey?

"So how are things in…where are you working? Oklahoma?"

"I was. I just resigned that post." She averted her eyes, knowing that he wouldn't agree.

"Why would you do that? Are you pregnant?" The hopeful tone was unmistakable.

"Daddy!" She swatted at his hand and shook her head. "You know better than that."

"You can't blame an old man for wanting to see his grandkids before the end comes, now can you?"

"Crimeny, Dad, you aren't dead yet." She stared at him then glanced toward the door.

"One foot in the grave, Punkin, the other foot is slipping." He shot her a crooked grin. "I've come to terms with it. I've lived a long and fruitful life. I have no regrets."

Laura shifted in her chair and glanced at the door again. "Dad? What if there was a cure?"

"Punk, we could play the 'what if' game all day, it won't change anything. I'm too far gone. All they can really do is try to manage the pain now and…"

"But what if there *was*?" She shot him a serious look. "Would you take it?"

He cocked his head and shrugged. "Are you serious? Of course I would. Nobody *wants* to die, Punk. Not really. But it's a moot point, because there isn't a cure."

"What if the cure had…side effects?"

Jim mustered his strength and sat upright a bit more in his bed. He turned and stared at his youngest child and narrowed his gaze. "What are you doing?"

"I'm just asking…what would you be willing to put up with if it meant beating this?"

"Are you being serious?" She noted the hope in his eyes, and it crushed her heart. She hated the idea of waving an 'out' for him only to drop a bombshell on him…attach a rider that he probably wouldn't believe.

Laura averted her eyes a moment and felt her head nodding. "Yes, Daddy, I'm being serious." She looked back to him and she felt the hot tears run down her cheeks. "It's real, but there's a catch. A *big* catch."

"Like how big? Do I have to sell my soul to the devil or join the Masonic Lodge or something?"

"Daddy, I'm being serious."

"I am too. I don't know if I trust grown men who ride little bitty cars in those parades."

"Those are Shriners and they do good things…why are we

even discussing this?" She threw her hands into the air. "You always do this to me when I want to talk about something serious."

"I'm trying to put you at ease, Punk." He shifted slightly in the bed, and his face couldn't hide the pain. "Just spit it out, sweetheart. If the price is doable, then I'm all for paying it."

Laura sighed and leaned in closer to him. "I need you to be open minded about what I'm about to tell you."

"I'll do my best."

Laura reached into her bag and pulled out the vials. She set them on the table beside her. "These can cure you." She turned and stared at her father. "But there *is* a catch."

*****

Mick had finished utilizing the gym and worked out much of his frustrations. He had received no answers to his prayers and his anger and frustration continued to build until he needed to exhaust himself or do something foolish that would get him into trouble. His muscles burned from the workout and his sinuses felt defiled from the scent of wet dog that permeated every inch of the place. He showered and changed and was hoping to put as much distance between himself and the lower levels as he could when he saw her.

Jenny didn't notice him lurking in the shadows, and yes, he was lurking. As soon as he spotted her, he dropped back to where he couldn't be seen and stared at her. She was smiling and seemed happy. She had her hair pulled back into a simple pony tail and it made her appear younger. He slipped further into the shadows and watched her as she went from place to place, simply touching things or stopping to stare, her smile broadening with each new experience.

Something inside of Mick changed as he watched her. He no

longer sulked. He was angry. Somehow…he knew. He could sense the difference in her. Before she arrived, she was apprehensive, frightened and wary of what returning to this place would do to her gentle psyche. Now, she darted from place to place, as if studying every inch, trying to get to know it as well as she could. The people she met were so open with her, treating her as though she were the Queen of the Dogs.

Mick felt his heart tearing itself from his chest. He knew. Somehow, he *felt* it as he watched her flit from place to place, her exuberance growing with each new experience.

She had mated with him.

Mick felt his legs go weak as the realization struck him and he all but collapsed. His breath came in ragged gasps and he stared up into the darkened corners. "Thanks for nothing."

He pulled himself to his feet and squared his shoulders. He had to know for sure what his heart already knew. His mind had to hear it come from her before he'd allow himself to accept it.

He stepped from the shadows and walked slowly toward her. She didn't notice him at first as she studied a bulletin board as though it were the most important thing in the world. Mick approached her from behind and stood with his hands behind him, a gentle smile painted across his features. "You seem awfully chipper today."

Jenny turned and at first, her face went through a dance of emotions. Happy, confusion, anger, betrayal, confusion again and finally, happiness. She nodded to him. "Yes. Yes, I am feeling quite chipper today, thank you."

"So I guess your fears of returning to this place are gone?"

She nodded as she turned back to the bulletin board. "Surprising, isn't it?" She placed a hand under her chin as she studied the board. "Did you know that whenever they get a 'hit', they first place it here until it's verified. Then the squads are rallied and sent out to deal with it. Amazing really, how this place operates."

"Truly," Mick replied absently. He glanced at the bulletin board and then at the notices to either side of it. "So, do you plan on staying for a while or will we be leaving anytime soon?"

Jenny turned and shot him a quizzical look. "Leaving? Why on earth would I do that?"

"Well…I just…" Mick cleared his throat. "I mean, you were going to come here just to meet the man who *claimed* to be your fated mate. Now you've met him and come to terms with your fears." Jenny nodded, her eyes still roaming the notices on the board. "I just thought that since you came and your dragon was slain, we could be on our way."

She froze and allowed his words to sink in. Slowly Jenny turned and gave him a look that he couldn't identify; or, perhaps, he didn't want to identify. "I'll not be going anywhere, Mick. Matt and I are mated now." She narrowed her gaze on him and shook her head. "It's forever."

Mick felt as though he couldn't breathe. A huge weight had been placed over his chest and he simply could not force enough air into his lungs. He actually staggered back a step and stared at her as the blood rushed out of his head. "You…you're…"

"We are mated."

Mick swallowed hard and stepped back again, his head nodding slightly. "Yes, yes, of course you are." He turned slightly and nodded to her, "If you'll excuse me."

Jenny had already turned back to the notices and was working her way down. She didn't notice, nor care that Mick had excused himself.

Mick staggered away and found a corner to lean on. Why had

her words struck him so? His heart knew already…why did hearing them have such an effect on him? He pushed away from the wall and forced himself toward the elevators. He had to get away. He had to get outside. He needed air. The walls were suddenly closing in on him and he had to get out.

*****

"What do you mean they left?" Little John paced the training area then turned and punched the door to the CQB trainer. "Nobody thought to tell me that she was leaving?"

Donnie stepped between him and the door exiting the training area. "Hey, big guy, nobody told us they were leaving. They just all walked outside and then left through the big rock out back."

"The big rock?" Little John threw his hands into the air.

Spalding had been leaning against the wall allowing the operator to vent before stepping in. "That's enough." His voice was quiet, even and low.

Little John turned on him. "Excuse me?"

Spalding pushed off the wall and stepped toward the towering man. "You heard me. That's enough."

Little John squared his shoulders and looked down at the much smaller man. "Who are you to tell me that?"

"I'm your Team Leader." Spalding stared up into the man's eyes, his jaw squared. "I've given you enough leeway on this. You throwing a tantrum and punching stuff isn't going to change anything."

"Well, you sure as hell haven't done anything to help in the matter, now have you?" Little John crossed his arms over his massive chest. "You were the one telling me to cool off, to give her time, that she'll come to me eventually. Well now she's done run off and I may never get another chance to…"

Spalding struck out so quickly that John didn't see it coming, but the hand that struck his chest pushed him back firmly. "I said, that's enough, and I meant it."

"Why you little…" John started to step forward when Lamb and Jacobs stepped in front of him, blocking his path.

"I really wouldn't do that if I were you," Lamb warned.

"Not a smart move," Jacobs added.

Little John glared down at the two men and ground his jaw. "Like you two will stop me?"

"No. I will," Spalding said softly. "If you don't calm yourself down and start thinking reasonably, you're grounded."

John shot him a wide eyed stare. "What?"

"You heard me." Spalding stepped forward and gently pushed Lamb and Jacobs out of the way so that he could stand in front of Sullivan. "John, your sister is part of another team. That *entire* team left out on a mission. She didn't just up and leave, to disappear into the night and never return." John took a half step back and looked to Donovan for verification. Donnie simply nodded. "She will return. And how do you think she's going to react to find out that her little brother went off the deep end because his sister left without leaving a note pinned to the refrigerator?"

John sighed and his shoulders slumped. "Point made."

"No, I don't think so." Spalding stepped closer and lowered his voice. "Look, I know that she's your sister. But somehow you have it in your mind that *you're* the big brother and she somehow needs you to protect her. You and I both know that's not the case. She's a decade older than you, even if she doesn't look it."

John opened his mouth to say something when Spalding held up a finger. "I'm not finished." He turned and motioned to the other men in the squad. "These are your squad mates. They're here to cover your ass in the muck and they expect to be able to count on you in a pinch. Right now, you don't have your head in the game. You're too wrapped up in Brooke."

"I just need her to…"

"I'm not done yet, rookie." Spalding turned to the door and pointed out the splintered wood. "You get a little upset and your first instinct is to strike out. That's not the level head I thought I was taking on here." Little John lowered his eyes and nodded. "And, word is that it's going to be a long while before Carbone is replaced. And since Jack isn't rejoining the squads, Major Tufo mentioned putting us back into two seven-man squads. That means somebody from First Squad will most likely be joining us. I do not want anybody coming into our squad and thinking that we have a loose cannon in our ranks."

"Especially one the size of a Buick," Lamb muttered. Donnie offered up an 'amen' and Little John could do little more than nod.

"Understood, boss." John exhaled hard and met his gaze. "Would an apology help?"

"It damn sure wouldn't hurt." Spalding slapped the man across the shoulder. "But for now, we have drills to prep for. I need you to get your head back in the game."

Donnie nudged John to get his attention. "Keep in mind, bro, she's been out there on her own for this long, kicking ass and taking names as a vampire assassin. Now she has a whole team to help cover her back."

Little John shrugged. "I guess you're right." He shouldered his weapon and turned toward the broken door for the CQB trainer. "Weapon, check. Armor, check. Head in the game, check."

"Alright, you dogs, let's do this," Spalding shouted. "Stack up."

*****

Gaius stood at attention as he reported to Lilith. “We have teams transporting the devices to different areas across the country. Other teams in other countries are dispersing with their devices and caches of them are being strategically placed so that strikes can be quickly coordinated with the least amount of down time.”

“Excellent, Commander.” Lilith turned and pointed to the map on her wall. “Show me the locations.”

Gaius stepped forward and made six circles, each covering major cities. “We have trusted strongholds or properties held by the human hosts that have adequate security for keeping the devices safely hidden until needed.”

“And how will our forces access these devices if they are locked away?”

Gaius held out an electronic keypad lock. “They all are unlocked by the same code. Anywhere in the world one of us should pick up a new host, we can go to a weapons cache, gain access, and lock up behind us, securing the facility for the next.”

Lilith smiled as she palmed the lock. “Excellent work, Commander.”

“What is he doing here?” Samael growled as he entered the office.

“Giving me an update.” Lilith tossed the lock to Samael. “Such a simple little device, but it will help us so much.”

Samael stared at the device with disdain. “Too simple.” He crushed the lock in his hand and let the pieces fall to the floor. “Anybody could get past something like this.”

Gaius stiffened and stared straight ahead. “Perhaps a god such as yourself, but not a human. And not without great difficulty.”

Samael snarled at the Roman then turned and marched to the wine casks. Lilith fought back the smile tugging at her mouth. She turned to Gaius and nodded, “Back to your duties, Commander. Let me know when the devices are all delivered and properly stored.”

“Yes, my queen.” Gaius bowed and quickly disappeared.

“He reminds me of a rat,” Samael muttered as Lilith slid next to him and wrapped her arms around him. “Vermin that needs exterminating.”

“He was hand-chosen to lead my legion, remember?” she purred.

“By who?” Samael spun on her, the wine spilling from the cask.

Lilith laughed as she fell into the chair beside him. “By you, my love, by you. You chose this legion to serve me centuries ago, remember?”

Samael growled low in his throat as he glared at her. He lifted the cask to his mouth and drank greedily. “I’ll never trust him.”

“And he knows it. You frighten him.” She lifted a leg and rubbed her foot teasingly against his large muscular thigh. “He knows that only you can give him the true death.”

Samael turned slowly and stared at her. “And you, my love. You *are* his queen. You have power over the dead, remember. You could extinguish his life as easily as I.”

Lilith raised a brow and smiled at him. “Truly?” She sat up and walked to the window looking out on her minions. “I simply must test this.”

She stared out at those working in the warehouse and chose a random male with bright orange hair. She concentrated on him for only a moment and watched as his eyes flashed a brilliant yellow glow then extinguish, his body collapsing to the floor. The others around him paused for a moment and stared at the corpse now lying down on the job. Two men walked toward the body and one kicked it with his foot. The two looked at each other, bent, and lifted the body, carrying it toward the Dumpster.

"See? I told you."

Lilith sighed and stepped away from the window, allowing the thin curtain to drop back into place. "And now I've wasted a perfectly good centurion."

"You have a thousand more." Samael lifted the cask to his mouth again."

"Actually, I have nine hundred and ninety-nine." She slid in next to him and ran a finger along the side of his mouth, wiping some of the wine from his face. "That's all you gave me." She licked her finger and gave him a wanting smile.

"And if you keep breaking your toys, you won't have any left," Samael laughed.

8

Mark hung up the phone and leaned back in his chair. His wife didn't like the idea of him putting in so many hours, especially so soon after the attack. She didn't care that he *appeared* normal. Hell, they both knew that he was never 'normal', even before the attack. But now with so many questions and so few answers, she worried even more. He tried his best to put her mind at ease about the whole thing, but she was a wife and a mother. She was pre-programmed to worry.

Mark promised her that he would try to take it easier over the next few days, but he still had a ton of work to catch up. He'd just sleep at the office. She knew how comfortable the couch in his office was. He'd be fine.

He rocked back and forth and stared at the leather couch, his mind still racing even though his body craved rest. "Maybe if I count sheep?" He stood and walked to the couch, still staring at it as though it were a foreign object somebody had thrown into the office and left to rot. With a sigh of resignation, he flipped off the light, lay down on the couch, and closed his eyes. Images flashed through his mind's eye so fast that he could barely keep up. The wolf attack, Doc telling him to drop by each day, the images of Apollo being shot…round and round she goes, where she stops…

Mark groaned and rolled to his side. He tried to count sheep but soon the fuzzy white shit factories had turned bloody and strips of flesh were hanging from their leaping bodies. He opened his eyes and stared at the leather that made up the back of the couch. Surely there was something he could do to help him sleep. He sat upright and stared into the darkness. It was almost as though a nightlight were left on. He could make out everything in the darkened office. Every detail was clear. More clear than if he were using night vision goggles. He blinked rapidly a few times and stood up. He walked to the desk and pulled out his hidden bottle of rum. It wasn't often that he'd allow himself a drink, especially at the office, but sometimes a nice, warming nightcap was necessary.

He pulled the lid and tilted the bottle back. The first swallow fell flat, a minor burn in his throat that left him bewildered. He stared at the open bottle and took a deep sniff from it. It smelled like rum. It even kind of tasted like rum. He lifted the bottle to his mouth again and chugged back about a third of it before replacing the cork.

"Good lord. No wonder Mitchell could drink this shit all day and never catch a buzz." He dropped the bottle back into the bottom drawer and kicked it shut. "What the hell?"

He plopped onto his couch and felt the burning liquid slosh in his stomach. He let loose a belch that caused his eyes to water. "Well, now I know." He slumped back into the couch and stared forlornly at the corner of his desk where the bottle lay hidden.

"The last vice I had left and I can't even enjoy it."

*****

Jack twisted the end of the flashlight to widen the beam and held it high. "I think we found it."

Azrael clapped his hands together and turned to smile at the others. "Weapons we know how to use."

Kalen felt a shudder under his feet and reached out to grab Azrael. "Wait. Something isn't…"

The cavern glowed with a green light that burned with brighter and brighter intensity. Jack swung the flashlight around to find the source of the light but came up empty. "I think we set off an alarm." He fought to steady himself under the shaking ground, Brooke holding on to his arm for balance.

"Perhaps we should leave, Chief Jack?" Kalen was backing toward the stone slowly, his eyes darting back and forth.

Before their party could move toward the door, a brilliant flash of green energy manifested in the middle of the room, blinding them all. Jack was reminded of a flash-bang grenade, just without the deafening sound to disorient. The group simultaneously raised their arms to shield their eyes and slowly lowered them as the light dissipated.

"You shall go no further!"

Jack stared at a bald figure standing between them and the weapons, his skin still glowing with the ethereal green light that had blinded them. He wore only what could be described as a cross between a loin cloth and a kilt, his feet covered in leather boots. His upper body was completely bare and heavily muscled. The light that jumped and arced across his body collected upward and flowed into his eyes, giving them an emerald glow that was more than a bit disconcerting.

"Easy there." Jack took a half step forward, his hands extended. "We were sent by the Wyldwood to—"

"You shall go no further!" his voice bellowed, echoing in the small chamber and causing the younger warriors to step back. The being lowered his gaze to Jack and gave a slight shake of his head. "You have brought abominations into this holy place."

Jack shot back a quizzical look. "Abominations?"

Brooke touched his shoulder gently. "I think he means me, Chief. We need to get out of here." She could feel the power emanating from the green glowing figure and it frightened her to her very core.

"No, hold on. We're not going anywhere." Jack straightened and gave the fellow his best stern look of authority. "We were sent here to collect weapons to fight—"

"Never!" The being threw his arms outward in a flexed position and green arcs shot up and down his extremities. "I am the Guardian and you shall not pass."

"Enough of this." Azrael positioned himself between Jack and green glowing Guardian, his wings flexing outward slightly to protect the team.

"Demon!"

The Guardian extended his hand and a metallic rod flew into it. Jack was instantly reminded of a lightsaber until the Guardian whirled it overhead and a golden lash flew out of the end. The Guardian whipped it outward toward Azrael who instinctively raised his arm to block the blow. The golden lash curled around his forearm and the two giants were locked in a tug of war with the golden lash connecting them.

"Azrael!" Brooke yelled as she tried to push past Jack.

"He is not Azrael, he is a demon! Can you not see!" The

Guardian loosened his pull and whipped an arc of power along the golden lash causing Azrael to scream out and stiffen, his body slowly encasing in stone.

"Stop it!" Jack raised his carbine and centered it on the Guardians chest. "He's not a demon. He's a gargoyle!"

The Guardian shot Jack a glare of derision then whipped another arc of jolting power into Azrael. As the gargoyle began shifting faster to stone, Jack lowered his weapon to the ground. "I don't want to have to kill you." He fired a short three-round burst into the ground in front of the Guardian.

The Guardian snarled at Jack then whipped the lash back from Azrael. He whipped it out again and wrapped the end of Jack's barrel with the glowing whip. Jack instinctively fired again, aiming for the Guardian's chest. The bullets ricocheted off before the weapon was pulled from his grip.

The arrows that Kalen fired from his bow glanced away and bounced back into the weapons cache behind the Guardian. He turned a worried eye to Brooke and shook his head. "Get behind me. Please."

Brooke started to step that direction before she squared her shoulders and pulled her katana. "This isn't over yet." As she turned, the golden lash wrapped around her blade; it was pulled from her hand as though she had no grip, her hand and wrist going limp. "What the hell?" She stared at her hand then at the ground by the Guardian's feet where her sword lay.

"You don't have to die this night." The Guardian lowered his eyes to Jack. "Take your people and leave this place."

A scream echoed through the chamber as Gnat launched himself from a rock outcropping in the cavern. He swung his hammer with all of his might and connected with the Guardian's jaw, sending the large glowing being tumbling to the ground. Gnat rolled with the blow and came up again, his hammer raised and ready to strike again. He stood on the Guardian's shoulder, hammer poised to crush his skull. "Stop!" Jack's voice held the tiny warrior mid strike.

Gnat swung his hammer to the side then rolled off the giant man. He reached down and lifted his face by his ear. "That man just saved your life." Gnat let go of his ear and let his head hit the rock floor.

Jack turned to Kalen and Brooke, "Check on Azrael." He slowly approached the Guardian, his prone body laid out on the cold stone floor. Jack hunkered next to the large man and gently slapped his cheek. "You still alive?"

The Guardian blinked rapidly and rolled his head to the side, away from Jack's slapping hand. "What hit me?"

"Our resident warrior gnome." Jack couldn't fight the smile tugging at his mouth. "You're lucky your head is still attached to your shoulders."

The Guardian rolled to the side and sat up slowly. "What did he hit me with, a train?"

"My hammer." Gnat smacked it against his palm a few times in warning. "You'll know better than to mess with my friends in the future."

The Guardian slowly shook his head and held a hand out toward Jack, pushing him away. "I cannot allow you access to the weapons. I am the Guardian…I must…protect…"

"Easy there, big guy." Jack grabbed his arm and pulled him to a sitting position. "I was trying to tell you that we were sent to collect the weapons."

"I cannot allow it." The Guardian turned his gaze to Jack and he couldn't be sure if it were sadness or fear behind those eyes. "My father would kill us all."

Jack shook his head in confusion. “Your father? I don’t get it. Who’s your father?”

The Guardian pushed himself to a kneeling position and inhaled deeply. He stared at the collection of unlikely warriors and blew out the breath. “I am Nephilim. My father is Rafael.”

“Rafael?” Jack shrugged. “I don’t know any Rafael. I only know that the Wyldwood sent us to collect these. Somebody told her that we’d need these weapons to defeat some darkness that is coming.”

Kalen stepped forward and knelt before the Guardian. “You are Nephilim?”

“Yes.” The large man tried to stand, and Kalen provided a shoulder for him.

Kalen turned to Jack, his eyes wide. “Chief Jack, he is Nephilim. A child of an archangel.” Kalen pointed to the weapons behind the Guardian. “Those must be angelic weapons.”

Jack stared open mouthed at both Kalen and the Guardian. “What the hell are we going to be fighting?”

*****

“Really, peanut? You expect me to believe that cock and bull story?” Jim Youngblood shook his head, his eyes betraying his disappointment.

“Believe it or not, Dad. It is what it is.” Laura stood and walked to the window, opening the blinds to allow in the sunlight. “You know how you keep asking me who I’m dating and I…” She turned away and pinched at the bridge of her nose.

“Let me guess. He’s a werewolf, too? Once a month he sheds on everything, and you have to put papers down on the floor or he’ll shit on the carpet?”

"Jesus, Dad, will you listen to yourself!" Laura threw her hands up in frustration.

"Mouth, young lady."

"I'm not seven anymore, Dad. I can say a lot worse than that, too. I can say shit, damn, and even fuck when I'm really mad." She thrust her chin out in defiance.

"I may be sick, but I can still bend you over my knee."

Laura stared at him and tried to imagine him, in his condition, ordering her to bend over his knee. Slowly she began to smile, fighting not to laugh. It must have been infectious because a moment later Jim was chuckling, then full on laughing until he had a coughing fit. Laura rushed to his side and patted at his back, offering him a drink of water.

She sat on the edge of his bed and held his hand. "Daddy, everything I told you is true."

"So what about this *guy* you're dating? I take it he's one of them?"

She shook her head. "No. Worse. He's a vampire."

"Oh, for shit's sake, Laura." Jim tossed her hand aside. "It's bad enough you want me to believe in shape shifters, but now vampires, too?"

"Daddy, you remember when I was little and you used to take me to the pow-wows? The elders believed in shape shifters."

Jim shook his head. "Hocus pocus mumbo jumbo. They didn't really. Not like this."

"I think they did. I think they knew." She reached for the vial and held it in front of her. "Daddy, this can save you. It will bring you back to full health."

"Will it make me young again?" Jim smirked at her.

She shook her head. "No, but you'll start aging from here on a lot slower."

"Well, why didn't you bring that crap by when I was thirty?" He laughed and reached for the vial. He stared at the blue liquid and shook it slightly. "You really believe this crap, don'tcha, Punk?"

She nodded. "And I promised the man I loved that I would tell you before you could take it." She sighed heavily and met his gaze. "I was going to just shoot you up with it and tell you after."

Jim raised a brow at her. "The man you love? You mean the vampire?"

"Yeah. I mean him. I told him it was easier to ask forgiveness than permission. He wouldn't have any part of that." She stood and walked back to the window. She stared out, but saw nothing…her mind back at Tinker with Evan.

Jim turned the bottle over in his hands then set it on the table beside him. "You were just gonna shoot me up with this stuff, but your *vampire* boyfriend talked you out of it."

"Pretty sad when an undead person had more moral fortitude than me, huh?" She sniffed back the tears she didn't want him to see.

"Sounds like I might actually like this guy."

Laura snorted a short laugh. "You probably would. He's a biologist and chemist and…hell, an engineer. He's probably the smartest man I know."

"Hey!" Jim actually sounded wounded.

She turned and gave him her warmest smile as she swiped at her cheeks. "Next to you, I mean."

"That's better." He opened his arms for her to lean in for a hug. She cuddled next to him on his bed while he stared at the vial. "So, what happens if I take that? Every full moon I have to lock myself up in the basement or I chase the neighborhood cats up a tree…or, what?"

"Actually, we have these pills you can take that will keep you from ever shifting." Her voice was low and quiet. "It's based off of wolfsbane, and it will keep you human. You'll still get antsy, and you'll be an even bigger pain in the ass during the full moon."

Jim pinched her in the ribs as she spoke. "Watch yourself."

Laura pushed herself up and met his eyes. "And once you and Crystal get married, you'll have to be doubly careful to never miss a dose. Or you could infect her as well."

"Sweetie, Crystal and I won't be tying the knot anytime soon." He patted her arm gently.

"Once we've cured you and you're on the bane, I don't see why not. There's nothing holding you back." She gave him a soft smile.

Jim nodded. "Actually, there is." He cleared his throat. "You see, I told her that…"

Laura pressed her finger to his mouth, silencing him. "You have my blessing, Daddy."

*****

As the wheels of the jet touched down, Foster was already on the phone making arrangements for cars, enforcers, security personnel, anything and everything he could get his hands on to strengthen their stance.

Rufus Thorn stepped to the rear of the plane and gently reached for the phone. "We won't be needing this, brother."

Foster stared at Rufus with wide eyes. "Are you nuts? You expect us to go up against Lilith alone? Just the two of us?"

Rufus shook his head. "*Non*, we have people on the ground looking for their hiding place. Once it is found, we will verify if she has been made whole. If she has, we alert the human hunters."

"And you think that they can do anything against her? She is evil incarnate. They'll be ripped to shreds."

Rufus chuckled. "Suddenly you are worried about the human hunters? How quaint."

Foster shook his head, his agitation and confusion fighting for dominance. "No. Hell no! I don't give two shits about the human hunters. I just think it's a waste of time to send them in to face her. She'll shred them…and they'll tip our hand."

Rufus smiled and patted his brother's shoulder. "They will keep her busy so that we might strike a killing blow. That is all they must do."

Foster stared at Rufus, his mouth opening and closing as a multitude of thoughts fought for pole position. "I think…I think I understand."

"Excellent." Rufus slipped past him and toward the door. "Have our car brought around."

*****

Bigby hung up the phone and stood from the chair. Everything he needed to bring the monster squad to their knees was beginning to fall into place. He stared out at the warehouse and the vehicles parked within. Pack enough of them with explosives and another wave of them with the gas, he could deliver a one-two punch that would remove them completely from the equation.

He whistled a little tune to himself as he walked through the warehouse and inspected everything. So little silver had been salvaged that they would have to import more to be able to create their rounds. That would take time; time he didn't want to spend, but it had to be done. He couldn't risk sending the men out into town and have them buy up silver trinkets to be melted down.

He walked by the lathe and studied the milled bullets that had already been fashioned. Milled from a silver rod, the shavings caught and melted down to create another rod, the rounds had grooves milled into them that would allow them to break apart once they hit a solid object. He had seen a similar design made of brass a few years earlier and the idea stayed with him. He didn't mind stealing it. It was one helluva idea. It was called a Trident PFP round and he'd seen the damage it could do first hand.

He ran his hand across the mill and felt the warmth radiating up from the machine. It had been well used the past few hours. Now to get more silver and form more rods…

Bigby spun on his heel and marched back to the office. There were places that offered precious metals in just about every form you could possibly desire. Surely somewhere, somebody offered it as a solid rod. The time saved from having to create their own would be worth the added expense.

Lifting the lid on his computer he opened a web browser. "Well, they say that Google is my friend…"

*****

Mick paced the grounds outside the hangar, his mind racing. *How could she have done that? How could she have mated with this guy? She just met him!* The disgust and pain rallied in his mind, each vying to take over his dominant thoughts.

Mick paused and stared at the sky, his heart hammering in his chest. "Oh no." His legs went out from under him and he sat staring, his weak mind just realizing what her coupling with Colonel Mitchell truly meant. "I have to call Walter. He needs to know!"

Mick dug through his pockets and pulled the satellite phone out. It still had half a charge when he punched the power button. He scrolled through his contact list and mashed the button for Walter Simmons. As the phone rang, Mick paced the parking lot. His eyes darted to and fro frantically. When the call was answered, he nearly shouted, "Hello! Hello? Mr. Simmons? This is Mick."

Mick waited for Walter Simmons to finish chewing his ass before he continued, "Mr. Simmons, there was no stopping her. They were going to hop a commercial flight. All I could do was find a way to tag along and…" He paused and listened to the man rant and rave about how a real man would have found a way to stop her. Finally, Mick had enough of being belittled. He clenched his jaw and gripped the phone a little too tightly. "I was just calling to let you know that it's too late. She mated with the son of a bitch."

Mick punched the end call button before Walter Simmons could begin a new tirade. He stared at the satellite phone and debated calling the old man back just to tell him to go to Hell. Instead, he squeezed the plastic case until it crushed in his hand, bits and pieces of the phone falling to the ground.

He stared into the sky once more and growled a deep, low growl. He bent low and threw the phone as far as he could. Mick stood and watched as the pieces disappeared from sight then turned and headed back toward the hangar.

She may have rejected him. She may have chosen another over him. She may have even tied her life to this asshole. But that was no reason to let her die just because her father was an ass. She needed to be warned that he was still on the attack…and her life was in just as much peril as her new mates was.

*****

"My queen." The demon bowed deeply and kept his eyes to the floor.

Lilith turned slowly and studied the man dressed as a security guard. "Report." She turned back to her maps and schedules, her mind on everything except the man at her door.

"Our sentinels that have been watching the human hunters? They have nothing to report." The demon remained prostrate, his eyes purposely avoiding hers.

"So? Why come to me if there is no news?"

"That's just it, my queen. If our reports are to be believed, then they surely have been informed of the cache. They would have sent people out to find them." The demon began to quiver as it spoke. "It is the belief of our sentinels that the human hunters were never told of the weapons cache. They believe that perhaps the supernaturals plan to handle this themselves."

Lilith stood slowly and strode to the doorway where the demon was now practically laying on the ground, his hands trembling visibly. "The *sentinels* concluded this? As if somebody gave them permission to think for themselves?"

"Apologies, my queen. I am merely the messenger." The demon backed away slowly, his eyes never rising to meet hers.

"Who are these sentinels that we have sent to watch the human hunters?" She placed her foot on the demon's arm to stop him from moving.

The man shook his head vigorously. "I do not know, my queen. I was only sent to report to you."

"You were a centurion for how long? You should act like it!" She kicked at the man and sent him sprawling.

The man turned his head, refusing to meet her eye. "Word has spread throughout the legion, my queen. You vanquished one of us for not working hard enough…nobody else wishes to be vanquished."

Lilith stared at the man trembling on the floor and smiled to herself. "How is it that you were sent to deliver this message to me?"

The man crawled to his knees and hung his head low. "We drew lots, my queen." His jaw trembled as he spoke. "I lost."

"Yet, you drew lots with the others, yes?"

The demon nodded his head. "I had little choice."

Lilith willed him to rise. "And yet here you are." She lifted his chin with her finger until his eyes met hers. "What are you to me, centurion?"

"I am your humble servant, my queen."

"Stop kissing my ass, soldier. What are you to me?" Her voice took on a hard edge and finally the Roman squared his shoulders and faced her, looking her square in the eye.

"I am your right hand, my queen. You meter of fate. I am your deliverer of pain and regret. I am your servant. My life is yours."

Lilith stepped back and gave him a wicked smile. "That's much better. I prefer my soldiers to have backbone."

"I wished only to avoid being vanquished, my queen." He met her eyes and she actually took a half step back. "To be sent back to Hell is one thing, but to be sent back as a victim instead of a servant? Intolerable."

Lilith nodded, understanding now what she had unwittingly done to the other centurion. "And now, what are you to me?"

"I am yours, my queen. To do with as you please. I am Death."

"Very good." She clapped her hands slowly. "Go back and tell the men you drew lots with that you are now their commander. Form your own unit of these cowards and beat some bravery into them. Do you think you can do that, *commander*?"

"As you will, my queen."

*****

The door pushed open into one of the many briefing rooms inside the CIA Headquarters building in Langley, Virginia. A haggard looking man dropped a stack of files onto the table then turned and greeted the two stoic individuals already seated. "So sorry I'm late. I forgot a couple of these files and…" He stared at the two men whose disdain for the analyst was palpable. "Right. Well, I knew you'd want them all, so…here they are." He pulled a chair out and sat down, sliding the files to the side.

"How long did it take you to acquire this information?" the older gentleman at the head of the table asked.

The analyst glanced at the stack of files and gave a slight shrug. "Actually, it took a while. This information was not easy to come by. You do realize that they keep everything locked down tight there. They have no servers connected to the outside so attempting to breach a firewall or do a brute force attack is nearly—"

"We know." The younger gentleman stated. He stood and clicked a button on a remote causing the lights to dim. An overhead projector came on and he began clicking through slides. "We at the NSA have been investigating this group for some time now. We had some data sent to us from a now dead Senator that triggered the investigation."

The analyst watched as the slides flashed images on the screen, and he turned to face the other men. "From what I gather, these guys actually think they're hunting bogeymen. Like there are some kind of monsters out there hiding in the dark, and it's their personal mission to waste taxpayer money to hunt them down." He chuckled as he glanced from man to man. Neither man showed any humor on their faces.

"The CIA has been working hand-in-hand with the NSA and the DIA to dig up what we can on this group, but so far…it hasn't been much. That's what we need you to do." The older man leaned across the table and turned a stern stare toward the young analyst.

"I-I know, sir. And I've been working diligently at this for quite some time." He slid the files over and spread them out before the two men. "These are the men that have been chosen from the field and reutilized within the group over the last six years. As you can see, there are quite a few that are dead. If you ask me, they probably drank too much and it was marked as a training accident to protect their reputations as Special Forces operators."

The NSA representative thumbed through the files then dropped them absently on the table. "They didn't drink too much."

"Well, whatever the cause, I doubt they were actually killed in battle. None were ever redeployed to a known combat zone while they were assigned to…"

"Key words there, son—known combat zone. These men died in the field, in battle." The CIA director tossed the files he was perusing onto the table and motioned back toward the screen. "Keep watching."

The NSA assistant director clicked through more slides until images of beings with fangs appeared. Other images of what could only be described as 'monsters' flashed before their eyes. The analyst stared in wide eyed wonder at some of the images, many apparently were stills taken from helmet cameras. "This can't be real. These things don't exist." He pointed anxiously at the screen.

"Yes, they do. We've verified it ourselves." The CIA director sat back in his chair and crossed his arms. "What I want to know is why weren't we told?"

The analyst shook his head. "Sir, I didn't know. I don't think anybody did. Otherwise you would have gotten a full briefing."

The NSA assistant director placed both hands on the table and leaned toward the analyst. "Cat's out of the bag now. We want everything that can be dug up on these assholes."

The analyst swallowed hard and nodded. "I can do that." He pushed away from the table then paused. "I have to ask though…why did you show me this? Surely it's classified above my current clearance."

The NSA assistant director glanced at the CIA director. The older man nodded, giving permission. The assistant director turned to the analyst and stated simply, "So you wouldn't discount the extraordinary."

"Sir?"

The CIA director stood and walked toward the door. "Stevens, if you ran across anything to do with these guys, and it had the words 'monster', 'vampire', 'werewolf'…any of those key words attached to it, what would you do?"

The analyst nodded. "I'd discount it as a redirect, sir."

"Exactly. Now you know what you're dealing with. I want everything." He opened the door for the analyst who slipped through, forgetting his files as he left.

Director Jameson sat back down and slid the files across the table. "What do you think, Robert? Will he be able to dig up anything on these guys?"

Robert Ingram sat back down and picked up the file for one Colonel Matthew Mitchell. For being a full bird colonel, the file was awfully thin. "He's supposed to be the best at digging up what doesn't exist. If it's out there, he'll find it."

Director Jameson leaned back in his chair and shook his head.

"What the hell has the world come to that we have men out there hunting monsters?"

"The monsters brought it upon themselves. They should have stayed in the shadows. Like we do." Ingram dropped the file and stood to leave. "Let me know when he finds anything."

"And you let me know when your super soldier is online and ready for testing." Jameson stood and began to stack the files together.

"We should be ready for testing in the next couple of months. Trust me, you'll be included in the shakedowns." Ingram winked at the older man as he walked to the door.

"Tell me something, Robert." Ingram paused and turned back to the older man. "Do you think there's any truth to the rumors? About what they did to these operators so they could stand against what's out there?"

Ingram shrugged. "I hope not." He glanced at the stack of files still on the table. "That's an awful lot of potentially good soldiers right there."

"But if it is true…" Jameson trailed off.

Ingram shrugged. "Once the cleansing begins, *all* monsters will be eradicated." He opened the door and turned back to Jameson. "Even the ones *we* created."

9

Mark rolled off the couch and turned off the alarm on his phone. He stared at the clock on the wall and sighed. He honestly didn't think he had slept at all. The oddest part was, the fatigue that he had felt earlier was gone. It had been brief, just a fleeting feeling, but he knew he should be tired.

He dug into his pocket and withdrew the black pill and swallowed it then washed it down with cold coffee. He flipped on the lights and squinted for a moment while his eyes adjusted. Mark pulled a clean uniform top from the wardrobe and swapped it out, sniffing the pits of the old one before depositing it in the pile of dirty laundry. He knew it was dirty, but he couldn't detect anything, scent wise. He fell into his chair and had just flipped on his computer when a knock at his door caught his attention. "Yes?"

The door opened slightly and Evan stuck his head in. "Is this a bad time, Major?"

Mark waved him in. “I was going to come down and see you shortly. I just wanted to catch up on some…”

“I’ve got some news…possibly.” Evan shrugged as he handed a manila envelope to him.

“What’s this?” Mark tugged the end open and slipped out the report.

“Your blood work. I had a sample sent off. I requested the work be expedited.” Evan sat quietly across from him as Mark stared at the cover.

He laid the report down and gave Evan a blank look. “Is this all? Was there anything else?”

“Don’t you want to read it?”

“I’ll read it later when I have more time. Right now, I have a lot of paperwork to catch up on.” Mark turned and pulled a folder from his IN basket and began perusing the papers inside, his eyes not truly reading the content.

“But…this could answer everything for you. It could tell you for certain if you were infected with both viruses, or if we need to consider another source for your…”

“Is that all, Doctor?” Mark shot him an angry glare that caught Evan off guard.

Doctor Peters stood and shook his head. “No, that’s all.” He turned for the door and paused. “I’ll see you in my lab within the hour.” He pulled the door shut behind him and left the man to his thoughts.

Mark slammed the file shut and stared at the report. He had no idea why he was so angry. He knew that Evan had run blood work. He knew that those results could be back at any time. He closed his eyes and clenched his jaw. When he opened them again, the report was in his hand. His eyes scanned the cover page and he found himself turning the page, reading the findings.

*****

"You're certain that your elder said a Heavenly being told her?" The Guardian sat atop the ledge that Gnat had launched his attack from.

Kalen nodded. "I have no reason to doubt her." He motioned to the cavern they all now sat in. "How else could we have found this place so easily if someone hadn't told her exactly where it was?"

The Guardian nodded, his eyes darting to each of the other warriors. "Still, he looks like a demon."

Kalen chuckled and sat down beside him. "But he has a gentle soul. Especially for one so effective in battle."

"He is quite strong." The Guardian nodded to Brooke. "But what of the undead female?"

"She feeds only on animals. She harms no humans." Kalen held his hand up and made the sign of the Oath Keeper.

"Still, she is *vampyre*."

Kalen nodded. "And Chief Jack is werewolf. But he is an honorable man and a great warrior." He pointed to Gnat who was combing his beard in the reflection of a large shield. "And Gnat is a gnome. A warrior from a clan of warriors, all sworn to protect their people from any harm. And I am Elf. Of the northern Greater Elves."

The Guardian shook his head and raised a brow at the unlikely assemblage. "My heart tells me you speak the truth, but my bond is to protect these weapons with my life. They shall not leave my sight nor shall they…"

"So come with us." Jack swung the sword in his hand and marveled at how light it felt. "That way the weapons don't leave your sight, you keep your word, and when we're done, the weapons are all returned here."

"You do not wish to keep them?" The Guardian shot him a disbelieving stare.

Jack shook his head. "Sorry, pal. Swords and crossbows just aren't my weapon of choice. I prefer things that go bang."

"But they're so ineffectual." The Guardian stood and placed his hands on his hips while he considered Jack's proposition.

"Chief Jack, why do you invite him to come along?" Kalen slipped beside Jack and tried to keep his voice low.

"Didn't Loren say that we are expecting another warrior to join us? Maybe it's him." Jack smirked at Kalen as he tossed the Elf a long bow.

"Yes, she said we are to expect another, and we are also to search out Allister the Griffin as well. We have made no efforts to do so."

"Maybe because she sent us looking for these." Jack held up a shield and tossed it to Kalen. "If she weren't so busy sending us on errands, we could accomplish something."

Kalen sighed heavily and leaned against the wall of the cavern. He pinched at the bridge of his nose then turned to the Guardian. "My apologies, friend. I do not know your name."

"I have no name. I am simply the Guardian. I have never needed a name."

"And calling you Nephilim seems impersonal." Kalen rubbed at his chin.

Brooke nudged the Elf. "How about just Phil?"

"If you like." The Guardian bowed slightly.

"Very well. Phil, if you would be willing to accompany us on our mission, we could most certainly use your help."

"He's coming." Jack brushed past Kalen and approached

Azrael. "You back in fighting shape?"

Azrael flexed his hands a few times and nodded. "The effects were short lived."

"Pick your poison. I want to bug out ASAP."

Kalen stared after him a moment then turned back to the Guardian. "I apologize for our leader. He's gruff, but he means well."

"Pay no mind." The Guardian slipped down from the ledge and chose a sword and shield from the pile. The whip handle hung from a rudimentary belt at his waist. "He seems adamant."

"Once he sets his mind to something, yes." Kalen sifted through some of the weapons and came up empty. "I see no quiver or arrows."

"Your bow requires none." The Guardian held out his hand and Kalen slipped the bow from his shoulder. As the Guardian pulled the bow string back an arrow materialized, perfectly nocked and ready to fly. He slowly let the string back and the arrow fell to the ground with a metallic clang.

"Impressive." Kalen bent and retrieved the arrow. "It's so light." He tried to bend the arrow and found that he couldn't.

"It is a holy weapon. You won't break it." The Guardian handed the bow back to him and watched as Kalen tried to find a place to stash the arrow. "There's no need. As long as your intentions are good, the bow will supply you. You shan't run out."

Jack reached for the arrow. "If his intentions are good?"

The Guardian nodded. "Holy weapons cannot be used for evil. They will…not allow it."

"Yet you were able to use the whip against Azrael." Jack raised a brow.

The Guardian nodded. "It did not kill him. That was why I was willing to allow you to leave."

"You mean that whip should have been deadly?" Jack took a half step back, his eyes narrowing on the Nephilim.

The Guardian nodded again. "Had his intentions been less than honorable, yes. It would have cleaved him in half. The energy surge would have set him aflame if nothing else."

Jack held up the crossbow. "And this?"

"Destroys your enemies from within." The Guardian put his hands together than quickly spread them apart, mimicking an explosion.

Jack rubbed at the back of his neck and tried to take in the power of the weapons. "Fine. Let's get these stacked up and ready to go. Kalen, open the door and let me out so I can call in transportation for the rest of these."

The Guardian stood to his full height and stepped between Jack and the weapons. "You claimed you wanted to arm your people."

Jack held his hands up and took a half step back. "Easy there, big guy. I *do* want to arm my people, but most of them are back at our base."

The Guardian shook his head. "You may not take them all." He crossed his arms and planted his feet. "You may only arm the warriors you brought with you."

Kalen stepped between the two. "He is right, Chief Jack. The others will not be needing the weapons, only we six."

"Now just hold on a goddam minute." Jack shoved a finger in Kalen's face. "This is news to me. I thought the whole point of us coming here was to arm up the squads."

Kalen shook his head. "No, Chief Jack, we are to arm ourselves so that we may face the threat. The others will not be needed other than to cover our backs as we do our job."

Jack narrowed his gaze on Kalen. "What aren't you telling

me?"

Kalen shook his head. "That is all I know! I swear it!"

Brooke stepped between the two and patted Jack's shoulder. "I'm armed. That's all that matters." Jack glanced at her and noted the crossed swords on her back and the numerous knives she had strapped to herself. She carried a small metallic handle that extended into a bow staff.

Jack sighed and threw his hands into the air. "Fine! Grab what you can carry and use. Apparently we're going this one alone."

"What is the task?" The Guardian picked up his weapons again and approached Jack.

Jack shook his head. "We still don't know. But apparently we're going to have to have angel weapons to do it."

*****

"Crystal, darling." Jim reached a hand out toward the woman as she entered his hospital room. "Would you be a dear and do me a favor?"

She reached for his hand and kissed his knuckles. "Of course, my love. Anything you want."

"Back at the house, in my top dresser drawer, there's a small photo album. Could you bring it here for me, please?" He gave her a loving smile and she melted inside.

"Of course." She kissed his hand again then stood. "May I ask what you need it for?"

"I just wanted to go over some family photos with Laura before she has to leave. That's all." He gave her a wink as she turned to leave.

"Is there anything else from the house I can get you while I'm there?" She grabbed her purse from the back of the chair and reached for the door again.

"No, ma'am." He gave her a cockeyed smile. "But I may have a little something for you when you get back."

Crystal smiled and shook her head. "Not even if they gave you a room with a locking door, my love."

"That wasn't what I meant." Jim smirked as she walked out.

Laura watched the banter and studied her dad. "You really love her, don't you, Daddy?"

Jim lowered his gaze to her sitting in the chair opposite him and nodded. "I have for a long time, Punk."

"Why didn't you just marry her then? I would have come to terms with it eventually."

"It just didn't seem right if my kids weren't on board." Jim pushed himself upright and pulled the rolling table closer. "I thought maybe it was too soon after your mother…" He paused and stared off into the shadows. "God rest her."

Laura stood and went to be by his side. "She knew you loved her." She gripped his hand tightly.

"You remind me so much of her sometimes." He stared at her with rummy eyes. "It scares me. I almost called you Margaret a number of times while you were growing up."

Laura tried to hide her smile. "It wouldn't have hurt my feelings."

"Oh, it was usually when you were testing my patience." Jim patted her arm. He glanced around then checked the door. "So, tell me more about this 'cure' of yours, Punk."

"You know the side effects, right, Daddy?"

"Yeah. And if I take the bitter black pills, the biggest one won't happen. But I'll get edgy around the full moon." He tried his best to read her face, just to see if she was pulling his leg.

"Does that mean you want to do this?" She tried not to sound hopeful.

Jim nodded almost imperceptibly. “Yeah, Punk, I think so.”

“You need to know so.” She lifted the vials and set them on the table. There’s no changing your mind once we start this.”

“Let’s see. It will cure me. I won’t age. I’ll get my libido back…”

“I didn’t say that.” Laura poked him with her finger.

“You didn’t say I wouldn’t either.” Jim reached around and pulled the port from his IV around so she could access it. “I’m positive Punk. If this will give me the opportunity to live to see my grandkids, then hell yeah.”

“It will let you live to marry Crystal.” Laura pulled the syringe from her bag and drew fifteen CCs from the vial. She tapped at the body of the syringe to knock the air bubbles to the top and vented them. “Last chance.”

Jim smiled at her and squeezed her arm. “Hit me, Punkin.”

Laura stabbed the needle into the port and injected the serum. Jim watched the port drip the solution into the tube feeding his arm. He stared as the saline changed color slightly and fed to his wrist then into his body. He took a deep breath and stared at his daughter wide eyed. He waited for something to happen. A pain to wrack his body. An explosion of energy. An electric jolt to shoot through him.

Nothing happened.

Laura packed away the vial and dropped the syringe into the sharps container in his room. “There ya go. Step one.”

“Step one?” Jim looked at his arm and lifted his sheet to see if he was growing hair in any funny places. “I don’t feel any different.”

“You won’t. Not for a little while. You have to give it time.” Laura glanced at her watch then patted her dad’s leg. “I have to make a call. You rest, and I'll be back in a moment."

"You mean I sent Crystal on a wild goose chase for nothing?"

Laura shook her head. "How would you explain your daughter having a 'cure' in her bag? It was for the best that you sent her on her way." She opened the door then leaned back into the room. "I'll be right back. I just need to call…my boyfriend, and tell him how things are going."

"You do that," Jim shouted after her, "and tell him I want grandkids!"

*****

Mitchell escorted Jenny through the lower levels of the base and hesitated as they stood outside the solid steel door. "Are you sure you want to do this?"

She clung to his arm and tightened her grip, her eyes glued to the dull silver door before them. Slowly she nodded her head. Her voice was a hoarse whisper as she spoke. "Not really." She turned and he saw the fear in her eyes. "But I have to, Matt. I have to break through this fear that's…buried deep inside me."

"We can do this later." Mitchell pulled her aside and held her tightly. "You don't want to overdo it too soon. Sensory overload and all that."

Jenny trembled in his arms but pushed away slightly. "I need to. I walked through the entire place and met the people. They're truly lovely."

"Lovely?" Matt chuckled and shook his head. "I can think of a hundred different ways to describe the people who work for me and lovely just isn't one of the words I think I'd choose."

She punched him lightly for teasing her. "You know what I mean. They treated me with respect and kindness. Not at all what

I…" She trailed off, her eyes falling on the door again.

"I understand, Jen." Matt slipped from beside her and entered the code in the keypad next to the door. "Just remember that, if at any time you want to leave, say the word."

She nodded fearfully and stepped forward, squaring her shoulders and screwing up her courage. "I'm ready."

Mitchell pulled the door open and stood to the side. Lights came on automatically overhead and Jennifer stood once again in the place where her nightmares originated. She stared wide eyed at the equipment that had once been her icy prison. The machines, now silent sat quietly in the dim light, the cameras no longer blinking, the monitors all shut down. She stepped closer and ran a hand along the cooling lines that had once fed the machine that kept her frozen. They weren't cold and it surprised her.

She turned slowly, her eyes taking everything in at once. "It's much larger than I remember."

"The power was out when you were here last." Mitchell tried to inflect as much compassion as he could in his voice. "And I'm sure you were still in a state of shock."

She nodded almost imperceptibly as she walked around the chamber that had held her for nearly a decade. She shivered involuntarily and lifted her eyes to his. "I-it's not as scary as I thought it would be."

Mitchell gave her a weak smile. "Yes it is." He stepped forward and took her hand. "You're scared to death right now. I can feel it."

Instinctively she leaned into him. "I was so angry for so long…"

Mitchell nodded, completely understanding. "I wanted to let you go so many times. They wouldn't let me."

Jenny sniffed back her tears and turned her face into his chest.

"I'm ready to go now. I don't ever want to come back here."

"You never will. I promise." He stroked her hair and withdrew her from the cryo unit. He found his own hands trembling as he pushed the door shut. Once it clanged shut and he entered the code to lock it he turned and found her staring at him. "Are you okay?"

"I will be. I just need to get away from here." She wrapped her arms around his middle, and he walked her to the elevators. "I have to admit something."

"Something tells me that I'm not going to like this."

She pulled him closer and they slowed their approach to the elevator. "The anger I felt toward you? The mixed emotions? The lack of trust? All of that disappeared once we mated. I don't know exactly what caused that, but I'm really glad it did."

Mitchell held her close and kissed her. "Me too."

*****

"You *will* stand down until further notice, do you understand me?" Walter Simmons growled through the phone.

Bigby leaned back in his chair and pinched at the bridge of his nose, a headache forming behind his eyes. "And why is that, sir?"

"I just got word that my daughter is inside their compound and she is *mated* to their leader! You are to take no action until I can get you more backup. I want her safety ensured above all else, do you understand?"

Bigby sighed heavily and slumped in his chair. "Understood, sir." He glanced out the window at the men doing hand to hand training and dry fire drills. "What are we supposed to do until you can procure backup?"

"I'm wiring you money. You said something about needing supplies? Use it to get them. And if you have plans for that building that they're in, build a mock-up. I want those men to know every inch of it."

"A mock-up? Seriously?" Bigby groaned. "Do you have any idea how long that will take?"

"I don't care! Until I am guaranteed of her safety, you are essentially shut down, do you hear me?" Simmons was practically screaming over the line.

Bigby stared out at the men and measured the odds of successfully taking the hangar with the crew on hand. If he ignored Simmons' orders and went ahead as planned, he could avenge Sheridan and take out the damned Monster Squad once and for all. Having to make special arrangements to save the girl? It might be too much.

Bigby opened his mouth to protest but found another thought forming as he spoke. "As you wish, sir. We'll begin building the mock-up as soon as we can get the supplies. How soon until the backups arrive?" His mouth said one thing, his mind raced in another direction. Who says they had to make every effort to save the girl? Collateral damage and all that. It happens all the time. And if she was truly mated to Mitchell, then she may well be the easiest way to cut the head from the snake.

"I'll get on the phone as soon as we hang up. I'll have them en route to you as soon as possible. I may have to buy mercenaries for this. Are you okay working with hired killers?"

Bigby chuckled. "I'm used to hired killers, sir. I know them best."

"Excellent. Just sit tight then, and I'll get back to you as soon as I have something solid."

Bigby nodded into the phone. "Standing by, sir."

He hung up the phone and stared out at the men training in the warehouse. Bigby stood and slipped Sheridan's beret on once more. It was time to fill Martinez in on the turn of events.

*****

Thorn slipped up the slope and rolled in the tall grass to settle in next to the chain link fence. The sun had just set and the ground still radiated it's warmth as he lifted the binoculars to his eyes and scanned the old auto manufacturing facility. He dropped a hand behind him and waved the rest of his party forward.

Foster slithered in beside his brother and lifted his own set of binoculars to his eyes. "Anything?"

"Not yet. But there are a lot of vehicles parked around the perimeter for this to be abandoned."

"Agreed." Foster scooted further to the side then tapped Thorn on the shoulder. "At the corner. In the shadows."

Rufus redirected his gaze and noted the two men standing near a steel door, their eyes scanning the parking lots. "Why would an abandoned building need guards?"

"Especially guards who weren't in uniform." Foster slithered back down the slope then stood, dusting off his clothes. "I think it's time we got a closer look."

"I can almost assure you that Lilith has been made whole, brother." Rufus slipped his binoculars into the case he wore on his belt. "But you're right. We need to know for sure before we contact the human hunters."

Foster planted his hands on his hips and stared at his brother. "I don't suppose you would trust this part of the mission to some of the enforcers?"

Thorn shook his head forlornly. "As if they would know what to look for."

Foster sighed heavily. "True enough." He cast a doubtful look back toward the building. "Our best bet is to come in at the roof and hope for a skylight."

"And if there isn't one, we drop down on the guards and kill them." Rufus motioned to Foster. "After you."

Paul grimaced. "Of course."

*****

"So this is the breakdown." Spalding paced slowly in front of all of the Monster Squad operators. "I sat down with Major Tufo and we worked out a tentative roster. As of now, squad two is moved up to squad one. We will not be taking the unit designator of Bravo, though. We'll stick with Delta for coms. Squad Three is now Squad Two. We will not be forming a third squad any time soon."

Lamb stood up and raised a hand. "Spank? Are we not gonna try to replace Carbone and Apollo?"

Spalding shrugged. "Not any time soon. We have too many irons in the fire to try to replace two squad members. It's easier just to go back to two squads." He flipped the page and scanned his notes. "Squad Two will be keeping their personnel and adding Wallace and Gonzales. My squad will be picking up Gus Tracy. Any questions?"

Dom stayed reclined but motioned with his chin. "How'd I get so lucky as to pick up two and you get one?"

Spalding shrugged. "We had an odd man left over. Major Tufo thought that, since your team was heavy with newbies, you could use a couple of more experienced operators to help train them."

A round of groans and mumbled epithets came from the newer operators assigned to second squad, but Dom held a hand up to hush them. "Probably good thinking on his part, but you know if we could get Phoenix to step up to the plate, we could round the teams out evenly." Dom shot Spanky a mischievous grin.

"Good luck with that. He's got his hands full with his own group." Spalding flipped his notes shut. "Look, I could stand up here and bore you guys with a lot of the thought processes that went into the split, but the short end is, this is what the major came up with, so this is how it's going to be. To be honest, I like the idea of having an extra man when boots hit the ground."

"Yeah, whatever." Dom stood and eyed his squad. "T.D., you and Popo work with Marshall and Erickson and work out a rotation for breaking in the new guys."

Chad McKenzie stood up and gave Dom a hurtful stare. "Haven't we proven ourselves yet? Jesus, you're still treating us like we're wet behind the ears here."

Dom pointed a meaty finger at the man. "As far as I'm concerned, you *are* still wet behind the ears. You're supposed to be a damned operator, so man up, grow a set, and act like one. What's our motto? Bleed in training so we don't bleed on the battlefield. So go bleed, asshole."

Ben Charmicael, the other new operator with Second Squad groaned. "Thanks, Mac. Your whining just got us an extra ass pounding in the trainer."

McKenzie shot him a dirty look. "Hey, maybe you're willing to be treated like a nub, but not me. I earned my stripes. I'm every bit as good as the rest of these—"

"Check yourself," Spalding interrupted. "Your little tantrum is liable to get you sidelined."

McKenzie clenched his jaw so tight that his jaw ticked. He exhaled hard and nodded to Spalding. "Roger that."

Spalding stepped back to the front and raised his voice, "Okay, hunters, get your gear together and get ready to train with your new battle buddy."

*****

"Isn't technology grand?" Lilith stared at the computer screen and smiled to herself.

"I'll take boots on the ground any day to…this," Samael snarled at the contraption that she continued to stare at. "Just because it is new does not make it grand."

"Oh, is somebody feeling unnecessary?" She stroked his chest as she poked at his fragile ego. "The big, bad angel is feeling left out."

"Stop." Samael stepped away from her and stared at the demon centurions as they continued to pack their suicide devices into crates and into trucks.

"I can track their movements with this. I can actually *see* them unload the devices at the drop spots. Once the time comes for us to strike, I'll be able to watch them come in and resupply themselves." She nearly squealed with delight.

"And if you were out there with them, you could see it firsthand rather than over a screen."

"And risk damaging this body? I just got it back, lover," she tsk'd at him and shook her head. "Not likely. I need to keep this body pristine in order to pull off my coup d'état."

"A coup? I thought you were going for world domination, my wilting flower?"

Lilith shot him a dirty look. "I am. But first, I must topple the largest and most powerful governments and at the same time, I *will* have my revenge."

Samael turned and raised a brow at her. "Revenge?"

"I intend to strike every Catholic church on the planet and

level it," she snarled. "They will pay for what they did to me."

"Just the Catholics? There are so many other religions that could be made to pay as well." Samael felt a swelling of pride as her eyes glazed over, imagining the blood and destruction.

"It was the Roman Catholics who hunted me down and…" She spun on him and pointed a sharpened finger in his face. "I will not be denied!"

Samael held his hands up in surrender and smiled at her. "I wouldn't dream of trying to stop you, my love."

10

Mark stared at the report in his hand and tried to make heads or tails of it. Why can't they just write these damned things in English so that normal people could read them? He could feel his eyelids getting heavier as the words blurred across the page.

"I could have used this when I went to bed." He closed the report and shoved it into his drawer. Who gave a shit what it said? As long as he could go out in sunlight and didn't try to eat anybody, he was happy.

He stood and poured another cup of coffee and stared out the window of his office. He didn't turn when the door of his office opened and Dr. Peters stepped inside. "I thought you were going to report to my lab."

Mark sipped his coffee and continued to stare out the window. "Did you get a copy of the report?"

"Not yet. I'm sure they'll send me one if you don't share the results."

Mark nodded and turned back for his chair. "I think I'm done being poked and prodded, Doc." He sat down and pulled the report out again. He slid it across his desk to him. "Knock yourself out."

Evan picked it up and gave Mark a wary eye. "What did it say?"

Mark shrugged. "A lot of words I can't pronounce." He sipped his coffee as Evan slowly opened the report. He watched as the vampire perused the papers, nodding to himself.

"As we expected." Evan closed the report and placed it gently back on his desk.

"Both viruses?"

"Two distinct variants detected." Doctor Peters sat down and studied him. Mark appeared unaffected by the news.

"So what did you call it? Werevamp?" Mark's eyes appeared cold as he stared at the doctor.

Evan simply shrugged. "It doesn't matter what you call it, Major. You are the only known case of an individual being infected by both at the same time. And being asymptomatic? That is absolutely incredible."

"We don't know that I'm asymptomatic yet." Mark took another sip of the coffee and sighed heavily. "We'll have to wait for the full moon before we know that."

"But don't you see? You are as much infected by the vampire virus as you are the wolf. Yet you are not affected by UV radiation, you have no thirst for blood, you can hold holy relics."

"For now. We can't know what tomorrow brings." Mark set his coffee cup down and leaned forward in his seat. "If I learned one thing from my time in the field, it's to never count your chickens before they're hatched."

"I'm not following you, Major."

“Don’t count on my staying asymptomatic. That could change at any given moment. For all we know, the virus is building up in my system, one of them waiting for the other to weaken so that it can become dominant.”

Evan sat back and nodded. “I hadn’t considered that.”

“Maybe it’s time you do.”

“Well then you definitely need to continue your daily check-ins with me. I’ll need to run tests and—”

“No,” Mark interrupted. “If it happens, it happens. I’m not going to try to maintain a balance with the two.” He stood and walked back to his window, his eyes focusing on nothing in particular. “If it happens, it happens. I’m not going to worry myself sick trying to prevent what’s meant to be.”

Evan groaned. “Don’t tell me you’re buying into this whole ‘fate’ bullshit, too?”

Mark turned slowly and gave him a tight lipped smile. “Why not? I am half wolf, aren’t I?”

Evan ran a hand across his face and sat up. “It’s all a crock, Major. There is no underlying ‘fate’ that runs the universe. Science can explain—”

“Says the vampire to the werewolf.” He raised a brow at the doctor.

“All explainable.” Evan held his hands out to stop him. “I know it sounds a little odd, but I assure you—”

“Doc, I’m busting your balls. I get it, okay?” Mark made his way back to his desk and sat down. “I’m just tired and cranky. I haven’t been sleeping well.”

“That’s understandable. With the changes that your body is going through, you probably don’t need sleep like you used to.”

“My mind does. My body feels fine, but my mind spins so fast that I feel like I’ve almost burned it out.”

"I think I have something that is safe for both halves to take that will help you sleep." He stood and turned for the door. "Just, please, reconsider the daily checkups. Even if you don't want to work on maintaining balance between the two viruses, we still need to monitor your systems. You truly are unique."

Mark nodded. "Aren't we all?"

*****

Jack checked his watch and placed a steadying hand on Kalen's shoulder. "Hold on there, Speedy. It's daylight back home. You might be able to open us something inside here, but we'd still have to trek across the grounds to the hangar."

Brooke flipped her hood up over her head. "I'm good, Chief. The sun won't bother me."

Jack hooked a thumb over his shoulder toward Azrael who was still nursing his arm. "You might, but Jolly Gray Giant over there would turn to stone faster than you could blink. I don't know about you, but I'm not up to carrying two tons of solid granite."

Azrael shot him a dirty look and crossed his arms over his massive chest. "I doubt that I would weigh two tons."

"Regardless, I'm not hefting you across the grounds. We're camping here." Jack popped a squat and settled in for the day. "Smoke 'em if you got…" He cast a glance at the group milling about the cavern. "Never mind."

Gnat settled in next to Jack and pulled his pipe. "Don't mind if I do."

Jack pulled the long stem pipe from his lips and set it aside. "We're in a closed environment. I'd rather you not. Besides, Sneezy, it will stunt your growth."

Gnat gave him a dirty stare and snatched his pipe back up off the ground. "I get the distinct impression from your tone that I've just been insulted."

"Who me? Never." Jack shook his head in denial and flipped off his flashlight, allowing the cavern to go dim.

"Would you care for natural light?" the Guardian asked.

Jack turned to Azrael who simply shrugged. "I could use the rest to heal."

"Sure, Phil, knock yourself out. Light us up."

The Nephilim placed hands on the large stone that was the hidden doorway and the group watched as it slid silently to the side at his touch. Natural sunlight washed partway into the interior and Azrael almost immediately began stiffening, his body covering in a light grey coating of stone. Within moments, he was solidly encased in the stone sleep.

The Guardian stepped closer and examined his still form in the light of day. "Incredible." He traced a finger over the gargoyle's folded wings and pulled his hand back carefully. "You're certain he is not a demon?"

Kalen nodded. "I am certain." He turned and stood at the doorway, his gaze cast outward as if waiting for something.

Jack pulled his radio and placed the ear bud in place. He tried to radio Tinker and found that either the rock encasing the cavern or the distance had them out of range. "Kalen, open me a channel."

The elf cast a weary glance at him then used the rock from the doorway to open a portal. Jack radioed the base and informed them of their situation. He sent word through the duty officer that they wouldn't need the transport that the XO had authorized and that at sundown they'd return.

When asked about the weapons they had gone in search of, Jack hesitated. "Uh, that's affirmative, but apparently there are just enough for my crew. I guess the Wyldwood left that part out." Jack chewed at his bottom lip as he lied. He hated to be dishonest, but it was much easier than trying to explain that the offspring of an archangel refused to allow them to use what was at hand.

As he flipped off the radio, Jack reached for an MRE. "Anybody hungry?"

Brooke stared at the foil pouch and narrowed her gaze. "Got any O positive in there?"

Jack hesitated and shot her a questioning look. "Roast beef count?"

"I was just messing with ya." She patted Kalen on the shoulder, "If I get too hungry, I'll take a chunk out of sugar cookie here." Kalen shuddered as he remembered his 'dream' and he gave her a knowing look that had Brooke blushing and turning away.

"What is a Wyldwood?" The Guardian bent low next to Jack, his voice low.

Jack patted the ground, inviting him to sit. As the Nephilim settled in, Jack pointed to Kalen. "She's the leader of his village. She has the ability to 'see' things. So do a lot of the elders." Jack washed down his mouthful with a swallow from his canteen then leaned back against the wall of the cavern. "Apparently they see some sort of threat headed our way, but whatever it is, it isn't clear to them exactly what it is. They just get bits and pieces as it's needed."

"And she is the one who told you where the holy weapons were hidden?"

Jack shrugged. "Well, she told us, but I think somebody else told her. I'm not sure of all the details as it seems that she prefers to go through Kalen now instead of talking to me directly."

The Nephilim eyed the elf still watching the terrain outside the doorway and nodded toward him. "Is he the leader?"

Jack grunted. "I'm supposed to be. I'm not sure how I got

roped into that job either." He took another bite from the MRE and shook his head. "I owe the Wyldwood. Maybe she figures this is a way to pay her back."

The Nephilim turned a curious gaze to him. "How?"

"How, what?"

"How do you owe her?"

"That is a very long story." Jack placed the MRE to the side and wiped his hands on his pants. "Suffice to say, she sent a small army of warriors to help us fight another big threat. She didn't have to, but she did. And like an idiot, I told her that if she ever needed anything, just ask."

"And she asked." The Nephilim nodded. "Perhaps her insight is more attuned than you are aware."

"Perhaps. Or perhaps she didn't have anybody else that she was willing to toss to the wolves." Jack gave the Nephilim a smirk. "Think about it, Phil. Whatever this threat is, we're going to need weapons made for angels to fight it. What the hell is as strong as an angel?"

The Nephilim rubbed his chin and glanced over his shoulder at the stockpile of ancient weapons. "I can think of only one thing: an angel."

*****

"I'm proud of you. I was afraid you were just telling me what I wanted to hear." Evan pressed the phone closer to his ear, his voice barely a whisper. "You do realize that you've broken nearly all of the rules there are, right?"

Laura pressed her forehead to the cool, painted block wall and sighed heavily. "It was worth it, Evan." She glanced toward the nurse's station and smelled the coffee brewing. She turned around and leaned against the wall, her foot propped under her. "You know, in all the years I devoted to the squads, I never once asked for anything. I figure *taking* a little something when I need it? It's justified."

"Ha!" Evan snorted into the phone and shook his head as he spoke to her. "Justified? Sweetie, if that's what you have to tell yourself, that's okay with me. You know I'm not going to judge you. But I also know you. Your conscience is going to eat at you until you confess to Mitchell."

Laura pursed her lips together and squeezed her eyes shut. "Dammit." Her voice was barely a whisper, but it may as well have been yelled across the phone to him. "It was tearing at me before I ever got here. You don't know how many times I nearly turned around or just picked up the phone or…I had to do *something*!"

"I know you felt like you did." Evan sat down gently and stared at the picture of her pinned to his corkboard. "Laura, I'm not going to say that Mitchell would have understood what you did, or that he would give you his blessing, but he's known you a lot longer than I have. Don't you think that if I can be understanding in the situation, that he could too?"

She shook her head. "No, not on this. I'll be lucky if I don't inherit your cell once he finds out."

"If you truly believe that, then you need to make sure he never finds out."

"Evan, they do inventory on the serum. He'll find out."

"Already taken care of." He smiled at her gasp on the other end of the phone. "I'm a man of many talents, and accounting for two broken vials was child's play."

She bit at her lower lip as emotion swelled within. "Have I told you how much I love you?"

"Not today you haven't."

"Well I do. Oh, and my father wants me to tell you that he wants grandchildren," she laughed.

Evan stiffened slightly and stared off into nothingness. "I would like nothing better. Unfortunately, it can't happen. At least, not with me."

"You don't know that for sure." She realized that she had hit a nerve and wished she had kept the comment to herself. "Evan, there's always a chance. Besides, our lifestyle isn't exactly conducive to raising children."

"True enough." He cleared his throat. "I hate to do it, but I need to let you go. Major Tufo is approaching."

"Okay. I love you."

"Love you." Evan hung up the phone just as Mark stepped into his lab.

"I take it that was Laura?" Mark fell into the chair opposite him.

"Yes, it was, but how did…ah, your hearing has improved already." Evan pulled a notebook out and began flipping through pages.

"What was that about broken vials and child's play?" Mark asked, slowly swaying back and forth in his chair. Evan froze mid pen-stroke and stared at him. "Excuse me?"

"I heard you say something to her about broken vials and child's play. I was just curious what that was about." Mark leveled his gaze at the good doctor then crossed his arms over his chest.

"Were you eavesdropping, Major?"

"Not at all. I just heard your voice and then…listened."

"From where?" Mark turned slightly and motioned toward the closed doorway leading to the hall on the other end of the open expanse. Evan shook his head. "That's impossible. Nobody could have heard our conversation from behind that wall." He stood slowly and he studied the Major.

"I assure you doctor, I was right over there, behind those doors and I heard you plain as day." Mark stopped swaying in his chair and cocked his head to the side. "So, what vials were you talking about?"

"Nothing important, Major, I assure you. I'm just shocked that you could hear from that distance and with that much—"

"Bull," Mark interrupted, coming to his feet. "Don't try to pull one over on me, Doc."

Evan pushed his chair back slightly and stared up at the man. "I assure you, Major, I wouldn't try to pull anything on you." He held his hands up and tried to calm the man. "I think perhaps you are reading too much into the small pieces of a *private* conversation that you overheard. That is all."

Mark narrowed his gaze at the doctor then stood tall and stretched his neck. "If you say so, Doc." He turned for the door to the lab.

"Aren't you going to stay for your workup?"

Mark turned and gave him a look he couldn't interpret. "I don't think so. I think you and I are done." He stepped through the doorway and crossed the expanse once more.

Evan watched as the man slipped through the double doors and out of sight. "Damn."

*****

Bigby leaned against the corner of the warehouse eating an apple as Martinez directed his men in unloading a flatbed truck of wooden studs, plywood and other building supplies. He shook his head as the men stacked the materials deep within the warehouse. "I guess we're supposed to be carpenters now." He took a final bite from the apple and tossed the core into a corner of the building.

Martinez supervised the offloading then motioned for the driver to pull the large flatbed out of the open doors and to return the rental truck. "Major Bigby, we'll begin constructing the mock-up once you've verified the dimensions on these drawings." He handed the papers to Bigby who glanced at them and shrugged.

"I have no clue, mate. I didn't draw these. A traitorous chap from within their own ranks did. I'd tell you to ask him yourself, but I shot him in the head." Bigby gave the man a wild grin that sent a shiver of mistrust down his back.

"Very well. We'll just have to the best we can." Martinez handed the papers off to one of his men then turned to direct the others in the first stages of construction.

"I can tell you one thing though," Bigby yelled as Martinez walked away. "You'll not be able to build all of that inside this warehouse. It's not tall enough."

"Didn't you say they have drones and could possibly do another flyover?" Bigby nodded and Martinez stared out the open doors. "Building outside is a no-go then."

"What to do, what to do?" Bigby laughed as he turned to make his way back to the office.

"I suppose we'll just have to build the floor plan with lower ceilings and go as high up as we dare inside here." Martinez stared upward into the rafters of the oversized warehouse. "We could easily get a three-story mock-up in here if we only made each level maybe seven foot."

Bigby stopped and ground his teeth together. "You're determined to do this, aren't you?"

Martinez nodded. "It's what Mr. Simmons wanted."

"Mr. Simmons doesn't know what he wants." Bigby threw his hands up in disgust. "Fine, build whatever you want." He stomped away, his anger building with each step.

"What would you have us do then?" Martinez appeared at his side, his voice held low so that the men wouldn't hear them argue. "Would you have us all study crude drawings that aren't even to scale?"

"You'd rather try to build a mock-up made from those same drawings that aren't even to scale?" Bigby shook his head. "You need someone on the inside that can get video of the innards of the place."

Martinez chuckled. "And I suppose you are volunteering?"

"Of course not you idiot. But didn't your boss say something about having a man that was *supposed* to keep his daughter away from Mitchell? Where the hell is he? I'm assuming he's with her, no?" Bigby watched as the light bulb came on over the warrant officer's head. "Perhaps your boss still has a way of reaching that man and can direct him to get us what we need."

"That is a very good idea."

"You don't say?" Bigby shook his head as he pushed open the office door. "There's a phone in here if you want to call Simmons."

*****

Thorn stretched a hand down and grasped Foster by the wrist, pulling him to the roof. The jump was just a little too much for him and he came up short the first time. "Why do they build these things so damned tall anyway?"

"To fit their equipment, I suppose." Thorn stood and stared across the large flat roof in front of them. Vent pipes, fan boxes, skylights and a myriad of other industrial looking devices were mounted across the broad flat expanse. "We must find a good vantage to see within."

"I'd think any of the skylights would work." Paul motioned with his hand, allowing his brother to take the lead.

Thorn paused and stared off to the horizon. "We must hurry. I don't want to be out here all night and be caught when the sun rises. We still have to drive back to our own lair before the dawn."

"Understood." Foster trotted across the roof to the nearest skylight and glanced down. It was too dark to make out much, if anything. He looked up and shook his head.

Thorn had made it to the next skylight and stole a peak over the side. He too raised his head and shook it. Foster passed him by and glanced into the next one. His head shot back up quickly and he waved Thorn over. "There are people down there doing something."

Thorn slipped in next to him and eased over the skylight, taking in the scene below. Men and women of all ages and races were packing things into wooden crates then shoving the crates into the back of trucks. "Do you see Damien?"

Foster shook his head. "No, either he's not here, or he's in a different part of the building." Paul raised his head and glanced across the massive expanse of the roof. "This place is huge, brother. We may not be able to spot him amongst the crowd."

Thorn squeezed his shoulder and pulled him back from the skylight. "There may be another way."

Foster turned to him, confusion painted across his features. "What's that?"

"Call to him. Call to his flesh. As his maker, *compel* him to come to you."

Foster shook his head. "No…no, no, no. That's craziness." He glanced around the rooftop in a panic. "Even if he answered, what would prevent him from bringing all of his people with him?"

"If they are truly his, then they are yours."

"You mean YOURS, remember? My people are your people now." Paul shook his head. "You call him. You're his master now."

"You are his maker, *mon ami*. His flesh must answer your call." Rufus stared into his brother's eyes and Paul groaned.

"I really don't want to do this."

"I know you do not, but it must be done. You said yourself, there are too many here and this place is too large to jump from skylight to skylight in hopes of finding him."

Foster whined and glanced around the rooftop once more. "Can't we just mail him an invitation to a costume party or something?"

"*Non*, this must be done. The sooner the better. We must know."

Paul sighed heavily and leaned against a vent pipe. "Fuck."

He stared up into the heavens and honestly wondered if this would be the last time he'd be able to look at those stars. For a fleeting moment he wondered why he had never taken the time to learn which constellation was which. After all, he was a creature of the night. This was *his* sky since the day he was born.

"Fine." He pushed off the vent pipe and stood before the skylight. "But if this ends up getting me killed, I am *so* disowning you."

*****

Little John watched as the other squad ran their drills. Charmichael and McKenzie vying for last place each time they ran the CQB simulator. On the first two run-throughs, Mac had shot the victim or innocent, earning a failing grade for each run. On the third run, he shot two, causing the entire squad to fail. Dominic actually accused the man of doing it on purpose and threatened to sideline him.

All of First Squad watched from the balcony outside Colonel Mitchell's office as Second Squad ran the drills again and again. Each time the CQB instructors reset the drill, the targets were moved, walls and doorways rearranged and each time the drill became that much tougher to pass.

Little John shook his head as he watched the squad exit the rear, their heads hung low and more than one muttering epithets. "I knew that Mac would be trouble."

Spalding watched the scenario play out beside the large man and sighed as they failed yet again. "How'd you know?"

"He tried to cause me trouble shortly after we cleared the training program. Remember all of the 'fitting in' problems and the issues that the team leaders thought that I had?"

Spalding nodded, his eyes still glued to the team below. "Yeah. What of it?"

"That was Chad's doing. He always seemed to find a way to paint others in a way to make them look their worst." John pushed away from the railing and fought back a scream. "I'm telling ya, the guy may have been good in the field before he got here, but now? He's not a team player."

Spalding looked to the giant standing next to him. "That's some pretty serious stuff to lay on a guy. Around here, everyone is a team player or they're out."

Little John nodded. "I know. And it kills me to say it." He glanced back over the rail and saw Dom in Mac's face. "The guy is poison. If he can't be *the* top dog, he wants to take down anybody and everybody who's above him until he is."

Spalding turned back to the scene unfolding below and sighed heavily. "I hope to God that you're wrong."

"Me too, boss. But I think we both know that I'm not."

*****

"Only the largest churches!" Lilith shoved the stack of papers away then swept the table clear. "I want maximum carnage!"

Her commanders watched as she threw a tantrum and screamed in a fit of rage. As she began to calm down, Gaius stepped forward. "If I may, my queen?" He held up a tablet and made a few keystrokes. The lights began to dim and the overhead projector displayed a map of the major cities. "We are only one thousand. But if we set up staging areas in these other cities, we can strike the largest churches at the beginning of mass, regain a new body and then strike the next largest church before mass lets out and before anybody can make moves to stop us." He punched a few more keystrokes and highlighted more areas. "Some of us may even be able to strike a third time."

"Especially when you consider that some of the largest churches will hold *two* morning masses because their attendance is so high, they can't all fit for one," another commander stated proudly. "If we arrange to hit those churches first…perhaps just before they let out of the first mass? Before word can go out over the media and prevent people from attending their regular mass?"

Lilith paced slowly, her eyes studying the map before her. "And we'll still have enough of the suicide bombs to take out the capitols?"

"We can ensure that we do, my queen." Gaius typed something else into the pad and the capitol building came up on the viewer. "We estimate that a force of less than a hundred should be able to destroy the White House and another forty for the Capitol

Building. But only if we strike both at the same time."

"Why so many for the White House?" She turned and gave him a curious stare.

"We'll have to strike from all sides and in waves. There is security everywhere. The roof, the fence, the gates, the perimeter…and since more than one citizen has jumped the fence and tried to rush the White House, they've tightened up their forces."

"It just seems to me that the first wave would kill more of their security personnel, no?" She stared at the screen again, her mind racing as she tried to imagine the destruction.

"Yes and no, my queen. Each wave will do more damage, but there are still many more inside. And we have to cut off every avenue of escape."

Lilith sighed heavily. "Fine, just make sure that any bombs left over are redirected toward the churches. I want them flattened."

Gaius stepped forward again and set the tablet down. "My queen? If I may be so bold? Once you have stepped in and have offered to 'save' the humans…wouldn't that be a good time to destroy the churches?" He saw her eyes widen with anger and he quickly added, "I'm just saying that you could easily blame the bombings on extremists from the church. The populace would believe it if it came from their savior and then you could simply *outlaw* Catholicism." He stepped back and studied her.

Lilith considered his words and slowly she began to smile. "I like the way you think, Commander."

Samael pushed past the Roman demons and walked jerkily out of the room. His face had a pained and contorted look about it. Lilith watched him with confusion for a moment then stood in his path. "Where do you think you're going?"

Samael continued to walk, slowly, his body fighting his commands to stop. "I…do…not…know."

"What is going on here?" Lilith opened her mouth to demand that he stop when Samael pushed her aside and marched past her. "Guards!"

11

Mark stood with his hand raised, knuckles poised to rap on Mitchell's office door. He paused and squeezed his eyes shut. Counting to three did no good so he counted to ten and slowly lowered his hand. He stood in place a moment longer then forced his feet to step away from the closed door and toward his own office. *What the hell? I think Doc is up to something, so I'm gonna run off and 'tell' on him?*

Mark shoved his office door open and fought not to slam it behind himself. He fell into his chair and pulled the bottom drawer open. He had the bottle open and to his lips before he realized what he was doing.

He pulled the empty bottle back and stared at the last drop clinging to the threads. He exhaled hard and dropped the bottle into the waste basket next to his desk. "What the fuck's come over me?" He dropped the lid in next to the clear glass bottle and stared at it. Thoughts raced through his mind as he continued to stare, his eyes not really focusing.

What the hell is Doc up to? Or is he up to something? Am I just being paranoid? What if I'm not? The guy fought like hell to save my life when I was bleeding out. Then again, he did infect me with the vampire virus. Maybe he did it on purpose? Maybe he wants to control me?

Mark sat up and stepped to the window of his office. He stared down into the labyrinth of workspaces and zeroed in on Dr. Peters diligently working in his lab. "What did you do to me, Doc? Were you trying to make me your slave?"

As soon as the words left his mouth, Mark rolled his eyes at his own comment. This is Doc he was talking about. He watched the spineless man going through the motions and shook his head. There was no way the guy had an agenda. His brain simply didn't work that way.

He walked back to his desk and rifled around in the bottom drawer again. There had to be another bottle down there someplace.

The phone on his desk rang and he nearly jumped. He snatched the phone off the hook and had to fight from barking into it. "What?"

"Duty officer, sir. Mister Thompson and his team checked in. They've retrieved the weapons, but he reported there wouldn't be a need for transportation. They'll be back at sundown."

"Very well." Mark slammed the phone down and turned back to his drawer. He stared at the mess he had made then caught a glimpse of the empty bottle in the trash. "Why do I bother?" He kicked his drawer shut and clenched his jaw.

He took a long cleansing breath and tried to relax. It did no good. He turned and grabbed the pot of coffee from behind his desk and poured a cup. He stared at the steaming brew and watched in stunned fascination as his hand reached out and grabbed the cup, brought it to his mouth and he gulped the steaming hot liquid down. He waited for a pain that didn't come.

He gently placed the cup down and stared at it, waiting for a reality check. He waited for the nerves in his mouth to start firing and send the message to his brain that he had just fucked up. They didn't come. He ran his tongue across the roof of his mouth and everything felt normal. He sucked in air and it felt surprisingly cold, the taste of the coffee finally biting his taste buds.

Mark turned slowly in his chair and stared at the coffee pot behind his desk. Slowly his hand reached out and grasped the handle, bringing the pot to his mouth. He took three long gulps of the steaming hot liquid before setting the pot back on the warmer. He smacked his lips and blew out a hot breath.

"This is messed up. That should have set my world on fire."

He glanced around his office and finding no other source of torture, his eyes fell on to the letter opener at the edge of his desk. He pulled it from the wooden block and slowly slid it into the flesh of his hand. Very little blood escaped as he withdrew the nickel plated dull blade and he watched in shocked fascination as the flesh stitched together and healed before his eyes.

"Aw, hell." He dropped the letter opener and quickly stood up. "I think something's broken."

*****

Thorn stood in shocked silence as the creature stepped into view below, numerous humans suddenly surrounding it. "That does not look like Damien."

Foster swallowed hard and shook his head. "I do not believe

that it is." He turned frightened eyes to his brother. "I think I'd remember if he had fucking *wings*!"

"Release him!" Thorn tugged at Foster's shoulder, pulling him back from the skylight. The two fell to the roof and sat quietly, each listening to the excitement below as the humans tried to stop the demonic looking creature from answering Foster's call. "We need to vacate this area now, *mon ami*."

"Try and stop me!"

Foster turned and ran for the edge of the roof. He leapt for the parapet and pushed off as hard as he could, Thorn beside him as they practically flew through the chill air. Both vampires landed with a roll in the parking lot then came to their feet and made for the fence as quickly as they could.

The enforcers saw the two running toward them and pulled the chain link up to allow them to slip under. Foster dove headfirst and slid under while Thorn slid feet first under the metal fabric. "Get the car! Now!"

"What did you see, m'lord?" One of the enforcers asked as he helped pull Thorn to his feet.

"The devil!" Foster tugged at Thorn's coat. "Quickly!"

The enforcers turned and stared toward the building, their eyes scanning the area looking for any sign of the 'devil' that Paul mentioned. They turned back when the black SUV slid to a stop behind the berm of earth they hid behind. The last enforcers stood watch while Thorn and Foster slid in followed by the other enforcers. He turned and pulled open the passenger door then glanced back toward the old factory. As the truck pulled away, he could almost swear he saw a very large man with black leathery bat wings standing beside the two guards at the far door.

"I think it's time to call the hunters in." Foster slid down into his seat and tried to keep his hands from shaking.

"*Oui, mon ami.* I believe you are correct." Thorn stared out the window as the truck sped away. "As soon as we return, I shall—" His words were interrupted by a thunderous boom and the ceiling of the SUV caved inwards.

A cacophony of curses and epithets were shouted as the SUV swerved on the road, its lights crisscrossing the road, the tires squealing on the dry pavement. "The devil is here!" Foster screamed, sliding into the floorboards of the vehicle.

Thorn shifted in his seat and stared up at the roof. "Destroy it!"

The enforcer in the passenger seat pulled his weapon and turned in his seat. He pressed the button for the sunroof then stuck his head and shoulders out through the hole. Weapons fire was heard then a scream as he was pulled through the small opening in the roof, the driver swerving, trying to shake the attacker.

Thorn shoved his shoulder, "Get us out of here! Now!"

The driver pressed the accelerator to the floor, doing his best to avoid obstacles in the nearly deserted part of town. He slammed on the brakes hoping to throw the attacker off the roof, but he clung to it like a magnet.

Rufus pressed himself tighter to the door of the SUV, praying that they did not lose control and that their attacker would soon be satisfied with the carnage he had already inflicted. He should have known better. He heard the screech of metal being rent and torn, large fingers tearing through the material of the truck as if it were tinfoil. Suddenly the top folded back and Rufus saw the demon in all of its horror.

The beast floated in the air, its wings extended and catching air like a sheet in the wind, the roof of the SUV caught between massive arms and clutched with taloned fingers. But what caught his attention the most were the glowing green eyes. As if lights shone from behind those glowing orbs, the light cast an eerie green hue to the scene below.

Thorn watched as the demon cast the roof of the SUV to the side then folded its wings and dove for the car. He grabbed the driver by the shoulder and jerked his arm. "Turn, damn you!"

The massive truck jerked to the right, its tires skidding, screeching into the night as the demon swooped in and missed. Rufus could almost feel the wind breaking off its body as it sailed by then arched back into the air for another assault. "Go! Go! Go!"

The driver mashed the accelerator again and tried to cut down a smaller street in hopes of limiting the mobility of their airborne attacker. The demon sailed overhead then swooped once more. With nowhere to turn, the truck would be easy prey. Rufus squeezed the driver's shoulder. "When I tell you, stand on the brakes!" The demon dove once more and Rufus yelled, "Now!"

Everyone within the vehicle was pitched forward as the truck slid to a stop, its anti-lock brakes protesting and vibrating under the driver's foot. The demon overshot and the driver accelerated once more hoping to hit the monster with the heavy truck. Just as the headlight closed on the beast, it disappeared.

"Get us out of here! Now!" Foster continued to squirm, trying to get even lower in the floor of the vehicle. He grabbed at an enforcer and pulled him over on top of him.

Thorn turned in his seat, his eyes skyward as he looked for the green eyed demon. He thought he caught a glimpse of it, but it was a traffic light ahead. He continued to watch, his head on a swivel, constantly searching for the monster.

Gunshots rang out and Thorn turned to see an enforcer firing at the rear of the vehicle. The demon had clung to the rear of the SUV as it bounced out of the narrow street. It climbed over the ruined rear of the truck and grasped the enforcer by the head, flinging him out of the vehicle as if he were nothing more than a ragdoll.

Thorn turned to Foster who was still cowering in the floor. “Control him! Compel him to stop!”

Foster had tears of fear running down his cheeks and he whimpered as Thorn barked at him. “I-I can’t!”

“Yes you can! You are his maker! This is Damien, you are his master! Control him!”

The demon wrapped an oversized hand around Thorn’s middle then extended his wings, the wind instantly lifting the pair into the night.

What was left of the SUV shot into the night, Foster cowering in the rear floor, crying and praying to whatever god would listen that he not be eaten.

*****

Laura watched as her dad sat up without grimacing. He smiled and inhaled deeply. “I smell something.”

She gave him a curious shrug. “I don’t smell anything.”

“It smells like meat cooking.” He smiled at her and waggled his eyebrows. “I’ll be damned if it doesn’t smell like meatloaf.”

Crystal leaned forward and patted his hand. “Jim, sweetie, they’re not going to allow you to eat something like that.”

He shrugged and glanced between the two women. “Why not? If my days are numbered, I might as well enjoy them right?” He gave Laura a slight wink that Crystal missed entirely. “Would you mind checking and if they have meatloaf, bring me some.”

Crystal shook her head. “I’ll check if you really want me to, but, Honey, you won’t be able to hold it down.”

“Indulge me, darling.”

She leaned over and kissed his forehead. “Anything for you.” She excused herself and slipped out of the room.

Laura gave her dad a skeptical smirk. “If you wanted to talk privately, I think you could have found something a little less—”

“No,” he interrupted. “I honestly smell meatloaf and damned if it doesn’t have my mouth watering.” He sat up taller in the bed and punched the button to raise the back higher. “Open the blinds again, Punk. I want to see some sunshine.”

Laura stood and opened the blinds, allowing the sunlight into the room. “I didn’t realize you couldn’t hold down…” she trailed off, remember her mother’s last days.

“Don’t, Punk.” He reached out for her and squeezed her hand. “It wasn’t anything you needed to know.”

“Still, I wish you had told me.”

He shrugged. “What’s to tell? Besides, I’m feeling much better already.” He gave a slight nod toward the port that she had used. “I haven’t been hungry like this in a long time.”

She lowered her eyes and nodded. “It’s to be expected, I suppose. That’s another side-effect.”

“If it means getting to eat again, I’m all for it. I really missed being able to eat.” Jim glanced to the door hoping that Crystal would come back in carrying a large tray full of meatloaf and mashed potatoes.

“You might find that your taste buds change some.”

He gave her a sideways look. “Like how?”

“Like, junk food won’t taste good anymore.”

“Ha! Junk food is called ‘junk’ for a reason, Punk.” He chuckled as he stared at the door. “I just wish she’d hurry up. I can smell that stuff, and I’m starving.”

“That’s another. Your sense of smell will be sharpened.”

“Again, not a bad thing.” He gave her a sideways smile.

"Until you decide that her perfume smells like road kill or that she doesn't shower often enough or…" Laura shrugged, "…any number of issues."

"I'm not bitching, Punk." He turned and gave her his full attention. "You've given me another chance. A chance to *live*. I don't care if I end up chasing the paperboy on his bicycle or marking the yard at night to keep other dogs away. I'm just happy for the opportunity."

Laura nodded but averted her gaze. "There may be others." She stood up slowly and turned for the door. "I'm going to check on Crystal and see if there was a problem."

"Tell her extra gravy on the taters. It smells so good."

"I will, Daddy." She turned and stepped out into the hallway. She lowered her eyes and exhaled hard, her heart suddenly heavy. She cast a furtive glance back toward his door and sighed. "What have I done?"

*****

Mick meandered forlornly. He debated with himself on how best to tell Jennifer that her crazy assed father was still on a killing spree. Every time that he thought he had a workable plan in his mind, he'd find her, start to approach her and then his brain would panic and he'd find a thousand reasons why the approach he had worked up simply wouldn't work.

He wanted to warn her. He needed to tell her. He prayed that he could find a solution on how to tell her. His mind kept running in circles and he fought with himself on how best to do what needed to be done. He even contemplated doing an end run on her and going straight to her mate. What would Mitchell do if he came to him with that information? He shuddered as he thought about it.

How could he explain that he knew this information? If he told them that Mr. Simmons had contacted him and told him?

"Hey, are you the pilot that brought the Simmons girl and Ms. Youngblood in?"

Mick lifted his eyes and he noted a young military man standing before him. He nodded slowly. "Yeah, mate. That's me."

"You had a call just a bit ago. I guess your dad was looking for you. Said you weren't answering you cellphone." The guy handed him a slip of paper. "He said that they were about to leave for vacation and he would be at this number."

Mick gave the man a confused look. His father was long gone and assumed dead; presumed to have been shot by a confused local while he was in werecat form. His father had been out hunting wild game and simply never returned. Had he been killed by a local and his body recovered, the local would panic when he found a naked man had been roaming the jungles and probably buried him in an unmarked grave.

Mick took the slip of paper and noted the phone number. He swallowed hard when he recognized Walter Simmons' phone number. He held the paper up and nodded to the young man. "Thanks, mate, wouldn't want to miss them before they left." The man turned to leave when Mick caught his attention again. "Say, is there a phone I could use? I, uh…well, my cell phone was broken during the trip up here."

"Yes, sir, if you'll follow me." The man took the lead and escorted Mick to a secluded office. He opened the door and pointed to a landline and desk. "The operator can get you the prefix you need." He pulled the door shut behind him as he left, and Mick stood alone in the room a cold sweat dripping down his back.

He sat and picked up the receiver, punching the numbers into the phone. He waited only a moment before Walter Simmons' voice came across the line. "Mick?"

"Y-yes, sir. I got your message. My cell phone is broken, and I had to use one of the landlines here." Mick prayed that Simmons would understand what he was trying to say.

The old man was no idiot and assumed the call would be bugged regardless. "I understand, son, I understand completely. Look, I just wanted to touch base with you before your mother and I left for vacation."

"Yeah, I got your note." Mick adjusted the phone and chewed nervously at his thumbnail. "Will you be gone long?"

"Not very long at all. We just had to wait for the right time. You know…we're very worried about your sister. She hasn't been heard from in a while, and we're worried about her. I understand she's okay, but it would be nice to know that she wasn't in harm's way."

"Yeah, well, she's awfully pigheaded. I think she gets it from you, Dad." Mick smiled at himself, knowing that Walter Simmons was probably steaming under his shirt collar at the comment.

Walter chuckled into the phone, "You're more right than you know, son. She definitely takes after me." He cleared his throat and lowered his voice somewhat. "Look, I'm not sure what you're doing up there in the States, and frankly, I don't care. Your mom worries. So, maybe if you just took some pictures of the sights and sent them to her…you know, to calm her nerves, so that she knows that you're okay. She may not be able to talk to her daughter, but if she could know that you were okay…it would put her at ease."

Mick thought hard about what he was saying. Pictures? "You want me to get pictures? And send them to you…er, to mom? To set her at ease?"

"Yeah, sure. Just whatever. You know. So that she knows you

aren't in jail." Walter laughed. "You're not in jail, are you, son?"

Mick exhaled hard and stared at the corner of the room. "No, I'm not in jail."

"Excellent. Then just snap a few photos, maybe pick her up a t-shirt or something. A souvenir."

"Yeah." Mick was deflated. How could he get pictures of the place where Jennifer was without getting caught? He was certain that Walter wanted to know exactly where Jennifer was so that the attack teams could avoid hurting her. "I'll see what I can do."

"Thataboy. Make your mother happy." Walter slapped the table. "Well, son, we have to get ready for our trip. Your mother sends her love, and she really looks forward to hearing from you as soon as you have time."

"Yeah. As soon as I have time." He laid the phone down in the cradle and stared at it. "It's not like you're asking me to risk my life here or anything, *Dad*."

*****

Kalen stared at his arm and nodded. He turned and left the mouth of the cavern. Approaching Jack, he removed the wrist band and handed it to him. "Chief Jack, the Wyldwood would speak with you."

Jack raised a brow and gave Kalen a look he didn't quite know how to interpret. "Oh, she'll grace me with her audience now, will she?" Jack stood and reached for the wrist band. "How does this work?"

"Simply place it on your arm. You will be able to see and hear each other. Nobody else will." Kalen averted his eyes as Jack slipped the golden-hued wrist band onto his arm. Immediately, the stone in the center seemed to glow and become translucent like the stone Loren had given him would do when they spoke through it.

Her image appeared and she gave him a pleasant smile that softened the hurtful feelings Jack had been feeling toward the elf. "Chief Jack, so good to see you again."

Jack bowed his head slightly, "Loren, to what do I owe this honor?"

"Our elders have reached a consensus on the threat. They feel confident what you will be facing." She glanced to the side and spoke in hushed tones then turned back to Jack. "I fear that this information may be coming to you too late."

Jack stiffened. "How's that?"

"The threat has manifested. We are most certain of that. We aren't certain how it intends to strike, but we are most certain that it is on your plane as we speak."

Jack peered through the cavern at his group of warriors, none of whom seemed able to hear the conversation going on. "Hit me with it."

Loren gave him a puzzled look and shook her head. "Hit you…with what, Chief Jack?"

Jack fought back a laugh. "It's a human expression. It means tell me everything. Even the bad news."

"Ah. Yes, well, we are most certain that the threat is Lilith." She waited for a reaction, but Jack simply stared at her image. "She is most dangerous. Perhaps the single most dangerous creature to have walked the earth since creation."

"Really? I can think of some pretty dangerous creatures."

"She is far worse. I assure you."

"Okay, so who is she?"

Loren explained to Jack the history of Lilith, her defiance of God, her rejection of the Adam, the allure of the Fallen Ones, and how it all played out in her downfall. Jack listened intently and tried to take it all in. “So, if she was defeated once, she can be taken out again.” He glanced to the Guardian. “You do know that we have a Nephilim in our group now. We sort of had to adopt him to get the weapons.”

Loren nodded. “The son of Rafael. He will be a good addition to your team of hunters.”

“Was he the one you intended us to pick up?”

“We only knew that one more would join. We couldn’t see *who*.”

Jack rubbed a hand across the back of his neck. “What’s the deal with them all being so young? You said it was necessary.”

“One of the elders saw it in a vision. The unending hope of youth. The ability to remain focused on the task at hand. The unyielding…”

“Wait a second. We’re talking about kids here, not battle hardened vets. Most kids I know can’t concentrate on anything long enough to see it through.”

Loren nodded slightly. “But these are not ordinary children. They are young adults. And they are battle hardened, each in their own way.”

He had to give her that one. “Okay, boss. You got your team, and now we got our target. I don’t guess any of your soothsayers happened to see where this Lilith was hiding, did they?”

“Not yet, but they have not given up. I am certain that she will raise her ugly head soon enough.”

Jack sighed and stared out the open door. “I’d feel a whole lot better if we could strike first.”

*****

“What is this?” Lilith stepped back slightly as the vampire was tossed against the wall.

"He was directing the others. He is the leader." Samael towered over the vampire and snarled, his wings extended and his hands opening and closing in anger. "They will want him back."

"So why didn't you remove the head from the snake?"

"I want to know how they controlled me!" His words echoed off the walls and caused the glass windows to vibrate. Centurions scurried back to their work, their curiosity no longer a priority.

"Whatever it was, they'll no longer be able to do it if he's dead, lover." She stroked his chest as she spoke, her words dripping with saccharin sweetness.

Samael pushed her aside and glared at the vampire trying to stand. "Who are you?"

Rufus got to his feet and adjusted his clothing. He squared his shoulders and turned to the Fallen One. "I am Rufus Thorn. Normally, I would say that I was pleased to make your acquaintance, but under the circumstances, I am sure you will understand why I cannot."

"Why have you come here?" Samael took a step closer and raised a meaty hand to strike the vampire.

Rufus did not cower, nor did he flinch. He stared the Fallen One in the eye and raised a brow. "I would be most pleased to discuss matters with you in a more civilized manner." He walked closer and extended his hand. "I assure you, brutality will get you nowhere."

Samael stared at the little vampire and anger rose within him. He couldn't explain why. All he knew was that he hated the man standing before him. He reached back to crush the man when Lilith yelled, "Stop!"

Samael turned on her, his eyes aglow. "Why would you stop me?"

"I'd like to hear what he has to say." She stepped closer and inspected the vampire. "He intrigues me."

"He shall be crushed."

"Not until I've heard what he has to say." Lilith stepped between the two and took Rufus' hand. "Lilith. So pleased to meet you."

"Lilith? As in, *the* Lilith?" Rufus kissed the back of her hand, his eyes never leaving hers.

"Of course. There can be only one." She gave him a wicked smile. "I take it that you know of me."

"I know that Damien Franklin was working diligently to see you made whole again. I see that he succeeded."

Her face wrinkled at the mention of the name, but she quickly recovered. "Yes, he did."

Rufus looked amongst the crowd hard at work inside the facility. "And is Damien still with us?"

Lilith chuckled and looped her arm through Thorn's. "In a manner of speaking, yes." She pointed to the demonic character behind her. "Samael took his body for his own."

"Samael? The angel?" Rufus glanced over his shoulder at the monster that had fallen into step behind them.

"One and the same. My lover needed a host body to transform." She lowered her voice to a whisper. "Unfortunately, by taking on dead flesh, there were certain 'side effects'. His wings…"

Thorn nodded. "I see."

"So, Mister Thorn, please, tell me what brings you here before we skin you alive and allow my demons to have their way with your bones."

Rufus raised a brow and cleared his throat. "We were…well, we were looking for Damien. We had heard that he was resurrecting you and we were going to see if we could assist."

"Then why would you run?"

"We didn't recognize any of the people here, and when we tried to summon Damien, we saw your friend here. The angel…"

"Samael."

"Yes. Samael. I must say, he did put quite the fright into us. So we decided that leaving was the best plan at the moment."

"Too bad you didn't leave sooner," Samael growled from behind them as Lilith pushed the door to her office open.

Rufus entered and the distinct smell of sex and stale food struck him. The unkempt bed in the center of the room and the myriad of tables with papers scattered about made him realize that this was definitely a multipurpose room.

Lilith stared at the vampire and shook her head. "What to do with you, little vampire?"

Rufus shrugged. "I'm not sure."

"We kill him." Samael stepped closer, and Lilith placed a hand on his shoulder to stop him.

"Technically, I am already dead." Thorn held up a hand. "However, I am probably worth more to you unharmed than not."

Lilith smirked. "How is that, little vampire?"

He turned to Samael. "Ask him. Didn't you say that he took Damien's flesh? Then certainly he still has some of his memories. Tell her who I am, baby vampire." Thorn's voice took on an edge that angered Samael. "Tell her the power I wield, the people under my command. Tell her the continents that I control, the sheer number of vampires who would stake themselves at my command!" He stepped closer and got in Samael's face. "Tell her, baby vamp!"

He struck quickly, a slap to the face that both stunned and silenced the angel. Just as Samael's eyes widened and his mouth opened to speak, Thorn released a wave of power that brought the angel to his knees. Rufus maintained the wave of power emanating from him until the angel lay prostrate on the floor, his mouth opening and closing as he gasped for breath, the green glow of life slowly fading from his eyes.

Rufus bent low and lifted the angel's head by the hair and whispered just loud enough that Lilith could hear. "Tell her who your real master is, baby vamp."

"Enough!" Lilith stepped forward and grabbed Thorn by the wrist. "Release him. Now."

Thorn turned his gaze to her and his face twisted into anger. "Unhand me, woman, or you'll beg for what the Romans did to you as a mercy."

She dropped his hand and stepped back, her eyes wide and her breath caught in her throat. She had seen evil in her life. She had experienced evil in her death. She thought she had been touched by evil while being taught by the Fallen Ones. But what she saw in those eyes made her heart turn cold.

"Please," her voice was barely a whisper, "Mister Thorn…please. Release him."

Rufus withdrew his power and stepped away from Samael. The angel rolled to his back and coughed, sucking in huge gulps of air as he tried to suck life back into his form. Slowly the green glow of life came back to his eyes.

"Thank you." Lilith dropped to the floor and cradled Samael, her eyes turned fearfully to the vampire before them. "I-I don't understand. You could have…I mean…you ran. But you could have…"

"He is not what I thought him to be." Rufus stepped back further and placed his hands behind his back. "But now that I know what he is and who you are…perhaps we can work together."

12

"Major, I'm surprised to see you again." Doctor Evans rolled his chair away from his workbench and stood up. "Is everything okay?"

Mark stepped deeper into the lab, the lights falling on his pale face. "I didn't know where else to go."

"You don't look well. Come, we need to run some blood panels and—"

"No." Mark took a half step back and held his hands up. "It's not…it's something different."

Evan moved around the bench and slowly approached him. "Okay, why don't you tell me what's going on then."

Mark slowly shook his head. "I'm not sure. Something's broken."

"A bone?"

"No." Mark threw him a frustrated look. "Something *inside*. I can feel it. I can…" He glanced around the lab then reached to the workstation and pulled up a phillips screwdriver. "Let me show you." He stabbed the end of the screwdriver into his hand then slowly withdrew it. There was little to no blood as the wound healed almost instantly.

"Remarkable." Evan moved in closer and stared at his hand. He took his hand in his own and turned it over. "There's not even a scar."

"I felt it, but there was hardly any pain." He turned worried eyes to the doctor. "What does this mean?"

Evan shook his head. "I honestly don't know. Vampires and werewolves both feel pain. You should have as well." He shrugged. "Perhaps because you heal so quickly, your body no longer registers it."

"I don't follow you."

Evan sat down and motioned for Mark to do the same. "Pain is the way your brain tells your body not to do something. Harm will befall it if it continues to do those things." Evan shrugged. "Since you apparently won't be harmed, your brain isn't registering the pain."

Mark ran a fingertip gently across his skin and felt the sensation normally. "Everything else seems to be okay. I mean, I can feel a normal touch. I can tell when my eyes are dry and I need to blink. I can tell when my mouth is dry and I need a drink."

"That's the only explanation I can come up with without running a myriad of tests." Evan shrugged. "I'm sorry, Major, but it's all speculation."

Mark stood and glanced around the lab. "There's no other way?"

"I'm afraid not. And even then, simple blood tests may not

give us the answer to this one."

"So it's a shot in the dark."

"Yes," Evan sighed. "Unfortunately, we simply have no other specimens to use as a baseline. You are the only known subject to be infect—"

"I know, Doc," Mark interrupted. "I'm unique." He rolled his eyes as he fell back into the chair and rolled his sleeve up. "This better tell us something."

Evan grabbed his blood drawing kit and donned gloves. "We can cross our fingers and hope."

*****

"It just grabbed him and plucked him straight from the bloody car! I'm telling you, it was a demon!" Paul screamed into the phone, his voice cracking as he spoke. "All I know is that he's still alive. If he had been killed, my people would have reverted back to me. I would have felt the shift in power."

"And you are in Detroit?" Viktor sounded more annoyed than worried.

"Yes, dammit. I've only told you this three times. He needs help. Whatever this thing is, I can't deal with it on my own."

Viktor sighed heavily and rubbed at his temples. "I have my own matters to deal with. Dropping everything to rush off and assist Rufus with a problem that is his own creation is not exactly how I planned to spend my weekend."

"Dammit, wolf! Are you not sworn to protect him?" Foster screeched into the phone.

Viktor leaned away from the speaker and glared at the offending device. "Do not use that tone with me, *vampire*. Why are you suddenly so worried about your brother's wellbeing?"

"I am his Second! When Thompson turned on him, he made me his…" Paul stopped and took a deep cleansing breath, trying to calm his emotions. "It doesn't matter why I am so worried, what does matter is that Rufus is in need. Will you help him or not?"

Viktor growled low in his throat then picked the receiver up, turning off the speaker phone. "I'll need time to assemble an attack force. And time to arrive."

Foster breathed an audible sigh of relief. "Thank you, Viktor. When can we expect you?"

"Morning at the earliest. Afternoon at the latest. By tomorrow evening, we will be positioned to strike."

Foster smiled into the phone. "Excellent." He hung up the phone and turned to the enforcers who surrounded him. "They're on their way. They'll be here tomorrow. Sometime during daylight. In the meantime, call in every enforcer we can get our hands on. I don't' care if they are hired mercenaries. I want to hit them with an army that will overwhelm them."

The enforcers bowed and left the darkened room, leaving Foster to himself. "Hang on, brother. We're coming for you. Just stay alive until we can get to you."

*****

Laura paced outside the hospital, a thousand thoughts racing through her mind at once. Something wasn't right and she knew it. Her father was exhibiting symptoms far too early and she bit at her lower lip. Had she used the vials in the wrong order? No…she remembered exactly what Evan had told her. Was he healthier than she thought when she came to him?

She paced and mumbled to herself, her eyes following the cracks in the sidewalk. "People will think you're nuts if you keep talking to yourself like that."

Laura looked up and saw her brother, Derek walking toward her. "They wouldn't be far off the mark."

"How's our dad doing today?" Derek squeezed her shoulder reassuringly.

"He's got his appetite back. He sent Crystal to get him something from the kitchen. Swore he could smell it cooking." She continued to stare at the ground, her feet wanting to pace.

"Really?" Derek rubbed his chin as he stared up at the window to their father's room. "I guess that's a good sign, right?"

Laura shrugged. "I guess."

He turned his attention back to his little sister. "What's wrong with you, Punk? You're acting like you got ants in your pants or something."

"Hmm?" She glanced at him questioningly. "Oh. No, I'm fine. I just have a lot on my mind, that's all."

"You're still a horrible liar." Derek walked past her and started toward the main entrance. "I'm going in. Want to go up with me?"

Laura nodded absently. "Might as well." She fell into step behind him and kept her thoughts to herself as they rode the elevator up.

"It's really good to have you home, ya know." Derek gave her a pat on the shoulder. "Maybe tonight we can go by and see mom?"

Laura paled. "I don't know if I'm ready for that, D. It's been hard enough seeing Dad in this condition and…Crystal. Maybe in a day or so we can visit Mom's grave."

Derek nodded. "Whenever you're ready, Punk." *It's not like she's going anywhere.* "Just let me know and I'll go with you."

"I appreciate it." The elevator door dinged as it opened and the pair walked down the hallway to Jim Youngblood's room. He had finished the tray of food that Crystal had brought to him and was leaning back in the bed, a satisfied look painted across his features.

"Hey, Punk, I was thinking maybe you had taken off on me."

Laura walked around to the other side of her father's bed and sat next to him. "I just got here, Daddy. I'm not going anywhere for a while."

"You going to stay at the house?" He searched her face and tried to read her.

Laura shrugged. "I hadn't thought that far ahead."

Crystal stood and let Derek have her chair. "You know your room is just the way you left it. Somebody refused to do anything with it just in case you decided to come home for a visit." She gave Jim a wink as she settled on the foot of the bed.

"Thanks, Dad. I may." Laura glanced around the room then her gaze settled on Derek. "Where are the rest of the boys?"

He shrugged. "They got families of their own that they have to see to. They usually come in on the weekends, don't they, Pop?"

Jim nodded. "Yeah. But maybe this next weekend we can all just meet at the house? We can have a barbecue like we used to."

Derek turned to Laura and shrugged. He didn't know that the old man was losing his mind, too. "Uh, sure, we can do that."

Crystal lowered her eyes and avoided Jim's gaze. Laura simply squeezed her dad's hand. "That sounds wonderful, Daddy."

"You guys think I'm joshing you, but I'm feeling better by the moment. I wouldn't be surprised if I didn't walk out of here in the next few days." He squeezed Laura's hand knowingly.

She kept her head down but glanced about the room, noting everyone else avoiding eye contact with her father. She caught his eye and gave a worried but subtle shake of her head. "I'm glad you're feeling better, Daddy, but let's just wait and see, okay?

Let's take each day as it comes."

Jim gave her a knowing smile. "Whatever you think, Punk." He quickly turned his attention to Derek. "So have you heard the news?"

Derek shrugged. "What news, Dad? I haven't been watching TV today."

Jim chuckled. "Not that news. I'm talking about your sister giving me and Crystal the go ahead to tie the knot." He waggled his eyebrows at Crystal. "I finally get to make her an honest woman."

Crystal smiled and patted his shoulder. "It's going to take a lot more than wedding vows for you to do that, mister."

Derek gave Laura a mocking smile. "Oh really? So you gave the old man your blessing, huh? Nothing like waiting 'til the last minute, little sister."

"I'm not dead yet, buster." Jim pulled Crystal up onto the bed next to him and planted a kiss on her cheek. "You better watch it or I might turn you into an older brother again."

"Jim!" Crystal poked at him. "You may be feeling your oats again, but that isn't going to unshrivel these ovaries."

"You might be surprised." He laughed and wrapped his arms around her. "The way I'm feeling, you may not need them!" He kissed her cheek again then howled playfully.

*****

Jack propped his weapons alongside the wall of the cavern and dug through the cache again. "All I know is, she said that this Lilith is one bad hombre."

"I do not know of an angel named Lilith." The Guardian watched jack intently as he dug through the weapons, searching. "I have heard my father speak of nearly all of the angels before, but never this Lilith."

"I don't think she's an angel, buddy." Jack picked up a mace and swung it a few times. Shaking his head he tossed it aside. "I want something that has a little more distance to it."

Kalen handed Jack his bow. "Perhaps this?"

Jack glanced over his shoulder and shook his head. "Naw, you're Robin Hood in this merry band of misfits. I'm hoping there's an angelic bazooka in here somewhere."

Brooke snatched the bow from Kalen's hand. "Yo, Chief. How about this?" She drew the bow string back, then let it slip forward slowly, the arrow that manifested dropping harmlessly to the ground. She picked it up and handed it to him. "Have your guys melt this down and make you some bullets from it. That should work, shouldn't it?"

Jack stared at the arrow and spun it around in his hand a few times. "I don't know." He turned to the Guardian. "Will it?"

The Nephilim shook his head. "I do not know what you ask."

"Can these arrows be melted down and made into another weapon? An *effective* weapon?"

The Guardian stared at the arrow then shrugged. "I cannot say."

Jack hooked a thumb toward the bow. "How many arrows does that thing come with?"

"As many as are needed."

Jack smiled as he turned to Kalen. "As soon as we get back, you're gonna make me a big pile of arrows."

"Very well." Kalen took the bow back from Brooke.

Gnat tapped the side of the cavern. "Chief Jack. It's time. It should be dark on the other side."

He looked to the Guardian. "Care to close the door and seal

out the light?"

The Nephilim rose and easily slid the rock back into place. Kalen waved his hands over the rock and the portal began to appear. Once moon glow shown through the portal, the fine crusting of rock covering Azrael cracked and crumbled off, falling to the ground like ash. He stretched and looked around the cavern. "Is it time to leave?"

"Grab your gear, big guy. We're out of here." Jack handed him the sword and hammer he had chosen.

"Excellent." Azrael hefted the oversized hammer and propped it over his shoulder.

The Nephilim paused at the portal and stared through to the other side. He glanced back at the weapons cache then back through the portal. Jack came up beside him and placed a reassuring hand on his arm. "It will be safe. In all the time you've guarded it, has anybody else come looking for it?"

The Nephilim shook his head. "But what if others come? I won't be here."

Jack peered back at the darkened cavern. "If anybody breaks in here while you're gone, I'll help you hunt them down and get back what they take."

The Guardian nodded cautiously and stepped through the portal. Kalen stepped through last and closed the portal behind him. The party took in their surroundings then turned to make their way to the hangar.

Jack had barely made it out of the gravel yard when footsteps were heard making a quick approach. "Chief Thompson!"

"Over here."

Lieutenant Gregory slid in the gravel as he skidded to a stop. "Your father-in-law has been trying to reach you. He said it was imperative that you contact him as soon as you returned." Gregory handed Jack a slip of paper with a phone number.

Jack tossed the man a worried look. "Did he say what it was about?"

"Negative. Just that you needed to call him as soon…"

Jack took off at a dead run, thoughts of Nadia and his unborn child racing through his mind.

*****

Mitchell escorted Jenny to his office and opened the blinds to the windows, giving her a command view of the different operations that went on under the hangar. "From here, I can see most of the day to day operations. On this side we have the different technical aspects. Dr. Peters' lab is down there on the left. There are the different machine shops. We have weapons designs and testing. Over there is the armory." He escorted her to the other side of his office and pointed out the window. "Over there is the CQB trainer and the hand-to-hand training areas. That room over there is the gym, and next to it is the lounge where the men rarely stand down."

"Amazing. And this is all just on this floor."

"It's a lot bigger than it looks from above." A loud banging sound caught their attention. The pair walked back and stared out toward Dr. Peters' lab. They watched as a large black pickup was lowered from the main floor on a lift. "Looks like Doc is about to start modifying another truck for us. We had one but it got tore up pretty good when we were attacked."

She turned and gave him sad eyes. "By my father."

He pulled her in close and squeezed her reassuringly. "I can't say that I blame him. If it was my own child and…" Mitchell trailed off.

"He knew that I was okay. And I told him that my fated mate was supposed to be here. He chose to attack anyway," she huffed in frustration.

"You don't think he'd try again, do you?"

Jenny thought about it and shook her head. "No. Not now that I'm here. He's stubborn and borderline crazy, but he wouldn't do anything to risk my…" She stared out the window and her words stuck unspoken in her throat.

"What's wrong, Jen?"

"Is that…Mick?" She pointed to the floor below and the man she had grown up with. He tried to act casual as he moved from piece of equipment to piece of equipment, stopping just long enough to bring something to his eye and pause then move on again. "What is he doing?"

Mitchell followed her arm and studied the man. "He's taking pictures." He turned and snatched the phone from his desk. "This is Mitchell. Get me security."

*****

Bigby walked through the makeshift munitions lockers that Martinez' men had built. He had to admire the craftsmanship. Somewhere amongst the warriors a carpenter was missing his true calling. He stared at the line of weapons and the filled magazines, the grenades, the tactical vests, the handguns…everything in its place and resembling a true armory. "They did good work."

"My men are nothing if not professional in everything they do."

"I'll give them that." Bigby glanced back to the area taped off to be where the mock-up would be built. "Maybe I was wrong about your plans, mate."

"Perhaps so." Martinez followed him a half step behind. "Once we have more accurate pictures of what to build, we shall be able to properly construct a training area."

Bigby sighed and rubbed his hand across his face. "About that, mate." He placed a hand on Martinez shoulder. "I've been thinking about our strategy. I'm thinking that our best bet is to gas them. Just shove some chlorine into their ventilation ducts and let nature run its course. No sense in risking anybody's life here."

Martinez glared at the man as if he had just stepped in dog shit. "That would put Miss Simmons' life in danger."

"Not if we time it right, it won't." Bigby smiled at the man and it reminded him of a shark. Dead, lifeless eyes. "If we wait until we know that she's not in there, then she's not at risk."

"But she is mated to their leader…if harm becomes him, harm becomes her."

Bigby shook his head. "That's a wives' tale. There's no truth to that."

"Yes! It is true." Martinez stepped back and pushed a finger in Bigby's face. "We will do nothing that will risk the life of—"

"Fine!" Bigby interrupted the rant. "It was just a suggestion. I was just trying to save your life and the lives of your men, that's all. You don't have any idea the caliber of men you're talking about going up against. If you could drop a car on their head and walk away from it, you bloody well should. These are the kinds of men that you don't just walk in and shoot. You need to put poison in their coffee and then while they're in the head puking up their toenails, you *might* have a chance of getting the drop on them." He shook his head and gave the man a tight-lipped smile. "You have no idea. These are the kinds of men that you could drop in the middle of the fucking Sahara desert with nothing but their skivvies and a pair of toenail clippers and a month later they're running some piss ant third world nation, sipping piña coladas on the beach."

"Weren't you one of these 'bad asses' once upon a time?"

Bigby threw his hands up. "Hey, mate, I still am. But I'm only one man."

"And you have all of us." Martinez motioned toward the men outside the office.

Bigby snorted. "And all of you together might equal one of them." He pointed out to the yard. "Do you remember all of the others that were sent here to fight them before? These blokes just waltzed in here and put a bullet in their brain like it was a day at the park. There was no challenge there for them."

"They shot them while they were caged."

"It just made the clean-up easier on them, that's all. Trust me." Bigby plopped into his chair and stared at Martinez. "If you want your men to stay alive, you need to listen to me. We can lure the little bitch out of the hole. And when we do, we need to drop a canister of fucking mustard gas on them, then go in guns blazing and drop the ones that the gas doesn't kill."

Martinez shook his head slowly and pointed an accusing finger at Bigby. "You're a coward, that's what you are."

"No, mate, I'm a realist. If you truly want theses bastards dead, then you need to listen to me." He pointed out the window. "Get your boys in gear making whatever kind of gas they can make with shit we can buy over the counter and make preparations to use it. Otherwise, you need to buy a whole lot of body bags."

*****

Little John heard the duty officer report that Jack and his team had returned. He breathed a quick sigh of relief and decided to make himself scarce. *Let her come to me. Let her come to me. Let her come to me.* He went to the gym and started hitting the weights. It didn't take long to work up a hot, sweaty lather and soon the fatigue set in.

Tracy and Donovan came in shortly after and started lifting as well. "Did ya hear about McKenzie?" Tracy asked as he slid plates onto the bar.

Donovan shook his head as he patted his hands down with chalk. "What happened?"

"Seems like the goofy fucker just kept getting out of hand in the CQB trainer."

Little John didn't mean to eavesdrop, but he found himself listening intently to the conversation. Tracy slapped the last plate on the bar and locked it into place. "Seems like when they kept screwing up and it was Chad's fault, the team sorta cornered him and told him to knock off his one-man-army shit. He got all kinds of bent out of shape."

"What did he do? Did he comply?"

"Negative," Tracy laughed. "He went off on 'em. Ol' Dom had to set him straight. Sidelined him from what I hear."

Little John sat up and turned to the two operators. "Couldn't have happened to a bigger dick." He pulled his towel and wiped the sweat off the bench he was using.

"Why you say that? I thought you two was tight?" Tracy asked.

John shook his head. "Nope. Mac is a hot head, and he's jealous of anybody who can one-up him. And his buddy Charmichael isn't much better. But Mac?" Little John draped the towel over his shoulder. "The guy just ain't 'team' material."

"What the fuck do you know?" All eyes turned to see McKenzie standing just inside the gym glaring at Little John. "You don't know shit about me, Sullivan."

"I know you're a liar and a manipulator. I know that you'll do anything to make somebody else look worse if you think it will make you look better." Little John bent and picked up his gym bag. "You don't play well with others, Mac. You're a liability."

"*You're* the liability, Sullivan!" Mac roared. "You're fucking nuts and everybody knows it. You want to talk about team players? Who keeps to hisself all the time? You do, that's who. Who doesn't hang with his teammates at all? You, that's who. If anybody around here isn't a team player, it's you, you jolly green fucking fag!" Mac screamed until his eyes bulged and the veins in his neck stood out.

"Jolly green fucking fag?" John rubbed at his chin. "I can think of worse things to be called." He turned to Donovan and Tracy. "See you guys in the field."

Little John walked past Chad as he left the gym. "That guy is a menace," Chad mumbled.

"That guy is an operator." Donovan stepped away from the weights and slowly approached McKenzie. "I don't know what your major malfunction is, but you need to get your shit together and learn how to become a part of the team."

"And you need to pull your head out of your ass." Mac turned and huffed out of the gym.

Donovan turned to Tracy. "I think Dom needs to know his boy is going off the rails."

*****

"Work together…how?" Lilith eyed the vampire warily as she clutched to Samael. The Fallen one soon rolled over and pushed himself from the floor. She rose with him, her hands steadying the large angel as he got his feet back under him.

"It would be in all of our best interest to work together, *non*?" Thorn walked slowly as he paced the small office. "You are Lilith, Queen of the damned. This is Samael, your first lover, the fallen Angel of Death, right hand of Lucifer." Thorn paused and studied her, looking to see if what he had learned from the ancient texts were correct and if his foreknowledge impressed her. She watched him, her head slowly nodding. "He has returned now that you have been made whole and…" He motioned toward the outer wall of the office, "I take it that these fine workers are your demon army, *oui*?"

"Yes, you are correct." She turned to Samael and whispered, "How can he know these things?"

"Hush, woman, most of these things were once common knowledge and taught by men." Samael stared at the vampire, his fear biting at his chest but his curiosity getting the better of him. "What do you want, vampire?"

Thorn smiled a soft and pleasant smile. "A partnership, of course." He stopped pacing and cocked his head to the side. "You are assisting her in her steps at world domination, *oui*?"

Lilith turned to Samael and watched as the angel slowly nodded. "That is the plan. What business is it of yours?"

Thorn gave a short, pleasant chuckle then sobered. His eyes narrowed and he glared at the pair. "You forget that humans are not the only creatures that inhabit this planet." Rufus gave them a moment for his statement to sink in. "We vampires have spent centuries setting up the infrastructure to many…*holdings* which we would like preserved. Not to mention that you will be endangering our very food supplies." He glared at the pair and shook his head. "This will not go over well with the numerous familias."

Lilith stared at Samael who squared his shoulders and

narrowed his gaze at the vampire. "What then do you suggest?"

"I suggest a partnership." Thorn turned and slowly began pacing again. "If you are to follow through with these plans, and I see no reason not to, then we need to ensure that no vampire businesses or safe houses or familial projects are damaged in the overthrow."

Samael turned to Lilith and the two exchanged unspoken agreement. "I believe that can be agreed upon." He turned back to the vampire. "What else."

"Of course, we'll have to ensure that certain humans are unharmed. They are protected familiars to the different *familias*."

Samael nodded. "I'm sure we can work something out." Lilith glared at him as he spoke. "Is there more?"

"Our food supply." Thorn turned slowly and eyed them both. "I do not know what percentage of the population you intend to destroy in your takeover, but we must maintain a high enough population that my people can be fed, and you will still have people to subjugate."

"But of course." Samael ignored Lilith and stepped forward, "If that is all, perhaps you could give us a few moments to discuss these matters?"

"Of course. Take your time." Rufus went to the door and stepped through. "Try not to be too long. Sunrise is not far off." He pulled the door shut and walked away.

Samael watched his shadow fade away through the covered windows, his hand held up holding Lilith's tongue until the vampire was far enough away to speak safely. "I know what you wish to say."

"I don't think you truly do, *lover*." Lilith's eyes blazed with hatred as she slapped at his chest. "How dare you!"

He grabbed her wrists and held her. "That vampire has a

control over me!" His whispered voice growled. "Don't you see? If he can control me, there's a chance he may wield some form of sorcery over you as well. Did you not see how he behaved once he realized who we were? There was not a single drop of fear within him!"

"I do not care! This is *my* world now!" Lilith stomped her foot. "I will not be denied!"

"And I am not saying that you will be." He pulled her closer and whispered into her ear. "I am saying that we agree to his terms until we know for sure what his hold is over us and then we kill him. Once we know that we can be safe, we destroy him. We can stake him out on the ground and let the sun take him. We can shove a wooden stake up his ass, throw him in a vat of holy water, lock him out in the sunlight, whatever it takes to reduce him to ash, but not until we know that it will not affect *us*."

Lilith calmed herself and forced her breathing back to normal. "Very well, I don't like it, but I'll play along." She turned and poked a finger into his thick chest. "But only as long as we have to. The very moment you discover his secret, we kill him!"

"Agreed."

13

Jericho met Mark as he made his way back to his office. "Major, we have some issues popping up on the boards. Thought maybe you should be made aware of them." He handed Mark a printout and stood by while he scanned the page.

"Any secondary confirmations?"

"Negative, sir. We have field spotters en route to both areas to see if they can get us a secondary ASAP." Jericho watched as Mark went over the list again.

"Why does this one sound familiar?" He tapped the page and Jericho leaned over to see what he was pointing at.

"That's where we picked up Sullivan's sister. Primary report is of a small group of vamps. From the mess they're making, the spotter truly thinks they're all baby vamps."

Marked scratched at his chin as he looked at the short list then handed it back to the man. "Keep me up on this. Is Colonel

Mitchell in his office?"

"Negative, sir. He had security pick up the pilot that flew Ms. Youngblood and…" He paused, unsure what to call Jennifer.

"The colonel's mate, Captain. It's okay. It is what it is."

"Yes, sir." Jericho gave him an embarrassed smile. "The pilot who flew both women here is in an interrogation room, and Colonel Mitchell is with him."

Mark raised a brow and glanced toward the stairwell. "I think I better check on this. Keep me informed on this alerts."

"Yes, sir." Jericho trotted back to the CDO office and Mark hit the stairs at a quick jog.

Taking the steps two and three at a time, he quickly hit the lower landing and came into the hallway leading to the interrogation rooms. Jennifer stood in the hallway watching through the small two way mirror. "What's going on?" Mark slipped in next to her and watched Mitchell as he cautiously questioned the pilot.

"We caught Mick taking pictures of the inside of this place." Jennifer's eyes never left her mate or her childhood friend.

"Pictures?" Mark gave her a questioning look, but she never turned away from the scene inside. He sighed and stepped around the woman. She obviously would be of little help.

Knocking on the door, he opened it without waiting for permission to enter. Mitchell looked up and gave Mark a barely perceptible wink. "Oh, well. It's too late now. It seems that Major Tufo has gotten wind of your activities. There's not much I can do to stop him." Mitchell closed the folder he had in front of him and stood from his chair.

"He was taking pictures?"

Mitchell handed him the digital camera. "He had worked his way down to third level before we spotted him. I can't believe that nobody here caught him in the act."

"Had I realized you had a window to your office up there, you wouldn't have caught me."

Mitchell turned and stared at the man. "That's the most he's said since we brought him in here."

Mark pulled the folder from Mitchell's hand and stepped around him. "I'll get answers. Why don't you go get a cup of coffee…or three." He narrowed his gaze at Mick who seemed totally unperturbed.

Mitchell shook his head. "I tried to tell you it was in your best interest but no…" He glanced at his watch. "I think I could drink a pot of coffee. I'll see you…whenever." He opened the door and let it shut behind him.

Mark stood on the other side of the table. He could almost feel Mitchell's presence through the two-way mirror. He continued to stare at the man on the other side of the table. "For a man who's about to experience untold amounts of pain, you sure seem uncaring."

Mick slowly raised his eyes and met Mark's. "There's nothing you can do to me that Simmons hasn't already done." Mick leaned back in his chair, his face stoic. "When his daughter went missing, he thought I had something to do with it. He *invented* new forms of torturing me…and all the while, you had her. Here."

"Oh, I assure you, the pain you felt at Walter Simmons' hand is nothing compared to what I have in store for you." Mark slammed the camera down on the table. "Why?"

Mick slowly looked up and met his glare. "Why do you think? Old man Simmons told me to."

"So you're still working for him." Mark sneered at the man.

"Hell no." Mick pushed away from the table as far as his chains would allow him to. "The old bastard still wants to flatten this place with everybody in it. He just doesn't want his little girl to get hurt."

Mark pulled the chair out and sat. "So…what? You were getting the layout so his men could…do what?"

"Now that…I honestly have no idea. I'm assuming it was so they'd have an idea what part of this place she'd most likely be in so that they could avoid shooting her or…well, whatever it is they have planned."

"And what do they have planned?"

Mick shrugged. "Beats the hell out of me."

"That sounds like a good starting point."

Mick shrugged again. "If it makes you happy, go ahead. I really don't care anymore."

Mark lashed out and grabbed him by the chains, pulling him into the edge of the table. Mick felt the air rush out of his lungs as the stainless steel table bruised his ribs. "Nothing makes me happier than beating the hell out of assholes that put my people at risk." He leaned in and lowered his voice. "And you are putting my people at risk."

Mick fought to push against the pull of the chains. "What did you expect me to do? There are still people in Belize that I care about and Simmons knows that."

"You could have come to us and told us!" Mark tightened the pull on the chains, choking him.

Mick felt his claws starts to push through his fingertips, fighting for purchase on the smooth table. "I didn't have much choice! And what would you have done? Put me right here anyway…so if I could have kept Jennifer safe…"

"I should rip your goddam head off you son of a—"

The door flew open and Colonel Mitchell stepped inside. "Major!" Mark turned and stared at him, his grip tightening further. "May I have a word with you? Outside."

Mark sneered at the man across from him then released the chains. Mick fell back against the chair and sucked in air as Mark stood and walked out. As the door shut, he turned past the wide eyed Jennifer and addressed Mitchell. "I think we can use this against her father."

Mitchell crossed his arms and nodded to him. "How's that?"

"Disinformation. We load that camera with false images. Give them a layout that doesn't exist. Get Simmons to think that he can trust Mick and get hairball hacker in there to work with us…we can use this."

Mitchell considered their options. "Whatever we do, it needs to be plausible. They already know that this place is larger underground than it appears."

Mark scratched at his chin. "Then maybe we convince them that we've moved our operations? Convince them that we just keep a skeleton crew here as a lure in case the hangar is attacked again."

Mitchell considered his suggestion. "Might work, but even that would be a hard sale."

"We moved to Nevada once. I'm sure we can make it look like we moved again."

Jenny stepped between the two. "Aren't you going to say something to him? About what he did in there?" She stared at Mark as though he were evil incarnate.

Mitchell nodded. "Good job, Major. You got us what we needed."

Jenny shook her head in disbelief. "That's not what I meant. Aren't there rules about how you treat prisoners?"

Mitchell took her by the shoulders gently and peered into her eyes, his face softening as he did. "Jen, I know that you care for that man in there, but he was working with the enemy. He was caught in the act of espionage. He was about to give them secrets that could easily have led to both of our deaths."

Jennifer opened her mouth to say something when his words finally sunk in. She paused and turned to look at Mick through the two way mirror once more. "You're right." Her voice was barely a whisper. "It's almost like I don't even know who he is anymore."

"No permanent damage done, ma'am." Mark patted her arm as he stepped around her once more. "I'm going to talk to him about doing the right thing."

Jen turned and grabbed his arm. "And if he refuses?"

Mark smiled. "I'll just have to persuade him."

*****

Jack gripped the phone tightly as it rang and nearly jumped when Viktor answered. "It's Jack. Is Nadia okay?"

"Nadia's fine." Viktor couldn't keep the displeasure from his voice. "If you truly cared, you would be here by her side."

Jack immediately felt relief and a huge weight lifted from his shoulder. Just as quickly, his anger flared. "You called me to chide me for not being there?" His voice growled low and deep into the phone, his eyes narrowing as he pictured his father-in-law.

"No, I called you because I…I require your assistance."

Jack held the phone back in surprise and stared at it. "Did I hear you correctly?"

"This is no time to gloat, hunter. Rufus has been captured. I need your—"

"Like hell!" Jack cut him off. "Rufus burned his bridges with me."

"You are his Second. You don't have that luxury," Viktor spoke matter-of-factly. "He does not have to explain his every action to you."

"He *stole* from my people and then built a Doomsday weapon. A weapon that could have killed every non-human on the planet."

Viktor stiffened slightly but maintained his composure. "You are still his Second. Your job is to trust his judgment."

"He forfeited that right when he—"

"Had he ever lied to you prior to this?" Viktor interrupted.

Jack paused and shrugged, not realizing Viktor couldn't see the action. "How could I know? He wasn't exactly been honest with me about the Doomsday weapon."

Viktor exhaled hard into the phone and rubbed at the bridge of his nose. "Jack…do you know *why* he had the weapon built?"

"It doesn't matter. He stole the plans and created it. As far as I'm concerned, he blew it."

"He knew that one of Foster's vampires was trying to resurrect Lilith. He has succeeded. The weapon was built to battle her. He needed an ultimate weapon to defeat the ultimate threat."

"Wait…what? Did you say *Lilith*?"

"You know of her?" Viktor finally saw a ray of hope as Jack spoke.

"Actually, yeah. I have my own team of…uh…*warriors* here. They were put together just to fight this bitch. We're just trying to figure out where she is."

"She is the one who holds Rufus." Viktor held the phone firmly, the corners of his mouth curling into a smile. "If you want to know where she is, you will have to agree to assist me in saving him."

Jack sighed heavily and stretched his neck. "Reverting to blackmail, *Dad*?"

"If you cannot do it for honor or because it is your duty as his Second, then yes."

*****

Laura threw her clothes into the dresser and dropped her duffel to the floor. She stood and stared at the room that she hadn't set foot in since she had screamed at her father for 'betraying' the memory of her mother. She plopped down on her bed and stared at the dresser, her reflection staring back.

She had been a grown woman when he tried to tell her that he'd met somebody that made him happy again…somebody that made him want to get up out of bed in the mornings. Somebody who shared the same beliefs, the same desires, the same…she shook her head, trying to rid the guilty thoughts from her mind.

How many years of potential happiness had she robbed him of? How long had it been since she practically spit in his face and stomped out of their family home? She fell back onto the bed and her eyes focused on the ceiling, the plastic glow in the dark stars still glued to the ceiling. Slowly a smile crept to the corners of her mouth as she remembered when her dad stuck them up there as a surprise for her. So many nights she had gone out to the trampoline to fall asleep under the stars only to have him carry her back inside and tuck her in bed. "Now you can sleep under the stars and I won't have to carry you back in at two in the morning. You're getting too heavy for me, Punkin."

She didn't have the heart to tell him that he didn't get any of them placed right. She couldn't tell him the names of the constellations, but she knew their shapes. She knew where the largest and brightest were supposed to be and she made her own constellations from the ones that she couldn't recognize.

Laura snatched a pillow from the head of the bed and stuffed it under her head. She glanced about the room and realized, he truly hadn't changed a thing since she left. She fished in her pocket and pulled out her cell phone. She punched the button and waited for Evan to pick up.

"Miss me already?"

She relaxed reflexively when she heard his voice. "You make me feel better."

"Uh-oh. What's wrong? Did he change his mind at the last moment?" She could hear him shuffling the phone and she could imagine him putting something away to give her his full attention.

"No, he didn't, but…I don't know. I think maybe I made a mistake." She sighed and kicked her shoes off into the floor. "Or maybe I didn't and I just feel guilty. I just don't know."

"Okay, let's back up. Tell me why you feel guilty."

Laura filled him in on her father and Crystal. She explained how her father's 'miraculous' increase in energy and appetite had struck a chord with her. Suddenly she just knew that it was 'wrong'. "Doesn't it say that death comes to us all? Who am I to intervene?"

"You're a worried daughter doing what she feels she has to do in order to save her ailing father." Evan leaned back in his chair and she could hear it creaking through the phone. "I can't say about any residual guilt you may be feeling about him and his girlfriend, but you felt this was something you had to do."

"Why didn't you stop me?" Her voice was soft and childlike.

Evan sighed into the phone and shook his head. "Like anybody could stop you once you set your mind to something. Besides, it was daylight outside. I'd have been toast before I ever reached you."

Laura rolled over on the bed and stared at the trophies on her shelf. "Do you think I messed up?"

"Don't ask me that."

"Why not? I trust your judgment."

"Because, regardless of what I think, it's too late to do anything about it. The deed is done. He's infected. All you can do now is continue the protocol so that he's eased into the transition."

Laura pinched her eyes shut and tried to force back the emotions she felt. "What if I messed up?"

"We'll just have to deal with the consequences." Evan shifted the phone closer to his mouth. "Did you note I said, 'we'?"

"Yes, I did. Thank you."

"I have to say though, I'm confused. Why the change of heart? You couldn't wait to get away from here and run off to save him. Now that you can, you're worried you made the wrong decision."

Laura opened her eyes and felt the hot sting of tears forming then running down the side of her face. "I can feel it in my gut. He won't be able to handle this and somebody…maybe even the squads will be called out to deal with him." She sniffed back the tears and clenched her teeth together. "It's one thing to die because it's your time. It's another to be put down because you lose it. If that happens, Evan…it will be *my* fault."

*****

Foster paced the tiny area as he waited to hear back from the hired enforcers. "Why haven't any of them checked in with us?"

"It is daylight. They may be asleep."

"Bah!" Foster slapped at the stack of papers on the edge of the desk and sent a chair flying into the wall. "Viktor could be here at any moment. I need to know what resources we have available to offer him!"

The enforcers bent and picked up the papers, shoving them haphazardly back into the files. "They will respond as soon as they see the message. With the money we are offering, they will not ignore the call."

"They'd better not. If they leave me standing here with nothing more than my dick in my hand once Viktor arrives…" He glared at the enforcer who simply nodded and backed away. "Do we have any resources left at the island?"

"The other hunter is in charge there. Mueller."

Foster threw his hands into the air. "Of course he is. Thompson's right hand man. They'd just as soon kill Rufus themselves." He paced the small room and tried to think, his mind racing. "What about the Russians?"

"I called them. Apparently they are tied up and can't release anyone right away."

"Tied up? Can't release anyone? This is the head of the *Lamia Beastia* we're talking about here!"

The enforcer nodded. "But he is not the head of their *familias*. Rufus is well respected and technically the head of all, but the *familias* can still supersede unless it is a time of war."

"Of course they can." Foster mocked their response while he continued to pace. "Is anyone overseas available?"

The enforcer shook his head. "The Sicarii's army destroyed many *familias* from within. Many are still trying to rebuild."

Foster paused and clenched his fists, his face contorting as he fought not to scream. "We have no wolves other than what Viktor may bring. We have no fighters because the vampire war destroyed them all. We have…nothing?"

The enforcer shrugged. "It is too short of notice for most to respond or send assistance."

"Because nobody has rebuilt their ranks." Foster plopped onto the hotel bed. "Short sighted, incompetent idiots."

"They are trying. Many have created new vampires, they

just…"

"What?" Foster turned a curious eye to the enforcer. "What do you know that I do not?"

The large vampire averted his eyes. "They get in too big of a hurry and they lose control. The packs of baby vamps end up loose on the humans." He turned and met Foster's gaze. "The hunters get them."

*****

Jericho stepped into Dominic's office and rapped on the door. "We have a couple of possibilities on the board. You might want to get your team prepped."

Dom set his paperwork aside and gave Captain Jones a crooked grin. "We just came in off the last one. Shouldn't First Squad take this one?"

Jones paused and lifted his clipboard. He flipped through the pages and scratched at his chin. "I forgot that they changed all the teams around. Team Two is actually Three and One was Two and…" He shrugged. "You want me to tell Spanky to take this one? I'm sure he wouldn't care either way."

Dominic stared at his after action report on Mac. Perhaps if he took the next op, the man would snap out of whatever funk he was in and develop a desire. A desire to be a part of the squad, to be a team player. "Let me talk to Spanky. I'll get back to you in two shakes."

Jericho gave him a thumbs-up and slipped out of the tiny office. Dom walked down the hall and knocked on Spalding's door. With no answer, he stuck his head inside to find the office empty. "If I were Spanky, where would I be?"

"Right behind you, you big oaf." Spanky poked him in the ribs as he walked past and flipped on the light to his office.

Dom jerked as his ribs were violated by Spalding's offending finger. "Dude, that ain't cool sneaking up on a trained killer like that."

Spalding laughed as he fell into his chair. "I'll keep that in mind the next time there's a spider in here." He pushed his chair back to make more room for the large Italian. "Don't be a stranger, come on in and…well…I'd say make yourself comfortable, but I swear this used to be a janitor's closet before they shoved a desk in here."

"Yeah, no shit." Dom leaned against the wall and smirked. "Hey look, Jericho just gave me a heads-up on a possible op on the boards. He was going to assign it to my squad, but I reminded him we just came in."

"Yeah, okay. We can take it." Spalding leaned forward in his chair and cleared a spot on his desk. He reached for the file in Dom's hand, but Dom held it back.

"No, this ain't it. I was just…" He sighed heavily then glanced out in the hallway to ensure it was clear. "I'm having problems with one of my guys."

"Just one? I figured Charmichael would be giving you fits, too."

Dom shook his head. "No, he's fitting in pretty well. It's all Chad. It seems the guy doesn't play well with others."

Spanky nodded. "All the things that people thought about Sullivan."

"Yeah, so how's he working out?"

"Actually, quite well. He was just misunderstood." Spalding gave him a lopsided grin. "He's a hell of an operator. A little emotional when it comes to his sister, but nothing I can't handle."

Dom smiled mischievously. "Feel like taking on another

project?"

Spalding shook his head. "Hell no. Little John would kill Mac. They can't stand each other."

"I sorta got that vibe too. I wonder why that is?"

Spalding shrugged. "Little John claims that Mac can't stand for anybody to outscore him on anything. He needs to be *numero uno* on everything. If he can't be, he undermines them every chance he gets."

Dom scratched the side of his head while he considered Sullivan's observations. "You know, that makes sense."

"So you think you have a handle on how to make him fit in?"

Dom shook his head. "Not a fucking clue." He slapped the folder against his thigh as he turned for the door. "But if you don't care, I'm going to take this next op. Maybe if he has to sit out for a rotation he'll realize I'm not playing."

Spalding nodded. "You got it brother. Let me know if you need anything."

"Just cover the fort while we're out protecting Democracy from monsters." He shot Spalding a wink.

"We're a Constitutional Republic."

Dom turned and gave him a blank stare. "Huh?"

"You said…" Spalding waved him off. "Good luck out there."

*****

Bigby drove back to the warehouse and hopped down from the truck. The greasy bag he carried dangled from his grip and nearly dropped as he listened to the sound of construction coming from within the warehouse. He rushed to the doors and found Martinez directing his men as they began building the mock-up.

"What's going on here?" Bigby marched to the work crews

that carried the lumber from the stacks. "Who told you to start construction on this?"

The man stopped and nodded toward Martinez with his chin. Bigby turned and saw the man flipping through pages within a file folder. "I'll get to the bottom of this." He turned and marched toward Martinez. "What the hell are you doing?"

Martinez turned and flashed the man a toothy grin. "We got the intel." He handed the folder to Bigby who dropped the greasy bag on the floor and began flipping through the folder.

"This…this can't be…are you sure?"

"We just got it. Mr. Simmons forwarded it to me just moments ago. I printed it out and my men have begun construction."

"There's even a blueprint in here."

"I know. Crazy huh?" Martinez pulled the file from Bigby's hand. "I have no idea where Mr. Simmons' man got it, but he delivered."

Bigby rubbed at his chin as he looked at the men hurriedly building the mock-up. "Yeah, mate, a little too convenient if you ask me."

*****

Kalen paused at Brooke's door, his hand raised but refusing to make contact with the painted metal surface. He could feel his heart rate increase and his breath caught in his throat. He lowered his head and stared at the floor. Slowly he turned and walked back to his room. What would he say to her?

As he sat down on his bed, his mind raced back to the night she invaded his dreams. It had felt so real. The knowing looks she had given him afterward convinced him that she had shared the dream as well, but he couldn't be certain.

Kalen sighed and slumped down into his mattress. What good would it do him to ask? Even if she admitted to having shared the dream with him, what would that mean? It didn't necessarily mean they were somehow connected. And who's to say that she would tell him the truth?

Kalen spun slowly on the bed and stretched out, interlacing his fingers and propping them behind his head. He closed his eyes and instantly, she filled his thoughts. Her eyes, her hair, the shape of her jaw, every minute detail of her face was burned into his memory. He sighed audibly and rolled to his side, facing the block wall. He instinctively reached out and placed his hand on the cold, painted wall and could almost imagine her on the other side.

"I wish I could know what you were thinking."

A soft knock at his door snapped him from his reverie. He rolled over and swung his feet off the edge of the bed. He padded to the door and opened it, his mouth dropping open as his eyes took in Brooke standing in the doorway.

"Brooke. I didn't…I mean…I was just…" Kalen closed his mouth and simply stared at her.

Brooke looked up at him and he couldn't read the expression on her face. "You gonna invite me in or what?"

Kalen startled and stepped aside. "Of course. Please."

She stepped inside and glanced around. "I see your place is just as fancy as mine."

He nodded as he shut the door. "It suffices."

He turned and gave her his full attention. "To what do I owe the honor?"

She averted her eyes and reached for the chair. "I was just…uh…I was thinking that maybe we should, you know…talk."

Kalen slipped past her and sat on the edge of the bed. "Very well." He brushed out imaginary wrinkles in the sleep tunic he wore. "What would you like to discuss?"

She finally raised her eyes to meet his gaze. "Why do you keep invading my dreams?"

*****

"Sir? I think I may have something."

Director Jameson looked up from the stack of papers on his desk and waved the analyst inside. "Talk to me, Stevens. What did you find?"

Stevens shoved a report onto his desk and stood smiling proudly as the man picked it up and browsed through the summary. "What is this?"

"Communications, sir." He glanced over his shoulder toward the door. "I thought your secretary was going to beat me over the head and take that from me, but I—"

"What kind of communications?" The director continued to sift through the papers behind the summary.

"Oh, uh…between the target party and their operatives in the field." Stevens leaned across the desk and tried to see what page the director was on. "I got to thinking, they need to have a way to *know* when a threat is real. They can't just wait for a civilian or a police agency to call them and say, 'hey, can we get a werewolf or vampire exterminator out here' now can they? No. So they must have field operatives. And if they have field operatives, then they have to communicate somehow."

"So…you utilized a satellite to track radio data?"

Stevens smiled. "Negative, sir. They're using old-fashioned telephone lines. I utilized the Patriot Act to pull their records of both incoming and outgoing calls. Then I started recording calls." He absolutely beamed as he spoke. "I uploaded the sound files to your G drive, sir. The hyperlinks are spelled out there so you can go straight to them and listen to—"

"English, son, in English." The director slapped the file shut and stared at the man.

"Oh…uh…I saved the sound files on a drive that only you and I can access. The directory to get to it is the last page of the report…the addendum there. I believe its attachment F, sir."

The director opened the file again and flipped to the last page. Slowly a smile crossed his face. "Okay, Stevens, I'm going to go listen to these files. If they are what you say they are then…good job."

"Thank you, sir."

Director Jameson looked up at the man. "You still cleared for field work, Stevens?"

The analyst paled as he tried to digest what the director had just asked him. "Sir?"

"Are you still cleared for field work?"

"Uh…I suppose, sir. But I'm an analyst. I work in the office here. I mean, I'm a data kind of guy, I don't actually go into the field and—"

"You're about to." Director Jameson reached across his desk and picked up his phone. "I've got to call Ingram and have him put together a surveillance team. I want you on it."

Stevens paled even more. "But, sir, I'm not really qualified to…I'm not a field operative!"

Director Jameson stared the man down. "If you're qualified to be one, then by God, you *are* one. Unless you'd rather be crunching satellite data in the fucking Yukon?"

The analyst stiffened and swallowed hard. "No, sir. I'd rather not."

"Excellent. Get your gear and prepare to assist Ingram's men in the field." Jameson began punching numbers into his phone then paused. He turned to Stevens once more. "That is all. You're dismissed."

CIA Analyst Robert Stevens walked back to his desk in a daze. He sat down in his chair and stared at his computer screen. His hands went through the motions of shutting down his station as his mind raced. Going out in the field was one thing. Going out in the field and facing genetically mutated, monster hunting, Special Forces soldiers was another.

He stared at the blank walls of his cubicle. For the briefest moment, he actually wished that he had a family or a sweetheart that he could tell good-bye.

14

"So what exactly did you send Mr. Simmons?" Mick asked as he leaned back in the metal chair.

Mark laid the camera back down and slid it across the table to him. "Those are pictures of another site. Then we snapped a few of different areas in here and in other buildings across the base. We had a draftsman draw up phony blueprints and artificially age them so that they'd look old." Mark crossed his arms and stared the were-cat down. "The big question now is, are you ready to become a part of the solution, or will you remain part of the problem?"

Mick held his chained hands up and rattled them. "You really think I want to spend the rest of my days like this? What's your proposal?"

"If I had my way, we'd take you out back and sink a bullet in your head. But seeing as how the colonel is feeling much more generous, he's offering you asylum. Of sorts."

Mick lowered his hands and cocked his head sideways. “Asylum? How does that work?”

“Considering that this Simmons character has a pretty long reach, we’re prepared to offer you a lifelong vacation on a really nice island. Surrounded by other shifters, too.”

“In exchange for?”

“In exchange for your help, as soon as Simmons is properly set up, we send you out on a chopper. It’s just a few hours away from here.”

“An island? Just a few hours from here?” Mick raised his brow at the man, obviously disbelieving.

“It’s in the Gulf. The fellow running it at the moment used to work here.” Mark scooted his chair back and glanced at his watch. “It’s a short-term offer.”

“Fine. I suppose it beats the bullet option. But what do you mean by lifelong? I’ll be a prisoner there?”

Mark ignored him as he flipped his folder shut. “Lifelong as in, as long as you want to stay alive. I truly doubt that a money man like Simmons is going to come out of the shadows to lead his little attack on us. As long as he’s out there, you’re going to need to keep a low profile.”

“So I’m either a prisoner there or a prisoner here.” He flung his chains toward Mark. “That’s some choice you’re giving me, mate.”

“There’s always option one.” Mark shot him a lopsided smile.

Mick sighed and pushed the camera back to him. “Just tell me what I have to do.”

“We’ll get you another cell phone. You call him and tell him that after the attack we decided to move to this location because of the damage done at this location. Make sure that he believes you.”

“And then?”

"And then make sure he knows that you are running out of minutes on your prepaid phone and have to go. Then we make you disappear."

Mick swallowed hard and averted his eyes. "What about Jennifer?"

"What about her? She's my CO's mate. We'll protect her with our lives." Mark crossed his arms and stared the man down. "From *anyone*."

"Yeah, I gathered as much." Mick leaned forward and held his hands out. "I'm not a threat Major. You may as well remove these."

Mark chuckled and shook his head. "Not until we've got what we want." He stood and pushed the chair back in to the table. "Then you'll get what you want."

"Yeah, I doubt that."

*****

"I don't understand. What do you mean that I invade your dreams?" Kalen was nearly floored by her question.

"Don't be coy with me, Sugar Cookie. I know that you did it, and you know that you did it. I just don't know how." She crossed her arms and squeezed herself tightly. "It's not like I'm going to tell anybody. I just want to know."

Kalen shook his head, his hands coming up in surrender. "I swear to you, Brooke, I haven't—"

"Raven." Her eyes pleaded with him. "Please, call me Raven."

Kalen's curiosity got the better of him. He could read her emotions, and they were all over the place. He sat down beside her and gingerly placed a reassuring hand on her arm. "Why? I don't understand why you would change who you are."

She shook her head, her hair covering her face. “Brooke is dead. She’s long since gone. Only Raven can do the things that need doing now.”

“You do realize you’re the same person, don’t you?” Kalen squeezed her arm gently. “You’re still you under all that black leather and bladed weapons.”

She pulled her arm back and leaned away from him. “No, Kalen, that’s where you’re wrong.” She stood and crossed the narrow room to the door. She stood with her back to the exit and still refused to meet his gaze. “Brooke was innocent. She was weak. She was…a child. Raven is strong, and she can do what needs to be done to survive. Raven can kill indiscriminately and she can…” Her voice broke, and he saw her bottom lip quivering.

Kalen got up and stood before her. His hands gently held her arms as they clutched even tighter to her sides. “Br-…I mean, Raven. You can be anything. You can become anything. You can even go back if you want.” He slowly stroked the sides of her arms as he spoke. “But changing your name doesn’t change what happened to you. It doesn’t change what you had to do in order to survive. Yes, it made you stronger and yes, you had to harden yourself in order to do it, but it doesn’t change the fact that you are Brooke Sullivan.”

He reached up and tucked a loose strand of hair behind her ear. He noted the tears running down her cheeks and a part of him wanted to wrap his arms around her and tell her that it would all be okay. He wanted to kiss her and tell her that she didn’t have to hurt inside any longer. He wanted to tuck her into his pocket and keep her warm and protected and hide her away from anything that might harm her. But the other part of him knew that she was as dangerous a warrior as any he had come across. He knew that she could just as easily best him in battle if he weren’t careful. She might have a fragile psyche, but she was far from broken.

He tucked away another strand of hair and gave her a gentle smile. "I'll call you whatever you wish. And we needn't speak of it any more if you don't want to." He pulled her gently into an embrace and he softly wrapped his arms around her.

For the briefest of moments, Kalen felt at peace; as though everything that could be right with the world suddenly was. Then he felt her shift under him and he knew that she didn't share the feeling. He broke the embrace and stepped back slightly, his eyes searching hers. Tears flowed freely, and she tried to wipe them away with the back of her hand. He reached across and grabbed the tissues from his desk.

"Thank you," she sniffed as she dabbed at her face.

"You are most welcome." Kalen stepped aside and allowed her to take the chair. "Not to change the subject, but you said that *I* had invaded your dreams." She looked up at him expectantly. He cleared his throat and shook his head. "I honestly thought that it was you who had invaded mine."

Her eyes went wide with shock and she stared at him. "I wouldn't…I mean, I couldn't even if I…"

"I understand. And neither could I." He sighed heavily as he sat down. "Perhaps it was happenstance that we shared a similar dream?"

She looked at him and shook her head. "What did you dream?"

Kalen's face flushed and he shook his head. "I don't really remember."

"You too, huh?" She chuckled as she wiped her nose again. "Yeah, mine was pretty steamy too."

"Did you rip out my throat in your dream?"

She gasped as she turned to him again. "No!"

He nodded. “You did in mine.”

“Oh, my God…” Raven suddenly stood and was searching for the door. “I need to leave.”

“No, wait!” Kalen jumped up and stood between her and the door. “Please don’t.”

“No, Kalen, this was a mistake. A giant, horrible mistake.” She tried to maneuver past him, but he sidestepped and stood in front of her again. She opened her mouth to protest when he leaned down and kissed her.

*****

Derek Youngblood stood in the living room of his childhood home and spun in slow circles. His mind raced as he tried to take in everything that Laura had told him. “And you just…shot him up with this stuff?”

“Yes, Derek, I did.” Laura groaned as her brother seemed to slip into shock. “But I did it to save his life.”

“Yeah, but at what cost?” His voice was raised and nearly at a panic level. “And why the hell would you tell me?”

Laura sat on the edge of the couch, her hands tucked neatly between her knees. “Because I think I’m going to have to go back and face the music for what I did. Dad’s going to need somebody to make sure he takes his medicine…and to keep an eye on him. Somebody to keep him grounded.”

“Oh, my God!” he screeched as he continued to spin in slow circles. “You want me to be responsible for your screw up? Isn’t that just priceless?”

“My what?” Laura glared at her brother, her head slowly tilting to the side. “Did you just say that saving Dad’s life was a ‘screw up’?”

"Yeah, I did. No, wait. I mean…I meant to say that…yeah, you…well…" Derek couldn't wrap his own mind around his thoughts, but the way Laura had twisted it back on him had him completely puzzled. "You did screw up. You know it and I know it. It was Dad's time. He had come to terms with it."

"But now he doesn't have to."

"Oh yeah. And he's supposed to just walk out with a clean bill of health and live forever and nobody will be the wiser for it." Derek threw his hands into the air and glared at her. "How the hell am I supposed to explain that one?"

"You don't have to, D! Medical miracles happen all the time."

"Not like this they don't!" He finally stopped his spinning and sat down hard on the brick hearth of the fireplace. "Jeezus, Sis, what have you done?"

"I saved his life." Her voice was soft and low, nearly pleading for her brother to understand her actions.

"At what cost? What if he does change? What if he likes the strength and power too much, and I can't stop him?" Derek shook his head. "If he decides to stop taking the meds, you know I can't force him. He's more pigheaded than you are."

"What do you want me to do, D? Shoot you up with the stuff too so you can overpower him?" She gave him a sideways look and Derek nearly fell off the hearth.

"Hell no! I don't want nothing to do with that stuff." He suddenly came to his feet. "In fact, as it is, you have me scared to death that if he scratched me or got mad and spit on me that I might get it."

"It doesn't work that way, Derek."

"How the hell am I supposed to know? It's not like I work with this crap every day." He began pacing, his eyes shifting back and forth as his mind raced.

"Will you just calm down?"

"Calm down? She wants me to calm down. You shoot our father up with werewolf venom and you want me to calm down. Sure, I'll just get right on that!"

"I've got a valium if you think that will help."

"No way, Jose. It's probably got vampire DNA or something in it. I'm not taking anything from you."

Laura chuckled and leaned back on the couch. "Vampires carry a virus as well. You can't get it from a valium."

Derek froze in place and slowly turned to face her. "Vampires? You mean to tell me that they're real, too?"

*****

Jack rounded the corner and tapped on Mitchell's door. "Come."

He stuck his head inside and nodded to his ex-commanding officer. "You got a minute?"

"Not really, but I'll make one. Take a seat." Mitchell poured him a cup of coffee and set it on the edge of the desk. "What's on your mind, Chief?"

"I just got off the horn with Viktor." Mitchell gave him a concerned look and Jack cut his question off before he could ask it. "Nadia is fine and so is the baby. No, this had to do with Rufus."

Mitchell leaned back in his chair and raised a brow. "So he's definitely alive and kicking?"

"And captured." Jack took a sip of the coffee and cradled it while he recounted the tale that Viktor had told him. When he was finished, he decided to drop the bomb. "I just recently got wind from the Wyldwood that our big dark threat is some chick named Lilith. Ever heard of her?"

Mitchell shook his head. "No, but something tells me I'm about to."

"She's apparently the original badass bitch created by God to be Adam's mate, but she rejected him and turned her back on God. She ended up with the fallen angels and…well, she turned to the Dark Side."

"Joy. So what is she supposedly up to?"

"World domination, slavery of all mankind, that sort of gig. And she's the one holding Rufus."

Mitchell's eyes widened. "Damn, when your boss steps in it, he really steps in it, doesn't he?"

"He's not my boss any more. But Viktor wants me to help him save the bloodsucker."

"And you're going to do it because it's Lilith that has him, right?" Mitchell could see where this was going.

Jack sighed and ran a hand across his face. "If this gal is everything she's made out to be, I don't know if my junior cub scouts can handle her."

Mitchell nodded as he sipped his coffee. "But the Wyldwood thinks they can?"

Jack shrugged. "She claims that it was foretold. These are the chosen warriors, and I'm supposed to lead them into battle."

"And you have your special weapons?"

"Angel weapons." Jack hooked his thumb over his shoulder. "The big guy we brought back with us is a Nephilim. That's the offspring of an angel and a human."

"Yeah, I know what a Nephilim is." Mitchell gave Jack a curious stare. "But I thought they were extinct. Old Testament legends."

Jack shrugged again. "I guess there's at least one angel that thought it was worth creating another kid."

"And this Nephilim is working with you?"

"Our new right hand man. He's stout as hell, pardon the pun. And he doesn't know what fear is."

Mitchell considered the creature they were going against. "Let's hope he doesn't learn it once he meets up with her."

"Yeah, well I'm about to gather my troops and gear up. You think you can have a team standing by as backup? I know we don't have any angelic weapons to arm them with, but I'd feel a lot better if I knew we had backup waiting."

Mitchell nodded. "We have a couple of blips on the boards but if push comes to shove, I'll divert a team to you. It sounds like this should be a priority anyway."

"I appreciate it, Skipper." Jack stood and turned for the door. "For the record…this is the first op I've ever gone on that I've actually been worried."

*****

Dom pushed Chad McKenzie back away from the leader boards. "You're staying here."

Mac grew red in the face. "No, that's bullshit! I'm still a member of this team. I deserve to—"

"You've been sidelined." Dom pulled his pack up and slipped an arm into it. "Maybe sitting by the wayside will give you the chance to see how a *team* handles things."

"You can't do this." Mac puffed up and stood between Dom and boards. "Major Tufo put me on this team and I…"

"I chose you for this team, and now I'm choosing to bench you until further notice." Dom picked up his carbine and checked the optics. "When I see an improvement in your attitude and your ability to work and play well with others, then I'll reconsider your position with my squad."

"So what am I supposed to do until then?" Mac stepped back, his eyes pleading with Dominic.

"I don't give a shit what you do." He packed an extra magazine into his chest pouch then turned his attention back to the man. "If I were you, I'd work on my interpersonal skills."

"This ain't right." Chad slowly walked back from the boards and pushed his way out the door.

Hammer slid in next to Dom and placed a hand on his shoulder, "Do you think you could have been a little gentler with him?"

Dom gave him a surprised look. "He's a grown-ass man. He should be able to handle the truth."

"Should be. But can't." Hammer shrugged. "I hope he doesn't piss on your pillow while we're gone."

Dom shot a quick stare toward the closed door that Mac had slipped through. He slammed a magazine home and chambered a round. "I'll kill him if he does."

*****

Bigby sat in his office cleaning his weapons while Martinez and his men continued their construction of the mock-up. He continued to play things out in his mind. How things had gone terribly wrong for them since Sheridan had made it his own personal mission to bring down the Yanks. How he had screwed the pooch by bringing in the huge fuzzy.

Bigby threw the cleaning rod across the counter and gripped the top so hard that he feared his knuckles would break. He blew his breath out slowly and unclenched his jaw. He'd never been one to be judgmental or racist. But after having Apollo turn on them, he wished he could think of a worse thing to call him. He wished he could kill him over and over and over again.

He closed his eyes and replayed the moment his bullet shattered the thick plate of Apollo's skull and sent the pink mist into the night air. He slowly allowed himself to relax as he replayed the moment. His only regret was that he didn't have the monstrosity of a man chained down so that he could have taken his time with him and did him up proper-like with his blades. "Aye, mate, I would have enjoyed making you scream."

"We're about done with the first floor if you want to check it out."

Bigby opened his eyes and saw Martinez standing in the doorway. "Why would I care?"

"I just…we're about to start on the second floor." He hooked his chin back out toward the warehouse.

"So get to it." Big spun in his chair and slid his pistol off the bench. "I'll look at it once you're done."

Martinez watched the man as he went through the motions of breaking down his weapon again. "Very well." He disappeared back into the warehouse, leaving him to his thoughts.

Bigby stroked the cold metal of the weapon as he field stripped it by memory. "Your mates will soon be joining ya. I guaran-damn-tee you that."

*****

"And I want to be there when the first of my troops strike." Lilith planted her hands firmly on her hips. "I won't take no for an answer. I need to watch as their great cathedrals are reduced to rubble."

Samael closed his eyes and clenched his jaw. "We cannot risk your being seen at any of the strikes."

"He's right." Thorn stepped closer and pulled a cell phone from his pocket. "Surely you are familiar with these? Nearly every human these days carry the damnable things, and they all have video capability. They all can take pictures. If any of them happened to record the carnage, and you were in any of the frames, your plan goes up in smoke." Thorn tapped a button which powered on his cell phone. He held it out to her and showed how simple it was to push an icon and the device instantly began recording. "You could just as easily have one of your troops record the action and transmit it to you at a safe location."

Lilith's bottom lip trembled with anger. "I *need* to witness the destruction of these interminable icons."

Rufus nodded as he slipped the phone back into his pocket. "I understand completely. However, imagine if you can…all of the buildings being decimated and all of them being recorded live and fed to you here or some other safe place." He slowly formed a smile as she considered his words.

"All of them?" she repeated cautiously. "At once?"

"*Oui*, all of them." Rufus waved his arms and turned a slow circle. "With the technology they have today, you could watch it all live from one safe vantage."

Samael stepped between the two and effectively cut Thorn out of the conversation. "We could set up our own…devices. That way we don't sacrifice any of the Centurions for the cause. They all go as planned."

Lilith paced slowly, her mind digesting the possibilities. She turned and gazed past Samael to the vampire behind him. "And how would we do this?"

Thorn shrugged absently. "Your people could purchase a disposable pre-paid phone, set it to record and transmit, set it in front of their target and then simply walk in and do their damage." He gave her a winning smile. "It would be as easy as *une, deux, trois*."

"And where should I observe this from?" She pushed past Samael and stood in front of Thorn, her eyes settling on him.

"From wherever you like, my dear. You could do it here in your own planning room, or if you prefer the security of a bunker, it could easily be set up there."

"What would I need?" Her voice betrayed the urgency and excitement she felt, and Samael placed a hand on her shoulder to steady her. She barely recognized his touch as she pressed the vampire further. "If I were to follow through with this? What would we need to have?"

Thorn shook his head. "Forgive me, my lady, I am not that knowledgeable in the setting up of such things." He watched her gaze darken and he thought quickly. "But I believe I know somebody who can." He held his hand up to stay her outburst. With his other hand he pulled his cell phone from his pocket again. "Allow me a moment, if you please."

Thorn turned his back to the pair and dialed the phone. He waited patiently until it was answered. "Rufus?"

"Ah, brother, I fear I need your assistance."

"Are you okay? I feared you were dead. I have called Viktor and he—"

Thorn quickly cut him off lest Lilith or Samael overheard the conversation. "I need your assistance in setting up a video monitoring system. Something that cell phones can call in and send video to. Is that something you can help me with or would you need to bring in technical experts?"

The silence on the other end of the line told him that Paul was trying desperately to decipher any hidden code that Rufus may have used. "Let me see if I understand you correctly. You need me to bring you technical experts who have knowledge in setting up a video monitoring system that can be…what now?"

"A video monitoring system that can accept video from numerous cell phones at one time and play them all in real time." Thorn glanced over his shoulder at Lilith and gave her a reassuring smile. He made a show of covering the phone, "If anybody can do this and do it correctly, it is my brother Paul."

Lilith nodded slowly as she watched him. "Where would we do this, Mr. Thorn?"

"Wherever you prefer, my lady. You are already established here. I see no reason why we couldn't set it up right here in this very room if you liked."

She glanced to Samael who grunted and turned his back on the two of them. "Here would be acceptable."

"We are at the facility where we trespassed. How soon do you think you could have a technical team ready and in place to install this?"

Paul cleared his throat and tried to think of appropriate questions to ask for such a task. "How many cell phones will be feeding the system at any given time?"

"Oh, I am not certain." Rufus turned to Lilith. "He needs to know how many feeds will be incoming at any given time."

Lilith shook her head, unsure. Samael turned and barked at him, "One thousand. We have one thousand Centurions and each have their own targets."

"One…*thousand*?" Rufus repeated.

"A thousand? Are you fucking kidding me?" Paul nearly screeched through the phone. "I'm not the NSA!"

Thorn gave a wan smile to Lilith. "Apparently it is quite the tall order."

"I don't need to witness them all. I only want the biggest. Can he do one hundred?" Her eyes had widened and her teeth were bared as she stepped closer.

"One hundred then, Paul. Can you set up a system that can handle one hundred?" He shifted the phone to his other ear and stood where he could watch the crazed woman and listen at the same time.

"That's still a pretty tall order." He sighed heavily into the phone. "But yeah, it can be done. You do realize that even if we split it into ten feeds per monitor, she's going to have ten wide screen monitors to try to keep up with."

"Yes, we understand. Just so long as it can be done. What will it take?"

"A shitload of satellite dishes, diplexers, splitters, computers, stable power supplies, rolls of cable…manpower…lots and lots of manpower." Foster paused as if catching his breath then added with a knowing tone, "Men who know what they're doing."

"Understood. Get the best men for the job." He smiled again at Lilith and gave her a nod. "I promised the lady the performance of a lifetime."

"The kind of manpower I'm talking about won't be cheap, you know. I'm thinking probably…Viktor. Specialists like…well, you know, Jack Thompson. Or at least somebody as good as him."

"Yes, of course. Only the absolute best." Both men knew that they were on the same page once Jack's name was mentioned.

"You know, I doubt I could get Jack on such short notice." Paul's voice was almost a whisper.

"I understand. Just get the best you can." Rufus gave Lilith a wink. "She deserves it."

*****

Robert Stevens checked back into his office long enough to grab a few things he had forgotten. He took one last look around and prepared to leave when his supervisor tapped on the wall nearly causing the small framed man to jump out of his skin. "Easy there, killer. Director Jameson wants to see you."

Stevens nodded sheepishly and put his duffle down. He surely wasn't dressed for a meeting with the director, but when called to Olympus, one did not simply ignore the call. He punched the number in the elevator and rode it up to the top floor.

Walking toward the director's office, his administrative assistance barely looked up as he approached. "He's waiting for you." She reached under her desk and pressed the button unlocking the door.

Stevens took a deep breath just as he pushed the door open. "Sir? You wanted to…" His voice trailed off as he looked about the room. NSA Assistant Director Ingram sat opposite Director Jameson, as did two other men that Robert had never seen before.

"Have a seat." Jameson didn't look up from the report he was rifling through. "Can you explain this?"

"Sir?" Stevens sat slowly, his confusion evident.

Ingram handed him a copy of the file. "This." Stevens opened the file and dug through it. He had never laid eyes on any of the intel within the folder before.

"I'm not familiar with…uh…sir?" Robert pulled out a sheet that was clearly marked DIA. "This is Defense Intelligence. I wouldn't have access to—"

"I didn't ask if you had access, Stevens," Jameson interrupted. "I told you to get me *everything* on this group." He glared at the analyst.

"Uh…yes, sir. And I did. Everything that I could access

legally, and even a few things that I obtained through questionable methods." He shot him a sheepish smile.

Jameson was stoic. "So why the hell weren't these reports included?"

"As I said, sir. These are DIA. I don't have access to their—"

"The hell you say!" Jameson slammed a hand down on his desk and Stevens jumped. "Are you or are you not a mole?"

"Sir?" Stevens squirmed. "A...*what*, sir?"

Ingram chuckled and held a hand up. "I believe they're called hackers, sir."

Stevens sighed audibly and slumped in his chair. "Oh. Yes, sir, I can hack systems but the Defense Intelligence Agency is a standalone—"

"I don't give two shits what they are, Stevens. When I tell you I want everything on these sons of bitches, I mean I want everything. I want to know their damned birthdays, their mothers' maiden names. I want their social security numbers. I want their fucking dogs' names!" He leaned across his desk and glared at the man. "Do you understand what I'm saying?"

Stevens swallowed hard. "I do now, sir."

"Good. 'Cuz I'd sure as hell hate to think that you and I weren't on the same page." He slammed the report down on his desk and glared at the two other men who simply stood and walked out. When the door shut he turned back to Stevens. "Can you do this task while you're running surveillance on this group?"

Stevens opened his mouth to answer then closed it abruptly. He averted his eyes and shook his head. "No, sir, not from a mobile unit, no."

"Of course not." Jameson sat down hard and tapped his pen against the desk. "So what do I do now, Stevens? You're the one man in my organization who has half a fucking clue the big picture and I need you in two places at one time."

Stevens looked up and squared his shoulders. "If I may, sir? I can get you the intel you want…the intel I *should have* already gotten for you. Two days, tops. If you can convince Assistant Director Ingram to put off the field op for that long…" He looked expectantly to Ingram who simply pursed his lips and rolled his eyes.

"I have a team standing by…" he trailed off.

"Two days, sir, that's all I need."

Jameson inhaled deeply and turned to Ingram. "How about it, Bob? What's a couple more days? These guys aren't going anywhere."

Ingram shrugged. "What the hell." He tossed the report onto Jameson's desk. "Two days." He turned to Stevens and gave him a stern stare. "But then we're going in with or without you."

"To observe. Right?" Stevens looked to both men for clarification.

"To observe," Jameson agreed. "At least for now."

15

Mark listened in while Mick made his phone call to Walter Simmons. If either party gave a hidden tell that something was up, he couldn't detect it. Walter kept pressing Mick to tell him exactly where Jennifer was staying, but Mick tried to explain that she was mated to the commanding officer. She had free reign of the entire facility. She could come and go as she pleased, or stay in any part, at any time. Mick's voice gave away his frustration at having no sway with the woman. She was as pig-headed as they came, and what little persuasive power he may have had as her friend was lost once she mated with the man in charge.

"There has to be something you can do. Can you convince her to step out? Maybe go shopping on a certain day?"

"Are you kidding me?" Mick flopped back into his chair and rolled his eyes. "It's like she doesn't even trust me anymore. I've known her since we were kids and now..." Mick paused as Mark tapped on the glass. He looked up to see him shaking his head and tapping at his watch. “Crap, my phone just alerted me. I’m almost out of minutes. I need to go.”

“Please, Mick, you have to try,” Simmons sounded desperate as he pleaded with the man.

“Mister Simmons, even if I could get her out of the place, there’s no way for me to let you know that she was out. We’d all be flying blind here. Besides, it’s like I told you, she just—” He clicked the end call button, letting Simmons assume the phone either died or ran out of time. He opened the back and pulled the battery from the device and placed the pieces on the table. “Happy now?”

“Ecstatic,” Mark deadpanned as he entered the room.

“Now can I get these chains off?” Mick held his hands up and shook the chains at him.

“Once you’re safely aboard the transport, I’ll think about it.”

“Oh for crying out loud.” Mick shoved the pieces of the phone away, sliding them off the table in frustration.

“Easy, kitty. You don’t want to go pissing me off or I might just toss you to the dogs.” Mark grabbed the chains between his wrists and pulled him from behind the table.

“Where the hell are we going?” Mick stumbled but fought to keep up with him.

“You want to spend all your time in the interrogation room before you leave, that’s up to you.” He allowed slack to build in the chain as he eyed the man. “I thought maybe you’d like to collect your personal items before we toss you on the chopper and ship you out.”

“Whoa…just like that? I mean…don’t I get a chance to say goodbye?”

Mark leaned in close. “Goodbye.” He tugged the chains and

pushed Mick out the door. Two security personnel were waiting beyond the doorway. "Take him to collect his crap then load him on the next chopper."

"Where's he headed, Major?"

"Thorn's island. Make sure Bob knows to expect him." Mark watched as the two men escorted Mick away then retrieved the pieces to the phone. He honestly had no idea what their tech guys could do with it, but maybe if they had the number, they could figure out a way to activate the GPS and pinpoint Simmons. At least they'd know if he ever left Belize. He slid the pieces into his pocket and shut the door of the interrogation room.

The alert warning on his two-way went off and he plucked it from his belt. "Time to make the doughnuts."

*****

"So that's what we're facing." Jack searched the young faces studying him. "Any questions?"

Azrael nodded. "Are we truly going to save your old employer?"

Jack squeezed his eyes shut and ground his teeth. "I really want to say no. But my father-in-law is expecting us to show up to do just that." He inhaled deeply and blew the breath out hard, his face twisting in anger. "So I suppose my official answer is yes. If the bastard is in trouble, we need to save him. But stopping Lilith is priority one, does everybody understand?"

Phil crossed his arms and gave Jack a puzzled look. "I do not understand. If you do not wish to save him, then why bother?"

"Because the only way we're getting Lilith's location is if we agree to this." Jack patted the Nephilim's shoulder. "I'm sorry we didn't get a chance to run through any training drills with you before this. It would have been nice to bring you up to speed before we went into battle."

Phil's featured twisted into what Jack interpreted as a smirk. "I have plenty of training for battle. I think I shall do well enough."

"Perhaps, big guy. But it's one thing to know how to fight and another to fight with a team." Jack pointed to the others in the group. "They know how to fight as a team."

Phil motioned to Gnat. "Even the small one fights?"

Gnat stuck his chest out and hefted his hammer. "Good enough to level your large arse, I do."

"Easy." Azrael planted a foot between Gnat and the angel spawn. "We don't want you to hurt him before we can take down the demon Lilith."

Gnat stepped back and leaned on his hammer, his eyes narrowing on Phil. "He just saved your life, he did."

"Okay, knock it off." Jack got their attention again. "As soon as Viktor calls me back, we'll find out where to meet and what his plan is. For now, we go with what he comes up with. If things go sour, we do what we do best."

Raven held a hand up to get Jack's attention. "Were you able to get bullets made from the arrows Kalen created for you?"

Jack sighed heavily as he shook his head. "They haven't had time yet. Doc is working on it, and the guys in the armory are trying to help, but whatever that metal is, it doesn't want to melt and it tears up the equipment when they try to turn it on a lathe."

She stepped closer to him and drew one of her swords. "I have an extra." She handed it to him and Jack waved it off. "Hey, you need some kind of super weapon, right? What if it comes down to you and her or if she grabs you and you're the only one with an opportunity?"

"Too big for my tastes. I prefer something more like this."

Jack pulled his Tanto-bladed survival knife and flashed it. "Small and quick."

Raven sheathed the sword and drew a dagger from her thigh. "Like this? It's not exactly the same, but it's as close as I have."

Jack hefted the weapon and nodded. "Nice balance."

She pulled the leather sheath and handed it to him. "This beats tucking it into your belt."

Jack strapped the knife to his leg then turned to face the warriors once more. "Look, I'm not very good at this stuff, but I just wanted to say be sharp out there. Keep your head clear, your eyes open, and always stay alert. I don't know what we're going into or what we're going to be facing. But I do know that whatever it is will be dangerous. We're walking right into the lion's den and punching the cat square in the nose." He squared his shoulders and set his jaw. "This whole ordeal could be over in a matter of moments or…"

"Or it could get very, very nasty," Kalen finished for him.

"Right. I just don't want to have to be the one to notify any of your next of kin that you didn't make it." Jack cleared his throat and shifted his weight from foot to foot. "I…uh…I've grown a little fond of you guys."

"I don't suppose the Nephilim could just call dad to come down here and kick her ass?" Gnat shot the giant Guardian a sardonic stare.

Phil shook his head. "I have no way to call an angel."

"Crying shame." Gnat shook his head. "Crying damned shame."

"Alright, boys and girls, enough chit chat. Finish gearing up and do what you need to do. As soon as I get the coordinates, I'll come get you." Jack turned and headed to the duty officer's office.

Kalen turned to Raven. "You ready for this?"

She stiffened slightly and shot him a sideways glance. She quickly noted that nobody was paying them attention so she pulled him aside. "That never happened, do you understand?"

"What didn't?"

"The…what happened in the…when you…" She clenched her teeth with frustration as Kalen stared at her questioningly. "You never *kissed* me," she whispered.

"Yes, I did."

"No, you didn't." She glanced over his shoulder to ensure nobody was listening in. "Kalen, we can't…" Her voice trailed off as she searched for the right words. "We shouldn't be getting involved. Especially now. It will muddy our thoughts. You'll be too concerned for my safety and that could get you hurt. Or worse, it could get you killed."

He smiled sheepishly and reached for her. She caught his hands and held them away. "No. I meant it."

Kalen's face fell as he stared at her. "But I know you. You are the most proficient warrior here. I wouldn't need to worry about you if we were in battle."

She exhaled hard and lowered her eyes. "And I don't need to worry about anybody else either." She finally brought her eyes up to meet his. "Jack says this is too important."

"But, Raven, this won't be forever. Then we could…"

"No." She let go of his hands and stepped back. "Just…no."

He watched her turn and walk away, an ache in his chest that he couldn't explain preventing him from breathing.

*****

Laura tried not to laugh as Derek stared at her open mouthed. "Seriously?" She leaned back and cocked her head to the side.

"You have no trouble swallowing that werewolves are real, but the idea that vampires might be real has you about to wet yourself?"

Derek was slowly shaking his head, his eyes unfocused. "For God's sake. What's next? Fairies? Elves? Oh wait, let me guess! Dragons! Dragons are real, too!" He threw his hands in the air then stopped his ranting. He turned on her, his face angry. "You're screwing with me, aren't you? There's no werewolf serum, is there? You just wanted to make me out to be an idiot!"

Laura sighed and shook her head. "Yes, there is a serum, and *now* you're acting like an idiot."

"Oh, I'm the idiot because you want me to believe in monsters. Right." Derek sat down on the hearth again and chuckled. "You really had me going for a bit there."

"It's real, Derek. And yes, vampires, elves, fairies, and yeah, even dragons are real. In fact most all of the fairy tales we heard as kids are based on fact."

He laughed a short snort and slapped his thigh. "Sure they are." He pointed toward the door. "Wait, you better let in the mummy, I think I hear him knocking!"

"No, Derek, mummies aren't real. Well…I mean, they're real, but they don't come back to life." She paused and scratched at her chin. "At least, I don't think that they do."

"Oh yeah. I'm sure you and the governor had a fun time cooking up this little joke to play on me." He shook his finger at her. "At least you got him to eat something."

"This wasn't a joke, dammit!" She threw a pillow at him, catching him off guard. "And stop calling him that. He isn't the governor any longer."

"He'll always be the governor to the folks around here and you know it. Just like Mom will always be—"

"I said STOP!"

He stopped talking and stared at her, seeing her for the first time since he started his rant. The tears running down her cheeks and the flushed color of anger painted across her features told him that he had gone too far. Way too far. He stood and closed the gap between them. "I'm sorry, Punk. I didn't mean to…"

"No. Just stay over there." She pushed him back and walked around him. She went back to her dad's chair and fell into it. "I'm pissed and I want to be left alone."

"You're pissed?" Derek stood in front of her and watched her turn her head to avoid having to look at him. "You pull a stunt like that on me and you're pissed?"

"It wasn't a stunt. It's real." She reached for her phone and tossed it to him.

"What the hell?"

"The wallpaper, jackass. That's my boyfriend with me. Notice anything?"

"Damn, he's pale."

"Anything…else?"

"He has the strangest colored eyes." Derek pulled the screen closer and stared. "Are they silver or blue?"

"His teeth, stupid." She finally looked at him and watched as his face contorted with confusion.

"Are those Halloween teeth?"

"He's a *vampire* for fuck sake!" She reached up and plucked the phone from his grip. "And no, those aren't Halloween teeth."

Derek stared at her, his mouth open as his brain tried to process what she was saying. He slowly shook his head again as a smile began to form across his face. "You're pulling my leg, aren't you?"

Laura inhaled deeply and her she ground her teeth. She sat up and pulled her hair back, exposing the freshest bite marks on the back of her neck. “Does that look like I’m pulling your leg?”

Derek leaned in close and traced a finger over the dual puncture wounds. “Holy shit, Punk.” His eyes widened as he turned to face her. “He *bit* you!”

“I wanted him to.”

“Why?” Derek screamed.

“Because I like it, you dimwit, why do you think?”

“I don’t…I mean…how could…but you…” He turned back to her, his eyes so wide she feared they would fall out of his skull. “Are you a vampire now?”

“What? No, it doesn’t work that way.”

“Yes it does! I’ve seen the movies.” He slowly backed away from her, his fingers coming up to form a cross in front of her.

“Oh for Pete’s sake.” She stood up and pushed his ‘cross’ away from her. “I wear a crucifix you dumbass.”

Derek stared at his crossed fingers then let his arms drop. “But, why aren’t you a soulless ghoul, too?”

“Oh, I’m soulless, but that’s from too many years of working for the government.” She walked into the kitchen and opened the fridge. She pulled out two beers and tossed one to him. “But I’m no vampire, and I’m certainly no ghoul.”

“There’s a difference? Oh wait…let me guess.”

She rolled her eyes at him as she unscrewed the top and tossed the lid into the trash. “It’s complicated, D.” She took a long pull from the cold brew and leaned against the wall. “All I know is that right now, I really wish I were back there with him.”

“Oh wow. So like, you’re in love with this guy?”

She rolled her eyes again. “Yeah, D, I’m like…in love with him.”

He sat down on the hearth again and stared at the beer in his hands. “That’s heavy.” He popped the lid and took a short drink.

"So…"

"Yeah. So."

"No, I was gonna say, so…dragons? They're really real?"

*****

Mitchell was bent over the operations console observing an overhead view of the area that his assault team would be soon be striking. He placed a gentle hand on the shoulder of the technician at the station. "ETA for drop?"

"Five minutes, Colonel." The technician adjusted the gain on the satellite relay and the feed sharpened. "We have movement in the northeast quadrant. Looks like our tangos are on the move."

"Heat signatures?"

"Negative, sir. Best guess based on speed and agility is they're vamps." The technician zoomed out on the display, broadening the area on the screen. "Small town south-by-southwest. At their current speed, they'll reach the outer markers in about ten minutes."

Mitchell leaned back in his chair and spun to the communications officer. "Notify Second Squad that the tangos are on the move. They need to insert ASAP and set up a moving screen along the northeast border of the town."

"Copy that, sir." The communications officer began relaying the information to the squad while still in transit. He held a hand up to the side of his head and closed off his other ear, trying to hear above the low murmur of the OPCOM. "Sir, Second Squad reports that they're facing some weather. The pilot had to increase altitude and speed to get above it. He's about to vector in now to gain them speed on the drop in."

"Roger that." Mitchell made adjustments to his calculations

and figured the team had bought at least two more minutes prep time. “It’s still a lot closer than I’d like.”

Mark stepped into the OPCOM and sealed the door to the harsh artificial light of the hallway. He leaned in to Mitchell and lowered his voice, “I got the pilot sent off to the island. He did his part.”

Mitchell nodded and motioned to the empty logistics chair. “Saddle up. It’s about to get messy.”

“Sir, their coms are choppy but reporting.” The communications tech turned up the gain and put it on the overhead speaker. “I’ve cleaned it up as best I could.”

“OPCOM, Second Actual, we’re about to depart Pterodactyl Airlines for the comfort of the storm outside. Com check.”

“We read you, Dom.” Mitchell punched the button to bring the satellite feed up on the big screen. “Damn, this isn’t working. Put the sat feed on the big screen.”

The tech nodded and typed the commands, the screen instantly switching to the satellite feed. His monitor now shown on the widescreen at the front of the center. “We have eyes on the tangos. They’re scattering their approach angles as they close on the town.”

“Copy that, OPCOM. We’re slowing for a low altitude drop. We’ll be boots down before you know it.”

The OPCOM personnel went about their business monitoring as they listened to the squad members attach their static lines and prepare for the jump. Jericho cut in on the feed and announced that he was assuming mobile command.

“Copy that, Mobile. OPCOM standing by to provide support.” Mitchell leaned back in his chair and exhaled a long sigh, his eyes staring at the screens overhead.

“Colonel, this is the first time using this drone. This one

replaced the one we lost against the aquatic trolls. Want to offer up a quick blessing on it?" Jericho couldn't hide the mirth from his voice as he brought the bird online.

"Sure." Mitchell leaned forward, his eyes narrowing as he watched the status of the drone on the screen to his right. "You better work right, you sorry piece of shit, or I'll personally melt you down into razor blades and use you to shave my ass."

A muffled round of laughter could be heard through the operators' mouthpieces. Jericho keyed back, "Couldn't have said it better myself, sir."

"Appropriate." Mark hiked a brow at him. "You just better hope you didn't piss off the drone gods or that thing will fall from the sky like a paperweight."

"He asked for my blessing, I gave him my blessing." Mitchell turned back to the screen and tried to switch it again. "Dammit, my remote isn't working." He banged it a couple times and it still wouldn't respond.

"Try kicking it into submission," Mark deadpanned. "I hear they have these newfangled things called 'batteries'. You should try them."

"It's hard wired, smart ass." Mitchell smacked it again then sighed. "Probably made in China."

"They're away, sir," the tech called from in front of Mitchell's seat. "Should be boots down in a matter of moments."

"Okay, people. Let's put on our A-game. It's time to make the doughnuts."

*****

Little John searched the mess decks and the gym. He walked through the showers and the library. He was working his way up from the lower levels floor by floor but couldn't find Spalding anywhere. As he walked past the second level overlook, McKenzie stormed past him. "Hey, have you seen Spalding?"

"Blow it out your ass, Sullivan." Chad's face was twisted in anger, his eyes narrowed.

"What the hell is your problem?" John turned and faced Mac as he marched away.

Chad stopped suddenly and clenched his fists. "You don't want to go there, Sullivan."

"Go where, Mac? You've been acting like somebody pissed in your Post Toasties for weeks now. What gives?" Sullivan truly couldn't understand where all of this misplaced anger was originating from.

Chad slowly turned, his face a mask of rage. "Even you can't be that dense."

Sullivan shrugged. "Well apparently I am. You've been stomping around here like you're pissed at the world, and it's everybody's fault but your own. You go against your own team, your Team Leader tries to set you straight and what do you do? You go off on him and get yourself benched." John shook his head in confusion. "I can't get a read on you, man."

Mac stood in the narrow hallway, clenching and unclenching his fists, his eyes boring a hole through John's chest. "You truly are an idiot, aren't you? I guess it's true what they say. The bigger they are, the stupider they are."

John rolled his eyes at the smaller operator. "Dude, you aren't going to bait me into smacking the ugly off of you. There wouldn't be nothing left."

"Keep thinking you *could*." Chad turned back and stormed off in the direction he was going.

John heard the footsteps approaching before he ever smelled

Spalding's aftershave. "Problems?"

He shook his head. "Not with me, but I think Mac is about to blow. There is something seriously wrong in the guy's noodle."

Spalding watched the other man reach the end of the hall and turn for the stairwell. "Well, it wasn't that long ago, people thought the same thing about you."

"Anger issues?" John shot him a puzzled look.

"No, just…something was off." Spalding shrugged. "Everybody's different. Chad is just…well, he's wound tighter than most folks."

"Aw, fuck. Don't tell me that you're going to adopt another basket case and nurse it to normalcy?"

Spalding snorted a laugh. "Not anytime soon." He clapped John on the shoulder. "One basket case is enough for me."

"Thanks." He turned and fell into step with him. "I was looking for you. For a moment I thought you were trying to hide."

"I was researching." Spalding handed him a file.

"What's this?"

"Everything I could dig up on Sheridan's old crew. Jack had a sit down with admin and together they thought things through. Best bet is our shooter is a guy named Bigby."

"Bigby? Never heard of him."

"Well, he's from Team One in England." Spalding held the door and the two entered his office. Spalding fell into the chair behind his desk and Little John stood, taking up the rest of the space. "Most of the guys on Team One are stand up guys. You know, for God and Queen, that sort of shit."

"Gotcha. But somehow this Bigby was a bad apple?"

"Well…" Spalding pulled another file from his desk. "Sheridan was his CO. Unlike our setup, their COs are field officers. They're out in the mud and muck with their troops. This

Major Sheridan had family and the blood suckers used them to get to him."

"That blows." John handed Bigby's file back. "So what's the score?"

"Jack and Sheridan were pals from way back. Jack was on an op that got his entire team wiped out, but he was saved and nursed back to health by this vampire named Thorn. The vamps that blackmailed Sheridan wanted him to assassinate Thorn." Spalding shook his head and shrugged. "Jack didn't like the idea of one of his buddies turning traitor and killing another buddy."

"So it was Jack that caught him?"

"Shot him in the foot and crippled him. But somehow he worked it out so that Sheridan's family could be shipped over here, put into Witness Protection and disappeared. Sheridan was supposed to be a part of it, but something inside him snapped."

"And he's the guy who recruited Apollo." John was nodding, the pieces finally falling into place. "And what? This Bigby was jealous or…"

"We think he recruited Bigby to work with him the same way he recruited Apollo." Spalding shrugged and stuffed the file into the stack with the others. "The thing is…I can't figure out *how* he got into Apollo's head like that."

John leaned against the wall and remained silent. He really didn't know Apollo well enough to hazard a guess. His eyes scanned the small office and eventually fell on the pile of file folders. "Are all of those tied to Apollo?"

"Yeah, most of them." Spalding leaned back and bit at the end of his thumbnail. "His briefings, field notes, the evidence that was found on scene. What we have on Sheridan and the guys from his team that went 'missing'. Bigby is the only one that really could be our missing shooter."

"It couldn't have been one of Simmons' guys?"

Spalding shrugged. "I suppose it could have been, but from what little we've gathered and from what others have said, he only trusts wolves."

Little John grunted, "With wolves like this Sheridan and Bigby, I don't know if that's such a good idea."

*****

"This will not be an easy task." Rufus walked through the warehouse and looked about, his eyes taking in everything. "They will need to run cabling from the roof and there will be much equipment that goes with this."

Lilith followed closely behind him, her eyes scanning the areas where he looked, unsure what he was looking for. "What do you search for?"

"My lady, we will need to run many wires and cables down from the roof to your office. These cables are heavy, and they will need to be secured." He patted one of the concrete columns. "I may be wrong, but I believe we can use these to run them down to those steel reinforcements up there, then along to that column beside your office and then down and into the area where they can set up the monitors."

"Very well." She turned to leave then noticed that he was still standing out in the warehouse, studying the ceiling. "What else?"

"Well, there are also the power supplies, the relays and…just very much equipment that we don't want lying about. They need to stay cooled and I'm curious if it would be better to mount them up and out of the way or…" His voice trailed off.

Lilith turned to Samael for guidance but the angel was disinterested. He was studying the Centurions still packing crates for their departure. "What are your thoughts, my love?"

"My thoughts do not matter." Samael turned his back to her and slowly made his way to the stack of crates along the wall. She ignored Thorn and followed the fallen angel.

"What bothers you?" She tugged at his shoulder, but he still continued to watch the workers.

"I think we should kill this vampire at first opportunity. Instead you are welcoming him into the fold." He turned a careful glance toward Thorn then eyed her again. "And he brings more of his people here. How do we know they are who they say they are?"

Lilith chuckled and moved around to the front of him. She wrapped her arms around his thick neck and pulled herself up to kiss him. "What can a handful of vampires do to us? You are an angel and I am Lilith, Demon Queen."

Samael's eyes widened. "You truly do not understand, do you? You *are* the queen. If anything happens to you, we are lost!" His whispered voice threatened to echo across the warehouse. "Your resurrection was what allowed us to return. It was the only spell I was allowed to cast when they…" He paused, his voice quivering, his eyes avoiding her.

She reached up and cupped his chiseled face. "What are you saying?"

"I'm saying that if anything happens to you, your demons and myself will be damned back to Hell. There is no coming back unless *he* permits it. And he won't permit it if we fail."

She nodded slowly, her eyes peering into his own. "What spell did you speak of?"

Samael sighed, his eyes darting to the side. "He wouldn't allow me to give you your demons when you first needed them. He said the timing wasn't right. The religion was too strong then. But now, people are losing their faith. They place their hope and belief in themselves…in science or in *things*. He made me wait until you were caught and being tried. Then he would only this spell be cast."

"A spell?"

"That once you were made whole, I could return to you. Your demons could be culled from Hell and allowed to take bodies for your bidding." Samael ground his teeth as he stared at her. "It was not my doing, my love."

Lilith inhaled deeply and steadied herself. She closed her eyes and turned from him. "Could you have saved me when they were torturing me?"

"No, he wouldn't allow it," Samael's voice cracked as he spoke. "He said you *needed* to experience that. That it would fuel your hatred toward the created ones. Toward the One who created them. That without that, your spirit couldn't *ripen*."

She exhaled hard and felt her hand tremble as her anger spread. "He said that I needed to be drawn and quartered. To have my organs ripped from my body and scattered to the four corners of the earth?" She ground her teeth so hard that she feared she would crack a tooth. "He thought that I needed that experience? To feel that kind of pain to hate even more?"

"Yes, my love." Samael brushed her neck with the back of his hand and felt her pull away. "I swear to you, it wasn't me. It was Satan. He knows that you are his loophole to the Armageddon."

"His what?" She spun and glared at him, shock painted across her features.

Samael groaned, his shoulders slumping. "He fears that the prophet's predictions of the battle of Armageddon are true. That he will lose. You are to be his loophole to destroy this creation."

An evil and defiant smile crossed her features. "Well, let's not dare disappoint your master, shall we?"

16

"Perimeter set and motion sensors active," the disembodied voice crackled over the speakers as the crew within the OPCOM observed their heat signatures from the satellite feed. "Distance to tangos?"

Mitchell did a quick calculation based on movement and trajectory. "Approximately half a click, Sierra One. At their current speed you should make contact in a few minutes. Stay sharp out there."

"Copy that," Dominic's voice dropped to a low whisper and his heat profile darkened as he slipped into a creek bed and began crawling up the other side. He laid out along the bank, his .308 caliber SCAR resting on its bipod. "Eyes open, ladies. Contact imminent."

A series of clicks responded as his team replied, their

individual heat signatures spread in a semi-circle between the oncoming vampires and the small town to their back.

Jericho broke onto the channel with a report. “Drone is away and at the ready. Call sign Vulture. Establishing a high altitude circular orbit. At your command, Sierra One.”

“Roger that. Stand by.” Dom switched his optics from thermal to night vision. Vampires wouldn’t give off heat, and the soft green glow of the night vision amplified the ambient light, turning night into an ethereal day. He shifted the stock against his shoulder slightly and reapplied his cheek weld, his eye adjusting to the optics once more. He caught motion in the corner of his field of vision and realized it was just a rabbit, scampering away and into a small stand of thickets. Dom strained his hearing, listening for the slightest sound. The snap of a twig, the rustling of a limb against a moving object, anything that would signify something large, moving quickly through the stand of trees.

“Movement,” Sierra Five called out quietly. Neils ‘Hammer’ Erikson was placed near the top of the arch, his field of view towards a clearing roughly half the size of a football field.

Dom tried not to turn his head in the general direction, his curiosity piqued. “How many?”

“Two,” Sierra Five responded, his whispered voice hesitant. “They’ve stopped…almost as if they expect something.”

“Let them close on us, Five.” Dom continued staring through his night vision optic, waiting for something to break through the tree line.

“They’re just sniffing at the air, One.” Neils studied the pair at the opening of the clearing.

Major Tufo keyed the coms. “Check your wind.”

“Wind is good, OPCOM. Our position is downwind,” Sierra Five reported, his eyes studying the pair who were slowly backing away and into the trees. "They're breaking back, One. Orders?"

Dom cursed under his breath. He keyed his coms, "Vulture, do you have eyes on the rest of the party?"

"Affirmative, One. They've slowed their approach, but are still closing."

"Orders, One?" Neils flipped the safety off his carbine and centered the crosshairs on the rearward vampire.

Dom sighed. "Drop them." He offered up a silent prayer that they weren't about to give away their position.

Suppressed silver jacketed rounds exited the barrel of the Colt M4, striking the first vampire square in the chest, the second in the temple as he turned to see what caused his friend to suddenly turn to orange ash. "Two tangos down."

"Report." Dom waited for each operator to report that nothing in their area had changed. Jericho continued to scan the area below with the drone.

"Tangos still on approach, but moving much, much slower." His voice hesitated then he continued, "The lead vampire has stopped, One. Two more are breaking away and heading toward the clearing."

"Shit!" Dom whispered into the mic. "We may have dropped two scouts. Prepare to pull up stakes. We may have to chase these rabbits down." He continued to stare through the optics then keyed his mic again, "Vulture, I need real time live feeds."

Inside the OPCOM Mitchell noted another group breaking away and swinging wide to the south. If they continued on their path, they'd either flank the operators or pass by them well beyond their effective range. "Dammit! Mark, flag those runners and feed the intel to Second Squad."

Major Tufo brought up the screen and placed designators on the group of six that had broken away from the main group. He keyed the commands that sent the intel to the squad. “Done and done.”

A moment later Dom had read the incoming message and keyed his mic. “Sierra Two and Three, break south and stop these asshats before they get past us. Double-time.”

“Copy that.”

Dom couldn’t see or hear the two operators as they broke from the group, but he knew they were on the move, their intercept course set at a sharp angle as they cut along the edge of the creek to cut off the small group of vampires. “Vulture, sitrep.”

“They’re still working their way toward you, but very slowly, One. It’s almost as if they waiting to hear back from the group sent to the clearing.”

“Check for radio traffic. Scan all frequencies.” Dom ground his teeth as he considered the possibilities. If these ‘baby vamps’ were using radios and flanking maneuvers before hitting a town? That didn’t sound like any baby vamp attack he’d ever heard of before.

“Bingo on the radio traffic, One. We have civilian two-ways being utilized in your area.” Jericho switched the coms over so that they could hear the conversation.

“…come in. Dale, are you there?” A moment later the radio crackled to life again. “Will, if you find Dale and he’s okay, give him your radio. We need to know that the coast is clear before we move closer.”

“Will do. We’re almost to the clearing now.”

Dom groaned. He keyed his coms. “Five, if they poke their heads out of that clearing, drop ‘em.”

“Copy that.” Neils scanned the tree line and waited for anything to break through. As soon as the two vampires stepped into the clearing, the first one only took a couple of steps before spotting the charred remains of their compatriots. He turned to run when he burst into orange flames, the silver jacketed round slicing through his midsection. The second vampire stood in shock, his mouth open and eyes wide as his friend fell to the ground in silent hellfire. He didn't have a chance to blink before he met a similar fate, his heart ruptured by the silver round that shredded through his chest. "Two tangos down."

"Second Squad, advance." Dom stood from the edge of the creek and brought the SCAR to his eye, scanning the area before him as he made a tactical advance into the trees.

*****

Jack stepped through the boulder and watched as the last of his team exited, the glowing light fading as Kalen closed the portal. "Kid, one of these days you're going to have to show me how to do that."

"You must be a Gatekeeper in order to—"

"Yeah, I'm sure it's really interesting, but not now." Jack stepped past him and approached his disapproving father-in-law. "As promised."

Viktor stared at the 'team' that Jack brought with him. "These are your warriors?" He raised a questioning brow.

Jack refused to take offense. "The best there are for kicking Lilith's ass. At least, that's what the head elf lady tells me." He waved Viktor onward. "Lead the way."

Viktor turned and escorted the crew inside. Paul immediately came to his feet and stared wide eyed at Jack, his feet stumbling as he stepped back and away from him. "H-how did…where did you find *him* at?"

Viktor rolled his eyes at the bumbling vampire. "He answers

when called."

"Only for a chance at Lilith," Jack corrected. "She's my main priority here."

"Well, she thinks we're going there to install a computer system so that she can watch…something." Foster kept his distance but tried to explain. "You can't just kick in the doors, guns blazing."

"No shit." Jack stared the vampire down. "Well there goes Plan A."

Foster paled and turned wide eyed to Viktor. "Surely he wasn't…"

"No, he wasn't." Viktor pushed past the vampire and to a makeshift table. "Foster gave me a rough layout of the place."

"As best as I could see it, anyway." Paul hurried to Viktor's side, putting as much distance as he could between himself and Jack.

"How did you get a look inside?" Jack closed the distance, putting Foster into a decidedly more uncomfortable state.

"I was on the roof with Rufus before he was captured."

"Tell me everything." Jack stared the vampire down and Foster swallowed hard.

Viktor placed a firm hand on Jack's shoulder. "We are all on the same side here."

"For now." Jack raised a brow at Paul. "Spill it. Everything."

Paul nodded and opened his mouth to speak but Viktor cut him off. "No. We are all on the same team. Not just for now. Not just until we get Rufus back. Not just until Lilith is dead. We are all on the same team. Period."

Jack turned slowly to Viktor, his eyes narrowed. "Apparently you've never been betrayed."

"Apparently you do not realize what it means to be

somebody's Second."

Jack squared his shoulders. "I'll only Second somebody who proves themselves honorable and worthy of my being their Second."

"And you still do not know the whole story. Have you spoken to Rufus? Have you heard his side of this?" Viktor would not be intimidated.

"I don't need to. I know the facts. He took the trust I gave him and he used it against me. He stole from my people and tried to build a Doomsday weapon. He tried to *use* it against wolves at the island." Jack pointed at Viktor. "Don't you get it Viktor? If that damned thing had worked, he could have killed ALL of the wolves there, including me…including Nadia and our baby. Perhaps even you and Natashia."

"But it did not." Viktor crossed his arms and glared at him.

"Only because it backfired on him."

"If I may?" Paul raised his hand like a school boy. "He only had that damnable thing built to battle Lilith."

Jack turned on him so fast that it spooked him. "Yet Lilith wasn't at the island, was she?" Foster shook his head, swallowing nervously. "No, it was only wolves at the island."

"Wolves who had you outnumbered and outgunned," Viktor added. "You surely would have lost had he not…"

"We beat them back without his Doomsday weapon!" Jack yelled. "Face it, Viktor, he's not the same man you once worked with. He's become paranoid and obsessed to the point that he'll lie and steal to meet his own agenda."

Viktor nodded. "And wouldn't you? If it meant staying alive? He's facing the Council, Lilith, and now you. You, who were supposed to be his Second."

"Don't you dare try to turn this around to make him the

victim." Jack turned to face his warriors who simply watched the two going at it. "I can take my team and leave you standing here with nothing but your dick in your hand."

"If it means that you'll do nothing to save Rufus, I'd rather you did." Viktor's voice was low and soft, much more effective than if he had yelled.

Jack had to force himself to slow his breathing, his anger trying to get the better of him. "I told you that we'd help you. But Lilith is our primary goal. If we can stop her, then Rufus isn't in any more danger."

Viktor studied him for a moment then turned to Paul. "What do you say? You are his Second now."

Foster sighed heavily, his head slowly shaking. "I say that it's better than nothing." He faced Viktor and as much as he hated to admit it… "There are few people in this world who scare me as much as he does. I'd rather get what I can from him."

*****

Laura and Derek stayed up into the wee hours of the night talking of dragons and elves and vampires and anything else that Derek could think of to ask her about. As the clock ticked on and the stories unfolded, headlights reflected across the living room windows. Derek picked himself up from the floor and walked to the curtains, pulling them back and staring into the yard. "Looks like James finally pulled himself away from his family." He turned and gave her a lopsided grin. "Somebody must have told him you were in town."

Laura stretched and lifted herself from the couch. "Great. Just remember, don't say anything to him about what we talked about, okay?"

"Like what? That you turned Dad into a werewolf? Or that you're dating a vampire? Or that everything we were ever taught wasn't real really *is* real?"

"Yeah, all that." Laura pulled open the front door and stepped out onto the porch. "Damn they stack it tall out here."

"You kiss your daddy with that mouth, little missy?" James jumped onto the porch and lifted her into a bear hug. "Good to see you again, sis."

"I'd say the same, but I think you cracked a few ribs." She pushed away from him and patted his midsection. "I see married life has made you soft."

"What can I say? I like to eat!" He chuckled as he pushed past her and walked inside. James plopped onto the couch and pulled Laura down beside him. "So tell me all about how things are in D.C. or wherever the hell you're working now. Got a boyfriend yet?" he teased as he pulled her close and tickled her.

She pushed away from him and leaned across the other side of the couch. "Crimeny, James, I'm not fifteen anymore."

"No shit." He gave her a crooked smile. "Fifteen-year-olds don't turn grey." He pointed to her hair and she slugged him in the arm.

"I am *not* turning grey." She pulled her legs up and sat on her feet. "I swear, it's like coming home from college during the holidays around here."

Derek handed James a beer and set one in front of Laura. "Some things never change Punk."

"Some things do. Heidi is expecting again." James popped the top on the beer and took a long pull. "This one makes four."

"You know what causes that, don't you?" Laura teased as she popped open her own beer.

James nodded. "Yeah, I shot the mailman, but she just *keeps* getting pregnant. Maybe it's the UPS driver?" He shot her an evil grin.

"You're horrible."

Derek stretched out on the floor again and watched the two. "Don't let him kid you, Punk. He's proud as punch that he still has lead in his pencil."

James threw the bottle top at him then flipped him the bird. "I'm not that old, butthead."

"You act it sometimes." Derek took a pull from his beer then set it aside.

James sat on the couch, absently peeling at the label of his beer. "So I guess you came out here to say goodbye to Pop?"

Laura gave him a sideways look. "I came out to see him." She shrugged. "He didn't look so bad to me."

James raised a brow but didn't look at her. "Really? Did you talk to his doctors?"

"No, but Dad was talking about maybe coming home." She watched him carefully and watched him simply nod.

"Yeah, he's been saying that ever since he went in this last time. Docs don't think he'll be leaving this time." James pulled the label off and flattened it on his knee. "I thought maybe they could let him come home just to…well, you know."

"To die?"

He finally turned and looked at her. "Yeah. Some place that he's comfortable with. You know, like a hospice or something."

Derek cleared his throat. "They wouldn't allow it. Said something about the pain meds he needs."

Laura nodded. "He didn't use any pain meds while I was there."

James took a pull from his beer then set it on the coffee table. "Yeah, they feed it straight in through his IV now. He kept throwing up the pills." He sighed and shook his head. "He's a tough old buzzard."

"What about Crystal?" Laura couldn't believe the words came out of her mouth until she saw both of her brothers turn to face her. "I just meant…couldn't she help him if he was here?"

James shook his head. "Not with the meds. They're pretty well controlled. I was trying to see if there was a nurse who could come by and…"

Laura reached out and patted his hand. "Don't give up hope. He may well outlive us all."

James gave her a confused look. "Don't count on it, Punkin."

*****

"So how come Admin isn't all over this?" Little John closed the file and shoved it back into the stack next to him.

Spalding rubbed at his eyes and sighed. "Honestly? I think they were ready to write off Apollo as soon as he turned on us. This? This is…low priority. They figure that whoever the shooter is will pop up on radar again soon enough. Then they'll sic us after him and we'll take care of it." He reached for another file and opened it. "I'd rather track the son of a bitch down and take the ass whoopin' to him than wait and see if he tries to hurt anybody else."

John stretched and tried to work the kinks out of his oversized frame. Working from the floor of Spalding's office was just a little too tight. "I can't say that I blame ya." He glanced at his watch and couldn't help but wonder where Brooke might be.

"You don't need to stay and help. I can stay on this."

John shook his head. "Naw, I don't mind. Besides, I'd just try to figure out another way to piss off my sister." He gave him a lopsided grin. "When it comes to death and destruction, I know just what to do. Trying to deal with family?" He shrugged his massive shoulders. "I'm completely lost."

Spalding pushed the file away and ran a hand through his hair. "I wish I knew what to tell you. I mean, I wish there was a quick fix, but there just isn't. She's just going to need some time."

John grunted a laugh. "Like she hasn't had enough of that." He shut the file in his hands and set it in his lap. "She's had since I was ten, I think that's plenty of time."

Spanky nodded. "True, that's her time. Time for her to adjust to what's happened to her, but not time for her to adjust to how to deal with you." He pushed his chair back and eyed Sullivan, his mind trying to find the right words. "John, she's inundated with all these old emotions again. Except here you are…a grown man. You're not ten any more. That brings a whole new set of issues to the table. She has to deal with her immortality, the fact that you've aged and she hasn't. She…" He sighed and tried to find the right words. "I get the impression that her abduction is still a very sore spot with her. Seeing you now…it brings it all to the forefront again and I don't think she wants to have to deal with it."

"Okay, I guess I can buy that. But if you're right, she's having problems dealing with my mortality and her immortality, she needs to realize that I may not be around forever now. Besides aging faster than her, I'm not exactly living a protected lifestyle here."

"True, but you're forgetting, you're wolf now. You age a lot slower. So you have a lot more time than you think. And as long as you're careful, your lifestyle isn't *that* dangerous."

John gave him a smart assed smirk. "Really? You say that to a guy who hunts monsters for a living."

Spalding shrugged. "Hey, it sounded a lot better in my head before it rolled out of my mouth, okay?" He pulled the file back closer and opened it. "Just…give her time. If she doesn't come around, we'll handcuff her to the interrogation table and you can tell her how much you missed her until she either gives in or chews her hand off to escape."

"Gee, thanks, boss."

"Any time."

*****

Samael watched diligently as the vampire walked through the warehouse, his eyes appearing to study the rafters and beams, but darting about as the demon Centurions went about their business. He watched as the intruder paused at key locations and seemed to take his time studying the columns or braces, all the while, the explosive vests were either being manufactured, test-fitted or crated for transportation.

The fallen angel slipped into Lilith's abode and pulled her aside. "I've been watching the undead one. He is studying every step of our undertakings."

Lilith shrugged. "So? What do I care? He is one man."

"He is more than a man. He can…" Samael lowered his voice and glanced out the window again. Satisfied that Rufus was beyond hearing, he continued, "He is a controller of demons. He can control *me*. I do not like what I do not understand."

Lilith tossed aside the maps she had been studying and turned to face him. "So why not call on your brothers and have them deal with him? If he is such a threat, remove him now. We will carry on as originally planned." She watched him carefully. "I'll just be certain to be very careful and not be seen."

Samael rolled the idea around for only a moment before shaking his head. "No. For this to work, we cannot risk you being seen." He fell onto the edge of the bed and folded his wings behind him. “You must remain unseen. The demons will rain down carnage and destruction and then you can step in and order them ‘away’. You will be seen as their savior. In exchange for keeping the demons at bay, they will have to put you in charge of everything. They won’t like it, but the demons will continue their attacks until they do.” He turned and faced her. “It is the only way.”

She smiled and caressed his cheek. “Especially once they see you. Once I order you, the big, bad demon, back to hell…they won’t have a choice but crown me queen.”

Samael nodded, rubbing his cheek against her hand. “Order it and I shall obey.”

“And how long before you can dump this body and obtain one more befitting your true stature?” she rubbed at his neck and shoulders as she whispered in his ear.

Samael shrugged. “A matter of hours I suspect. It will be days though until I can transform it as I did this one.”

“Just be sure and choose a human one this time.” She clucked in his ear. “No more bat wings.”

“White feathers from here on.” He kissed her palm and raised his eyes to meet hers. “But the moment the vampire has the system in place…”

“He will be dealt with.” She gave him a soft smile. “He may be able to control you, but let’s see what he can do when he has a thousand demons attacking all at once.”

*****

Analyst Bob Stevens stared at the screen in front of him and had to remember to close his mouth. He swallowed hard and routed the print command to his local printer. He couldn’t risk anybody stumbling upon his find before he picked it up, and he certainly didn't dare it showing up in the server queue.

He waited while the pages printed then pulled them from the print tray. He thumbed through them and felt his chest tighten. "This can't be right. Director Jameson will flip shit." He shoved the pages into the file folder and clutched it tight to his breast. He stood slowly and peered over his cubicle, paranoia creeping upon him.

Stevens reached across his desk and picked up the other two file folders and wrapped the info he had just printed in between the others. For some reason he felt that if he could bury it, nobody else would be able to see it as he worked his way to the director's office.

As he stepped off the elevator and worked his way around to the open area where the administrative assistant sat, Bob clutched the folders tighter. "I really need to see him."

"He's on a conference call."

Bob stared at the door then back at the assistant. "I can wait." His head bobbed up and down as he shakily sat in a chair.

"He may be a while."

Bob stared, his eyes not really focusing. "This is important." His hands automatically clutched the files tighter.

He had no idea how long he sat outside the office. He fought the urge to open the files and go back over the material that he had found, the information burned into his memory at this point. He vaguely remembered the administrative assistant raising her voice to get his attention.

"He'll see you now." She pointed to the door and Bob slowly stood.

He pushed the large mahogany door open and pulled it shut behind him, his mind racing as he closed the short gap to the man's desk. “Did you find what I wanted?” Jameson didn’t even bother to look up as Bob stopped in front of him.

“Y-yes, sir. That…and more.” He placed the stack of file folders on his desk and stared at the man.

Jameson finally glanced up and noted the pale pallor of Stevens. “Good heavens. You look like you’re about to pass out.”

Bob Stevens swallowed hard and nodded. “I found something that…” He shook his head.

“Well, spit it out, man. Don’t just stand there.”

Bob pushed the short stack of files toward him. “It’s all in there.”

Jameson stared at the stack of folders as if Bob had just placed a flaming bag of dog shit on his desk. “You expect me to dig through all of that now? Just tell me.” He leaned back in his chair and crossed his arms.

Stevens couldn’t find the words. “Do you have any idea what…what we’re…what they’re doing?”

“What *who* is doing? Make sense, man!” Jameson was beginning to lose his temper.

Bob reached into the pile and pulled the fresh printouts. He handed the file to the director and waited while the man opened it and perused the information. Jameson pursed his lips and slowly closed the file. “Where did you find this?”

“You told me to look at our own files. Not just theirs, but other agencies. I did. I found that.” He swallowed hard.

“How?” Jameson tossed the file onto the stack and stared at the analyst.

“How?” Stevens took a half step back. “You mean you already knew about that?”

“Of course I knew. I authorized it.” He sat forward and leaned across his desk. “Do you really think that we could discover that monsters were real and not actually *do* something about it?"

"B-but…they…I mean, the Monster Squad? They do something about it now. Why would we…I mean…"

"Why would we create a *better* monster hunter?" Jameson pushed his chair back from his desk and crossed his legs. He continued to stare at the analyst, watching as the wheels spun in the man's mind. "Think about it, Stevens. Why would we allow monsters to hunt monsters? You read the reports. You know what they're doing. They're playing God. They're deciding who are the good guys and who are the bad guys."

"But, sir, even we have allies that you wouldn't normally consider an ally." He shook his head, his mind trying to wrap around the concept.

"True, but they're *human* allies. Not monsters." Jameson blew out a breath hard and eyed the analyst firmly. "We can't allow the inmates to be running the asylum. The monsters cannot be policing the monsters."

"But…to create…*this*?"

"This? This what? At least they're human." Jameson pulled the file from the stack and opened it. "Project Gladiator is a super soldier program that was shelved in the early Nineties. We simply revived it."

"But, sir…genetically engineered humans?" Stevens' mouth went dry as he tried to speak. "*Are* they human?"

"Of course they're human, Stevens. They're stronger, faster, smarter…and they aren't monsters." He narrowed his gaze at the smaller man. "They're soldiers, and they'll do what they're ordered."

"But—"

"No buts, Stevens." Jameson shut the file and tossed it into his waste basket. "You never saw this information, do you understand me? You aren't cleared for this."

"But, sir—"

"What did I just tell you?" Jameson glared at the man.

Stevens nodded. "Yes, sir, I never saw it. I know nothing about it."

"Very good, Stevens." Jameson waved him out. "I think you have a surveillance party to get ready for, don't you?"

Stevens nodded. "Yes, sir." He backed away slowly.

"Don't let the door hit you on the way out, son."

17

Mitchell adjusted the chair he was in and continued to work the buttons on the arm of his chair. “Dammit! My kingdom for something that worked around here.”

Mark spun in his chair to face him. “Just give the word, sir.”

“It’s easier to do it myself, XO,” Mitchell huffed as he slumped back and crossed his arms. “Pull up the helmet cams from Sierra One. Run it side-by-side with the overhead from the bird.”

“Aye, sir.” Mark punched up the commands and nodded to the tech in the front row. “On my mark. Three, two, one, shift.” Both men switched the feeds and the dual view came up on the large screen above.

Mitchell watched as the live feed from Dom’s helmet camera played out in a green glow, the artificial night vision adjusting contrast much too rapidly as he moved within the trees. Mitchell leaned forward and tried to study the images. “Can you clean that up any?"

"Roger that, Colonel. On it." The tech ran an algorithm that input best guesstimates for the fuzzy data, sharpening the image. "Best we can get, sir."

"Very well." He turned to Tufo, "Distance to the tangos?"

"About a quarter-click, sir. They're slowly moving out to the flanks."

"Feed that data to Dom and his crew. They need to be made aware."

"Roger that." Mark spun back to his console and began typing the data into his keyboard. "Update sent."

Mitchell watched the screen as Sierra One paused and glanced at his ruggedized PDA. He punched a button and glanced at the screen. The coms snapped with static for just a moment then Dom's voice filled the overhead speaker again. "On your toes, ladies. Spread out and contain."

Mitchell watched the heat signatures begin to widen their spread and close the distance to the slowly moving dark targets. "Vulture, let's drop altitude and prepare to provide support."

"Copy that, OPCOM." Jericho didn't complain as Colonel Mitchell seemingly took over operational command. He half expected the man to step in once the team had closed the gap.

Dom's helmet cam slowed, and his fist came up into the frame, indicating the squad should stop. For those within eyesight of him, they would pass on the order to those further out. Stopping the advance, he waited and listened, his ears straining to pick up anything out of the ordinary. He slowly turned his head and closed his eyes. His fist turned into two fingers and he pointed ahead and to his right. He stepped off in the general direction of the noise. "Advancing."

Mitchell watched nervously as the group began moving again,

slowly closing the gap. They should be making contact at any moment. He knew that once they did and the first of the vampires were dropped, the rest would scatter into the wind. With their speed advantage, he could only hope that the Predator could catch openings in the tree canopy to effectively stop the targets.

Dom crested a short rise, his barrel scanning left and right, his night vision scope lighting up the darkest of shadows. He stepped through a thin thicket and was suddenly thrust forward, a grey-white hand grasping his ankle from under the ground and pulling him backward, his forward momentum forcing him face first into the mossy floor of the woods. He grunted as he impacted the floor and tried to roll to the side to bring his attacker into view. The hand continued to pull, effectively pulling the owner up from the dark rich soil as it did so. Almost simultaneously, the other members of the squad swore epithets into their mics as their bodies impacted the earth.

"It's a trap!" Dom leveled his barrel to where he assumed the owner of the arm would be and pumped a half dozen rounds into the soil, waiting for the arm to erupt into orange ash.

He reached for his silver-plated survival knife and thrust it as deeply into the shoulder attached to the offending arm as he could, watching with morbid satisfaction as the flesh immediately flashed into orange flame and ash rose from the soil, a depression forming where the body once lay.

Dom rolled to his side and brought the SCAR to his eye once more, scanning the surrounding area. "OPCOM, Second Actual! It's a trap! They were waiting underground for us."

Mitchell was up from his chair and staring at the satellite feed as the darkened figures converged on the squad, more and more 'bodies' appearing from nowhere and joining those moving en masse. "Good heavens…Vulture! Engage! Repeat, Vulture, engage targets!"

Jericho's voice was stone as he responded, "Negative, Colonel. Tree canopy is too thick to engage tangos."

Mitchell stepped down from his command platform and approached the big screen as dozens of dark figures turned into fifty, then into a hundred. "Oh, my God…"

*****

Jack sat as quietly as he could as he listened to Viktor play out his plan. He really didn't want to listen, but if Lilith truly had hundreds of flunkies working for her at this place, he needed to know every bit that they did. "The two larger…beings should probably head straight to the roof when we get there. They can use the excuse of mounting the satellite dishes and running cables."

Foster stared at the crude drawing of the old auto plant, his eyes studying the exits. "They have multiple guards at each entrance. We'll have to keep them busy so that they don't notice the…big guys."

"The gargoyle and Nephilim."

"All the more reason to keep them hidden until they're needed. If Samael is truly with her, he may be able to sense the offspring of an angel." Viktor held a level gaze on Jack, waiting for him to argue.

Jack merely nodded. "A smart precaution. No sense in tipping our hand."

Viktor blew out a long breath and tapped the drawing. "There are numerous skylights across the ceiling where they can maintain watch. You can give them a sign that means to enter and bring the wrath of the giants with them."

Jack nodded, his eyes studying the drawing. "I think the

screaming and people bleeding will be a good enough sign."

"This is no time for light hearted banter, Jack. We may need to all strike at once in order to save…to take down the demon Lilith." Viktor eyed his son-in-law, waiting.

"Agreed. I'll come up with something that isn't too obvious." He tapped the drawing. "What is this?"

Foster cleared his throat. "That is, what appears to be, an office of some sort. We saw the winged demon exit from there."

"And you think this is their headquarters?"

Foster nodded. "It's the only part of the warehouse that affords any privacy. We saw makeshift bunks set up on this far end here." He pointed to the northern most part of the warehouse. "The equipment that was left appeared to be mothballed, but they were utilizing this area here. We couldn't tell what they were doing."

Jack gave him a skeptical glance. "Why not just move to another skylight and observe until you had a better idea what was going on?"

Foster sighed and shook his head. "Rufus wanted me to attempt to call Damien. When I did…the demon answered."

"The demon answered?" Jack shrugged. "Why the hell would the demon answer?"

"I have a theory on that." Viktor pulled a book from his satchel. "I relieved this from my…well, from a witch." He flipped through pages then laid the book out. "For an angel to manifest on this plane, it must have a willing host. A *body*, if you will. I believe that the demon is actually an angel, and that it took Damien's body."

Jack fought off the urge to laugh. "Wait, a demon isn't an angel. A demon is a twisted human soul. An angel is—"

"A *fallen* angel, Jack." Viktor flipped back through the book and tapped the page. "A third of the angels rebelled after the creation of man and were cast from Heaven. A fallen angel is still an angel."

"So…you're talking one of Lucifer's minions?" Jack raised a brow.

"Technically, Satan gave up the title Lucifer when he fell. He was no longer the light bearer, but yes. One of the angels that fell with the bright and morning star." Rather than explain angelic history, Viktor continued on. "If history and lore are correct, Samael was Lilith's first lover. If I were to bet money, I would bet that the angel is he."

"Okay…so we have this demon bitch, Lilith. We also have a fallen angel named Samael and a couple hundred minions that are most likely demons?" Jack shrugged. "No fucking problem. Nothing my tiny little band of warriors can't handle." He rolled his eyes and glanced at the group who stood and watched the exchange.

"Not a few hundred, Jack." Viktor flipped through the book again and propped it open on a section that dealt with Lilith. "Samael promised her a legion of demons."

"A legion?"

"One thousand." Viktor closed the book and stared at him.

Jack felt his knees grow weak. "I knew I had a bad feeling about this when we left the city." He leaned across the table and lowered his voice, "I did *not* bring these kids here to run some kind of suicide mission!"

"Nor did we." Viktor placed the book back into his satchel and tapped the drawing. "The secret here is to find the lynchpin. That one target that, once it is dropped, the dominos fall with it."

"Great. And how do we find that amongst a thousand demons?" Jack ground his teeth so hard that his jaw ticked.

Foster interjected, "It is either the angel or Lilith. It has to be.

The angel promised the legion to her so he has authority over them. But she is recipient of the legion, so she has control. It *has* to be one or the other."

Jack sighed. "Well I guess that narrows it down." He rubbed a hand across his stubbled chin. "But how do we know which one?"

"We must strike them both at the same time. That is the only way." Viktor stabbed a knife into the paper to emphasize his point. "We strike them both and watch the demons flame out."

Foster nodded. "There is even a small chance that once they do, the humans they inhabit will be restored."

"Joy," Jack groaned. He turned to his crew and motioned them over. "New game plan. Everybody huddle up."

*****

Jim Youngblood sat up in his hospital bed and turned slowly to stare at Crystal sleeping quietly beside him. He smiled as he watched her in the soft glow of the monitors and the silvery shaft of moonlight that beamed through his window.

He turned slowly and dangled his feet from the edge of the bed, feeling the blood flow into his extremities for the first time in a very long time. He held his hand out into the silver-white light of the moon and turned it slowly, watching the shadows play across the surface of his skin. He watched as the shadows formed and disappeared over the thick veins and ridges of his thick hands. He watched the shadows play off of the tubes sticking out of his forearm and he shook his head.

Since nightfall he'd had a surge of energy unlike anything he'd felt in a very long time. He slid gracefully from the edge of the bed and felt the IV tubes tug at him. His first instinct was to pull the damned things from his flesh and toss them aside, but he didn't dare. Should he set off an alarm or worse, waken Crystal, he'd be forced back to bed, and he really didn't want that right now.

He carefully reached across the bed and unhooked the tubes from where they were caught on the rails and lifted them carefully over the mattress. He then turned and took the single step toward the window. He carefully and quietly pulled the curtains back and stared out into the darkness of the night. His eyes rose into the sky and settled on the moon hanging lifelessly in the sky. He could feel a 'pull' from that giant piece of rock hanging up there. He couldn't explain how, or why, he just knew that it was there.

Jim didn't know how long he stood and stared at the glowing orb, but he allowed his mind to drift. He imagined that he was outside, in the woods, naked and running; his heart pounding in his chest as he raced through the woods. He lifted his nose and caught a scent…prey! He didn't know exactly what it was at the moment, but he knew it was food.

He turned and followed the scent, his sharp ears picking up the sounds of a rushed scurrying. Rustling leaves, twigs breaking as something small darted about, trying frantically to dart first one direction then another to escape the certain death that it knew was coming.

As he closed on the sound, his nose picked up a stronger scent. Fear. He now knew what he was chasing. A rabbit. Not a huge meal, but it was red meat nonetheless. He increased his speed and darted between two large pines, his feet gaining purchase in the loose pine needles. He darted under a fallen tree then jumped over a thicket, coming down nearly on top of the startled animal.

Jim saw the fear in its eyes as he suddenly appeared out of nowhere and that fear exhilarated him. He felt his mouth water and his heart rate increase at the potential meal. The rabbit froze for just a moment before darting off, Jim hot on his heels.

He could see the rabbit now, its rear feet kicking up little tufts of pine needles and dirt as it fought like hell to escape, but he knew it was for naught. He had the little creature and it would soon make a nice snack.

He watched the rabbit approach a small fallen branch and he knew it couldn't go under…it had to jump over. He poured on the speed and leapt, his mouth opening and then snapping in the air, closing like a trap on the soft body of the hare as it attempted to escape in mid-jump.

Jim felt himself slide to a stop, the warm blood of the rabbit running down his throat as his jaws closed tighter, snapping the hare's spine, his canines tearing flesh. He trotted off to a small clearing and laid down to enjoy the small snack.

Just as he ripped the head off the rabbit, Jim snapped out of his daydream, his body slowly rocking as his mind sucked back into his body. He glanced about the room and saw that Crystal still slept soundly just feet away. He smiled again and slowly pulled the curtain shut.

Jim Youngblood draped his IV tubes back over the edge of the bed and slipped back into his bed, pulling the covers over his cold body. As he slid down into the bed, he paused. He wiggled his bare toes in the sheets then pulled the covers back to investigate.

At the end of his bed, his feet lay on the bleached white sheets, covered in rich, black soil…pine needles stuck between his toes.

*****

"Hey, wait up. Where you headed?" Little John trotted to catch up with Spalding as the man marched topside.

"I have a theory I want to test."

"Okay. So share." Little John stepped between Spalding and the doorway leading out to the top level of the hangar.

Spalding stopped and stared at him. "Look, Sullivan, this isn't your fight. You should really stay here."

Little John crossed his arms and effectively blocked any way past. "Like hell. You're still my Team Leader. Your fight is my fight."

"No. It isn't." Spalding tried to step past him and found the way blocked. "I mean it, Sullivan. Stand down."

Little John raised his brows at him and cocked his head to the side. "You said you had a theory."

Spalding sighed heavily. "Look…it's just an idea really. But the colonel and XO are both balls deep in an op, so I can't get it approved."

"And…"

"And, if I catch hell over it, I'd rather not catch hell for dragging any of my people with me." Spalding shrugged. "Besides, it's a wild goose chase at best."

"I like chasing geese." Little John shot him a crooked grin. "I guess I'm in."

"No, John, look…"

"Never leave a man behind." He turned and opened the door for Spalding, ushering him out. "If you're about to run out and do something stupid? Try and get rid of me."

Spalding walked slowly toward the armory. "Look, this is a long shot, but…I was just thinking, Bigby was an operator. SAS, true, but an operator is an operator at his core. If he was the one who pulled the trigger on Apollo, maybe if I go back there and try to put myself in his shoes, I can figure out where he went."

"I thought the techs scoured the area and came up empty?"

Spalding stopped and turned to him. "That's the thing, the trail is never completely empty, is it? I mean, not to a trained eye. The techs are just techs. They're no operators."

Sullivan nodded. "Okay, I'll grant you that. But buddy, it's the middle of the night. It's dark as hell out there."

"Exactly!" Spalding slapped his shoulder. "The same conditions that he was in when he pulled the trigger. He probably didn't know the area well enough to have an escape plan. Neither do I. So…I go out there, try to put myself into the same mindset and then take off into the woods. Take the path that *I* would take. See where that leads me. Every so often I stop and check for signs."

Sullivan slowly nodded. "You realize this is a one in a million, right?"

Spalding shrugged. "It's all I got right now. I can't just give up and wait for the bastard to come back and try to hit us again."

Sullivan fell into step behind him as Spalding headed for the armory again. "And you really think he will?"

"He blames us for everything. We're the reason that his old CO is pushing up daisies. We're the reason that Apollo turned on them in the end. We're the reason that all of their wolves got gunned down. He's out there right now, alone and pissed and plotting revenge. I guarantee it."

"You sound awfully confident." Sullivan stopped as they reached the armory. "How can you be so sure?"

"Because it's what I would do if I were him."

*****

Dom fought off the urge to panic as multiple hands thrust up from the earth like slender mushrooms, fingers grasping at empty air as he and his crew slowly closed in on each other, silver rounds firing into the soil. Occasionally, the owner of a set of hands would go up in orange ash leaving a depression in the soil as their body disintegrated. "Second Squad, converge on me." Dom spun a slow circle, his suppressed SCAR pumping whispered round after whispered round into the soil around him.

"Look alive, Second Squad. Tangos closing fast on your twenty," Jericho's voice echoed Mitchell's warning from just moments before.

"Sierra Two, Sierra Three, have you neutralized the flanking tangos?" Dom tried to keep his voice calm as he called Marshall and Wallace.

He was about to call a second time when his earpiece finally came alive with the sound of muted gunfire and Marshall breathing hard while trying to respond. "Negative, One. Flanking group maneuvered us into an attempted trap. Clearing our way back now."

"Dispatch with all due diligence. Converge on me, ASAP!" Dom slapped a fresh magazine into the heavy SCAR and brought the scope back up to his eye. "We're about to have a shitload of company, boys. Mow 'em down!"

His earpiece erupted with a cacophony of 'Copy that' and 'About damn time' as the vampires broke through the tree line. Dom brought his barrel to bear on each of the forward most vampires, converting each to a pile of glowing ash as they ran to intercept him.

"Sierra One, drop back your position five-zero yards to the southeast. There's a clearing where Vulture can assist." Jericho scanned all of the video feeds that the Predator had fed since being airborne and the clearing he directed them to, while small, was by far the closest.

"Copy that, Vulture!" Dom began backing up as he continued

sending hot, silver coated lead toward the onrushing attackers. "You heard the man, fall back."

Each operator began back stepping, averting their eyes from the oncoming targets just long enough to ensure they didn't step into the waiting hands of a buried tango. Hammer felt a hand grip his BDU trousers and he reacted so quick that his arm was a blur. He pulled his knife, cut the offending hand off at the elbow, and re-sheathed his blade before the next attacking vampire could advance more than a few feet. The handless stub quivered violently before bursting into flame then orange ash rose from the hole in the ground.

As the operators cleared the line of buried vampires, Dom keyed his coms again, "UV grenades!"

Each operator deployed a grenade. Some close to handle the vampires still in the ground, other threw theirs into the oncoming crowd. The operators all turned and double timed it toward the clearing as the quick succession of UV blasts bought them a few precious moments of time.

"Vulture, get your bird ready to lay down cover fire!" Dom yelled into the mic.

"Standing by." Jericho had the Predator in a tight circular flight path ready to pull out and strafe the northwest tree line of the clearing once the team had broken clear. He watched the same satellite feed that Mitchell and the OPCOM were watching, the heat signatures of the squad quickly closing the gap on the clearing. "You're almost there, Sierra One. Just the other side of the dry creek bed."

Jericho saw the creek bed ahead and pushed himself harder. He knew that the clearing would be the only thing that would buy them a reprieve. They needed the cover fire of the drone to thin the herd or his team would be hamburger. "Don't let up 'til you're on the other side of that clearing. Put some distance between yourself and the drones field of fire." Dom leapt and jumped the dry creek bed. He pushed hard and came out of the tree line in a roll, tumbling and coming up on his knees.

He brought the SCAR back up to his eyes and scanned the trees, watching as his team each jumped the dry creek. Each man broke through the trees and into the clearing, establishing a staggered formation as they began to work their way back.

Mitchell's voice broke through the coms, "Sierra One, cover your six!"

Dom instantly spun, his SCAR scanning the trees behind them. Movement deep within the shadows of the woods left him scanning left to right, but with no clear shot. "OPCOM, no clear target."

"Those woods are alive with tangos." Mitchell's voice gave away the tension he felt.

"Two by two formations, each group take a quadrant." Dom pointed to Hammer. "You and I will each take a quad."

Neils smiled as he slapped a fresh magazine into his carbine. "Roger that, boss man." He dropped to his knee and leveled his M4 on the trees ahead of him.

"Dammit, Jones, we could really use some backup about now," Dom cursed through gritted teeth.

"Vulture going hot," Jericho announced as a sound ripped through the night sky. What always reminded Dom of a giant zipper being unzipped cut through the air, red tracers leaving a trail of death as the woods erupted into an explosion of leaves, pine needles and bark. Twigs, small branches, and soil flew into the air as hundreds of rounds ripped into the stand of trees opposite the clearing. Dom could see dozens of plumes of orange ash rise into the air as the Predator turned and prepared for another pass.

"Now that's what I'm talking about." He brought the SCAR back to his eye and watched for more plumes of ash. He didn't expect to see the line of angry vampires break through the trees and make a rush for the operators in the middle of the clearing…

*****

Loren the Wyldwood pulled her cloak tighter and shrugged her shoulders, allowing the hood to cover her face more. She could barely see as she tried to maneuver through the torch lit cave. The dripping water was glacial and sent a chill through the air that bit her skin even from the protection of the heavy material she wore.

She paused at a Y in the path and looked for some kind of sign showing her which direction she should go. She looked along both walls, the ceiling, the floor…nothing could be found. "Allister, where are you?" Her voice was barely a whisper, but the fog from her breath carried on the small currents of air.

"Where I always am."

She spun and nearly tripped on the loose rock of the cavern floor.

"Who dares disturb me in my own domain?"

Loren stood erect and lifted the hood from her face. "It is I, Allister. Loren, of the Greater Elves."

The griffin stepped from the shadows, its nails clicking on the stone floor. "So it is." He cocked his head and eyed her warily. "You've aged well, elf."

"As have you." She bowed slightly, her eyes never leaving his.

"Now you may feel free to leave." He turned with a fluid motion that belied his massive size and slipped back into the shadows of the cavern.

"Wait. Allister, please." She stepped forward to follow him

and paused, her eyes unable to focus in the darkness. "I must speak with you."

"And so you have. You may feel free to leave me now." His voice sounded far away, but she knew that he was still close…watching her.

"I am in need of your talents. Your wisdom." She listened intently, straining her ears in the underground cavern to discern anything. A scrape of his nails, the inhalation of breath, the swish of his mighty tail…any sign to indicate where he was. "The demon queen has returned."

"Impossible." His voice sounded close, but the echoes made it impossible for even her to discern where he was. She knew it was just one of his many talents, but it caused an unease that she simply couldn't stand.

"It is true. She has been made whole."

"Again, impossible. The cardinal assured me that she would be sent to the four corners of the known world." He suddenly appeared from behind a rock outcropping, his mighty bird-like head twitching as his eyes studied her.

"It is truth. I have seen it. I have already assembled a group of warriors to meet the threat."

"So why have you come to search me out?" She could see his tail swishing behind him, curiosity eating at him.

"Because they need your guidance." She stepped closer, her hands held outward, pleading. "They need your wisdom."

His massive body leapt up onto the outcropping, his feline like legs gripping the rock under their claws, his wings spread to keep him steady. "And why would I do this?"

"Because you want her destroyed as much as anybody." Loren gave him a knowing look, her eyes probing his own.

"I have accepted my fate." He spread his wings wide and

stood on his hind legs. "I have my library. What more could I want?"

"You've had how many thousands of years to study these ancient writings? Surely you've memorized it all by now." Loren shook her head. "You've secluded yourself to this place with nothing but your scrolls…aren't you the least bit curious what *new* knowledge there is to learn?"

"Bah! All that is fit to learn was writ eons ago." He hissed at her and settled back onto the outcropping.

Loren crossed her arms and smiled at him. "Truly? You think that nothing worth learning has been writ since the days of Alexander? My, my, talk of hubris."

"It is not hubris when speaking of the wisdom of others."

"It is not wisdom, dear Allister. It is the philosophical meanderings of humans. Humans long since dead and buried." She opened her arms and spun a slow circle. "Imagine the great things writ since you raided the library of Alexandria! The thousands of years of ideas, of technology of…"

"Technology?" Allister stepped down from the outcrop and slowly moved toward her. "Tell me of this."

She smiled again and sighed. "Oh, the wondrous things that humans have invented since the days of the Empire. They have flying machines now."

"Bah. Any bird can fly."

"They have horseless carriages."

"Horses are better eaten than used for pulling carriages. Tell me something to whet my mental appetites."

Loren nodded knowingly. "These days, men can remove the beating heart from one man and place it into the chest of another and give life. They perform surgeries daily without infection. They have almost conquered all known diseases. They have ships that can cross the entire world in days rather than years. They have sent men to the moon and walked upon it."

Allister narrowed his gaze on her and slowly shook his head. "You lie."

Loren's features hardened. "I cannot, and you know it."

"A man on the moon?"

"Many men. They have even built machines that go to other worlds and report to them like sentinels."

Allister sat back and nodded. "Perhaps there are *some* things still left to learn."

"So you'll help me?"

Allister stood and spread his wings. "If it means finally destroying the demon bitch that cursed me to *this*…yes."

18

"What a clusterfuck." The technician didn't realize he'd spoken aloud until Mitchell turned a disapproving eye toward him.

"Cut the chatter and let's see what kind of support we can provide." He spun his chair to Tufo. "Do we have any assets in the area?"

"Negative, sir. Not even a repair facility within range." He shook his head forlornly. "They're on their own."

"How soon before we could get First Squad on scene?"

Mark sighed heavily and pulled his headphones off. "Too long. Whatever they're going to do, they're going to have to do it with the resources at hand."

Mitchell cursed and spun his chair back to the big screen. "Give me a grid matrix view from their helmet cams. I want to see what they're seeing. Move the satellite feed and the drone feeds to the smaller screens."

"Yes, sir." The technician began tapping furiously at his keyboard and the feeds switched on the large screen before him. He watched nervously as the vampires broke through the tree line and rushed the circle of operators in the open. "Jesus Christ, Jericho! Bring the rain! Bring the fuckin' rain!" He pounded the side of his chair as he waited for the massive C-130 to rain down silver plated terror from the twin mounted chain guns.

"Bringing the rain, Colonel, but be advised, the targets are too close to the…"

"Just do it!" Mitchell interrupted.

All eyes were glued to the screens above as the trees erupted behind the advancing vampires, orange tracers looking very much like liquid fire falling from the heavens. Plumes of ash and smoke rose from the woods surrounding the clearing and the helmet cam views showed the operators continuing to fire into the onslaught of vampires.

The Predator drone designated Vulture came in for a low pass between the operators and the rain of hellfire from above, slicing a wide swath through the advancing horde. Those not immediately incinerated slid to a stop and stared both ahead and behind them as their compatriots met the true death. Some broke and ran for the far edge of the clearing, others stood and stared, picked off by the human hunters while yet others still advanced, fearing their master more than death.

Mitchell watched in fascinated horror as two vampires grabbed a third and literally flung him past the others and directly into the circle of operators. The vampire rolled with the landing then came to his feet ready to strike. Before anyone could turn to confront the intruder, it sprung, tackling Hammer. The pair rolled away from the group as the vampire slashed and bit at the man.

Neils tried to hold the creature's arms away and work a knee up between the two in order to push the gnashing face further from his face and neck. “A little help here!”

Dom shot a glance at the two then swung his barrel toward the vampire. “Stay low!” He snapped off a single round then swung his barrel back to his quadrant, picking his targets with care, ensuring the lead vampires were the ones he ashed.

Neils came to his feet spiting as blood, gore, and ash rained down upon him. “Thanks. I think.” He scooped his rifle back from the ground and slapped a new magazine in, charging it as he brought it to his eye. “Ya think next time you could try for a body shot?”

Dom shrugged, a stupid grin crossing his face. “I was aiming for his body. Guess I missed.”

Neils shot him a worried look and turned back to the task at hand. He was running dangerously low on ammo and feared that the other operators must be as well. “I’m about to have to switch to my pistol.”

“We’ll use our damned knives if we have to,” Dom spat as another vampire fell close to their makeshift perimeter. “This is getting nuts. Did they turn the entire town?”

Just as quickly as the attack started, the vampires stopped coming. It was as though they all ran through the meat grinder and came out hamburger on the other end. Dom continued to stare through his scope into the tree line as smoke and ash blew across the clearing. “OPCOM, Sierra One, I think we’re clear.”

Mitchell zoomed in with the satellite feed and watched as the horde dropped back further into the trees, maintaining their circle around the operators. “That’s a negative, Sierra One. Tangos have dropped back but they are still on—”

“Stand by!” Dom interrupted. He slowly came to his feet and stared at something his mind simply couldn’t wrap around. In the shadows of the trees something was moving, waving back and forth. He brought his scope back up to his eye and stared at the white flag swinging with purpose. "Hold fire." He turned to Hammer and tapped his shoulder. "You seeing what I'm seeing?"

"If you're seeing a white flag, then yeah." Hammer came up from his kneeling position and rested his rifle at the ready. "Damndest thing I've ever seen."

"Second Squad…I can't believe I'm saying this, but hold fire."

Dom watched as a lone figure stepped from the woods, the white flag waving over their head. The figure strode carefully toward the team and slowed their approach as it came into view. What appeared to be a young woman held the flag, her eyes darting from hunter to hunter. "*Parlez*?"

Dom looked to Hammer and shrugged. "English, sweetheart."

She cleared her throat nervously and stuck the stick in the dirt. "I have come to invite your leader to speak with our master in order to prevent the unnecessary loss of any more lives." She glanced to the edge of the trees and nodded slightly. "There are many more of us out there that even your…*thing* can't see." She pointed upward toward the drone.

"Just means more work for us, darlin'. It's all in a day's work." Dom heard a magazine slam home and the charging handle rack on a rifle behind him. "My men and I have faced much worse than this."

The female vampire shifted uncomfortably and glanced back toward the trees. She quickly turned to Dom, her voice pleading, "Please, sir, just speak with him."

"Unless he's a *Lamia Beastia*, I got nothing to say." Dom rested his arms on his rifle as he glared at the woman in the moonlight. "And if he were *Beastia*, he wouldn't be out here munching on folks."

She turned back to the trees and stared at it again, obviously communicating with somebody, but how? She lowered her head and nodded. "You were given a chance. Remember that." She turned and pulled the stick from the ground, the white flag dragged behind her.

Dom watched her walk back as Hammer's rifle barrel came into view. He gently placed a hand on the barrel shroud and pulled it down. "Let her go."

"We're just gonna have to kill her later."

"True enough. But I'll honor the white flag until she's clear." Dom turned to his men and made a circular motion with his hand. "Rack 'em and stack 'em. Prepare to loose the hounds of war."

"Hoo-yah!"

*****

The van rocked as Viktor brought it to a stop near the abandoned auto factory. All eyes peered through the tinted windows to size up the facility. "How are we going to do this? That place is huge." Brooke felt a shiver as she realized the enormity of the building they were about to enter.

"They're all in this main building over here." Foster pointed to the only structure with lights on. "As we get closer, you'll see the guards at the doors."

"Remember the plan." Jack stiffened as he eyed his crew. For the most part, they seemed unfazed, but Brooke's nervousness bothered him. She was used to operating alone and on a much smaller scale. "Stick with your battle buddy. He'll keep you alive."

Her eyes continued to stare at the building but she nodded slightly. "Battle buddy, got it."

As Viktor pulled the van into the parking lot a rental truck pulled out from the side of the building and drove past them. The driver seemed unperturbed by their presence. Foster watched the truck pull out on to the street and disappear at the next corner. "I wonder what that was all about?"

Viktor snapped his fingers in front of the vampire's face. "We have a job, remember?" He pulled the van up beside the largest double doors and killed the engine. Opening the doors, he noticed the two guards simply stood at their post. His best chance for pulling this off was to immediately act as though he had done this numerous times before. He walked to the doors and faced the largest of the two guards. "Is this where we're to install the system?"

The guard shot him a questioning look then glanced at the other guard. Both men shrugged.

"Cat steal your tongue?" Viktor asked louder. "We're to install satellite feeds and servers. Somebody wants a state of the art server here."

The smaller guard held up a finger. "Wait one." He stepped inside and a few moments later returned with Rufus in tow.

"*Mon ami*! You have finally arrived." Thorn grasped Viktor and kissed both cheeks. "You are truly a sight for sore eyes, my friend."

Viktor offered a rare smile and a slight bow, doing his best to hide his shock that Rufus was not in a cage. "We have brought all of the equipment you requested."

"Excellent." Thorn stepped past him and barely cast a glance at Paul and Jack as they unloaded large tubs and crates from the back of the van. "The sooner the better. Get your people moving and in place. Time is definitely of the essence."

Viktor nodded and turned to the assembled crew. "You heard

the man, get moving. You two," he pointed to Azrael and Phil, "on the roof, now. Start installing the dishes. The rest of you, get the stuff inside."

The guards held the doors open as the work crew began unloading and carrying in boxes. Demon centurions came out and carried in the rest of the material. Viktor walked slowly through the facility, his eyes taking in everything. He tried to get an approximate head count on the number of demons there but quickly lost track with all of their movements. It certainly didn't *feel* like a thousand souls, but he'd been wrong before.

Thorn clapped him on the back. "I've been looking over the place. I think if you bring the cabling in from up there and along those beams, you can easily feed them down these two columns and into that office."

Viktor nodded as he glanced about, trying to get a feel for the place. "And the…customer?"

"She is in her office. She won't be a problem as you are working, I assure you." Thorn smiled as the two walked toward the office area.

"And her…consort?"

Thorn paused, his painted on smile unwavering. "He is…about." He nodded slightly as the two began again. "He's easy to spot, I promise."

Viktor pulled Thorn aside and turned him around, pointing up to the rafters. He lowered his voice and leaned in close. "Jack came up with an idea that may assist in our endeavors." He continued to point up and into the overhead, his fingers pointing out different areas. "There are explosives placed inside the monitors and the server equipment. If it doesn't kill them, hopefully it will stun them long enough for our team to strike."

Rufus nodded and quickly turned him back toward the office.

"You were wise to bring him."

Viktor grunted. "That is yet to be seen."

"Come, let me introduce you to our queen." Thorn maintained his façade as the two approached the offices. He opened the door and allowed Viktor to enter first. "And this is where you will be installing the equipment," he announced a bit too excitedly.

Lilith turned from the window and smiled at the tall dark haired man. "And who have we here?" She strode purposefully toward him, her movements fluid.

Rufus stepped between them and bowed slightly. "Lilith, my queen, allow me to introduce one of my oldest and most trusted friends, Viktor Verissimo Veranus."

Lilith held her hand out for Viktor to take it. He bowed slightly and kissed the back of her hand. "Your highness."

She eyed him suspiciously then broke into a toothy grin. "You're a wolf."

Viktor nodded. "As is my father. I am a natural born."

"Interesting." She eyed Rufus with a raised brow. "Natural enemies and you're both *friends*?"

Rufus simply smiled and waved a hand toward Viktor. "Perhaps my friend would prefer to tell how our friendship bloomed?"

Lilith turned to Viktor, skepticism in her eye. "Yes, please do."

Viktor shrugged. "It is a very long story, and I wouldn't dare bore you with the details. But the short version is…both my family and Rufus valued human life. We made an oath to provide protection to him and he to us. We kept other wolves from his properties and he kept other vampire familias from our territories." Viktor shrugged. "I was assigned to his personal protection and over time we became friends."

"He was my Second for a very long time," Rufus stated proudly.

Lilith turned to Thorn and narrowed her gaze. "You both *valued* human life and yet here you are, assisting me?"

"*Oui*," Rufus agreed as though it made perfect sense. "Valuing human life doesn't mean they don't need to be ruled. All sheep need a shepherd. As we agreed upon before, the *familias* would need assurances that their holdings would not be lost and that their personal human familiars wouldn't be killed." He searched her face to ensure that she remembered their bargain.

"True enough. We did agree upon such terms." Lilith spun back to Viktor and took his hand. "Show me what you have brought."

Viktor lead her to the door and pointed out the crates and boxes being placed just outside the office. "We have eleven monitors for you. A spare in case we have issues with one…and servers and power supplies and everything we should need to have you up and running soon."

She stepped back and waved him through the door. "Then let me stay out of your way. You have work to do." She turned and glided out the door nearly silently.

Viktor turned to Rufus and gave him a questioning look. "You are not a prisoner?"

Rufus shook his head. "Perhaps I would have been, but I offered to assist her in her attempt to take over the world."

"You…" Viktor found the words stuck in his throat. "You are assisting her?"

"Just as you are." Rufus patted the man's shoulder. "Stick with your plan. It's definitely on the right track." He gave him a slight wink as he stepped toward the door.

*****

Laura was shaken awake by Derek, a concerned look across his features. “Get up, Punk.”

She sat up and rubbed at her eyes groggily. “What’s wrong?”

Derek thrust a cup of coffee toward her. “We need to get going pretty quick.”

She took the mug and stared up at him through bloodshot eyes. “What’s the rush? You kicking me out already? I just got here.” She smiled to herself as she sipped the bitter wake-up juice.

“It’s Dad.”

Her eyes shot open and she scooted to the edge of the mattress, her coffee mug set on the nightstand. “What’s happened?”

“They can’t keep him in bed. He keeps swearing that he’s fine and that he wants to go home.” Derek pulled his t-shirt over his head as he spoke through the door. “Crystal wants us down there to talk some sense into him.”

“Oh, my God…” Laura scooted off the bed and took a quick gulp of the coffee. She threw on her jeans and pulled a shirt from her bag. She stuffed it into her jeans and started pulling her boots on when Derek pushed open her door again. “Gah! For crying out loud, drag a comb through your hair or something. You look like you’ve been scared half to death.”

“I just woke up, you jackass. Give me a minute.”

She threw a dirty sock at him as he scooted back through the door. She took another drink of the coffee and pushed her way into the bathroom. One look in the mirror and she knew why he had teased her. She grabbed her brush and pulled her back and into a pony tail. No time for anything fancy today. She threw on her Bronco’s ball cap and looked in the mirror. Other than some darkness under her eyes, she didn't really look any worse for wear.

"We're stopping at a real coffee house on the way there." She finished the mug o' mud that Derek had given her and set the cup in the sink. She noticed all of the empty beer bottles scattered around the living room and poked her brother. "You'd better hope Dad doesn't get to come home today. He'll kill you for leaving all the dead soldiers out on the battlefield."

Derek groaned and grabbed the kitchen trash, sliding empty bottles into it. "Go warm up the car."

"It's fuel injected. It doesn't need to warm up." She scooped her keys from the coffee table and headed for the door. "But I'll wait for you out there."

Derek played on his phone while she drove and didn't really speak until she pulled out of the drive through all night doughnut shop. He finally put his phone down and turned to her. "Do you really think there's a chance they'll let him leave?"

She shrugged. "I don't know, D. If they decide to run a bunch of tests, then no. But if he insists on going home, I don't think they can stop him."

"Crap." He ran a hand through his dark hair and stifled a yawn. "I'd hate to think what could come of this. It's one thing if he slowly started recovering but for it to happen seemingly overnight?"

She shrugged. "He was in a lot rougher shape than I thought." She took a sip of her latte and didn't taste it for the fear running through her. What if they tested his blood and found the virus? What if a lab tech accidentally got infected? How would she explain to the squads how a wolf was accidentally created in her home town without having been attacked?

"You couldn't have known, Punk. Even Jimmy didn't want to tell you how bad he'd gotten," Derek's voice was soft and apologetic.

"But if I'd known, I could have come sooner." She pulled into the parking lot and shut off the Jeep. "I tried to come home about six months ago but…" Her voice trailed off and she averted her eyes.

"It's okay. I understand. You had to save the world from monsters and shit." He shot her a crooked grin.

Laura shook her head. "No. Actually I'd quit at probably the worst possible time." She turned and faced him. "But we were facing probably one of the worst possible situations and I was afraid. If something happened to me? I'd never be able to make it to dad in time and…"

He reached out and gripped her hand. "Hey, you made it in time. He's still kicking. And he wants to get the hell out of there."

She looked out the window and the deep black of the sky. "Why couldn't he have waited until morning?"

Derek laughed. "It's Dad. 3AM *is* morning!" He opened the door and stepped out of the Jeep.

Laura got out and walked to the doors of the hospital. A creepy feeling fell over her as she entered the foyer of the hospital and the reception desk sat empty.

*****

"Odds are slim we'll actually find anything, you know that, right?"

Spalding turned his eyes from the road and grunted. "That's the fourth time you've said that since we left."

"I just don't want you to get your hopes up." Little John held onto the Oh-Shit handle as Spalding took the turn into the industrial complex. He relaxed when the truck straightened out then stiffened again. "Whoa!" He slapped Spalding's arm and pointed. "Lights."

Spalding killed the headlights and let off the accelerator, allowing the truck to coast along the empty paved street. "Nobody's supposed to be there." He pulled the truck to the side of the road and jumped the concrete curb, letting it come to rest on the dirt shoulder.

"You don't think our shooter would be stupid enough to return here, do you?" Little John reached for the rifle in the back seat of the truck came to his knee across the console. He poked his head out of the sunroof and brought the rifle scope to his eye.

"I have no idea who it could be. Hell, it could be teenagers coming up here to drink and get laid." Spalding killed the engine and hit the button for the window. He watched from a distance but couldn't make out anything discernible. "See anything?"

"I've got two moving near the gate." John slid back down from the sunroof, his jaw set. "They're armed."

Spalding rubbed at this chin, his gears turning. "By all rights we should call this in and get the team together."

John gave him a knowing look. "So they can scatter like roaches before we can get back?"

Spalding glanced back up the hill toward the warehouse. "I guess if we were quiet, we could take a look. Get an idea how many we're talking about."

"And kill them." John shot him a wink.

"Let's see who they are first." Spalding reached behind him and grabbed his own rifle. Since so many operators had made the switch to M4s, he found himself grabbing the familiar rifle rather than using the venerable P90. He still often carried one slung to his back as they were lightweight and delivered a hell of a punch, but when you really wanted to reach out and touch somebody, the extra power of the 5.56 round made him much more comfortable.

Both men slipped from the truck and Little John brought the heavy SCAR to his shoulder, his eye scanning the area as the two made their way up the hill in a crouched advance. The waist high grass rustled against their uniforms as they moved silently up the hill, using what little cover there was to conceal their movement.

John slipped in behind a rather large oak tree and stole a quick glance toward the gate. Both guards had their backs turned to the drive and seemed to be in a heated discussion. He motioned to Spalding to advance and watched as the man slithered up the hill, the grass barely moving as he settled in next to a small stand of brush. He brought his scope to his eye and scanned the area.

John stole another quick glance and motioned to Spalding who shook him off. Using hand signals he indicated that another guard was on the roof. Little John settled in low on the tree and pulled the suppressor from his pack. He quickly attached the canister to the end of the .308 and slipped around the base of the tree. The grass concealed him as he scanned the rooftop. Finding the guard sitting at the peak, the orange glow of a cigarette flaring as he inhaled, Little John adjusted his scope for distance and elevation. There was no wind to speak of as he settled the crosshairs on the guard.

Spalding watched through his own scope as the guard's head exploded in a silvery mist when the SCAR coughed its deadly round. The bloody spray reflected the small amount of moonlight and made the spray appear silver rather than pink. He nodded with satisfaction as the man slumped and fell to his side. He gave a thumb's up to Spalding and the two turned their attention to the guards at the gate.

Spalding gave the hold sign and the two would-be snipers waited to ensure that another guard didn't appear to throw a monkey wrench into the works. Once he was satisfied that the immediate area was clear, he signaled Sullivan. Almost simultaneously, both rifles spit their deadly silver plated rounds, decimating their targets. Spalding took the head shot and Little John went for the heart. Both shots struck with deadly accuracy.

The two men scrambled to their feet and made for the gate. Spalding pushed one side open first and grabbed a guard by the ankles, dragging him out and into the tall grass. John grabbed the other guard by the belt and carried him out, stacking him unceremoniously next to his partner. "I think it's safe to assume our shooter isn't alone."

Spalding glanced over his shoulder and stared at the building, the rows of shipping containers still in position in front. "What do you want to bet they have a whole new army?"

"Ya think?"

"Well, that is the way our luck runs, ain't it?" Spalding slipped back across the open yard and fell into the shadows of the shipping containers. Little John cleared the next corner and the two advanced. "We may have no choice but to engage."

"You don't call those three guards we shot engaging?" John shot him a smirk.

"That's not engaging the whole damn lot of them." Spalding slipped ahead and cleared the next corner. They could hear the sounds of construction and people talking. Spalding slipped in next to the building and peered through a window. The sight of numerous people within the building sent a chill through him. "Fuck, if I'd had any clue, I'd have brought coms."

"Given a choice, I'd have brought the rest of the team."

*****

Bob Stevens knew he was risking more than his career as he slipped the keycard into the reader and pushed open the doors. He had the keycard made for an employee that transferred almost immediately to a field office. With instructions to destroy the card and delete the permissions, Bob thought then that it might one day come in handy. He never actually thought that he'd be the one using it.

He pulled the hood up and over his face before approaching the building. He knew where almost all of the cameras were and he prayed that his precautions would protect him. When the door light turned green, he let loose the breath that he hadn't realized he had been holding and quickly pushed his way through before he could change his mind. As soon as the door shut behind him, he turned and began taking the stairs two at a time.

He finally reached the top floor and pulled a small pouch from his pocket. He fumbled with it as he walked across the padded carpet floor toward the director's office. He pulled the lock picks from their pouch and quickly went to work on the door. He prayed the entire time that the director wasn't so security minded that he had different locks installed. Bob knew he could pick the standard locks used throughout the building, but the *director's* office?

He nearly fainted when the lock clicked and allowed him to turn the barrel within the cylinder. He pulled the lever and pushed the door open slowly. He glanced around the darkened office and looked for anything out of the ordinary; red lights in the corners or along the floors that would indicate a laser grid security system. Heat scanners or pressure monitors in the floor. He paused just inside the door and felt his shoulders slump. He'd watched too many spy movies.

He quickly slid in behind the desk and began tugging at drawers, a penlight pinched tight between his teeth. He scanned the files in the desk drawer and came up empty. He reached for the other side of the desk and found the drawer locked. He quickly dug out his lock picks and went to work again.

He could feel the sweat forming above his lip and across his forehead as he worked the lock, a sigh of relief escaping as the lock turned and the drawer slid open. He pulled it out and began digging through them. Nothing on Project Gladiator that he could find. Bob sat down in the director's chair and glanced around the darkened office. "If I were a paranoid dictator, where would I hide shit?"

His eyes fell on a portrait of the president on the wall. Bob's head cocked sideways as he noted the deep shadow along one side of the portrait. "Surely not." He pushed up from the chair and went to the photo. He tried to lift it and found it attached to one side with a hinge. The frame pulled out and Bob stood facing a safe built into the wall. "Fuck me."

Fingerprint scanner, retina verification, and a combination lock all built into one safe? How paranoid was this guy? Bob's shoulders slumped as he pushed the frame back into place.

He turned for the door and paused. His computer! How could he have been such a dolt?

He slipped back into the chair and pushed the power button. He waited for the login prompt to come up and smiled when it asked for the login and password.

Being a computer analyst for the agency had its perks. Having had to repair the man's computer more than once, Bob had become familiar with the pattern he used for his passwords. He clicked his username and tried the last known password that he had stolen from his login logs. The screen instantly came to life and Bob smiled to himself again. Even if the old bastard deleted the files, Bob could reconstruct them. Nobody bothered to use the DoD shredder that came installed on their computers. They simply moved everything to their 'trash' and then on occasion deleted those files. That meant they still existed.

Bob clicked away at the computer and grunted happily when he hit pay dirt. He pulled the USB thumb drive from his keychain and plugged it in, transferring the files to the thumb drive before shutting everything down and slipping the drive back onto his keychain.

He stopped at the door and pulled the hood back over his face before slipping out into the lobby. He purposely left the director's office door open. He wanted him to know that somebody had been in his office…even if he honestly thought there was nothing to be had.

19

Mitchell watched the monitors as the drone made slow circles above the battlefield. “Keep ‘em busy, boys. We got another drone headed your way.”

“Copy that, OPCOM. Be advised, we’re running dangerously low on ammunition here.” Dominic’s voice sounded tinny coming across the overhead speakers. “I’m beginning to wish I’d have listened to what the little vamp had to say.”

“It wouldn’t be anything good, Sierra One.” Mitchell studied the radar feeds and knew that it would be too long before the second drone could be onsite.

“Any idea how many are in the shadows, OPCOM?”

“Negative. They just keep coming. We can’t even pinpoint a staging area. It’s like they’re just materializing in the woods and advancing on your position.”

Marshall nudged Dominic. “See all that dirt on the bodies?

You don't think they buried themselves out there just waiting for us, do you?"

"I have no idea, Two." Dom pulled rounds from his partially emptied magazines and used them to top off his others. He tossed the empty mags aside and shoved the two full ones into his vest and brought his rifle to his shoulder. "But with as many of them as were buried in the ground just to trip us up and grab at us? Who knows what they were thinking."

"We were thinking of capturing you so that we could speak."

Dom spun and leveled his rifle on the vampire standing beside him. "How the…" He felt the color drain from his face and heard the other operators shift their weaponry to aim it at the man now standing beside him. He made no effort to move, his smile unwavering.

"Would you believe I come in peace?" The man held his hands up, palms out to show them empty and raised them slowly. "I could easily have struck at you while you were distracted."

"You'd be dead." Dom flipped the safety off and moved his finger onto the trigger.

"Very true. And that is not what either of us desires." The vampire stepped back and the moonlight highlighted his features. Long blonde hair trailed behind his ears and brilliant blue eyes sparkled with intelligence. He kept his arms raised and stood erect. "You may search me if you like. You may even take me as a hostage. I wish only to speak with the leader of your group."

"You getting all this, OPCOM?" Hammer asked as Dom reached forward and pulled the vampire unceremoniously into the middle of the circle of operators. Wallace did a quick pat down and declared him free of weapons.

"My people are waiting beyond the trees. They have strict orders not to advance so long as we are speaking. Should you release me right away…or kill me, they will attack again." The vampire looked to Dom. "May I sit?"

Dom took a step back and shrugged. "Suit yourself. It's your funeral."

"I certainly hope not." The man was dressed in blue jeans and a flannel shirt. Had they been anywhere else, he might have passed for a hiker or lumberjack. He sat on the ground, crossing his booted foot. He motioned to Dom. "Please join me. We have a lot to discuss, and I think your superiors would like to know what we know as well."

Dom turned to Hammer, "Keep an eye on the tree line. If anything moves, drop it. That goes for all of you. Keep the perimeter secure." He turned to the vampire and sat across from him, his rifle resting across his lap so that the barrel faced the man.

"Allow me to begin with an apology. You were not who we thought you were at first. Once we realized you were the human hunters…I sent one of my people to make contact."

"And who did you think we were?" Dom couldn't hide the distrust from his voice.

"It is a very long story, but suffice to say, we thought you were hired mercenaries sent to exterminate us."

"Not too far from the mark."

The vampire stiffened and nodded slightly. "You are the human hunters, no? The ones who lead the attack against the Sicarii in the desert?"

"One and the same." Dom sneered a smile.

"Then you are not the mercenaries we thought you to be." The vampire's voice grew silent as he spoke. His face took an almost reflective appearance as he turned his attention back to the hunter across from him. "We were crossing through this area and discovered a small group of very young vampires. They had done…unspeakable things."

"We know." Dom raised a brow at him, not believing him.

"We are *not Lamia Beastia*, but we do not adopt the tenets of the Humanus either. We do feed on humans, but we have familiars who volunteer their blood to us. We do not kill in order to feed."

Dom didn't like what he was hearing, but he got the distinct impression that he was truthful. He shrugged. "I should care?"

"You should. We took it upon ourselves to remove the troublesome vampires from this area and were about to move on when we got word that they were simply bait."

Dom's eyes narrowed. "Bait? For what?"

"For you, we think. Perhaps for us. We are not sure." The vampire shrugged slightly, his face displaying worry.

Mitchell came across the coms, "Who would be doing the baiting and who told him this?"

"Who told you the baby vamps were bait? Why would they do this?" Dom repeated.

The vampire shook his head. "The only survivor from those we removed is who told us. He wasn't…new. He was much older. He was ordered to do this thing."

"By who?"

The vampire averted his eyes a moment and inhaled deeply. "He *claims* that he was ordered to by the Council."

"Who?" Dom leaned forward, unsure what he was hearing.

"The Vampire Council?" Mitchell asked.

The vampire looked up and nodded. "Your superior is correct. The Vampire Council. We tried to ask him more questions, but he had a suicide pill. Silver. He swallowed it before we knew what he was doing. He would rather accept the true death than betray his masters."

"And you thought we were mercs sent to kill you?" Dom

shook his head. "Why?"

"Hunter, you have much to learn about our ways. It is the true death for any who takes the life of another vampire. But for one who takes the life of a Council's agent?" The vampire shuddered. "Everyone he has ever cared about shall pay. They will see to it."

"Pass him coms, Sierra One," Mitchell ordered. He turned to the communications tech and nodded. "Enter this into the permanent record."

"I can hear him fine," the vampire stated as Dom pulled his earpiece and lip mic.

"I think it's so they can hear you better." He handed it to the vampire and watched as he fumbled with it. Dom laid his rifle aside and clipped the mic in place then helped him run the wire for the earpiece. "You're good."

"To whom am I speaking?" Mitchell asked.

"You may call me Reginald." The vampire listened to the sounds in the background as Mitchell took his seat again.

"Reginald, I am Colonel Mitchell, I think maybe you should go into a bit more detail here. If there's a threat coming from the Council, I'd like to know about it."

*****

Jack watched Gnat run through the rafters unrolling cables as he jumped through the narrow gaps. If he didn't know any better, he'd swear the little guy had been doing it his entire life. He smiled to himself knowing that the performance his people were putting on would go a long way toward convincing those around them that they were who they claimed to be.

He lifted another stack of monitors and carried them into the office space and set them on the makeshift station that Viktor and

Foster were setting up. "I'll get the power supplies set up on the backside of the office here. The closer to the station, the better." He gave Viktor a knowing look and the older wolf simply nodded.

Jack went out and picked up the crate with the power inverters and carried them to the backside of the office. With explosives embedded into the monitors and the power inverters, he hoped to direct the blast inward toward whoever was at the station, disintegrating them with one fail swoop.

He ran the heavy extension cords to the inverters and plugged them in, the outputs fed through the wall and to the computer station where Lilith could watch her attacks take place. He hoped that they could convince her to test the system prior to the attacks. If they could remove her and the Fallen one from the equation before any suicide bombers could detonate, maybe they could save a whole lot of lives.

He nearly fell over when he was told what the targets were planned to be. Every major Catholic church across the world and then political heads of state. Capitols, monuments, anything that they could think of that would shake up the people enough that they would lose faith in their leaders. The crazy bitch was adamant that the churches would be her first targets though. She was obsessed with making them pay for what was done to her in a previous life.

Jack mulled over the whole idea of her obsession while he ran the cabling. He knew what it was like to become so focused on something that you lose track of a bigger picture. He had become obsessed with revenge when he found out about the wolf virus giving them their strength. He was so disillusioned with the program and the people running it that he actually ran the opposite direction and joined forces with a vampire. He sighed as he realized once again that he'd set himself up to be let down.

Disillusioned by the flaws of the four hundred-year-old being who saved him from the attack that killed his team, he wasn't ready to admit that people can do the wrong thing for what they believe to be the right reason.

Jack paused as he ran out another run of cabling. He glanced at Thorn inside the office with Viktor and Foster. Was he really that different than Mitchell? The colonel had used the wolf virus to transform the men into fighting machines. True, he damned them, but he made them physically more capable of facing what was out there. Was Rufus that far out of line by creating the Doomsday weapon?

And Apollo. He was obsessed with Maria. When Sheridan got to him and twisted his mind…Jack closed his eyes and tried to shake the gut wrenching pain that he'd been ignoring since he had heard of Apollo's death. He ground his teeth and clenched his fists as he fought off the urge to scream. One of Sheridan's men had put a round through Apollo's skull like he was a rabid dog.

He blew out the breath he'd been holding and let his body sag. At least Apollo didn't suffer.

"What's the hold up?"

Jack turned to see a rather large man staring at him. He had to assume it was one of Lilith's demons. He tried to smile as he shrugged. "Sorry, just got a little frustrated. The cabling keeps getting twisted up…knotting up on itself."

The man eyed him cautiously then stepped off, back to his own duties. Jack watched him walk off and turned back to his own work. He finished running out the cabling and hooked the proper ends to the power inverters. With power applied, it would feed the computers inside the office. For a little while anyway, before they overheated and shut down.

He patted the detonator in his pants pocket and smiled to

himself. Hopefully it wouldn't take that long.

*****

"Everybody out." Jim Youngblood didn't raise his voice as he spoke, but he had that commanding tone that made everyone in the room stiffen and take note. People started filing out of the room when he reached out and grabbed Laura by the arm. "You. Stay."

"I'm not a terrier, Dad." She glared at him as the others walked out and quietly shut the door.

He didn't apologize as he released her arm, but he stood from his bed and pulled back the sheets. Her eyes fell on the dirt, detritus, and pine needles at the foot of the bed. "When did you go out?"

Her father crossed his arms and stared at her. "I didn't." He pointed to the mess in his bed. "But when I crawled back into bed, this was here waiting for me. It was stuck to my feet. Any idea how that could have happened?"

She looked to him and saw the accusatory look in his eye. "I have no clue." She stepped back and shook her head. "What? You think I came in here and planted this stuff when you weren't looking?"

"Crystal was asleep right there in that chair. I stood up and stared out the window. I get back into bed and…*this*."

"Well I sure as hell didn't do it." She crossed her arms and stared at him.

Jim pointed to her travel bag. "Didn't you?"

She glanced at the bag she kept the serum in and gave him a shocked look. "Really? You think that the shot did that?" She reached down and picked up a small handful of the dirt and pine needles. "You really think that this is a figment of your imagination?"

"Hell no I don't. I know it's real." Jim Youngblood stared at his daughter and waited for an explanation.

"What do you want me to tell you, Dad?"

"Tell me how I can have a…a…*vision* of running in the woods, hunting down a rabbit. And when I snap out of it and climb back into bed, my feet are covered with the forest floor."

Laura shook her head. "I can't."

Jim sat down heavily on the bed and shook his head. "Do I have this to look forward to from now on?"

"No!" Laura sat next to him and cupped his hand. "Daddy, I've never heard of any of the others ever having this happen."

He turned and gave her a questioning look. "What others?"

Her eyes widened and she swallowed hard. "The…men that I work with. They're infected with the wolf virus, too."

Jim nodded knowingly. "That's how you knew what to expect."

"Yes," her voice was soft and nearly silent in the darkened room.

"And these men…how did they get infected? Were they about to die as well?"

She shook her head. "No. They were just…men." Her eyes met his and she gave him a wan smile. "Extraordinary men. SEALs, Green Berets, Rangers…the best of the best. They volunteered."

Jim Youngblood sat up and gave his daughter a serious stare. "And why would they do this?"

Laura sighed. "Because there are monsters out there that need killing. And to do that, we needed supermen." She looked at him and shook her head. "I don't expect you to understand. I don't expect you to condone. Just accept that it happens."

He looked to her and narrowed his gaze. “Something tells me that you and I need to have a much more in depth and serious talk about what you do for a living.”

*****

Little John pulled Spalding back from the edge of the warehouse. “We need to call this in and get the team out here.”

Spalding’s eyes went wide and he shoved John back. “Are you nuts? They could scatter in the time it takes them to saddle up and get here,” his whispered voice threatened to rise as he glared at the large man.

Little John cocked his head and shot him a quizzical stare. “Dude, you’re chasing the white rabbit. There is *no way* the two of us can handle this many of them with the firepower we have and ammo we brought. We thought we were reconnoitering an escape route, not facing down a small army.”

Spalding shook his head. “No, we have to find that British bastard and—”

Little John pulled him closer and slapped him. “Snap out of it.”

Spalding’s eyes widened and he set his jaw, prepared to go on the offensive. “I know you didn’t just—”

Little John interrupted his tirade. “You need to come back to earth. There are at least thirty operatives inside, all armed. We know that Bigby was SAS. That means Seriously Awful Sonovabitch in my book. There is no way the two of us can do this alone.” He pulled Spalding further back into the shadows and lowered his voice. “The team can be here in less than thirty minutes. We monitor these bastards and if they try to move, we pluck em off one by one.” He prayed that Spalding would see reason.

Darren Spalding stared into the eyes of the big man and almost accused him of being a coward. He knew better. He felt his heart rate and breathing and knew that he was amped up. He had to take a step back and reevaluate.

He stared off into the blackness of the night and tried to put everything into perspective, but all he could see in his mind's eye was the spray of bone and grey matter from Apollo's skull as the sniper's bullet entered his skull. He shook his head and rested a hand on Sullivan's tactical vest.

Sullivan leaned in close and whispered, "Look, man, I know. You want to charge in there and send them all straight to hell. Believe me, I know. If it had been you, I'd be feeling the same thing. But you're the most level headed guy I know and right now, I need you to get your shit together and call in a strike. Get the team geared up and high tail it out here so we can do what we do best." He pulled Spalding up and stared him in the eye. "As a *team*."

Spalding took two long deep breaths, his eyes never leaving Little John's. He nodded his head. "Call in the strike. Get them out here. We'll go to high ground and take sniping positions in case they try to bug out."

Little John smiled. "Now that's the Team Leader we all know and love."

*****

Bigby walked the warehouse and sighed. The constant sounds of construction and the men training on the completed 'levels' was enough to drive him mad. He wondered if these guys were ever going to sleep as they worked around the clock. It wasn't until tonight that he realized they were working in shifts.

He stretched and yawned, fatigue wearing him thin as the constant noise and activity worked together to form the worst sort of distraction. He entered the office that he was now sharing with Martinez and fell into his chair. He reached for the headphones to his laptop and slid them over his ears. Pulling up his sound files, he put on Mozart and set the volume just high enough that he couldn't hear the noise outside the office.

Slumping into the supple leather chair, his head slipped to the side and he was soon asleep, visions of revenge dancing in his head.

*****

Lieutenant Gregory slipped into the OPCOM and quickly shut the door behind him. Mitchell cast an accusatory stare in his direction as the man walked behind him. He approached Major Tufo and handed him a sheet of paper. "I just got off the horn with Sullivan. He and Spalding went to investigate a hunch. They may have stumbled on the group that attacked the OPCOM. They require backup pronto."

Tufo read through the sheet quickly then shut down his station. "Colonel, I'll be setting up the secondary Command Center for this."

"Now, Major?"

Tufo leaned in close and lowered his voice. "They've already engaged. Outer perimeter guards have been neutralized. Eventually those guards will be missed. We need to get First Squad on the scene before shit hits the fan."

"Go. Keep me informed." Mitchell watched the two men leave the OPCOM and he ran a hand down his face. He prayed that

Second Squad had seen the last of the action for the night. He turned back to the communications tech. “Open coms.”

Tufo marched down the darkened hallway, his eyes scanning the report again. “Has the secondary command response team been notified?”

“On their way, sir.” Gregory was a half-step behind him.

“Notify First Squad to make ready and get their asses over there. If we can get…” Mark paused and let out a long breath. “Both drones are in action.” He looked back toward the OPCOM and considered going back to see if the second drone could be redirected but thought against it. “Notify First Squad that air support will not be available.”

“Aye, sir.” Gregory turned and took off down the hall as Mark kicked open the door to the secondary command center. He flipped the breakers bringing the smaller version of OPCOM online. The red lights overhead switched on almost immediately as the computers and monitors began booting up. Mark stepped up onto the command console as personnel began to file into the command center.

“This is gonna happen close to home and we have zero air support. This one is by the books, gentlemen. No mistakes.”

He spun the chair and tested the controls built into the arm. Monitors on the main wall came to life and he switched views, keyed coms and tested the various functions. He quickly realized Mitchell’s frustration with the shortcomings of the unit he was using. “Communications, feed Delta One’s coms to the overhead.”

“Sir, Delta One isn’t online.”

Mark spun the chair to shoot a questioning stare at the tech. “How the hell did they call in the report?”

“Uh…cell phone, sir,” the tech reported, obviously flustered.

“Then pipe that in until we can get him coms.” Mark shook his head as he punched up the secondary satellite feeds. "Give me their location the big screen. Go to IR."

Within moments the main screen showed a familiar scene and Mark's brow rose as he stared at the facility where Apollo was shot. "Is that…?"

"Yes, sir. Apparently the bad guys decided to go back once we cleaned it out."

Mark grunted as he zoomed the image in. He made a mental note to set up motion sensors and cameras at future locations where they clean out bad guys. "I wouldn't have thought they'd return."

"Probably why they went back, sir." The tech brought up the satellite controls and switched the feed to IR. Almost immediately the screen went to shades of black with orange, red, yellow and white hot spots.

"Mark our people and start painting designators on the bad guys." Tufo spun back to the communications tech. "Do we have that cell feed yet?"

"Negative, sir. They're…they aren't answering."

Mark groaned and leaned back in his seat. "Let's assume that the two assholes set up in sniping position are ours."

"Safe assumption, Major." The tech marked the two snipers as friendly.

Mark squinted at the screen and zoomed the image to a cooling mass outside the gate. "Let's assume those *used to be* the guards."

"We have another on the roof, sir." The tech painted a red 'X' on the cooling figure sprawled on the roof of the warehouse.

"Somebody give me their best guess on numbers here." Tufo began typing intel into the scrambler to feed to the squad's ruggedized PDAs.

"Best count at present is twenty-five, sir."

"Very well." Mark entered the info and sent it to the commandos who were now en route to the scene. "Saddle up, gentlemen. Time to make the doughnuts."

*****

"What a strange and eclectic group." Lilith watched as the newcomers went about making her dream a reality. She smiled to herself as the strangers worked diligently, installing things, running black wires, connecting electrical things and just...working as a team. "And they're so quick."

"Another truck is ready to leave." Samael scowled as she beamed with pride.

She gave him a furtive glance and waved him away nonchalantly. "Then send them on their way."

"What of the others? The ones you would have work in Europe?"

"Charter a plane. Surely they are capable of doing that."

"Planes take money," Samael sighed, realizing that it was the one thing they lacked.

"Then have one of your damned demons jump into a pilot and have him steal the plane. I do not care. Just get the devices and the bombers there and have them ready." She threw her hands into the air and stomped her foot. "Must I think of everything?"

Samael bit his tongue and took a long, deep breath. Her unreasonable attitude was wearing very thin with him. She had invited the vampire into their stronghold, allowed him to see everything they were doing and even though he showed himself to be a threat to them, she embraced him as a long lost trusted advisor. He glanced around the warehouse and saw the vampire's people working about the place, free rein to do what they wished, as they wished and nobody watching them. He felt his lip curl into a snarl and tried to fight the growl rising in his throat. "You've become too trusting, my love."

She spun on him and glared at him. "What do you mean?"

He clenched his jaw and waved his arm about before him. "I mean, these people are doing as they wish." He lowered his voice and leaned closer, "They could be plotting against us."

She rolled her eyes and turned her back on him. "And what if they were? Do you truly think that I wouldn't have a plan in that event?" She spun and pointed a finger at his chest, her long nail poking against his flesh. "They are but a handful. If I sent two-thirds of my demons to the task, I'd still have over three hundred minions left to rip them limb from limb. Or do you think they are so mighty that they could beat three hundred of your best demons?"

Samael stiffened and squared his shoulders. "Never!"

"Then why do you worry so?" She poked him harder with her nail. "Why do you fret like an old maiden?"

Samael grunted with frustration. "You were not the one being lead about like a puppet on a string. I was." He bent lower and stared her directly in the eye. "That vampire has the touch of a witch."

"A witch, you say?" She chuckled low in her throat as the words bounced around in her mind. "A witch?" She laughed now, deep and hearty. "What do you know of witchcraft?"

Samael sneered at her. "I know of witchery. Or have you forgotten that it was I who cast the spell for—"

She snapped around, interrupting him. "I have not forgotten! You bowed to your brother like a sniveling snot. Rather than stand up for me, you allowed me to be tortured, drawn and quartered…my innards ripped from my body and scattered across the face of the earth." She spat at his feet. "All because your brother said it would make me more bitter?"

Samael lowered his eyes, his shoulders slumping. "I told you it was not what I wanted."

"But you allowed it. You refused to stand up for me. After all that we went through together." She turned her back on him again, not wanting him to see the tears forming in her eyes. "I gave up paradise for you."

"I did not ask you to give up paradise." His voice cracked as he spoke, his mind racing back across the millennia to when they were first together.

"You didn't have to. I chose to." She sniffed back the tears that threatened to fall. "I did it for you. I did not want the *Adama.* He wanted me to prostrate myself to him simply because he was created first. I refused to submit to his whims. I refused to bow to him and I…I rejected his…"

Samael reached out and wrapped his mighty arms around her. "I know what you gave up. I know why." He kissed her lightly upon the neck. "I was there, remember?"

"His God would have none of it." Her voice cracked this time as she remembered. "I remember what the world was like outside that garden." She spun on him. "Do you?"

Samael nodded. "And that is why I carried you off, away from that desolate place."

She withered in his arms. "Tell me again it was worth it."

"How can you say that? Had you not, we never could have been together."

"I was marked. Barren. Never to bear children." She turned and buried her face in his chest.

Samael stroked her back with a loving caress. "There are

worse things than being cursed childless."

"Like living forever."

20

Mitchell keyed the coms again, "Reginald, tell me more of the Council. Why do you think they're targeting either of us?"

He watched the vampire through Dom's helmet cam. He inhaled deeply and shook his head slightly. "I cannot be certain. There are rumors amongst my people. Those who fought with your people in the desert were marked as traitors. We continue to hear the same rumors from different groups and then they…" He trailed off, unable to finish.

"They what?" Mitchell pushed.

"They disappear. No trace. As if they were targeted for the true death."

Mitchell leaned back in his chair and was about to turn to Tufo when he remembered his XO wasn't there. "Your people fought with us at Area 51?"

"Yes, we were there. We were asked to by the *Lamia Beastia*. We felt it was in our best interest to stand against the Sicarii." Reginald saw the helmet cam and directed his gaze directly toward it. "We didn't agree with the Sicarii's agenda."

"Yet, you aren't *Beastia*."

"No, sir, we are not. As I explained to your man here, we have people who volunteer to feed us. We do not turn them, nor do we kill them. We take only what we need for survival."

"Yeah, I heard that." Mitchell wasn't sure if he quite believed him, but he accepted the man at face value for now. "And the altercation my people and yours have already had? I'm supposed to believe that you're ready to let bygones be bygones?"

"Colonel, we have a common enemy. A very *powerful* common enemy. As I understand it, they are breaking covenants daily in order to push their agenda. They want only those who are fully loyal to their old ways." Reginald squared his shoulders. "Had we announced who we were, and simply attempted to speak with your people, then there's a very good chance no lives would have been lost." He bowed his head to the camera. "I place all responsibility on my own shoulders and hold your men blameless. That is what a leader does."

Mitchell watched as the man finally brought his head up and stared into the camera again. "I have told you all that I know. I can show your men where we disposed of the young vampires who caused so much mayhem. We ask only that we be allowed to pass through these territories untouched."

Mitchell nodded to himself aware that the vampire couldn't see him. "And where will you go?"

"North. Perhaps to the Canadian border."

"You do realize that we cover Canada as part of our protected area of coverage as well."

"Yes, we do. If you prefer, I will personally check in with you and give you our exact location. If anything out of the ordinary occurs in our lands, you will have a point of contact." He stared directly into the camera again. "We police our own, Colonel."

Mitchell inhaled deeply and nodded again. "Reginald, call me crazy, but I believe what you're telling me. Put my man back on the line." He watched as the Dom helped transfer the coms back over. "Sierra One, Reginald here is going to show your team where they disposed of the vamps who stirred up trouble. Get his contact info and wish his people well. Remind him to check in with us when they reach their destination."

"Copy that, Colonel."

Mitchell nodded to the communications tech and had the coms cut. "Deploy resources to Major Tufo as needed. Set a watch to maintain surveillance on Second Squad until they're in the air and on the way home." He leaned toward the tech running the satellite. "If there's any way to keep tabs on the group as they're traveling, do it. Tag them for automatic monitoring. I want to know everywhere they go between now and when they contact us again."

"Trust but verify, sir?"

"Exactly." Colonel Mitchell stepped down from the command platform. "Shift command back to Captain Jones. Make sure Jericho is up to speed on everything that happened here."

"Where will you be, sir?"

"I need a drink."

*****

Mick sat in the helicopter, his anger and frustration growing with each passing landmark. He stared out through the windows and saw the blackness of the coast approaching. He knew that once they reached the water, there was no turning back. If he was dropped off on that stupid island, he would be stuck there.

They had unshackled his hands, but his feet were chained to the floor. He stared at the simple lock and a panic rose in him. He extended a claw and slipped it into the keyhole of the lock. He wiggled it around and prayed that it would give. It didn't.

Mick fought the urge to scream and then his eyes fell on the shackles around his ankles. He almost began laughing as he stared at them. He slipped his shoes off and allowed his body to begin shifting. He watched as his feet elongated and narrowed. The shackled slipped and fell from his legs, clattering onto the floor of the helicopter. He quickly shifted back to human form and slipped his shoes back on. He slipped forward and watched the two pilots as they controlled the rotary wing craft.

He wrapped one clawed hand around the throat of the pilot on the right and gripped tightly. "Turn us around! Now!" he growled into the man's ear.

"I can't. We have orders." The man struggled against his grip, and Mick reluctantly ripped a jagged hole in his throat. He quickly jumped forward and caught the other pilot's hand before he could bring the pistol to bear.

"Naughty-naughty, mate. Your chum here didn't want to play nice. How about you?" He twisted the pistol from his grip and pressed it to the man's temple. "Let's turn the craft around nice and gentle."

The pilot sneered at him. "Go ahead and kill me. Who would fly this thing?"

Mick smiled back. "I'm a pilot, mate. I only have about thirty hours in a rotary, but I think I could figure it out." He pulled the hammer back on the pistol and pressed the 9MM Beretta to the side of his head again. "Your choice."

The pilot cursed and began turning the craft around. "Good choice, mate." Mick dragged the other pilot to the rear of the craft and dumped him over the shackles. Taking his position in the front seat, he pulled on the headphones. "Let's be sure and land this thing far enough away from the hangar that they won't know we're back."

"And then you kill me, right?"

Mick gave him a sideways stare. "Nobody else has to die tonight, mate. Your buddy there? I had to make my point. I knew that saying please wasn't going to work."

*****

Thorn pulled Jack aside. "Is everything in place?"

Jack tried not to react. Although he had worked through things in his mind, his heart still considered Rufus a traitor. He stiffened slightly and the reaction did not go unnoticed. "I…yeah. Everything is in place." He reached into his pocket and pulled the miniature detonator. "As soon as they're both in place, we flip this and…blooey. It's done."

Thorn gave him a confused look. "Why both of them?"

"We're not sure who is the…" he trailed off, trying to remember what term Viktor used. "The…the main key to making it all fall apart."

"It is she. She is the 'key'. The blast will most likely only slow her. We will need to dismember her." He glanced around to ensure there was nobody listening. "We will need a distraction for the angel and demons though."

Jack gave him a sly smile. "I can arrange that."

"Very well. I will do my best to get her inside. Perhaps a demonstration."

"I'll get my people ready." Jack turned to leave when Rufus grabbed his arm.

"What do you have planned?"

"Trust me. You'll know." Jack gave him a wink. "I've got a couple of people on the roof that should be able to keep the others busy."

"Then it will be up to me to convince her she will be safer inside." Thorn gave him a slight bow. "Good luck."

Jack took off and Rufus turned to find the demon queen. He approached the office and nodded knowingly to Viktor. "Find Paul and prepare your people. Jack is going to provide a distraction."

Viktor stiffened. "What is he going to do?"

"He said he has people on the roof that can keep Samael and the demons busy enough for us to deal with Lilith." Rufus looked around for her. "But we must hurry."

Viktor rounded the corner quickly and found the vampire and elf loitering near the crate with the angelic weapons. The gnome was still in the rafters. Viktor made a few subtle hand signals and the trio responded in kind. Kalen opened the crate and dug through the coconut fibers, his hand resting on the handle of his bow. He stayed bent, his eyes scanning the area.

Rufus found Lilith and approached her smiling. "My queen, I believe they have the system up and running if you'd like to see how it operates."

"Perhaps later. I have an issue to deal with now."

Thorn bowed slightly. "As you wish. I just thought that since the technicians were here, if any problems arose then they could make repairs." He turned to leave. "We'll just have to hope that they got everything right the first time."

Lilith stiffened and turned to him. "They are leaving?"

Rufus paused and turned back to her. "Well...*oui*. They are not part of our effort. They have other projects to finish for other clients. They simply rushed this one as a favor to me." He gave her a smile and turned back to leave.

"Wait." She came beside him and gave him a condescending smile. "Perhaps I can make time to ensure that everything is working as it should."

"As you wish, my lady." Rufus offered his arm which she ignored and walked ahead of him. He quickly fell into step behind her. She waited at the door of her office for him to open it and she stepped inside to see the command center they had put together for her. Ten flat panel monitors set up in a semi-circle, each of them displaying a slowly moving icon.

She sat gingerly behind the screens and waited for him to tell her what to do. "Move this small device. It is called a mouse."

She moved it and the screens came to life. "Oh, brilliant!"

"Once the cell phone feeds start coming in, they'll be fed to the main screen here, then you can decide which ones you absolutely *must* see." Rufus beamed as she stared at the screens.

"How will I do that?"

"The mouse has two buttons. Simply click the left button with your finger." He stiffened slightly. "Ah, but you need something to 'click' do you not?" She looked at him as if he were daft. He held up a finger. "Give me a moment. I believe we can simulate that for you. It won't be the actual feed from your people, but it will give you an idea of what to expect. Just one moment."

Rufus stepped outside the office and pulled the door shut. He looked to Jack and nodded. Jack keyed the coms on his collar and two of the skylights exploded inward.

Azrael glided inward, sword and shield in hand. The Guardian dropped from the other skylight and landed with a crash amidst a handful of demons. The mighty sword and hammer he held made quick work of the minions close to him.

Samael lifted his mighty head to see what the noise was. He tossed the crate aside that he had been loading into another truck. The crate cracked open, spilling the suicide vests onto the concrete floor as he stomped toward the noise. He watched as the soft glow yellow glow of his demons leaving their human hosts flew up and out of the warehouse. "Who dares?" he bellowed.

Jack flipped the switch on the detonator and the warehouse was nearly leveled by the concussive blow of the C4 exploding in two different directions. The directed blasts had no place else to go but up, destroying much of the ceiling above what was once the office. Each of Jack's crew took shelter behind the heavy concrete columns.

As the shock wave passed, they stepped out and wielded their angelic weapons. They watched in silent fascination as hundreds of demons departed their broken human shells, yellow beams of light shooting upward and into the night sky.

Thorn and Viktor pushed past the debris of the office and began to dig for the remains of the demon queen. She had to be dismembered before she could revive herself.

Samael picked himself from the broken machinery he had been blown into and shook his mighty head, trying to regain his bearings. "What happened?" He glanced around what once was their safe haven. His eyes fell upon where he knew Lilith was and they shot wide with fear. "Lilith!" He clambered and fought to free himself from the twisted metal just as the Nephilim appeared before him.

"Demon spawn," the Guardian sneered as he lifted his mighty hammer.

"A Nephilim?" Samael's eyes widened and he lifted his arm to block the crushing blow just as Phil brought the great hammer down. The hammer glanced across Samael's arm and smashed into the metal remains of the machinery.

"Son of Rafael, you Fallen abomination!" Phil swung the sword intending to decapitate the fallen angel, but Samael fell back into the twisted metal and lifted his free foot.

He caught the Nephilim in the midsection and kicked him back and away. Samael pulled himself free and jumped from the metal, his hand pulling up a twisted beam to use as a weapon.

Phil swung both the hammer and the sword as he came back to finish the angel. Samael ducked, blocked and dove, knowing that without an angelic weapon of his own, he had little chance of defending himself from the Halfling for long. He leapt back and took to the air, his great leathery wings beating rapidly, scooping large pockets of air and lifting him higher. "It will take more than you to defeat me, Nephilim."

A spine shattering blow knocked the wind from Samael and sent him spiraling to the concrete floor below. He rolled to his side and saw the light skinned gargoyle flying above him, an angelic sword and shield in his hands. Samael groaned as he rolled to his hands and knees, and he felt the blood roll down his back and sides, splattering upon the broken concrete below. He lifted his mighty head and saw the Nephilim charging, hammer and sword pumping as he ran across the great warehouse.

Samael reached out and grabbed the broken body of one of his demons and hurled it at the Nephilim. He then leapt to the side and with a mighty jump, landed in the middle of the wreckage of the office. Both Viktor and Thorn fell back with surprise as the Fallen one landed amidst the rubble. "She is *mine*!" he growled at the pair as he thrust both hands into the rubble and scooped her broken body from the ruins.

Kalen and Brooke paused in their battles with the demons who survived the blast and watched as the bloody demon looking creature jumped into the air and with a mighty push of his wings, shot through a broken skylight and into the night air.

Jack looked to Azrael and pointed upward. “Stop him!”

The gargoyle clenched his jaw and made for the skylight himself. He tucked his wings and lowered his weapons to shoot through the jagged skylight.

Kalen turned his attention back to the demons. “Kill them all!” He raised his bow and watched as each demon suddenly fell to the ground, a yellow beam of light shooting from the host’s body as the demon escaped into the night.

Thorn turned a slow circle staring at the destruction. “*Sacre bleu.* We almost had them.”

Viktor placed a reassuring hand on his shoulder. “We live to fight another day.”

Thorn shrugged his hand away. “Do we? We will never have another chance to defeat her.” He kicked at a piece of the rubble and stormed from the remains of the office.

Jack motioned for his people to converge on him. “There’s still a chance that Azrael will catch them.”

Phil shook his head. “He cannot stop a Fallen abomination.” He hung his head. “Even with the weapons he has, he does not have the power to stop him.”

“He put a hurt on him,” Jack added. “If it can bleed, it can die.”

“True. But it can also heal.”

*****

Laura squirmed as her father stared at her. “Spill it, Punkin. I want to know everything.”

"I think I pretty much told you everything." She picked at her fingernails as she chewed at her lower lip.

"I don't think you did. You mentioned that monsters were real. You said that you are dating a vampire. But you said nothing about the men you working with actually *being* infected with this stuff like I am."

"Well, how else did you think I'd know it was safe?" She shrugged as if he should have simply connected the dots.

Jim inhaled deeply and sighed. "Tell me, how many are there?"

"Enough." She shook her head. "Dad, I'm not really supposed to talk about it."

"Just like I'm sure you aren't supposed to smuggle that stuff out and shoot me up with it, yet, here we are." He narrowed his stare at her and watched her squirm.

"Daddy, really. It's classified, and I could get into a lot of trouble for just mentioning them."

Jim nodded. "Fine. I can understand that, I suppose." He pursed his lips as a multitude of thoughts ran through his mind. "Can you at least tell me *why* they volunteered for this?"

She nodded. "To better fight the real monsters out there. So that they could keep up."

"So, in order to fight the monsters, they had to *become* a monster? Fight fire with fire."

"In a manner of speaking."

"And that's why you were so…adamant about me knowing the rules you expect me to live by? Because if I don't live by those rules…"

She nodded, tears starting to form in her eyes. "Then they would definitely come and hunt you down."

"And then somebody would put two and two together and

realize what you did."

She shook her head and finally met his gaze, her tears falling freely. "I don't care if they find out. Hell, I'll probably end up spilling my guts to them as soon as I get back anyway. I just don't want anything to happen to you. If it did it would be…" Her voice cracked and she trailed off, burying her face.

"What?"

She lifted her face and wiped the tears from her cheeks. "It would be *my* fault. They would hunt you down, and they would kill you and it would be all my fault. Don't you see?"

Jim shook his head. "No, Punk, I don't. It isn't your fault if I do something I shouldn't. It's called personal responsibility." He pulled her tight and squeezed her. "I know I taught you better than that."

"I'm sorry, Daddy. I should have told you everything." She sniffed as he stroked her arm.

"You told me enough, Punk." Jim stared off into nothingness.

"What's wrong?" Laura pulled back slightly and stared at him. "I know when you're not telling me something."

Jim inhaled sharply and let the breath out slowly. He leaned over and picked up something that she couldn't quite make out. He lifted it in the low light and held it out to her. She wrapped her hand around it and recognition hit her like a truck. It was the vial that held the wolf virus she had infected him with. It was empty.

She pulled back from him and stared at him with shock. "Daddy? What did you do with the rest of it?"

*****

First Squad advanced on the warehouse and caught the light from Spalding and Sullivan's positions. Donovan approached the pair and handed them their coms. "Boss ain't too happy you're here."

"He'll get over it." Spalding plugged in his coms and did a check.

"Don't be so sure, Spanky," Major Tufo corrected. "I tend to hold a grudge."

Spalding sputtered and responded, "Sorry, Major. Didn't realize the coms were hot."

"Apparently." Mark took his seat again and keyed up the helmet cams. "Make this a clean op and I'll consider forgiving you."

"Copy that, sir." Spalding gave a quick rundown of what was he spotted inside the warehouse.

Sullivan added, "They're working on a mock-up of some kind and running drills at the same time."

Mark smiled to himself. "Those would be phony plans, gentlemen. I wish I could tell you what to expect, but honestly, I didn't think they could be built."

"Understood, sir." Spalding motioned his men forward, "Two by two standard, run silent, suppressed fire."

"Be advised, Delta One, you're running without air support. Drones are inbound, but ETA is so far out that clean-up crews will probably be finishing up before they arrive."

"Copy that."

The squad made a slow advance with Lamb and Jacobs breaking left and working around to the rear of the building. Donovan and Tracy broke left and stacked up on the west roll away door. Spalding and Sullivan stacked on the south maintenance door.

Tracy broke coms first, "West entrance open, clear view through the structure."

“Tangos?” Spalding asked.

“Negative, Delta One. West side is clear. Nothing but gear and machinery on this end.”

Spalding nodded to Sullivan. “Breach west side, Delta Five. Delta Two, provide cover.”

Lamb came over the coms. “North side is locked tight. No entry without blowing the door.”

“Copy that, Delta Three. You and Four stand by until bingo.”

“Roger that.”

Sullivan tiptoed and glanced through the window next to the maintenance door. “We’re clear on this end, boss. You ready?”

Spalding nodded. “Delta One and Six are breaching south entrance.” Sullivan opened the door and Spalding slid in, scanning left to right. Little John came in behind and above him, sweeping right to left. The pair slid to the right and behind a stack of crates.

Spalding pulled a small mirror from his vest and checked the corners. “Clear.”

The pair slipped out and made a tactical advance along the wall until they came to a door on their right. A row of cots inside lay empty and it was obvious that was where the small army was using as sleeping quarters. Spalding moved them further on until the stack of crates ended. Using the mirror again, he could see where a group of men were constructing a mock-up while another group were running drills on the lower level.

He looked to Sullivan and smiled. “Want to come in the back of that mock-up and give them a real surprise?”

“We got a warehouse full of unarmed guys and you want to go face the ones with automatic weapons first?” He shook his head. “You got a death wish I don’t know about?”

Spalding chuckled. “Buddy, that sure sounds like simunition to me. They aren’t putting any holes in that plywood.”

Sullivan's brows knitted and he took a quick glance. "Good eye, boss. I've been listening to them run drills all this time and wishing they'd run out." He checked the safety on his rifle and nodded. "Let's do it."

Spalding keyed his coms, "We're heading for the mock-up. Advance and engage. Delta Three and Four, you have the bingo." The pair scooted across the stack of crates and came to the rear of the mock-up. Spalding glanced down the length of the warehouse and could just make out Delta Two and Delta Five making their way down the length of the structure. Sullivan pushed through the flimsy back door and brought his rifle to his shoulder. Spalding slipped in behind him and followed suit.

The pair worked their way from the back to the front, taking turns spitting suppressed rounds through their rifles, watching as wolves reacted violently to the silver jacketed rounds. As they worked their way closer to the front, they waited for the next wave to enter. "Anybody got eyes on the mock-up?"

"You may come out now. We have your people," a heavily accented voice spoke directly in his ear.

Spalding froze and glanced at Little John who visibly stiffened. John tightened his grip on his rifle and took a half step forward, but Spalding reached out and grabbed the man by his massive bicep. "Don't." Little John glanced back the way they had come and Spalding shook his head. He keyed his coms. "To whom am I speaking?"

"Chief Warrant Officer Martinez, we have your people. You may come out now or they will die." Spalding slowly lowered his rifle and sighed.

"You ain't giving up?"

"The only way he can come across our coms is if he has one of our guys." He looked up at the low ceiling and shook his head.

"And they probably have a signal blocker in place or Major Tufo would be screaming in our ears right now."

"You have five seconds."

Spalding keyed his coms. "Okay. We're coming out."

John grabbed his arm and shook his head. "We don't surrender."

"We're blind in here and they have our people. As long as we're breathing, we have a fighting chance."

Spalding stepped to the front of the mock-up and pushed open the door. He was greeted with multiple rifle barrels in the face.

*****

Director Jameson waited for Ingram to pick up the phone. He wasn't surprised that the man's voice wasn't groggy when he answered. "What is it?"

"You were right. I'm watching a video of someone rifling through my office now."

"Is it him?"

Jameson sighed into the phone. "I can't be certain. I want to say yes." He paused the video and stared at the low light image. Whoever it was had a penlight in their mouth that cast them into silhouette. Even when they got on his computer, the screen blocked his face from view. "I just can't tell."

"I would say it's safe to assume it's him."

"As would I. The question is, what are his intentions?"

"Only he can tell you that." Ingram shifted the phone and he jotted a few notes. "Do you want me to send a team to pick him up?"

Jameson considered it for a moment. "No, let me handle him. If he has the balls to break into my office then I may have misjudged him." He leaned back and stared at the assuredness of the man in his office. "He may well be the man for the job."

"How do you want to play him? Let him in on the plan or keep dropping crumbs and see if he goes running to them?"

Jameson pinched the bridge of his nose and shook his head. "I'm not sure. I want to test him a bit more first."

"Did he get anything?"

Jameson chuckled into the phone. "There's nothing *to* get. All of my files are hard-copied and locked tight in my safe. Without my palm print, eye scan and the combination, nobody is getting into it. You should have seen his reaction when he realized that."

"Are you absolutely sure? The little shit can be pretty creative."

"Oh, I'm sure." Jameson closed the video file and closed the lid on his computer. "There's nothing out there for anybody to tie us to the program except what we tell them."

"You'd better be right. We're not just talking about a slap on the wrist here." Ingram shifted the phone again and Jameson got the paranoid thought that perhaps he was recording the conversation. "They could put us both away for a very long time."

"Oh, I'm very aware of the ramifications." He sat back in his chair and spun it to stare out his home office window. "When will they be ready for a field trial?"

"Very soon. They're finishing the medical tests now." Ingram's voice dropped to a near whisper, "You won't believe what these guys can do."

"They'd better be good. These monster hunters are nothing to sneeze at."

"Oh, they're good. Good enough to get the job done," Ingram chuckled into the phone. "And for the amount of money we're being paid, they'll do everything we promised and then some."

"If the Council finds out we intend to double cross them after all of the monsters have been eradicated…they'll send somebody after us."

"That's why we save them for last. There won't be anybody *left* for them to send after us." Ingram laughed as he hung up the phone.

Coming Fall 2015

MS8-Specters

From the desk of Heath Stallcup

A personal note-

Thank you so much for investing your time in reading my story. If you enjoyed it, please take a moment and leave a review. I realize that it may be an inconvenience, but reviews mean the world to authors…

Also, I love hearing from my readers. You can reach me at my blog: http://heathstallcup.com/ or via email at heathstallcup@gmail.com

Feel free to check out my Facebook page for information on upcoming releases: https://www.facebook.com/heathstallcup find me on Twitter at @HeathStallcup or via my Author Page at Amazon.

My stories so far:

The Monster Squad Series

The first saga:

Humanity has spent its time enjoying a peace that can only be had through blissful ignorance. For centuries, stories of things that go "bump" in the night have been passed down and shared. When

creatures of the night proved to be real, the best of America's military came together to form an elite band of rapid response teams. Their mission: to keep the civilian populace safe from those threats and hide all evidence of their existence.
This time, they face the largest threat ever to rise against mankind as it prepares its own twisted Apocalypse. The only thing standing in its way is the Monster Squad. Man and monster will fight side by side in an epic battle to the death to try to defeat an evil so great, it could only have been created by the hand of God Himself.

The second saga:

An ancient evil is awakened by a naïve pawn. Planned centuries in advance by fallen angels, the reign of Lilith is put into motion. With a legion of demons at her command, she plans to enact her revenge upon the world's largest religious group before thrusting herself center stage and taking her seat upon the throne as Queen of the World.
With threats coming at them from every angle, the Monster Squad turns to an ex-member to form a new team—a team made up of the most unlikely warriors to hunt down and face the Demon Queen.

However, when it comes time to remove the Queen in this grand game of chess, will they be able to sacrifice their own game pieces to do it?

Caldera

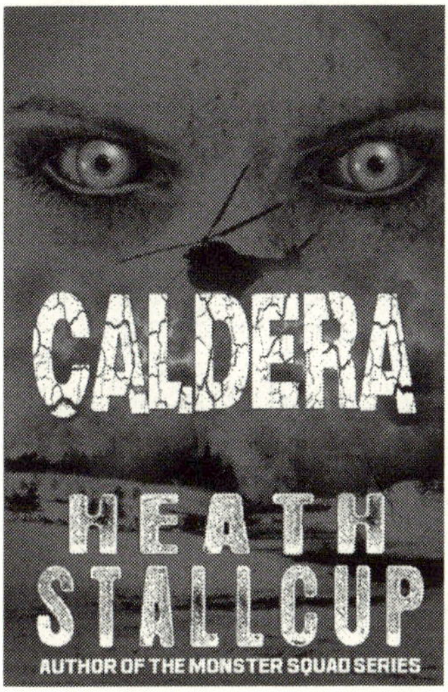

For years, the biggest threat Yellowstone was thought to offer was in the form of its semi-dormant super volcano. Little did anyone realize the threat was real and slowly working its way to the surface, but not in the form of magma. Lying deep within the bowels of the earth itself, an ancient virus waited.
Recently credited with wiping out the Neanderthals, the virus is released within the park and quickly spreads. A desperate plea for assistance reaches the military, but are they coming to help those battling for their lives or to wipe out every living thing in an effort to prevent a second mass extinction? Can humanity survive the raging cannibals that erupt from within?

Whispers

How does a sheriff's department from a small North Texas community stop a brutal murderer who is already dead and buried?
When grave robbers disturb the tomb of Sheriff James 'Two Guns' Tolbert searching for Old West relics, a vengeful spirit is unleashed, hell bent for blood. Over a hundred years in the making, a vengeful spirit hunts for its killers. If those responsible couldn't be made to pay, then their progeny would.
Even when aided by a Texas Ranger and UCLA Paranormal Investigators, can modern-day law enforcement stop a spirit destined to fulfill an oath made in death? An oath fueled by passion from a love cut down before its time?

Forneus Corson

Nothing comes easy and nothing is ever truly free. When Steve Wilson stumbles upon the best-kept secret of history's most successful writers, he can't help but take advantage of it. Little did he know it would come back to haunt him in ways he'd never have dreamt... even in his worst nightmares.

With his life turned upside down, his name discredited, his friends persecuted, the authorities chasing him for something he didn't do, Steve finds himself on the run with nothing but his wits and his best friend by his side. When a man finds himself hitting rock bottom, he thinks there's little else he can do but go up... unless he's facing an evil willing to dig the hole deeper. An evil in the business of pitting men against odds so great, they risk losing their very souls in the attempt to escape...

For a refreshing change of pace, check out this exciting new Young Adult Zombie thriller from JJ Beal.
Lions & Tigers & Zombies, Oh My!

The cold war has heated up again. This time the battle will be fought in every street of America.
Trapped in a major city, hours from their small town country home, a team of young girls find themselves cut off from everyone they know and left to fend for themselves as the world spins out of control.
With nothing but their wits, their softball equipment and their friendship to hold them together, they face incredible odds as they fight their way across the state. Physical, emotional and psychological challenges meet them at every turn as they struggle to find the family they can't be sure survived. How much more can they endure before reaching the breaking point?

ABOUT THE AUTHOR

Heath Stallcup was born in Salinas, California and relocated to Tupelo, Oklahoma in his tween years. He joined the US Navy and was stationed in Charleston, SC and Bangor, WA shortly after junior college. After his second tour he attended East Central University where he obtained BS degrees in Biology and Chemistry. Heath then served ten years with the State of Oklahoma as a Compliance and Enforcement Officer while moonlighting nights and weekends with his local Sheriff's Office. He still lives in the small township of Tupelo, Oklahoma with his wife and three of his seven children. He steals time to write between household duties, going to ballgames, being a grandfather to five and being the pet of numerous animals that have taken over his home. Visit him at heathstallcup.com or Facebook.com for news of his upcoming releases.

CUSTOMERS ALSO PURCHASED:

SHAWN CHESSER
SURVIVING THE ZOMBIE APOCALYPSE SERIES

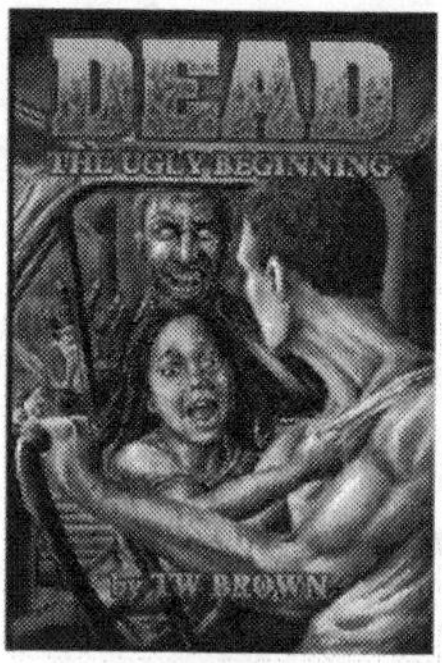

T.W. BROWN
THE DEAD SERIES

JOHN O'BRIEN
NEW WORLD SERIES

JAMES N. COOK
SURVIVING THE DEAD SERIES

MARK TUFO
ZOMBIE FALLOUT SERIES

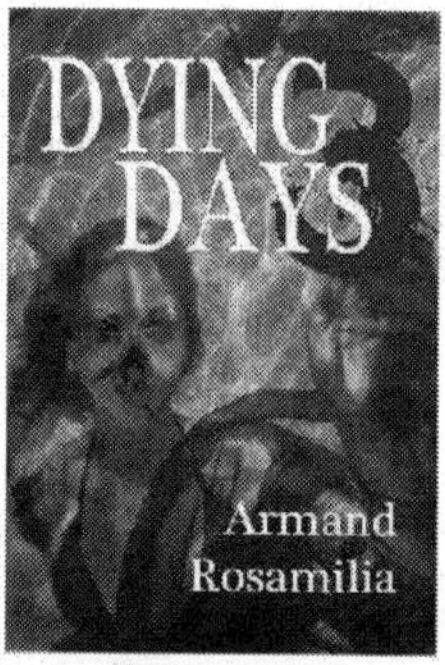

ARMAND ROSAMILLIA
DYING DAYS SERIES

43920177R00238

Made in the USA
San Bernardino, CA
03 January 2017